S0-BZV-791

"Your answer, my lady?"

Willa lifted her gaze to his. "You have your mistress."

Raiden schooled his features, snared in a trap of his own making.

"However, you must prove yourself, prove you can help me first."

His expression darkened. "I am not above honor, Willa."

She made a nasty sound. "You have asked me to whore for you, Raiden. Whilst history writes of the Black Angel and his feats of daring on the high seas, my name will be naught but a slur for my son to bear!"

"Then in this we have a common bond, for I *am* the slur of my father's actions."

A bastard was he? "Well, then, this blackmail has confirmed you have not risen above it," she snapped, hurt that he would force her into this.

Suddenly he advanced on her like a dragon let loose from his cave, swooping down on her, his arm shooting out to snare her waist and slam her flush to his length. "Did I not warn that you swam in waters too dangerous for you?"

She stared defiantly back, shoving his chest and his grip cinched tighter, imprisoning her. "You will regret this, Raiden."

"Montegomery," he added for her and her brows rose. "Raiden Montegomery. Bastard. Thief. Outlaw."

"Kidnapper, flesh peddler," she shot back. "Is there no end to your debauchery?"

"Apparently not." He insinuated his knee between hers, unbalancing her, the motion erotic, parting her for his will.

"You will not win me like this."

"I do not have to." His free hand rode her shape and she squirmed. "You, my lady, have agreed to the price."

Suddenly he ducked, his mouth slashing heavily over hers. He expected the claw of her nails, the bite of her teeth, yet when she suddenly plowed her hands into his hair and returned his kiss, Raiden knew he'd fallen into a cavern with no way to the surface. He should have known she'd give no quarter. And brigand that he was, he stole more. Needed more.

BOOK YOUR PLACE ON OUR WEBSITE AND MAKE THE READING CONNECTION!

We've created a customized website just for our very special readers, where you can get the inside scoop on everything that's going on with Zebra, Pinnacle and Kensington books.

When you come online, you'll have the exciting opportunity to:

- View covers of upcoming books

- Read sample chapters

- Learn about our future publishing schedule (listed by publication month *and author*)

- Find out when your favorite authors will be visiting a city near you

- Search for and order backlist books from our online catalog

- Check out author bios and background information

- Send e-mail to your favorite authors

- Meet the Kensington staff online

- Join us in weekly chats with authors, readers and other guests

- Get writing guidelines

- AND MUCH MORE!

**Visit our website at
http://www.zebrabooks.com**

RENEGADE HEART

Amy J. Fetzer

Zebra Books
Kensington Publishing Corp.

http://www.zebrabooks.com

ZEBRA BOOKS are published by

Kensington Publishing Corp.
850 Third Avenue
New York, NY 10022

First Printing: August, 2000
10 9 8 7 6 5 4 3 2 1

Printed in the United States of America

Dedicated with much love and friendship
to Maureen Child
a.k.a. Kathleen Kane

For Diva-hood, and beautiful jammies just because.
For delicious "purring" and keeping my secrets,
especially the really weird ones.
For Dan'l Boone and Hogless One
and a hundred ways to cook venison.
For wanting to share this last hurrah with the Corps.
For believing I have brilliant moments when I really don't
Here's to kindred spirits, propping each other up,
and "kickin' butt and takin' names" as we march on.
You're the best, girl, and
I hope you never get tired of hearing,
"Tell me if this stinks?"
If you do, I'm sunk.

Books by Amy J. Fetzer

MY TIMESWEPT HEART

THUNDER IN THE HEART

LION HEART

TIMESWEPT ROGUE

DANGEROUS WATERS

REBEL HEART

THE IRISH PRINCESS

RENEGADE HEART

Published by Zebra Books

Articles of Piracy

I. Every man shall have an equal vote in affairs of the moment. He shall have an equal title to the fresh provisions and strong liquor at any time seized, and shall use them at pleasure unless a scarcity may make it necessary for the common good that a retrenchment may be voted.

II. Every man shall be called fairly in turn by the list on board for distribution of prizes. Over and above their proper share, they are allowed a shift of clothes and incidentals. But if they defraud their mates to the value of even one shilling in plate, jewels, gold, or money, they shall be unmercifully marooned. He that keeps secrets or robs another in his company, shall have his nose slit and ears severed, and put ashore under conditions of severe hardship.

III. Aboard the ship, none shall game for money, either with dice or cards.

IV. Each man shall keep his piece, cutlass, and pistols at all times clean and ready for action.

V. No boy or woman to be allowed on board except on special occasions such as socials. If any man shall be found carrying any of the latter sex to sea in disguise for purpose of selfish lust and seduction, he shall suffer severance of his organ.

VI. He that shall desert the ship or his quarters or exhibit cowardice in time of battle shall be punished by death.

VII. None shall strike another on board the ship, but every man's quarrel shall be settled on shore by sword or pistol in the proper manner of a gentlemen's duel.

VIII. Any man who shall become a cripple or lose a limb in this service shall receive 800 pieces-of-eight from the common treasury, and proportionate amounts for lesser hurts.

IX. The captain and the quartermaster shall each receive two shares of a prize, the master gunner and boatswain one and one-half shares, and private gentlemen of fortune and adventurers one share each.

One

Fresh blood colored his blade.

"Decide now, man." Raiden arched a brow, the point of his sword tucked beneath the man's jaw near his ear. "I offer only once." When the East India soldier stalled, he pushed the razor tip into his flesh far enough to make it bleed steadily "Are you prepared to meet Yama? Or is it Allah who will greet you?"

The man swallowed hard, his glance darting to the two dead soldiers at his feet before he tossed down his sword, his hands thrown up in surrender. He back stepped. Raiden inclined his head, and the man made a hasty escape down the street and into the thick crowds of the marketplace. Raiden had not taken a step before three of the man's brethren slipped from dark alleys and arched doorways, spitting at their fleeing comrade and lunging for Raiden. English cutlasses and vicious curved swords swiped the air before his face.

Steel clashed, his blade sliding against his opponent's and bringing him face-to-face with a man only half his length.

Raiden took pity and, grabbing him by the coat front, lifted him off the ground. "Drop it."

The sword clattered to the parched dirt. With a heave, Raiden sent the man into a vendor's cart. The merchant cursed. Blue-coated soldiers charged. Quick sparring, and Raiden sent two back. *Persistent little buggers,* he thought as he kicked the crude scaffold covered in ropes of fabric. Like a house of sticks, it collapsed on his attackers, wet dye coating his assailants red and deep blue.

Raiden seized the moment and put distance between them. But the wiry, dark-skinned men were quick to chase, each with a mission in mind—his death. *Not this day,* he thought, turning to face them and wishing he'd time to reload his pistols. Metal sparked. One turbaned man advanced enough to bleed his arm. Raiden repaid in kind, yet even in the fray, he noticed their gazes slip past him.

He whipped around just as a beautiful woman, elegantly dressed and looking far too fresh for this heat, smashed a terra-cotta jar over a man's head. The man slithered to the ground, the blade meant for Raiden's back toppling from his hand.

The woman dusted her hands and shrugged. "The odds seemed terribly unfair," she said, then gestured beyond. "Attend to your own, sir."

Raiden faced forward as more East India soldiers slipped around corners, from under carts and tables of the marketplace. Vastly outnumbered, he knew when to cut the mooring and take the wind. Grabbing her hand, he ignored the woman's protests and pulled her none too gently down the avenue. Apparently, he'd been betrayed. The soldiers were expecting him. 'Twas not the first time he'd fled for life in the last sennight, except now he was saddled with a bit of feminine baggage wearing twenty pounds of panniers and petticoats, and threatening their escape.

Willa grappled for footing on the rocky street. " 'Tis unnecessary, this," she gasped, grabbing up a fistful of gown and trying to match his pace, the brute. "They are after *you.*"

"They do not see lines in this battle, m'lady."

She jerked on his hand. "I will take my chances."

"I will not." He hauled her into an alley, shoving her behind him before peering into the street.

" 'Tis not your choice." She tried moving past, but without looking, he pinned her back with one arm.

"Nor is it yours."

Willa's gaze fell on the bloody sword clenched in his fist and she swallowed. Had she aided the wrong man? Then she saw the two flintlock pistols and knives jammed into his wide belt at his back and knew she had.

"You *chose* to interfere in my affairs, woman." He lurched back from the edge; then, moving deeper into the alley, he forced her ahead. "And you wounded their comrade."

She stopped and faced him, her hands on her hips. "Do not speak to me of a mere bump on the head when *you* were hacking at your share." She waved wildly, her beaded reticule swinging from her wrist.

Ahh, she had too much fire for her own good, he thought. Just his luck to be saved by a redheaded hellion with, God forbid, an opinion. "I hacked two, clean to the bone," he took pleasure in clarifying, then watched her features slacken with horror. His own callousness hit him like bad beef in his gullet, angering him, and in two strides, he was inches from her, saying, "And were you mayhaps expecting my everlasting gratitude for braining that soldier?" as he forced her around and pushed her on ahead.

"A simple thank-you would suffice." She threw a contemptuous look back over her shoulder. "But obviously polite manners are not common amongst bloodthirsty barbarians such as yourself." He reached. She sidled away from his bloodstained touch, but he caught her wrist, wrestling with her a bit before his grip turned painful.

"Do not fight me, woman. They would kill you for those alone," he growled in her face, nodding to the jewels adorning her neck and ears. "And so could I."

Her chin lifted, her eyes brittle. "I would give them freely afore allowing my life as forfeit." Sweeping her finger under the necklace, she jiggled it, taunting him. "Would you prefer to take it now?"

A deep growling rumbled in his chest, and she clearly expected to see fangs appear.

"I do not rob defenseless women," he gritted, though she was not without weapons a man could resist.

"So, 'tis only armed ones you thieve upon, then?"

"Aye. I require at least a musket or a dagger." He pulled her along behind him. "Makes it a bit more challenging."

Oh, the rogue, she thought, her lips twitching helplessly. He spared her a thin-lidded glance when she dug in her heels.

"Well, you needn't be so rough."

"Then move your pampered arse."

She gasped, twisting in his grip, then drove her dainty toe into his shin. Grunting, he let go, the abrupt release sending her reeling backward. Before she hit the wall, he caught her about the waist, dragging her up against him.

Her gaze locked with eyes as black as midnight, hypnotic, fathomless—chilling. Sight and sensation assaulted her; ribbons of sable-dark hair, carved features hewed by events she could only imagine, the immovable hardness of his body, the steely strength circling her waist and denying any escape ... and the intoxicating heat spiraling through her every cell and threatening her composure.

Raiden felt her soften against him for the briefest instant, warm and womanly supple, and the impression tortured him with what he could never taste. "Careful, lass." He backed her up against the stone wall. "You swim in waters far too rough for the likes of you."

She struggled, her bravado fleeing as quick fear raced up her spine. "I know only that I do not want to be here."

He pushed his body into hers and kept pushing, sandwiching her to the wall and crushing the breath from her lungs. "Then mayhaps you should have let them kill me."

His ominous expression gripped her by the throat, enthralling her.

He meant it to taunt her, show her she'd interfered in something far more volatile than a brawl in the avenue. But she saw the truth in his eyes, his gaze scoring her every feature and revealing a strange entreaty. He courted death. Mayhap not this night, at this moment, but he'd nothing in his blackened soul. No hope. No tenderness. A blend of fear and sympathy swept her, even when he dared her not to come near.

"I could not allow it. Not even to a man like you," she breathed, mesmerized by the challenge in his eyes.

"Your bravery is misspent, little fox," he rasped, his face inches from her. "I could cut your pretty pale throat and be done with you."

"If 'tis so," she tipped her chin up, exposing her slender neck, "then you'd have left me to those soldiers."

Raiden scowled, not wanting her trust—or her innocence. He deserved little of either. " 'Tis still possible." He withdrew a wickedly long dagger and watched her eyes widen. "I could steal more than jewels from you." He ducked, his mouth nearing hers in open threat.

Her breath caught, her gaze flashing between his empty eyes and his chiseled lips, the very thought of kissing him tightening her throat.

Just then the shouts of soldiers echoed in the streets beyond.

Willa arched a russet brow, her lips pursed with triumph.

He smirked. "You have chosen the same evil," he said, his hand suddenly beneath her skirts, warm and heavy as it swept up her bare thigh.

Willa squelched her fear and met his gaze. "I saved your life," came through gritted teeth as she shoved at his chest. "Now do me the courtesy to remove your hand!"

The disgust in her voice struck Raiden like a slap, and his expression turned blacker. "Hush, woman! You slow us down with all that frippery." He shoved her skirts above her waist, and in two swipes of his blade, cut away the tapes and ties of her pannier and several petticoats.

Willa sputtered, utterly mortified and slapping at his hands.

Unaffected, he lifted her out of the pile, dropped her to her feet, and pulled her along. She tripped twice on the overlong skirts, then swept up an armful of green silk, glancing back at the stack of expensive lace and caging, then to the men coming around the corner.

This time they had long rifles.

"Oh, lord a'mighty!"

Raiden didn't look back. "Run!" The soldiers fired, balls plunking into the dry-mortared walls just as they rounded a corner.

Showing more leg than was proper, Willa ran behind him through the west end of the marketplace. She'd no notion of where exactly they were, and in the haze of the setting sun, she could scarcely see the area around her. She was forced to trust him, yet he never let her go, keeping her prisoner to his game. Merchants hurriedly closed up their carts and shops, pulling fabrics swept over rods and poles as they passed. She bumped into a table weighted with bowls and jars, toppling crockery to the dirt, but when she bent to the shattered pieces, he jerked on her arm, commanding her to run. A woman sitting amongst black kettles and pots like a witch to her cauldron cackled and called out, giving away their position. Raiden snarled at her in Hindi as they passed, and the woman cowered.

The scent of curry, cardamom, and ginger mixed with the odor of fish as they neared the wharf. His boots thumped on the hard dirt road, then sounded hollow when they met the wood slats of the dockside. Willa's heel caught, and without hesitation, he scooped her up, ducking behind a stack of timbers.

Setting her to her feet, he shielded her with his body, then immediately went about reloading his pistol.

Leaning back against the woodpile, she tried to catch her breath and said, "Considering your nature, I could speculate for hours, but what in the name of heaven did you do to warrant this attention?''

''Asked questions.''

Well, she certainly understood that. She'd made one inquiry after another about Mason and received nothing but silence and a patronizing pat on the head. ''Who *are* you that these men are so . . . persistent?'' she asked, peering around his rather large body.

''No one of consequence.''

She scoffed delicately. ''Practice your lying, sir. It lacks that fine degree of sincerity.''

Raiden shook his head, then looked down, again caught in her cat-green eyes. Eyes to entrap a man's soul, he thought and admitted she was truly lovely; voluptuous, flame-haired, and exotic. And she wore the most intriguing French undergarments. ''I am Raiden.'' He darted a look into the street. ''And you are?''

''Willa.'' Wisely, she, too, withheld her last name. No sense in becoming any more . . . familiar. *Oh do not think on it,* she scolded herself, the warm imprint of his hand lingering on her thigh.

The exclusion did not escape him, setting a boundary he needed and glancing over his shoulder, he let his gaze roam over her long enough to be rude, then looked down the street again. ''Come, we cease this running now.'' His pistol and sword a'ready, he took a step.

She grabbed his arm. Hard muscle flexed beneath her grasp, and her hand dampened with blood. ''Outnumbered, wounded''—she showed him her palm—''and you still seek a fight? I took you for a smarter fellow, barbarian.'' She lifted her hem, intent on tearing off a piece of petticoat; then, with a disgusted sound over its absence, ripped the lining of her skirt. ''You may not value your life''—she straightened, wrapping his bicep—''but I intend to grow old and doddering, talking out of turn and coddling my grandchildren.''

Raiden gazed down at her bowed head, something working

through his chest at the sight of her smooth hands on him. "What? No stomping about with a cane? Masticating your food to mush?"

She pursed her lips. "How kind of you to add that." She tied off the wound. "But I fully intend to keep my teeth."

A smile threatened, yet the picture she painted was foreign to him, a future he would not allow to materialize. It made him see his worth and loathe her involvement in this mess. But she was right. He'd much business to tend to, and he'd not perish in the streets of Calcutta like a damned dog. "You are marked because you aided me;"

Without looking up, she wiped her bloodied hands on a handkerchief from her reticule. "To my eternal regret."

Aye, he thought, and any longer in his presence could get her killed. "If the soldiers approach and it looks to be another battle, scream and run to them."

Her brows rose. "What? But you will be accused—"

"Of stealing all you have," he finished smoothly, his smile barely there, yet his eyes spoke of a pleasurable theft. "Come." He stepped away, and like a lamb to the slaughter, she followed.

He led her through narrow alleys, behind taverns and shops, his pace quick, yet cautious. People scattered at the sight of him, mothers shielding their children and herding them indoors. His sword held before him, he was heads above most and dangerously dark from his long hair to his tall jackboots. Willa admitted that being near him made her heart quicken, and even the looks he cast her, irritated over her interference in his gloriously eventful day, gave her only foolish thoughts she should never entertain. But she did, and as they ducked into an arched doorway, she knew that beyond his crude language and threats, he would die to protect her. He'd already offered his freedom for hers.

'Twas a startling revelation, especially since she'd no trust to offer him. Her gaze swept the hard set of his features, yet could see nothing but the moon's glitter in his gaze. A predator's eyes. Without comment, he grasped her hand and stepped out into the street again, keeping her tucked close to his back. The heat of his body penetrated her gown, bringing his scent—dark, musky, and completely male. Willa scolded herself for noticing.

Sheathing his sword, he held the loaded pistol a'ready, his head twisting and turning, midnight eyes darting to every shadow and cavity. When a squad of troops trotted down the far end of the street, closer to the wharf, he pulled her into the dilapidated stable and kept moving deeper into the hovel, releasing her hand to duck under the low-slung loft and edge toward a cut in the wall serving as a window. He gestured for her to move behind him. She hesitated, aware of the danger in remaining in his presence a moment longer. Not only her reputation was in jeopardy.

His brow lifted, a dark slash against bronzed skin. "Frightened of me still?"

"Hardly," she said, yet reluctant to join him in the dark. "I do not trust you."

"You grow wiser by the moment, little fox," he murmured, folding his arms over his chest and leaning back against the wall beside the window, his gaze on the street beyond. The East India soldiers did not appear, and he looked at her. "Do forgive the less than stellar accommodations, m'lady." He tipped a slight bow totally lacking in respect. "But 'tis the best I can offer."

His caustic tone stung and she sniffed the air. " 'Tis but a temporary state." She didn't elaborate that she'd spent the last months in places near as crude as this and took a step, tripping on her overlong skirts. She bit back a curse. Without the bone cage and petticoats, the fabric dragged horribly, and she scooped up an armful, sending him a glare he didn't see.

But he felt it. Raiden looked up and glimpsed her shapely calves wrapped in stockings with tiny bows securing her garters. His insides twisted violently at the purely feminine sight, and he tore his gaze away. He didn't want to think on the last time he'd been with a woman of her caliber and forced the image into the wasteland of his memory. 'Twas a time he did not wish to revisit.

Damn and blast, he should have left her behind. The soldiers might have let her go without harm, especially since she was a lady of quality and, likely, of considerable influence. He scoffed. East India soldiers saw nothing but protecting the company's interests and destroying anything in their path. Experience had taught him that. Unexpectedly, memories surged, and with a snarl, he jammed his pistol into the back of his belt and removed the other, reloading it. Covertly, he studied her.

She withdrew a respectable distance away, sitting on a crate, half in the shadows and wisely far back enough from the window not to be seen. Poised demurely in a pile of green silk, she plucked at bits of flax, then resecured her hair into its elaborately braided coif. Yet nothing would take away the alluring disheveled look about her. He wanted to ruffle her more and did not doubt 'twas the woman's first occasion to perspire. Her breathless state spoke of it.

His back flat against the wall, he packed the wad and shoved it into the barrel, then tapped powder into the pan.

She was a rare beauty, beyond compare, her accent unlike any he'd heard recently, cultured and pleasing. When she was not sharpening it on his hide, he thought, as a dozen questions darted through his mind. Why was she in the marketplace alone? What sort of man left her to travel without an escort or even a maid? And whose woman was she, for she was too old not to be wed? His gaze dropped to her hand and he found no ring, though he cast the implication off. 'Twas his experience that women left the question of vows up to the moment and the man.

The sun crowded the moon in the Indian sky, the red haze of heat conquered by the blue coolness of night. The colors danced across her face and smooth bare shoulders, glittering off the emeralds and diamonds surrounding her throat and twinkling from her ears. Even the most honest of souls would be tempted to slit her throat for the wealth they posed, or sell her into slavery to some pasha who'd a taste for pale-ivory skin. His gaze moved over her green gown, turned a deeper shade in the dark; watered silk, costly and beaded. A bored lass out for a bit of adventure? She fished in her reticule, withdrawing a handkerchief stained with his blood and blotting her face and throat. Raiden's gaze remained riveted to the cloth as she passed it over her skin, the plump swells of her breasts. A fine, lush piece she was. And leagues of trouble if he did not put her off somewhere.

And he would. Quickly.

He returned his flintlock to his belt. "Have you a home or a room here?"

She met his gaze. " 'Tis not your concern."

"You are under my protection."

A delicately arched brow lifted. "I am a *victim* of your protection. How long must we remain here?"

He didn't answer, only staring, and Willa felt the flush of embarrassment warm her damp skin. His eyes might offer the blackness of a Carolina river, yet they bore a strange, turbulent power, like lightning. Each time they lit on her, her insides flinched and her heart jumped a full beat. Lord a'mighty, he was a handsome devil. Devil. An apt description,. There was a savageness in him she'd never encountered in any man, none in her circles. Command, that was it. He garnered attention for no reason other than his formidable presence, his countenance impenetrable, his big muscled body as much of a weapon as the arsenal circling his trim waist. His legs were a'liken to tree trunks, his breeches a bit too snug for modesty's sake, she thought, suddenly a little lost for thought. Clad from head to toe in black, his hair was but a shade or two lighter, the fashion of it alone, beyond his shoulders, loose and side-parted, would set tongues to wagging. His shoulder braced on the wall, he gave the appearance of a grand sphinx, unaffected by their situation, her, or their surroundings. He simply stared. Then, with a flick of his head, he sent his hair back, the motion revealing a crescent-shaped scar on his jaw. And a gold loop piercing his ear. How exotic.

What did he do for a living? she wondered suddenly, then decided 'twas best not to know. Given their meeting, 'twas undeniably dangerous. She sighed, pulling her gaze away and staring out the window. A fine fat mess, this. A fitting end to a completely unpleasant day after spending hours at the Ship's Chandlers, trying to book passage to the Banda Islands. But no seaman of reputable quality would take her, most refusing to discuss it. The last man even had the nerve to laugh in her face, the hairy wastrel. Needing time alone, she'd sent her bodyguard, Manav, against his protests, back to the hotel. She'd taken a stroll through the market when she'd come upon that greasy little man creeping up behind Raiden.

Manav will be worried, she thought, and impatient to be gone, she stood, moving nearer to the spot between the window and the door. In the street, the city started its journey to bed, and a young boy lit a multitude of candles, each wedged into the stone walls. Her gaze hungrily followed the child, her heart clenching painfully as he raced from lamp to globe, brightening the black streets. Did Mason have a light to protect him against the dark? Was his nurse, Maura, with him? Was he hungry and cold this night? Was he calling out for her? Oh, that tortured her the most, that he might think she'd abandoned him. She covered her mouth, smothering her grief and uncertainly. Then, seeking fresh air, she took a step.

"Stay back."

She twisted, meeting his gaze.

Raiden frowned at the unmistakable sheen of tears and straightened. "M'lady?"

"Do not call me that," she snapped, gathering her skirts and moving to the door. "Blessed saints, I loathe hearing that."

He was there before she could take two steps, grasping her arm and wrenching her around.

"Where think you to go?"

"Home. I am done with this little escapade, sir." She pried

off his fingers and threw his hand back at him. "Good evening."
She had barely turned away when a figure shadowed the doorway. She sucked in a breath, lurching back into Raiden.

"Sahib?"

In the space of a heartbeat, Raiden shielded her with his body, his sword out and tucked under the chin of the intruder.

"Sahib Raiden, it is me." The voice trembled.

Raiden's stance relaxed. "Sanjeev?"

A young man, no more than eight-and-ten, stepped into the stable, his body clad like a soldier, yet his dusty uniform was in poor condition. He wore far too many weapons to make her comfortable, and she remained behind Raiden until he pulled the lad inside.

"A most valiant fight, sir."

Raiden scowled, sheathing his weapon. "And you chose to watch instead of lending aid?"

Sanjeev smirked. "You already had help." His gaze flicked beyond him to the woman.

Raiden twisted, his gaze sliding over Willa in one luxurious sweep. Her blush brimmed with innocence, and if Raiden needed more evidence that they were worlds apart, that was it.

Willa sucked in a deep breath. Oh, that man was too bold for certain, she thought, making her feel entirely too . . . exposed under his gaze. 'Twas rude and calculating and oh, she didn't want to consider anything beyond that. Straightening her clothing, Willa was smoothing her hair, when the entrance filled with men. The most disreputable-looking men she'd ever seen, she thought, her arm lowering slowly. Were these his friends, his associates? Again she wondered what he did to survive—besides hacking at soldiers.

"Captain?" Tristan Dysart interrupted, then gestured behind Raiden.

He turned in time to see Willa's skirts disappear beyond the rear doorframe. He strode to the door, glancing left and right into the empty alleyway, then let out a long tired breath, shaking his head. She was either stupid or utterly fearless, he thought, then flicked a hand toward the alley entrance.

"Dysart, Vazeen, come with me." Brows rose, his crew's expression questioning his motives. "Your captain lives because of that little bit of fluff." Their looks doubted, but Raiden could not walk away without seeing to her welfare. "The rest of you find safety this night. The British are pressing any man still on two legs into service, and I suspect if Siraj-uddulah attacks, this city will fall. And we fight for no country."

Two

Willa was yards from her hotel when she heard, "By the gods, are you always so disobedient?"

She sucked in a huge breath and whirled, a knife in her hand. Sweet mercy, a man that big had no right to possess so silent a step. "Aye, constantly," she quipped, her heart pounding. " 'Tis my greatest dream to irritate you right out of my life." She gestured with the knife. "Now go."

Raiden arched a brow at the little folding blade, his look questioning its presence.

Her chin rose a notch. "Had you investigated more than my . . . accouterment . . ." Words failed when he darted close, too close, towering, smothering, his voice low and seductive.

"Is that an invitation?" He snatched the blade from her grasp, inspecting it with a critical eye. Then, with a deft movement, he snapped it closed.

"Give it back," she said, refusing to reach for it.

"Demanding *and* disobedient? You must be the very bane of your father's existence." And incredibly brave, he thought.

"And I shall be yours if you do not return my blade." She'd had it too long to lose it now.

His expression darkened. "Threats, Willa?"

Her eyes flared hotly, and unable to resist the taunt, Raiden pressed the blunt edge of the knife to her chest. She went as still as shallow water, her gaze locked with his as he pushed it, ever so slowly, down into the lush valley between her breasts. The motion brought forth an entirely different image he'd no right to possess.

"Raider," she gasped, and he felt unhinged at the breathy sound of his name on her lips.

"You've no need of it now, my lady." He tapped once more, his fingertip resting on her skin.

His touch seared, radiating like a cloudy promise of more, and she caught his wrist. "I am capable of taking care of myself."

She was a fool to believe that, then. "And I will see you safely home." He withdrew a step, loosing her grip. "Make no mistake."

She eyed him, and when he motioned her ahead, she went. She could sense more than see or hear his vigil as he walked behind her. She could not be seen with him. And when she was near the doors, the elaborately dressed hotel guards in sight, she asked, "Why do you insist on continuing this association? You owe me naught."

"Do I?"

She frowned at his odd tone and glanced back, freezing in her tracks. He was gone, and her gaze swept the narrow streets. No footsteps. No shadows. She felt strangely disappointed, and defenseless. She raced the few steps to the hotel.

The danger of what she'd done truly hit her when she reached the hall leading to her rooms and finally drew a decent breath. She fell back against the wall beside the door, her hand trembling as she pressed it to her stomach. She closed her eyes. *The fixes I managed to find,* she thought glumly. Ten times she regretted her walk in the market. And now, how was she to explain the lack of a pannier and a half-dozen petticoats to Manav and the prim Rajani? Not to mention the scandal of how she lost them. Unwillingly, her lips curved as Raiden's dark image unfolded in her mind, and her hand rose to her breasts, his touch lingering, stirring her still, and for a moment she almost wished he'd . . .

A scuffling sound came from her rooms and she frowned, rolling around and reaching for the latch. Then she realized the door was unlocked.

She pushed it open and sucked in her breath.

Chaos greeted her, drawers ransacked, her cases upended and torn, clothes strewn everywhere.

"Manav? Rajani?"

Cautiously, she edged around the carved screen near the door and froze. Her gaze dropped to her bodyguard sprawled on the floor.

"Manav!" She rushed to his side, sliding to her knees. "Oh, Manav," she cried, gently lifting his head onto her lap and using her hem to wipe the blood from a gash on his temple. 'Twas deep and bore the look of a claw or hook. Calling his name, she blotted his battered face, and his lashes fluttered, then swept up.

"Memsahib!" His gaze darted around the room before coming back to meet hers. "I feared you . . . were dead." He struggled for each word, his breathing a gurgling rasp.

"I am unharmed. Nay, lie still," she said when he tried to move. "Who did this?" Where was Rajani? She glanced around, calling for help.

Footsteps sounded beyond the door and she looked up as Mr. Romhi stepped inside, Rajani behind him.

"Oh, Rajani, thank God," she said, then put up her hand when the girl approached. "Nay, return to your room till it's safe." The innocent did not need to see this.

She obeyed as the innkeeper turned back into the hall, calling for servants to get the British authorities, clapping his hands and meting out orders. Then he crossed the room, pouring water into a bowl and searching the debris for a cloth.

At the sight of Mr. Romhi, Manav lifted his trembling hand, cupped the back of her head, and drew her closer. Despite his wounds, his grip was fierce in her hair, his voice desperate. "It was . . . you . . . they sought, Memsahib." His words warmed her ear. "Trust . . . no one!"

Bowed over him like a protective shield, she whispered, "Why me?

Before he could respond, his grip slackened, his hand falling from her hair. She sat upright, staring at his darkly tanned face. "Manav? Don't you dare!"

The innkeeper neared, kneeling with a bowl and damp towel. She took the cloth, wiping Manav's face and throat and calling his name.

"Memsahib?"

She glanced up. Mr. Romhi gestured off to her right and Willa looked, her eyes widening at the pool of blood spreading on the wood floor beneath Manav like a slow-moving tide. *Lord save him,* she thought, quickly checking for a pulse. She found none, and a low moan spilled as she wrapped her arms around the brave, slender man. She rocked him gently, pushing off his blue turban and stroking his inky black hair. *Oh, my trusted friend.* He did not deserve to die, and not like this.

Mr. Romhi reached for her. "Come away from here. This is no place for you."

She flinched from his touch, meeting his gaze. "Manav had no family, no one to mourn him. This *is* my place. Leave us, please."

Romhi nodded and stood, ordering the servants out and closing the door. Willa didn't see him post a guard outside.

Beyond the walls, in the street, the even cadence of boot heels came to her as she tipped her head back, releasing her grief in hot tears and quiet sobs. Manav believed in *Puner Janam,* that death brought his soul to another life, and she prayed that when he was reborn, 'twas in a gentler place than this horror. Suddenly, the door shoved open and she looked as a British officer strode in and stopped a few feet from her.

He snapped to attention. "Captain Atcheson, my lady."

The East India insignia glared from his shoulder, and she wondered how he'd arrived so quickly. "Did your mother not teach you to knock, captain?"

He reddened, keeping his gaze forward. "My apologies, my lady. Given the situation, I thought it best not to waste time."

"My bodyguard is dead, captain. How much time do you need to deduce that?" Willa knew she was taking her grief out on the soldier, but she couldn't help it. This was her fault, and she felt her life slipping out of her control.

"I promise to see this matter to the end." His gaze swept the room, assessing and cataloging the disorder before he brought it back to the body. His eyes flared slightly, yet he showed no remorse or sympathy for the Hindu man. Willa wanted to slap him for it.

Romhi entered behind him, cowering a bit, and Willa hated seeing the man's dignity scarred. Damn the English Army, she thought. Was their own country not enough that they had to subjugate everywhere they stepped?

Atcheson motioned to three uniformed men, and they stepped close, laying a stretcher on the floor beside Manav. Willa replaced his turban, smoothing his hair beneath and kissing his forehead before she scooted back and laid his head gently on the floor. She stood, her blood-soaked dress leaving a trail as she moved back, and in a cool voice warned the attendants, "Be gentle with him."

They nodded and did as she bade, her gaze never leaving her bodyguard until they carted him beyond the door. Servants moved around her, collecting her things, returning order, but Willa didn't see them as she stepped to the window.

"Lady Eastwick?"

She flinched at those words, hunching her shoulders as she wiped tears from her cheek. Willa Delaney Peachwood, Lady Eastwick. What rubbish. She was no more a member of the

British aristocracy than the maid who tidied her room. She was a Carolinian, born and reared, yet in the last years she'd slowly grown to loathe anything about the mother country and most especially the highbrow society that bred men like her husband, Alistar. No longer did she ask herself how she could have married such a man, a man so ignorant of anything but his surroundings, how to improve them, and how people viewed him. She knew why. Alistar was a peer and he had money. 'Twas that simple. Her father had needed it for his shipping company in these hard times in the Carolinas, especially when Father refused, bless his tired soul, to barter in slaves and was losing money on his spice and coffee imports because of the East India Company's monopoly. 'Twas a profitable match. She admitted Alistar was refined, handsome, impeccably mannered, and well turned out, but he bore an unmerciful quality she'd never suspected. Until their son was nearly three.

"My lady?"

She tipped her head and met the captain's gaze. If he noticed her tears, he was gracious enough not to mention it.

"I beg you to come to the compound. We can supply suitable quarters for you where you can be properly protected."

"Citizens are amassing, captain, and if Siraj-ud-dulah enters this city, the East India offices would be the first attacked and the first to fall."

He straightened with indignation. "The insurgents will be put down, my lady. This I assure you."

She waved him off. 'Twas useless to try to convince him or any other official that this was the Indians' country and men defending their homes were far more successful than those defending it for England. "You do not ask a thing about this incident, no questions to the staff? To Mr. Romhi?"

"We will do our utmost to find the culprits, your ladyship. However, 'tis your safety that is our first concern."

"Then get me a pistol."

He looked at her as if she'd grown horns and wings, then offered a tolerant smile. "My dear lady. Truly, 'tis not your concern to defend yourself. 'Tis why we are here, and his lordship would never forgive me if I did not see to it personally.''

If *his lordship* had any say in the matter, Willa suspected he'd like her to disappear.

''I heartily agree with the captain, your ladyship.''

She looked up to see East India Director Barkmon stroll in, wigged and powdered, impeccable in white. He reminded her of a leek, pale, with a slight green tint, and in bad need of peeling and boiling. Three nights ago, at dinner at his residence, he was congenial, obsequious, even partnering her with an admiral and a charming general. Now he had the audacity to inspect her from head to toe. She turned her back on the man.

''Have you been in contact with Lord Eastwick?'' she said coolly, sparing them a look she'd seen a dowager duchess give anyone who was not family. She'd learned early that to show kindness or vulnerability, especially to East India nabobs, was to lose the advantage in a situation. And she did not want her loyalties to her husband to become suspect. 'Twas her *only* advantage right now.

The men exchanged glances. ''Nay, I have not.'' The director cleared his throat. ''But I have received word that he is in country.''

That was a lie. She knew by his forced smile, his faltering gaze. They were under Alistar's supervision.

''Where were you when this incident occurred?''

Raiden's image filled her mind like an overflowing cup of port wine, strong, potent. ''In the marketplace.''

''Alone? At this hour?'' His gaze lowered to her skirts, his attention on the missing shape the panniers normally offered.

She met his gaze head on and dared him to mention it. ''I was lost.

He seemed to consider that for a moment. ''Who would want to harm your bodyguard, your ladyship?''

Apprehension slithered up her spine, and Willa felt cornered. If she responded with the truth, that 'twas quite possibly her husband's people searching for her, they could force her under English guard and all opportunity to find Mason would be lost. If she lied, surely she would be caught in it. She was never very accomplished at it. She decided on hedging the truth. "Ask yourself who would want to harm *me,* sir. For there was no reason to kill Manav other than to get to me." She lifted her gaze to the captain and the director and offered them a look of pure innocence. "I am only Lord Eastwick's wife."

The captain looked thoughtful for a moment, then crossed to her, taking her hand and patting it. "For that reason alone, I beg you again, your ladyship, reconsider coming with us. Or mayhap returning to your home?"

She pulled from his grasp. She was not returning to the massive, empty house the Crown provided in Bengal. Not without her son. "I need privacy, at least for a day," she said, her tone regal. "I shall remain here."

Neither man argued, and that added to her suspicions.

"The captain, here, will post guards and assign an escort for you. We can only hope you will not meet the same fate as your servant."

Was that a threat? she wondered, a chill running down her spine. "I accept the guard for the evening, captain. I wish to know any and all information gained in the investigation of Manav's murder."

" 'Tis a simple burglary," Barkmon said.

His lack of concern angered her and she strode to the small trunk tucked beneath her vanity, kneeling. Opening it, she shifted the false bottom and removed a velvet bag, pouring the contents into her hand and holding it out. "There is naught simple about this."

Jewels, in necklaces, earbobs, and bracelets, glittered from her palm in diamonds, sapphires, and blood-red rubies. It actually made her ill to remember that Alistar had given them to her after he came to her bed. As if bedding her deserved payment. Like a whore. She'd done it out of duty, loneliness, and the crushing want of a child. 'Twas a shame Alistar did not love his child as much as he loved the trinkets he draped on her so lavishly. She stuffed them back into the pouch, stood, and dropped them into a vanity drawer.

She did not see Atcheson and Barkmon exchange a glance. *Trust no one.* Manav was the only person she'd trusted in months, beyond her father. And without the Hindu man, she felt alone and hunted.

Could Alistar really have done this? Nay, she thought, for he'd have sent someone to beat her guard into revealing what she knew and her location, for he loathed soiling his clothes, let alone tainting his hands with another's blood. She was suddenly glad she'd encountered Raiden, or this same killer would have undoubtedly stolen or attacked her. Manav had not revealed her, she knew beyond doubt, but his death meant Alistar was either near, being informed, or laying orders. If he was not party to this, then she'd another pile of twine to unravel.

She pushed the vanity drawer closed, stealing a covert glance at the director. Slightly round across the middle and short, he had the look of a well-nourished nabob with no notion of the lives he was altering. She'd been in the city a sennight before he'd paid her a visit, gently chastising her for not making herself known to him. And she, tisk-tisk, a peer's bride. Hah. The man was looking for a way to better himself, and since Alistar was sent by the Crown to inspect East India ships, properties, and accounts, if he had to, he'd serve her up on a platter like a plump, roasted pigeon.

She could not reveal why she was here, yet suspected these men knew little regardless. Alistar did not reveal his private affairs to a soul, yet he wanted to be informed of her movements. He was her husband. 'Twas his right. He was close enough to either gain a message, or send one. Was Mason with him? she wondered, her heartbeat quickening. Were they still in the city? She had plans to make.

"Leave me. Mr. Romhi will see to aught I need. He has done so with great care thus far."

Behind the Englishmen, Romhi smiled at her.

Atcheson gave them both a superior look. "Really? With such care that someone entered your rooms?"

Willa went to the window and lifted a rope, the end tied to a grappling hook, yet when she offered the curved iron up for inspection, 'twas stained with blood. She dropped it, realizing that Manav could have been killed with it.

Frowning, Captain Atcheson snapped his fingers at the soldiers in the corridor and they stepped inside. "Post yourselves at the rear doors and beneath Lady Eastwick's windows."

She nodded agreement, but before the soldiers left, she called out. "But not outside my rooms. I do not want to alarm the other guests." She swept to the open door, maids trotting in and out with her things, one with a bucket and rags to clean up the blood. Willa could not bring herself to look at the spot where Manav breathed his last. Not and keep her composure. "Now, if that will be all, gentlemen?"

The men stiffened, bade her good evening, and left. Romhi remained. "Your things will be moved to a new room, Memsahib. This one has a view of the street and a private exit."

They exchanged a smile and she whispered her thanks. "I will pay for aught that is necessary for Manav's funeral. Will you see to the arrangements?"

Agreeing, he offered his laundress to clean her gown. She looked down at her bloody fabric, and her heart constricted. She simply shook her head, and he left her alone with Rajani. Willa moved around her rooms, returning order.

If Alistar was a part of this and could beat an innocent man to death, what would he do to her . . . or to their son? Did he not know that she would tell his peers, his father, what he'd done? She scoffed rudely. They would not believe her. For five years she'd done everything to be accepted, but she lacked the proper background, a lineage noted in books and by kings. To them, she was a lowly colonist and whispered that Alistar was a fool for marrying her. Though she was rather proud of her Carolina home, here the colonists were still England's bastard children, and the Crown intended to keep a tight leash on them or punish them for profiting from the relationship.

Dispirited, Willa finished collecting her things into trunks, and two hours later she was settled in her new rooms, bathed and sleepy after a meal. In her night rail, she sat on the window sill, slices of paper she'd risked her life to gain clutched in her hand. Her husband would not allow anyone to discover his deeds, she realized, for he never intended for her to return to England. And what would Mason's life be worth then? She made the sign of the cross and bowed her head, praying for her son's life. Praying to any god who would listen to keep him safe.

Raiden stood across the street, sunk deep in the shadows, staring up at the window, at Willa sitting on the sill, praying useless prayers. Her guard's murder made for lively speculation over a cup of *sarai* this night, and he did not want to examine how he'd felt when he heard. Although he'd waited until she entered the hotel, when the news traveled, he'd thought for a moment she'd met her death after saving his life.

And for the first time in over ten years, his heart ached.

God above, if he'd failed her too . . . He swallowed tightly, absorbing her, her sadness reaching him as if he wore it beneath his skin. He did not want it, did not need any attachment to her, yet when she tipped her head back, her hair spilling over one shoulder, catching the breeze and spreading back across the stark white of the building, Raiden felt almost honored. The light beyond her offered no more than a gauzy silhouette, embellishing the sweet—*ah, Christ above*—the sweet outline of her body beneath the white batiste, the smooth pearl of her shoulder where the night rail slipped low. The fabric molded her breasts, and the look of her green eyes, the flare of emerald heat when he'd pushed the knife down between her breasts, burst in his mind. He swallowed hard, crushing the images he didn't want—of her, bare and brazen for his touch, beckoning when he knew she would never call to a man like him.

Suddenly, her head turned toward him, and though he could see little of her features now, he felt her frown, felt her gaze dart and shift over the vapid streets.

He clenched his fists against the urge to step into the light. Did she have to be so damned beautiful? Did she have to bait him fearlessly at every turn, create a fire in him like none before her? She was beyond him, his dirty world, further away than the mere yards dividing them now.

When she left her perch, he turned away, motioning to Dysart and Vazeen, and the men melted out of the doorways and into the inky-black streets of Calcutta.

"There's more than a bit of fluff sitting up on that sill." Dysart didn't look at him.

But Raiden heard the smile in Tristan's voice. "She is only a woman."

"A most lovely one, sahib," Vazeen piped in.

Raiden slid him a wry glance. "Careful, lad, you drool."

Vazeen smiled, white teeth stark against his dark skin. "If it would gain me a visit to her bed, then I would walk on my hands for her."

Raiden's fingers tightened around his sword hilt before he considered that the boy was at the age when every woman he clapped eyes on meant a chance to ride between her thighs.

"Barkmon was there," Tristan said.

Raiden glanced at the man, his ragged appearance belying his elegant voice and mannerisms.

"She could assist us—"

"Nay," Raiden cut in.

"But if she, mayhaps, takes tea with Barkmon, she can gather information."

"We do not involve women. Especially not that one. And she already has the British looking after her." Raiden wondered briefly who she was to garner the attention of the director and what the bloody hell was she doing in India alone? He planned to find out, then decided 'twas best to leave their association where it belonged, at a doorstep he could not cross.

Three

Willa twisted, leveling a hard look at the British soldiers standing off to the side, talking amongst themselves. They snapped to attention when they noticed her and ceased their disrespectful prattle. The four red-coated men had been shadowing her since last night, testing her patience, and she needed a plan to ditch them.

She glanced to the left, at her maid Rajani sniffling behind her veil, before she faced the stack of oiled wood. Atop lay Manav, dressed in his finest garments, his dark hair wrapped in a gold turban. A tear slipped down her cheek as she whispered her farewell, and Willa sucked in a breath when a man—a distant cousin, she'd learned—covered her friend in a shroud, then lifted a torch to the wood pyre.

The blaze caught quickly, engulfing Manav's earthly body, and she imagined his spirit fleeing within the curls of sandal-wood smoke reaching for the sky. She remained so, offering her thanks for her life and for his bravery. For without Manav's sacrifice, she'd no longer have the chance to find her son.

The sound of hoofbeats made her spine stiffen, yet she did

not turn, pressing her palms together close to her chest and bowing slightly, giving her friend the respect he deserved. Willa turned toward the carriage as Captain Atcheson slid from his saddle. Rajani hurried ahead.

"An unexpected visit, Captain." She kept walking, not liking the way he leered at her maid. "Have you no insurgents to put down? Sailors to press?"

Atcheson sent her an amused look. "The director wishes you to join him for luncheon."

Her hand looped in the carriage lighting strap, she glanced back at him. She'd been obligated to dine with Barkmon four days ago. That was quite enough. "Inform Mr. Barkmon that I'm not up to it."

"The director insists."

Her expression tightened. "Does he now?" Willa stepped into the carriage, and the footman closed the door.

Atcheson stood at the window. "My lady, I am to bring you to—"

"You've made his wishes clear." Seated beside Rajani, Willa turned her head to meet his gaze. "Relay to Mr. Barkmon that he is never to summon me like chattel. His poor manners prove him to be an ill-bred beast of the company and unworthy of my attention." She tapped the roof. "As do yours."

The carriage lurched, forcing him back, the four soldiers rushing to follow behind and leaving Captain Atcheson alone as the body burned into ashes.

"Order me about, will he?" she muttered, jerking off her gloves.

Rajani peered out the window. "He is most unhappy, Memsahib."

"I care little of the captain, nor should you." She rubbed her forehead, a headache brewing. "And I've a mind to attend, just to slap Barkmon's pudgy pale face."

Rajani gasped. "He would beat you."

Willa lowered her hand, frowning at the innocent girl. "He

would not dare.'' She was a wife of a peer, and regardless of
his power, he respected that. Yet the implication reminded
her to see Rajani protected and returned to her family should
Barkmon decide to overstep his authority.

'Twas foul enough to have those four troops following her
about and reminding her of her precarious position. How was
she to ferret out information on Alistar's whereabouts if they
followed her everywhere? And this carriage, for pity's sake.
'Twas elaborate and ridiculous in the narrow streets, sent by
Barkmon and bearing the British East India Company crest on
its glossy black door. To turn it down would prompt too many
questions she would not answer, yet sadly, not a soul would
speak with her whilst she plodded about in this contraption.
Twice it had been hit with rotten fruit. She longed for the
freedom of a horse. Pish-posh, she'd settle for an elephant or
a camel to avoid feeling locked in this rolling coffin.

The word brought a wave of guilt and she closed her eyes,
her head lolling with the roll of the wheels. *It was you they
sought,* Manav had said. To steal her? To hurt her? And what
for? For none knew she was searching for Mason save Manav
and the timid English maid she'd sent home. Not even Rajani
knew. And if 'twas true, there were any number of ways to
get to her. Manav would not be dead if she'd not left their
Bengali home and come to Calcutta; if she'd not insisted on
the private stroll; if her husband had not taken their son . . .
Damn the man, she thought, kicking out at the opposite seat.
A hollow sound responded. She glanced at Rajani, giving her
a mischievous look before sliding to her knees and shoving the
cushion up.

''Well, well. So very good of the English to be prepared.''
Willa immediately removed the pistol and powder horn, rummaging through the blankets, fans, umbrellas and—good lord,
there was even service for tea in here. She spied a thin silver
flask and snatched it, knocking off her veiled hat, then pulling
the stopper.

Rajani gasped, her gaze moving to the weapon and the decanter.

"Manav, forgive me." Willa saluted, then tipped it to her lips. Liquid fire raced through her blood, banishing the chill that had been with her for so long.

"Memsahib!" Rajani whispered, shocked.

Willa licked her lips, then held out the flask. "Would you care for some?"

The girl shook her head, a bashful smile curving her lips.

"French brandy, and a very fine year, I might add," she said, taking another healthy sip before climbing back into her seat. Handing the flask to Rajani, she inspected the flintlock, the East India seal on the stock. With a disgusted sound, she set it aside and took back the liquor, capping it.

The conveyance slowed to a patient roll as it entered the city. People milled and shopped, the heat oppressive as her gaze swept the streets, then slid back to a figure standing close to a building, beneath a merchant's awning.

Her brows knitted and she scooted closer to the window, his height and the width of his shoulders catching her attention. Indian men were rarely so large. A sand-hued turban covered his hair, the free end drawn across the lower portion of his face against the dust and blending with his *kurta,* the mud-dark tunic buttoned from waist to throat, long and slit at the sides over close-fitting brown breeches. Hidden in the shadows, he spoke to the vendor; slivers of sunlight glittered off the medallions and strands of gold adorning his neck as he doled coins into the vendor's palm. At the edge of the street, men loaded a wagon already brimming with baskets and crates, and when a worker called out in Hindi, the tall fellow looked up, his movements gone still. She felt the strength of his gaze as the carriage inched past, saw one worker follow its direction, and she sat back suddenly, frowning. Nay. 'Twas folly.

"Is there trouble?" Rajani leaned to look, but Willa motioned her back.

The carriage stopped to allow pedestrians to pass, and Willa poked her head out the window, looking back. The man shifted around baskets and barrels, toward her and into the sunlight, yet the carriage jolted forward, hurling her back into her seat in an undignified heap.

It could not be Raiden, she thought, waving off Rajani's help and struggling in the heavy skirts to sit upright. She twisted to look out the small window behind her head, but the soldiers on horseback blocked further view. She sank into the leather cushion, fanning herself and wondering why her heart picked up its pace at just the thought of him.

She opened the flask and hurriedly tipped it to her lips, knowing, with painful clarity, exactly why.

"You stare at her like the lad once gazed upon a platter of food."

Raiden kept his attention on the carriage as Tristan moved up behind him. "That boy no longer hungers and neither does the man." Yet 'twas the same as in his youth and always would be. The richest feast lay out of his reach.

"Forget the lady. She is well protected, and you have already stated you will not make use of her."

Raiden slid him a glance. "She knows my name." Tristan muttered a foul curse, and Raiden's brows rose high. "Swearing, Master Dysart? I'm appalled."

"By all that is sacred, what possessed you to—never mind. I have seen the lady." Tristan's expression soured. "I know what part of you was possessed."

Raiden scowled and looked back at the carriage as it turned the corner toward her hotel, the finest in three cities, yet the expensive fortress could not protect her manservant. Then how could it protect her? What business did she have that would warrant such a fatal attack? And was it meant for her, or was it retribution for something she or another had done? The sight of her in the company carriage made him burn with suspicion, for 'twas the director's own. Was she Barkmon's mistress?

Raiden knew the look of the man's wife, and Willa was a far reach from the short woman as round as her husband.

"Know you her family name?"

Raiden shook his head.

"I could ascertain it easy enough."

"Vazeen has tried," Raiden said. "Apparently the hotel servants are rather fond of her and would offer naught that was useful."

"What did they offer?"

"She arrived alone, except for servants. One English maid she sent away, replacing her with an Indian girl, and the other is, of course, dead."

Tristan's blue eyes narrowed. "Could that attack have been meant for her?"

"Considering her sharp tongue, 'twould not be a surprise." Raiden turned back toward the vendors as a horse and rider barreled down the street, scattering dust and people in his wake. Raiden lurched back as he passed. "Atcheson," he muttered, watching the captain steer his mount toward the East India Company headquarters.

A glass smashed against the wall to the left of Raiden's head, spraying liquor and crockery over his shoulder. He spared it a glance, flicking debris off his clothes as he warned his comrades back from the fight threatening to brew in the Red Raven Inn.

" 'Tis not our battle," he reminded them, relaxed in the chair, his leg flung over the arm as he sipped *kallu,* wishing 'twas Madeira. He popped a date into his mouth, his gaze sweeping to Vazeen, a girl of no more than ten and six on his lap and nearly in his breeches. She was English, if he had to guess, for this tavern catered to every class but the upper— Portuguese merchants, Mongols, English and Spanish sailors. A few Dutch. Yet like the locals, the East India soldiers did not step inside. One did not enter a lion's den and not expect to be picked apart by the predator.

Around him men, mostly his crew, enjoyed the freedom of drink and the whores lazing about, seeking a penny for their services. He considered paying for time with that voluptuous redhead talking with a Mongol, then dismissed the notion, looking away and knowing from whence it sprang.

He drained his drink, calling for more.

The girl with Vazeen straddled his lap, her hand in his breeches.

Raiden tossed a coin on the table, and Vazeen twisted to look at him, his eyes glazed. "Take it elsewhere," he growled, his thinning gaze telling him there were some things even he would not tolerate. "And conceal some of those." Raiden gestured to the stolen British weapons Vazeen wore proudly. "Do you want the world to understand who we are?"

The lad sent him an irritated look, then pushed the girl off, scraping up the coin before he ushered her toward the back rooms. The pair barely made it into the room before he had her up against the wall, pushing into her with hot, rhythmic strokes. Raiden looked away, cursing as he shifted in the chair, his gaze landing on Tristan as he nudged a plump little man toward his table.

"This fine gentleman has consented to join us."

Raiden's gaze flicked to the pistol his quartermaster pressed into the little man's back. He kicked out a chair and nodded. Winston Pendergast dropped into it like a petulant bear, casting a suspicious glance around. Tristan slid into a chair across from them both, the pistol concealed beneath the table.

"What do you here, Pendergast?"

If the man was surprised Raiden knew his name, he did not show it, shrugging before staring sullenly at his drink. Raiden called for *kallu,* and the man's face brightened slightly. The servant poured only after he gave up his coin, and Raiden threw Tristan a disgruntled look as his quartermaster whipped out a handkerchief to clean his glass prior to service.

Pendergast greedily drank the palm-tree wine, then swiped

the back of his hand across his lips and met Raiden's gaze. "I've come to see you."

Raiden arched a brow. "That is why you hide in the corner like a beaten animal?"

Pendergast looked affronted. "I do not hide, I wait. Even you can see the wisdom in that?"

Raiden's smile was thin and icy. "Yet you enter here?" He waved to the tavern full of the Calcutta's most disreputable creatures. "When there are dozens finer." His gaze flicked down the man's elegant clothes. He stood out like the white barnacle on a black hull, and if he thought no one noticed, he was wrong. They simply did not care.

"But 'tis not where I'd find a Montegomery."

Raiden's expression did not alter a fraction at the slander, only his gaze hardening on Pendergast.

"I see your mother neglected the manners portion of your education, Winston," Tristan said without a show of anger. "If you've a mind, Captain, I can kill him for you." Tristan, settled comfortably in the chair, spared neither man a glance, yet Raiden knew the pistol barrel was pressed to Winston's belly.

"That won't be necessary, Mr. Dysart."

"You're certain? 'Tis nay a bit of trouble."

Raiden took a small bit of pleasure in watching Pendergast pale to the shade of an unripened turnip before he waved away the offer. Tristan returned his gaze to their surroundings, covering Raiden's back.

"You have my ear," Raiden said, and Pendergast straightened his shoulders, his gaze dropping briefly to what lay beneath the table.

"I learned you pay handsomely."

He could only imagine who was stupid enough to tell him that. He'd killed for less.

"I am a clerk for the East—"

"I'm aware of your employer. Are you prepared for the

price of betrayal?'' 'Twould be a life sentence, if the directors allowed it to go that far.

Pendergast hunched over his drink and committed treason. "A ship sails in a sennight."

"One?"

"Aye. The *Persephone*."

Tristan and Raiden exchanged a glance. That was a lie. The English ships sailed in pairs as a defense posture. "Where bound?" Tristan asked.

"Ceram. The Banda Islands."

Raiden scoffed. "Even the English Navy is not reckless enough to weigh anchor there now." One crew complement and a few cannons? In the Spice Islands? Did not having their last expedition served as their supper warn them to the dangers? But then, the English would do anything for the scented coin, the spices. Even slaughter every soul from here to Guinea. They'd never learned that patience worked better than force with tribal kings and sultans. And 'twould be their undoing.

He eyed the man, then said, "Who owns your tongue that you would lie so easily?"

"No one owns me!"

Raiden sneered "The company possesses your soul, Pendergast. You simply do not recall losing it."

Pendergast flushed, rolling the glass between his palms. "The admiral will put to sea again."

Raiden did not respond, showing no interest, and waited for the trap to be laid.

Pendergast cleared his throat, glancing around, then leaned close, his face stretched in triumph that Raiden instantly distrusted. "In a month's time, he will command the *Queen's Regard* headed to Malacca—"

A sudden cry vibrated in the smoky tavern. Raiden scowled, and on reflex, drew his pistol, cocking the hammer in unison with Tristan's. Pendergast shoved away from the table, out of the line of fire.

Raiden searched the crowd for the source and found Bidda,

the owner, skinny and haggard with yards of tangled black
hair, shouting at a smaller woman. The shrouded, sari-wrapped
woman replied, her tone too low to be heard above the din of
the tavern as she offered coin. A lady. Raiden would stake his
life on it, and as his gaze swept the tavern, he was not the only
one who noticed. Men converged on the strange pair, interested
more in the sport of females battling than the women themselves. Bidda dismissed her and walked away.

But the lady was not abiding and grabbed Bidda's arm. 'Twas
unwise, that, Raiden thought, then winced when Bidda's balled
fist impacted with the woman's cheek. The lady reeled from
the blow, falling back against a man. The Portuguese sailor
pushed her on, but not before squeezing a handful of breast.
The lady spun and slapped him, but the sailor only chuckled.

Then she turned, stepped up to Bidda, and kicked her.

Raiden groaned, his chin dropping to his chest. *God save
me from impulsive females,* he thought as he stood.

"Raiden," Tristan said. "Is not that—?"

"Aye." Tossing a few coins at Pendergast, he paused long
enough to meet his gaze and level his pistol. "If I discover a
falsehood, there is no place safe for you to hide."

Pendergast's Adam's apple bobbed in his throat. Raiden
shoved aside tables and chairs, heading toward Willa. God
above, she wore a green sari. And her hair was dyed black.

"You're lying!" she shrieked, grabbing a handful of Bidda's
dirty hair and pulling a pistol from God knew where.

Swiftly, Raiden came up behind her, wrapping his arm about
her waist and yanking her back. "For the love of Triton, are
you mad?" He wrenched the loaded flintlock from her fist.

"Aye. Quite. Though 'tis nay business of yours." She tried
taking the pistol back, but he held it out of her reach, like a
parent denying a child candy.

"Sweet Christ, woman, did you not think your green eyes
would give you away?"

Willa had little choice. This was the last place Alistar had been. Likely hiring the brigands who beat Manav to death. ''Release me!''

His grip tightened around her as he growled in her ear, ''They are more fond of Bidda than you, woman. Or would you care to discover such on your own?''

She shook her head, helpless and loathing it.

Suddenly the doors burst open, hinges fracturing as British soldiers filled every exit. For a moment no one moved, then an officer shouldered his way inside, gold braid gleaming his rank on his red coat.

''You ain't welcome 'ere,'' Bidda snarled, sauntering up to the man.

He shoved her, sending her into the barrels supporting the counter. ''The Crown needs soldiers and sailors,'' he said to the crowd.

''Needs cannon fodder, I believe he means,'' Tristan said.

Women scattered as over two dozen men drew swords and pistols.

And Raiden held a struggling Willa in the center of it, an unwanted gauntlet thrown at their feet.

The officer fired into the ceiling, the dry mortar sprinkling them with red dust. ''Do not move,'' he shouted, a second weapon and gaze on Raiden.

He smiled thinly. If the man thought he'd be pressed into service, he was sadly mistaken. ''Shoot, captain, or die.'' The soldier's gaze slid to Willa's pistol in his hand and Raiden prayed 'twas properly loaded.

A split second passed before Raiden realized the officer was not aiming at him.

But at Willa.

Four

The officer extended his aim.

Raiden twisted, shielding her as best he could, and fired.

Willa looked as the uniformed man folded like a rag doll at her feet, a clean hole between his eyes. Her stunned gaze swung to Raiden, but before she could open her mouth, he yanked the sari's fabric further over her head and tossed her up on his shoulder. The tavern erupted in chaos. Immediately he drove into the crowd toward the window as Vazeen lifted a chair, smashing it. Raiden kicked at the sharp glass still in the frame, then climbed out, and kept moving.

"You killed him!"

"Are you amazed at my aim or that I live, when he does not?"

"He was just following orders—oh, that was awful! You are a vile, murderous beast!" She pummeled his back with every word.

Yet he kept running.

"Put me down! *Raiden!*"

"Now is not the time for sniveling, Willa."

"Sniveling! I'll have you know—!"

He smacked her behind. She gasped, outraged, kicking wildly, but gaining nothing. *"I know* I constantly find you where you do not belong, and I grow tired of it." His hand rode her bottom in warning and wisely, she heeded it.

Shouts followed them as he ran, his long strides eating up the terrain as if Lucifer barked at his heels. The ground passed rapidly before her vision, and Willa closed her eyes, the breath pounding from her lungs with each hard step. Her head felt as if 'twould explode, and when she smelled the sweetness of grass and trees, she thought they were safe. He dumped her on her feet, then swung up onto a horse, bending to slap his arm around her waist and drag her up.

"You can ride face down," he said when she struggled, "or take your chances with them."

She twisted to see a dozen soldiers racing for their mounts, three already in pursuit, weapons out. "Merciful heaven, the trouble I find around you," she groused, flinging her leg over the horse's neck and shoving her skirts down as Raiden heeled the beast around.

Bent low over the animal's neck, they rode hard into the jungle and he withdrew his sword, hacking through the heavy vegetation before it struck her face.

She fished in her tight bodice for her knife, but he clamped a hand over hers, pushing it away. Then he dipped his fingers inside, feeling her tense at the first touch and he let his fingers play over her soft skin before he withdrew the folded knife. "Is there aught else I should search you for?"

"Nay."

"You are dangerous, woman." He tucked the blade inside his vest.

Willa was still reeling from his invasion to be witty.

"Your name, Willa."

She hesitated, and his arm about her waist tightened, chasing her breath. "Delaney." She gave her maiden name without hesitation and elbowed him. *"Mrs.* Delaney." He tensed behind her, and though she wanted to ask his last name, she suspected he would not tell her.

"What man allows his bride to walk into a tavern unescorted, or stroll the marketplace at nightfall?" came in an angry snap.

"A dead one."

He stilled for an instant, his sword raised to chop before he brought it down, slicing open a path.

Shame swept her, those three words the start of a fresh lie. Her marital state was not his business, meant little to this race they were running. 'Twas not as if they were readying for a lasting relationship, she and this barbarian. She'd be done with him the instant the danger was gone, although she suspected he'd have little honor for a married woman should he want to take her to his bed. Nor did she want him to know her husband was a peer. Not for Alistar's sake, but her reasons were twofold. If Raiden ransomed her, 'twould be too humiliating when Alistar refused to pay, provided he could locate him. And she feared she'd be used against others, for 'twas clear Raiden loathed the aristocracy. Not that she was a viable member of it, she thought bitterly.

Behind, riders approached, and when he did not bother to increase his speed, she knew they were his friends. Friends? Hah. What sort of man, who killed without thought, had friends? The ride jolted too hard to question him, the thick, vine-draped trees stealing the sun, and more than an hour passed before the jungle thinned slightly and he turned down an unused road. She smelled the sea and moments later, the animal bolted from the forest and onto the beach. They rode the treeline, following it to the water's edge, his men not far behind.

"Where are you taking me?"

"To safety." He reined in at the jungle's end, swung from the saddle, then pulled her unceremoniously down.

"What think you to save me from this time?" She scoffed. "That foul-smelling innkeeper?"

Immediately, he cut away the palms and vines concealing two longboats in the underbrush. "Nay. From that captain aiming at your heart.'' Grabbing saddlebags and pouches, he tossed them into the boat, then loosened the saddle's cinch.

She frowned, following on his heels. "He sought you—" Her words faltered when he swung around to look at her, crowding her vision.

"Know that I have lived this long by prudence and skill, Willa. Nor do I kill carelessly. Believe me when I say, his intent was to murder *you.*" He shifted past her.

She spun about. "Me? But why—?" Willa looked away as the realization hit her. Of course he spoke the truth, and if it was not, 'twas close enough. She was a risk, for she could talk, tell of Alistar's misdeeds. Manav had died for all the secrets she'd uncovered. Mayhaps someone wanted Alistar dead or harmed and would use her to do it, she tried reasoning, still hoping her husband had not turned against her. Had that been Barkmon's intention when he summoned her to his quarters? But to abuse East India soldiers to do it? 'Twas the reason she would not tell Raiden who her husband was; Alistar's influence was wider than she'd anticipated. But the fact remained, Raiden had saved her life.

"Aye, lass," he said when the truth dawned in her incredible eyes. "The question now is why?"

She met his gaze, and knew she believed him. "I've done naught to warrant death, and I've no need of your protection."

She was coloring the truth, he thought, and it surprised him that he could tell. He slapped the horse's rump, and Willa watched her only escape disappear into the jungle.

"Well, that was stupid. I needed that horse to—"

Raiden dragged her toward the longboat.

She dug in her heels. "I will not go anywhere with you!"

"I did not ask your permission." He picked her up and dumped her in the boat. When she tried to leave, he leveled a pistol at her head. "More than your life is at risk now, little fox. Behave."

She turned her head till the barrel pressed against her forehead. "So ruthless, Raiden, and yet so contrary." She held his gaze a moment longer, then pushed the pistol aside and tried climbing out. He shoved her back down and swiftly tied her hands. She fought him until he jerked on the bindings.

Gazes locked and clashed.

"Do not fight me, woman."

"Or what? You will beat me? Drown me?" They were nearly nose-to-nose. "Oh, nay, silly me, I forgot. You do not attack *defenseless women!*" She yanked her bound hands free and found a proper seat.

Raiden snarled at her back, jamming the pistol in his belt before tossing in his bags and pushing the longboat off the sand. He climbed in as his men approached, sliding from saddles, some splashing into the water, some pulling the second craft off the sand, then throwing themselves in. His men rowed furiously, Raiden at the rudder. The crew sent her disgusted glances, and the same to Raiden.

Apparently she was not welcome. Good. She did not want to be here either, and though she'd little idea where they were, precisely, she was certain she could find her way back to the city. Mayhaps. How was she to find her boy now? she wondered with a longing glance at the shore as the oarsmen labored to pull the boat around a jetty, muscles straining to take the curving land.

Then she saw it.

A massive, three-masted ship rocked in the lagoon. A black ship. The sails, the hull, gun ports, were all black and though the dark wood gleamed, the fittings were painted ink-black too. She flew no colors, and as the longboat drew swiftly closer, her heart rolled in her stomach at the sight of the figurehead. An avenging angel gripping a sword and shield. Polished to a glossy sheen, only its garments were painted silver.

And only one kind of man sailed a ship like that. Slowly, she turned her head to stare at Raiden. His expression was as impenetrable as his composure.

The Black Angel. Oh, lord a'mighty.

"Pirates?" She looked at the others. "The lot of you are pirates!"

The men simply grinned at her.

"Oh do not look so proud." She shoved at the nearest man. "What would your mothers think?"

" 'ell, lady, 'alf of us ain't got one."

"You want to be me mum, luv?"

She made a face at the young man looking at her as if she were slathered in mint sauce with an apple shoved in her mouth, then turned her gaze on Raiden. "I knew you did something disreputable, but this?"

Raiden did not respond, the disappointment in her finds twisting like a wire in his chest and quelling any argument. She suspected before. Now she understood the whole of it.

They sailed alongside the ship as a rope ladder tumbled down. Crewmen tied off the craft to lead lines as Raiden reached for her, cutting her bindings. Willa smacked his hands away, but he was bigger, stronger, and with one jerk on her arm, he put her on his shoulder like a grain sack and climbed.

Below in the boats, his crew scrambled to board, paying them no mind. "Do not do this," she hissed, gripping his shirt.

He had to. The image of the soldier aiming for her heart pushed him to steal her away as quickly as possible. Flinging a leg over the rail, Raiden leapt to the deck, and strode to the passageway, barking orders to weigh anchor as he ducked through the hatch. He moved to his cabin, shouldering open the door and walking straight to the bed. With a heave, he dumped her there. She bounced, shoving her hair from her face and scrambling to her knees as he headed to the door.

"Put me ashore this instant!"

Her imperious tone stopped him, and with his hands on hips, his insolent gaze raked her like claws. "Do not make demands on me, woman."

"If you keep me, it shall be my utmost concern to make your life miserable."

"Threats? Or is my lady afraid to live without her servants and riches?"

She tipped her chin up, her green eyes flashing with contempt. "Do be more observant, pirate. If it a'tall mattered, would I have been in the tavern alone?"

"I see," he said thoughtfully. "Then you are merely dim-witted, to risk your life and now mine?"

She fumed. "I did not recall asking for your assistance—and I was armed."

"But could you have pulled the trigger?"

"Give over the pistol, barbarian, and I will prove it on you!"

She opened her mouth, but Raiden did not give her a chance to sharpen her tongue on his hide. "Enough! Consider yourself duly captured, m'lady." At least 'twould keep her alive.

"You will gain naught from taking me, pirate, I swear it!"

His gaze, heavy and speaking volumes, moved over her body like the stroke of his hand, leaving her unexpectedly breathless. "We shall see." He turned away. A slipper hit him square in the back, and he paused on the threshold, twisting, his black eyes narrowing to slits. "Shall I bind you to my bed?"

She dropped to her rump and slammed her fists on the bed at her sides. "This is kidnapping!"

"So it is." He closed the door, the click of the lock making her flinch.

She threw the second shoe at the sealed door, then sighed in defeat. Arrogant cur. Her shoulders slumped, and she rubbed her abused stomach, then fell back onto the cushions.

Pirates. Bloody fine, Willa. Fine, fine. *Fine.*

She stared at the white mosquito netting falling in delicate waves to the bedpost, then cocked her head. From a string, a strip of pungent sandalwood twirled overhead. Propping herself up on her elbows, she surveyed the cabin.

Oh my word.

It hit her like a strong fragrance, capturing her interest and wanting to name it. Power and a dangerous sensuality permeated the black and deep-blue decor, as if secrets lay hidden in the rich fabrics and furnishings. Just to look upon it, knowing he lived here, slept in this bed, made her skin tingle. 'Twas generously appointed—Persian rugs covering the deck; a carved rosewood desk, polished near blood red, lying in a corner near the aft windows; the slanted glass draped in blue damask and brushing the bench beneath. His desk chair bore the look of a sultan's throne in elaborately carved wood, leather, and gold, and she could almost see him there, planning attacks, deciding fates, lording over the East Indies as if they were his private playground of thievery.

With a disgusted sound, she swung her gaze to her right, to the racks of swords lining the wall like black pins about to prick the deck. The ward table was scarred but polished and surrounded by at least twenty chairs. He had lattice screens, a copper tub, six barrels of water, and a tea cart heavy with china, locked cabinets of books, and a trunk at the foot of the bed, with another two across the room near the desk. She twisted to study the bed, its pineapple-carved headboard, blue coverlet, and silken sheets. Pillows were piled on the mattress like a sultan's divan, tasseled and plump, the fabric shot with gold and silver. More of them were scattered on the bench and on the floor before his desk, and without will, seductive images bloomed, bodies entwined, his big hands smoothing . . .

"Oh, for pity's sake." Abruptly, she straightened and swung her legs over the side of the bed, banishing the erotic notions.

So. He was successful at pirating. A thief of the first water. And Willa put his face to the legend. The Black Angel. Even the name conjured death and destruction, and a glimmer of fear shot up her spine, tightening her scalp, yet she found the very idea of legend and man almost difficult to believe, especially after he saved her life. The dead captain's face filled her mind, and with it came the horrible stories and rumors she'd heard. Night attacks, hundreds of sailors slaughtered or left for dead. 'Twas reported he leveled the deck so a ship could not sail from the barrage of cannon fire, and after all this time no one could identify the leader. And there was talk of more than one ship painted black.

Every East India sea captain sought his head, the Crown's high price on it sending hunters into the seas for the prize, yet the thought of Raiden's head on a spike made her stomach churn. An outlaw, a barbarian thief marked for death, and she wondered suddenly, that if he stole for a living, could he be bought and convinced to put her ashore? She had to leave his presence and find her son. She had to. And not even a handsome pirate was going to stop her. Much talk and little recourse, she thought. She was his prisoner. Captured booty and no more. She did not want to think what he'd do with her now with no one to stop him, but the fear that he'd give her over to his men was real.

Leaving the bed, she retrieved her slippers, then glumly moved to the aft window bench and sat. The ship moved at incredible speed now, the shore growing smaller by the second and stealing any chance for freedom. At least she'd had the forethought to see to Rajani's welfare, yet she knew the girl would still worry. Sighing, she grasped a pillow, pulling it to her chest and burying her face in the elegant woven fabric. Instantly her little boy's face loomed in her mind, his dark red curls, his plump cheeks. Then she saw him weak and dirty and hungry, crying out for her, reaching for her, and her silent torment brought hot tears.

Mommy's coming, my sweet. I swear to you. I will find you.

Tristan rested his rear against the quarterdeck rail and studied his captain. The wind snapped at his black shirtsleeves, lifting his hair, and Tristan wondered why the man never tied it back. Shamefully unkempt, Tristan thought, thinking he'd taught him better. "They've a right to know what you plan to do with her."

Raiden gazed back at his crew gathered on the deck below. "I am aware of the rules, Quartermaster Dysart."

Tristan smiled at the tension in his face and voice, for the man rarely allowed his emotions to show.

"We 'adda run 'cuz of her, Captain," a seaman shouted.

"Aye, I say we put 'er ashore. She be bad luck already!"

"Aye, maroon 'er or share the lass!"

Raiden folded his arms over his chest, raking each man with a glare meant to maim. "The soldiers would have entered the Red Raven even if the woman were not about. And if any one of you drunken idiots with their hands up women's skirts were alert, we'd have seen them coming."

Several laughed; a few looked away guiltily.

"What say you of her, Captain?"

He scanned the hundred men and laid claim. "She is mine."

Talk scuffled around him, surprise mixed with distrust.

"I forfeit my share of the next prize for her."

Men snickered. "Got ye by the rocks, does she, Cap'n?"

Raiden smirked. Willa had him by something. What exactly, he could not name. Aye, she was a pretty thing, and as rebellious as a yard mongrel, but she had too many secrets to set her free just now.

"A vote?" Tristan asked and Raiden nodded.

The men agreed, most wanting nothing to do with a woman aboard or to deal with the captain's anger.

"I've never had the need of women's clothing. Therefore I pay to any man for aught they've in their shares."

"Leave 'er in the sari, captain. She fills it well."

Possessiveness reared and he shot Mr. Cheston an exacting look. "What Mrs. Delaney wears is not your concern."

"Mrs.?" Tristan said, straightening.

Raiden glanced at him. "Widowed, she claims."

"And you do not believe her?"

"I wonder even now if the woman was ever wed."

Tristan chuckled softly. "Pitying her husband, eh?"

Envying him, he thought, then smothered the notion. He'd no time or patience for wandering thoughts and wishful fantasies.

"Pity me, old friend, for I suspect she's torn apart my cabin like a cat let loose in a room full of mice."

Tristan smiled at his tired tone. "Why did you take her? Because she was in the East India carriage and chummy with the Brits, or because she was in danger?"

Raiden met his gaze. "Are you saying you'd have left her there to be shot?"

Tristan tugged at his coat hem. "Despite my profession, I am a man of honor, Montegomery."

Raiden scowled darkly. "Then why do you question mine?"

"I've seen you look at her."

He scoffed. "She is beautiful, aye, but never forget that two men are dead because of her. She is thick in the Company, make no mistake. Just how deep I will discover in time." Raiden suspected she was Barkmon's mistress, for a widow alone had to have means. Unless she married wealth. Either way, she was in league with the East India Company and that alone made her motives suspect.

"And have a bit of fun doing it, I imagine."

Black eyes slid to greet his. "A fondness for the lass, Quarter-master?"

"I can find my own women, Raiden. I need not kidnap them."

Raiden threw him a deadly look, then strode to the ladder, turning and climbing down. "You have the watch," he said, before he disappeared from sight.

Five

Raiden stepped into the cabin, his gaze instantly lighting on Willa sitting on the cushioned bench. Something hard ground through his chest to see her so dispirited when he knew her to be willful and impulsive. Yet the only image constantly baiting him was that captain aiming for her heart. It made his own pinch to know how close she'd come to dying in his arms, and he was determined to discover why the officer was ordered to kill her. And who ordered it. What could she have possibly done to warrant an execution? As more questions tumbled through his mind, he understood she'd not take kindly to his prying. She hated him, thought him no better than a street thief, which was painfully accurate. Yet had he not stolen her, she'd have run right into the arms of a man instructed to end her life. He would not let her go until he knew why and was certain she could travel without hazard. Even if it meant she must remain his prisoner. Even if she was the temptation of a lifetime laid before him like a sumptuous feast.

He closed the door, and she looked up as he crossed to his

desk, removing his cache of knives and pistols before unbuckling his sword belt and laying it down.

Slumped into the nook near the window, she glared at him. "You must put me ashore."

He did not answer, reloading the pistols.

Willa's nerves stood on end as she remembered the soldier and the clean hole between his blue eyes. "Can you not consider it?"

"Nay." He shoved the shot home.

"I beg you."

"As appealing as that sounds, little fox, the answer is still nay."

She stood, angrily tossing the pillow aside. "I must get to shore, Raiden. A life is at stake."

"Aye, mine, my crew's . . . yours."

"Nay. My son's."

He froze, his gaze climbing slowly to meet hers.

"He is lost and I must find him."

"How does one lose her own child?"

Her chin went up, regret staining her features. " 'Tis unimportant now. He is gone."

His eyes narrowed. Coloring the truth again, he thought. "And where do you plan to search for your child?"

His condescending tone did not escape her. "The Banda Islands."

He laughed rudely, the harsh sound telling her he thought her a fool and did not care. "Few skilled men have survived the jungles, Willa."

"Have you?"

He hesitated before admitting, "Aye." She took one step closer, the movement bespeaking a plea he must resist.

"Then 'tis the perfect solution. Help me find him."

Was she mad? "Nay."

"Please."

He arched a brow, sliding his dagger against the whetstone.

She rushed the desk, clutching the edge. "But you have been there! You would know where to look."

He returned his focus to the weapons, ignoring those soft, imploring eyes. "I have an agenda of my own."

She scoffed. "Killing and thievery goes by a schedule?"

His look was benign.

"Have you no heart? He is but a child. A baby. He needs me! We've been parted so long, and he's afraid and—" She swallowed hard, refusing to cry before him. "Take me to the islands."

"Willa," he groaned, a tinge of sympathy in his tone as he laid the knife down. "*Men* have perished from a mosquito bite on those islands, *men* with guns and ships. Can you not see that a child—"

In the space of a breath, she was against him, her hand covering his mouth.

"Nay! Do not speak the words, pirate. Please. He is not dead. I would know!" Her eyes teared softly and Raiden felt his knees collapse. "I would know."

Ah this woman will be the death of me, he thought, sagging against his desk even as her lush body lay against him like warm velvet, stirring his darkest desires. Even when he understood her need all too clearly. And he wished someone, years ago, had hunted for him with such determination. How had they been separated? And if her son was on the Banda Islands, how did he get to so deadly a place? Fierce in her faith that the child lived, when Raiden was certain he did not, he knew 'twas best to spare her more grief. He himself had scarcely survived his first encounter with the natives of the Indies. Resisting the urge to wrap his arms around her, he pulled her hand from his mouth. "The danger is tremendous, Willa. You do not know what you ask."

"I am his mother," she whispered, squeezing his shoulder. "I would suffer any price to hold him in my arms again. I would die for him."

Raiden closed his eyes, painful memories threatening to

destroy his resolve. Every bone in his body felt as if it would snap, making him flinch. Crushing the memories beneath necessity, he set her back from him and turned slightly away. His past had nothing to do with this.

Willa swallowed repeatedly, glancing around as if a solution would present itself in the rich furnishings. Then she fumbled beneath her sari, offering a velvet bag. "I can pay you." She opened it, spilling the priceless jewelry, the last of her valuables, on his desktop.

He spared it a glance. Then, without a word, he lifted a small chest from the floor under the desk, flipped the latch, then threw back the lid. She gasped at the piles of sparkling gems in every color imaginable, strands of silken pearls, gold coins, and silver medallions.

"As you can see, I've no need of it."

Willa glanced between her wealth and his, and her shoulders drooped. She scraped her jewels into the sack and turned away.

Regret slithered through him and he sighed, pinching the bridge of his nose. He hated crushing her hope. The child was dead, of that he was certain, and he would like nothing more than to drop her in the next port and sail away without a thought or a scent to haunt him as she had since they'd met. He had his own purposes to attend, his men to give answer to, and he could not sail around the Indian Ocean searching for a child.

Yet 'twas the woman herself who lured him; her beauty, her temper, the faint memory of her touch strapped his restraint right now and he wanted nothing but to hold her, comfort her— and taste her riches. His body tightened at the mere thought, images struggling to bloom in his mind when he wanted them to die a quick death. He'd known women like her, cultured, refined, and he'd been invited to many a scented chamber for the single reason of his lowborn breeding. Those women wanted excitement, a dangerous assignation, a lover to make them cry out, to teach and to play with, always slipping through the servant's doors in the dark of night and never acknowledged in the morn. He was a bastard, a thief, an outlaw. His life was dangerous, of his own making, its end marked by the price on his head.

And because of that, he was not worthy of this woman. Of the thoughts crowding his head, of this incurable need to experience her touch, her kiss. Their association could bring her death. He'd little honor left, shredded deeply over the years, and yet with all he'd done, she made him want to hold tight to the tattered pieces. Widow or nay, he'd no right to touch her. Even if Barkmon had. She weakened him, made him already alter his plans for her safety. Having her as he desired, he knew, would make him a mindless buffoon.

"You saved my life, and for that I am grateful. We are even, you and I, and I see no reason for you to keep me prisoner. This"—she touched the velvet bag—"is all I have left—save my son."

"You know too much of me and mine."

She looked insulted. "I will not reveal you."

"I cannot trust that. Nor will my crew." She opened her mouth, but he cut her off with, "Nay, do not plead your case, for 'tis impossible. My entire crew is at risk, and I will not have a mutiny over you when I have already placed their lives in jeopardy to see you unharmed."

"Do you expect to keep me till you are dead?"

"Take heart, lass, it could be a rather short association."

Her features slackened. "You speak of death so easily, yet you risk yours for mine. Why?"

'Twas a long moment before he said, "You did not deserve that fate."

"How do you know? I could be a murdering thief like—"

His gaze sharpened. "Guard your tongue, Willa."

"I do not believe the pretenses of polite society need be observed here. Especially when you are condemning my son to a fate he does not deserve."

The catch in her voice hammered through him. There was no fate to be had. The child was dead. But her faith bred the image of a small boy, so lost and tormented with his fear, his loneliness, that he almost reconsidered. For this time, the child wore Raiden's face—and *that* innocent was most assuredly dead.

Hitching his rear on the edge of the desk, he banished the images and stared at her long enough to make her squirm. "What business have you with the East India Company?" He gestured to her weapon baring the seal.

"Ah, so now we come to the heart of it," she said bitterly. " 'Twas you I saw in the markets."

That she could recognize him so easily, even robed as he was, made him more determined to keep her hidden. "Why did you not ask your lover to find your son?"

She gritted her teeth. "I am asking you to help me."

"And I have given you my answer," he said casually. He had an entire crew to answer to, and even the suggestion of hunting the child and losing riches in the process would bring a mutiny. "How came you to travel in Barkmon's personal carriage? Trading your favors?"

His insult stung; the look he shot her, of disdain and something else she could not name, made her turn away. *Oh, Raiden,* she thought, dispirited, *the lies I've told, the things I have seen.*

"Willa," he warned.

"You needn't be involved in my affairs."

The word burned through him, and he crossed to her, spinning her around. "What is he to you?" Her expression was bland, unrevealing, and Raiden's imagination broke free. The thought of that overstuffed nabob's hands on her made him seethe, leaving a sour taste in his mouth and the burning need to wring his fat neck. "I'd have thought you'd better taste in men, Willa."

"It appears that my acquaintances have gone to the chamber pot of late," she said with a meaningful look that included him.

"I do not take kindly to insults from Barkmon's mistress."

"Insults? You have accused me of whoring for Barkmon and denied me any hope of finding my son." The last piece of information she had found was that a ship sailed south with a child aboard. Only she could not match her son's presence with the right vessel, and now she'd lost all chance. " 'Tis all you will gain from me."

He advanced on her, forcing her to back step or press against him. "I *take* what I want, Willa, understand that here and now. You are a threat. To my ships, my men, and though I believe you seek your son, if he is in the Spice Islands, he is dead." She shook her head violently and he caught it between his callused palms, the simple touch softening him down to his wretched soul. "Tell me why the East India soldier would want to kill you."

"I do not know!" She batted his hands and moved quickly away, rubbing her face, the warm imprint of his touch heating her blood.

"You lie!" He slammed his fist onto the desk, making her flinch with the jump of his weapons. "Your manservant, the captain, both killed because of you!" The guilt spread over her features and he took the advantage. "Who have you angered?"

"Aside from you?" He would not help her find her son, she reasoned, therefore he need not be involved in her troubles.

He wanted to shake her. "How can I guard your life if I do not know what from?"

She could not tell him, not of Alistar and what she suspected. With his avid interest in the East India Company and Barkmon, 'twould be only a stronger reason for him to keep her. And if she revealed Alistar's involvement, she would never see land again. "Remember, sir pirate, I did not ask for you to guard my life. I asked you to save my son and you are too afraid of a jungle bug to do so."

His eyes narrowed. "I do not fear the jungle. I do not care to die because of a woman."

"Then what would you die for? Gold? Jewels? The thirty pieces of silver to pay Satan on your way to hell?"

"Aye."

"Damn you. You say aye to saving my life, but not my

child's, because he does not benefit anyone but me.'' Her lip quivered and briefly she bit down on it, wanting to fling useless curses at him. When she met his gaze again, her expression was as cold as the Nordic sea. ''I have no information, or I would not have been in the tavern. As to my life''—she shrugged carelessly—''the troops will tell Barkmon I have been taken by marauders, and they will cease looking and think me dead.''

He shook his head. ''East India will not cease a chase on so little evidence. They will hunt us now too.''

''They hunt *you* regardless, Black Angel. Admiral Dunfee has made it his personal quest!'' His dark eyes flared briefly at that. ''If you do not want more ships combing these waters, put me ashore.''

''To die?''

''To search for my child!''

''Or to return to Barkmon's bed?''

The thought of Barkmon even touching her turned her stomach. ''You think of beds when all I can think of is my son. Have you never loved so much that you'd risk all for it?''

Raiden stared at her, thinking of the love so brief and innocent, and so long ago, the memory of it no more than an ache, yet in its place grew a vengeance that would not be satisfied. But risk his life for love? 'Twas for the foolish and the young, certainly not for a man like him.

''Have you?''

He looked up and found her close, her soulful eyes gazing into his with a thread of hope. ''Love is too fleeting to sacrifice a thing for it.''

Her expression fell. ''Then I pity you, outlaw. For you have denied yourself a gift, and because of it, you have denied me the only person I have left to love.'' She turned her back on him, her arms folded over her middle.

Behind her, Raiden clenched his fists, anger and sympathy rampaging through him. He did not want this empathy and tenderness that called him to be her champion for more than a day or two, but for a century. She was a plague on a heart he thought was dead, and on a body he'd always commanded. He felt inexcusably weak around her. She held too many secrets for one so small, and he needed to be away from her, above decks where her seductive presence could not insinuate itself beneath his armor.

But the mere sight of her kept him rooted to the floor, and his gaze slid over her figure, the green sari skirt molding her hips, the sheer head covering sweeping beyond her waist, tinting the bare midriff exposed beneath the snug bodice. She was more than a mother—she was a temptress, and lethal when armed. He remembered her knife hidden between her breasts, the search for it, and he frowned, patting his leather vest, then withdrew it. The bone handle was worn smooth from much handling. He moved to the desk, gathering his weapons and placing all but his pistols in a trunk. Those he tucked in his belt.

She twisted to look and he met her gaze before dropping her blade in the pile and locking the lid.

"What do you want from me, Raiden?" His dark eyes flared with a look so potent that Willa's breath caught in her lungs.

"The truth."

She faced him. "You've denied me help. What does the truth matter?"

He moved toward her, and her heart picked up pace with each step. His stride was lazy, the rolling gait of his hips briefly snagging her attention, and Willa felt small and helpless by the simple power of the man—and desired by the look in his fathomless eyes. Her gaze swept him, from the tall jackboots to his flowing dark hair, before he stopped within inches, the heat of his body penetrating her thin garments. Her breasts strained inside the tight bodice, her skin gone damp and flushed at the anticipation of his touch. And even as the scandalous thought raced through her mind, she tipped her head to look him in the eye, almost daring him.

"I will uncover your secrets, Willa. 'Tis but a matter of how and when."

"Threats, my lord pirate, will fail."

Damn if her defiance wasn't like an aphrodisiac, luring him, taunting him, and Raiden fell prey to the singlemost temptation he'd suppressed since he'd first held her against him in the alleyways of Calcutta—since he'd put his hand beneath her skirt and felt the supple flesh of her thigh. His honor screamed denial, yet his need smothered it, and he bent, his mouth a fraction from hers. He felt her tremble, the inches separating them radiating in her every fiber like a beacon. Raiden thought his legs would fold beneath him on the mere suggestion of kissing her.

"I will not need them," he whispered. Her breath quickened against his lips, her stillness like a vase about to shatter. He reveled in it.

"You seek to torture me? Surely, you—"

"There are many forms of torture, lass," he interrupted smoothly, tilting his head. "And I am well skilled in all of them."

His tongue snaked across her lower lip and she gasped, reaching out yet never touching. Hungering for the hot press of his mouth, but never tasting. He offered another enticement, his tongue sliding wetly, slowly, over her lush lip, and a tiny sound escaped her. A breath, a whimper, she did not know, could not think for the heat rushing in her blood, for the rich entreaty hidden deep inside her, now begging for more than a single, tantalizing touch. 'Twas erotic, consuming; like a frothing wave it spilled over her, and she fought the pull, knew she hadn't the strength for this kind of battle. Not with him, never with him.

And Raiden knew it, felt her pulsing need saturate him, this untamed craving crackling between them, waiting to be awakened, and the wall separating him from this dark passion crushing through him—fractured. His muscles locked. His heart pounded hard and heavy. He clenched his fists. And in that moment, he understood the danger of this woman lay not in the joining of bodies, but in the gamble of his soul.

Raiden instantly retreated, holding her confused gaze for a moment before he turned and strode from the cabin.

Willa staggered back and fell numbly onto the window bench. Torture? Oh nay, she thought. This would not do. An instant later she heard a loud thump, and the wall housing the line of swords rattled.

Beyond the sealed door, his arms braced on the wall, Raiden raised his fist again, then let his arm fall to the wall without vengeance. He pressed his head to the wood, resisting the childish urge to thump his head till he knocked some sense into himself. What was he thinking to toy with her like that? To tempt with his own want of her? The lady did not need another weapon to wield over him. And the true source of his turmoil was, she would have let him kiss her. If she'd any doubt of his desire for her before now, he'd just hammered it home.

Yet he'd recognized the flicker of alarm in her eyes, the confusion and wonder of what he'd do with her. Pirates had a notorious reputation for taking women, but only the sorriest lot of brigands killed them and tossed them overboard when they were used and had lost their worth. Or they'd ransom them. His head jerked up and he stared at the knotholes in the wood, frowning. Did she think he'd ransom her? Was that why she refused to tell him anything of her life, her association with Barkmon, and why she was in that tavern? Had her man been killed protecting her wealth? Was it that simple? Then why hide it?

God above, his head ached with thinking on it overlong. Pushing away from the wall, he called to his cabin boy and gave orders before heading above decks. The blast of sunlight forced him to squint as he made his way forward, then climbed to the quarterdeck. He paced, forming and dismissing one plan after another for controlling the woman in his cabin before he dismissed the notion completely. Stopping, he tipped his head back and drew a deep breath.

"The lady giving you a bit of trouble?"

He slid Tristan a look. The man was sunning himself, booted ankles crossed, elbows braced behind him on the rail. "Have you naught better to do than laze about, Quartermaster?"

Dysart straightened at his sharp tone. "We've another crewman." Tristan gestured, and Raiden followed the direction to a man near the fo'c'sle, coiling rope. He was tall and broad in the shoulders, a cap pulled low and his dark hair queued.

"How does he come by us?"

"He saved Cheston and Curry's life last night, and mine."

Raiden spared him a glance.

Dysart shrugged. "British soldiers did not take kindly to us availing ourselves of their stores."

Raiden cursed. "Damn you to hell, man, we can pay for those goods, and thieving in that port brings attention."

"You needn't remind me of my mistakes and the risks. I have unfortunately experienced them in close quarters." Dysart opened one side of his coat, revealing a faint stain of blood on his pristine white shirt.

"How bad is it?" Raiden said with genuine concern.

"I will survive."

"Good, for I've no time to nursemaid you."

Dysart scoffed. The man never nursed a soul, he thought. In fact, on more than one occasion, Tristan had seen him disregard his own wounds to get at another East Indiaman. "I could entreat to the lady to care for them."

Raiden called for his spyglass and sighted behind them. "I would not chance it."

The calm warning sent Tristan to his feet and he winced, favoring his side as he moved to stand beside his captain.

"I expect better judgment from my second," Raiden said in a low voice, then looked at him, the glass still poised. "Having difficulty at this pirating?"

Tristan smiled. 'Twas a frequent jibe from Raiden, for he'd

been raised a peer's son. The second son of a lord, unfortunately, and whilst Tristan did not expect a bloody thing handed to him, there were parts of his rearing he could not dismiss. Nor his flaws of recklessness. Which had sent him into the belly of a prison ship with Raiden as his bunkmate. "I grow accustomed."

"After only ten years?" Raiden scoffed good-naturedly, closing the glass and giving his shoulder a squeeze. Dysart, ever the gentleman, and forced to seek his fortune without his heritage, had schooled Raiden in deportment, reading, ciphering, and a few other gentlemanly attributes, in exchange for his knowledge of the sea and ships. It had made them strong friends, of which Raiden had few. His quartermaster was not only trusted by the crew to divide the spoils and pay the recompense for severe wounds, he was the *Renegade*'s first mate. "Assemble the men."

Tristan called to the bos'n, and the sound of his whistle bit the air. The crew meandered toward the quarterdeck, and Raiden hitched his rear on the rail, staring down. "Who joins us?"

The man raised his hand, and Raiden gestured him close. The sailor kept his head bowed. "I suspect a man who cannot look me in the eye." The man tipped his head, and Raiden frowned. Strapping in size, he was much older than he'd expected, especially to best young British soldiers. "Your name."

"Nealy Perth, Cap'n."

"Swear your oath now, Mr. Perth, and be held by the laws of this vessel and crew, or be set ashore in the first port. We take none aboard who do not wish to be here."

The man swore his oath, and after a cheer and a jostle from Cheston and Curry, they grew quiet as Raiden stared at each in turn, the look telling them this new crewman was their responsibility till his oath was tested. Cheston and Curry nodded, knowing failure meant marooning.

"What found you in Calcutta besides women and *kallu?*" he said to the group.

The men offered bits of information, locations and rumors

of ships sailing for the Spice Islands. With their information, and all he'd garnered himself, Raiden offered his plan to take the next prize.

"Then we lay a course out of this river, then south into the Indian Ocean," he said to the men assembled. "We meet with the others. Then, if winds are fair and monsoons hold, we come round and take the *Weston* from behind. And aught else we see along the way."

His crew smiled, agreeing to the tactics. Raiden dismissed them and gestured Dysart and his helmsman, Kahlid, to the rear of the quarterdeck, out of earshot. "The soldiers were waiting for me outside the offices."

Kahlid and Dysart exchanged a glance. "The East India has lost three ships of late, only one to us," Tristan said, then flashed a grin.

Raiden braced his forearms on the rail and watched the land disappear on the horizon.

"They might have sought another and assumed it was you, Captain," Kahlid said.

" 'Twill be difficult to discern a traitor among us, especially with a new crewman, but think, mates—who would have known I was headed there?"

"I would cut off my fingers before I revealed your plans, Ibn Montegomery," Kahlid said.

Raiden turned his head and stared at the tall, slender Arab for a moment, then straightened. "I believe you, friend, and I ask that you keep an ear to the talk. And their duties. No one steps into the hull without the quartermaster's notice."

If he carried a disloyal crewman aboard, he'd find a way to ferret the man out. And if there was such a man aboard, what did he hope to gain? And for whom? Raiden looked down the length of the ship, searching for Perth, finding him talking as he labored with heavy sails.

He'd trust the lot of these men at sea, a fistful on land, and none he'd not fought beside.

Six

India's moon was high in the sky when Raiden headed to the passageway. Working above decks, he'd put his priorities in order, and now felt well guarded against his unexplainable need for the woman imprisoned in his cabin. Yet, as he approached the hatch, angry voices came to him, and instantly he flung open the door—and stopped short. Wrapped in nothing but a long blue Turkish towel, her red hair dripping wet, Willa stood in the center of the room, a sword poised on Balthasar, the *Renegade's* cook. The cabin was in slight disarray, watery footprints on the floor, a stool tipped on its side, and while Willa looked a bit frazzled, Balthasar's turban listed to one side.

She shielded Jabari, his cabin boy, like a lioness protecting her cub. "Get him out of here!"

His hands on his hips, the tall, robed Bedouin spared his captain a glance. "She is a most troublesome female, my captain."

"Though only, I thought, for me," Raiden said tiredly, moving toward them.

"You should beat her."

Willa fairly shrieked her outrage, and with two hands swept the heavy sword point under Balthasar's chin. The towel threatened to fall. "You or anyone else had better keep their hands off me and this child or—or I shall run you through!"

Raiden's gaze shot to Balthasar. "What have you done?" came with deadly calm.

"She is a woman. What does it matter?"

Raiden batted the sword aside and stepped between the dueling pair. "This is my ship and my cabin, Bedouin, not your harem." His fist clenched and unclenched in an effort to contain his temper. "She is mine."

Willa's eyes widened at the blatant claim, yet Balthasar only shrugged. "So be it." He stepped back, his gaze landing on Willa. "Eat, woman." He gestured to the tray on the table. "You are too skinny to fill my leader's bed and pleasure him."

Willa could not contain her outrage and shifted around Raiden, but he caught her, pushing her behind him. "Never touch her, or I will cut off your fingers," he told the cook.

Balthasar's gaze thinned. "Then how will I cook or fight for you?"

"You won't." The Persian's insolence just added him to a list of suspects, Raiden decided, his temper boiling. He'd known Balthasar only a year, and although his indifferent behavior was a part of his rearing, it would not be tolerated.

Balthasar's black eyes flared at the warning and he nodded respectfully, then turned on his heel and left.

The sword clattered to the deck, and Willa backed up as Raiden swung around to face her. "Did he hurt you?" His gaze swept her body, webbed with dripping hair, dampening the towel till 'twas nearly transparent.

Willa crossed her arms protectively over her chest, glaring. "Aside from mauling me as though I was naught but breasts and bum laid out for his pleasure and slapping this child when he tried to defend me, nay. You say you want to protect me, yet you cannot even do it on your own ship!"

The truth of her words hit him like a slap. He'd never brought a woman aboard and underestimated his crew's reaction. ''Balthasar was below decks when I—never mind. Be assured my crew will not touch you from this moment on.''

Her expression bespoke her doubt and when he moved toward her, she retreated, eyeing him like a cornered animal and clutching the little dark-skinned boy protectively to her side. She looked down at Jabari, whispering to him, stroking his black hair off his forehead, and the temptress faded, the mother unfolding before his eyes. How tenderly she looked upon the boy and how quickly he soaked up her attention. And gave his loyalty, Raiden thought as Jabari nodded, spoke to her with a glance at him, then moved away to right the cabin and tend to his duties.

Willa straightened and faced him, clutching the towel at her breasts. His attention slid to her shoulders. Instantly he was inches from her, pushing her hair off and revealing finger marks on her delicate skin.

''I swear,'' he growled. ''I will kill him.''

Willa knew he meant it when he turned toward the door. She caught his arm and met his gaze. ''Is killing your only solution, pirate? I do not bleed and only my dignity is truly bruised.'' What a strange battle flickered in his dark eyes, she thought, before it faded to something softer, warmer, and Willa felt her insides shift at the glimpse of tenderness.

Just how fragile she was showed in the tiny bruises, and he wanted to apologize, to offer her something to ease her fears. He reached for her shoulder, to soothe the unfair blemish, but she stiffened, gripping the towel protectively, and although her expression was gentle, he was duly warned off. He needed the reminder, he thought, releasing a long breath. Then, bending, he scooped the fallen sword off the floor and replaced it on the wall. God, but she was a wild one to hold a blade on a man twice her size and ten times as mean. ''Try not to stab anyone while you are here, my lady.''

''We would not have these complications if you'd release

me." His look dismissed all hope, and resolutely, Willa moved to the bathing stool, gathering her fallen clothes. "I will not cease asking, you know."

"I live for your badgering, lass," he said, rocking back on his heels. "Jabari, I see you've met Mistress Delaney." The lad tipped a bow and Willa smiled back, dipping a quick curtsy that looked utterly delightful in the towel. "You will bring her all she needs. And that would start with something suitable to wear on the morrow," Raiden said, unable to drag his gaze from her. "Inquire of Mr. Dysart."

"But—Captain?" Jabari hesitated, handing Willa a towel for her hair.

Raiden frowned. "Speak up, lad."

"You should not be here. Alone with her."

Willa smiled to herself. She and Jabari had become fast friends before that oaf, Balthasar, strode into the cabin and proceeded to take leave of her. The half-Egyptian child was gallant and protective, and she wondered what had happened in his life to bring him here when he should be running the beaches, searching for critters and fishing.

"So it would seem, lad." Raiden's gaze sharpened on Willa. "But I am not going anywhere. Off with you." He waved.

The child cast a look between the two with beautiful eyes too old for his innocent face, and she recognized his apprehension. "I will be fine, lad," she assured him.

Raiden's lips thinned as his cabin boy grabbed the buckets and headed back out. "You have bewitched him," Raiden accused her, then realized how ridiculous that sounded.

She wrapped her hair in another Turkish cloth. "No more than I have bewitched you, I suppose."

She had done *something* to him, he thought, for he'd never felt so much for one troublesome female. Especially one who held his life, his identity, in her hands.

"I need no other clothing." She held up the bundled sari and started for the screen. "This is fine."

"Nay. 'Tis filthy and reeks of the boot polish from your hair."

She blinked, surprised he knew, and when he crossed to the chest at the foot of the bed, throwing back the lid, Willa inched close. He withdrew a white shirt, holding it out.

" 'Tis too short and far too thin for modesty's sake." It would scarcely come below her knees.

"I've had my hand beneath your skirts, little fox," he teased in a husky pitch and her eyes flew wide. "Hiding aught now seems a bit unnecessary."

She reddened viciously. "You are an insufferable cur." She snatched the shirt, replacing it neatly in the chest before rummaging beneath it.

Raiden folded his arms over his chest and leaned against the bedpost, a smile threatening. "Feel free to plunder, my lady."

She ignored him, pulling out a long blue robe. "This is sufficient." She moved behind the carved screen Jabari had placed around the tub and let the towel fall.

Every muscle in his body locked. The ornate wood screen offered no more than a shadowed vision of her lush body as she eased into his robe. And bastard that he was, he looked his fill till she belted herself inside the garment.

Willa jumped when Raiden stepped around the screen, offering a wooden box. Frowning, she opened it. Inside lay a bone comb edged in gold, a boar's hairbrush, and a dainty hand mirror. "Spoils of battle, pirate?" she said with a sour look.

"Nay." He moved away, returning the screen to its spot against the wall. "They were my mother's, I'm told."

"Told? You never knew her?"

He went to the aft windows, sliding one open. Cool air and the mist of the sea filled the cabin. "Except for the moment she delivered me, nay."

Willa frowned, watching as he returned to the tub, lifting it, then carting the copper bath to the window. 'Twas nearly full, and his muscles strained against his dark shirt as he poured the contents into the ocean. His strength reminded her that he could snap her neck with his fingers, yet 'twas the brush and comb that garnered her attention, making her wonder what life this man had lived till now. To never have known his mother left her open for a wealth of speculation.

Would Mason one day not remember her? The thought was unbearable and she went to the table for the tray of food, then, with the wooden box tucked under her arm, she moved to the window bench, taking a seat at the far end. "What happened to her? How did you get this?"

"She died soon after I was born, I understand." A pause and then, "The set came anonymously with a note."

"And what of your father?"

His steps faltered before he continued, setting the empty tub in a corner. "Only once have I been in his presence." His back to her, he spoke softly. "He named me." Raiden did not want to see the sympathy in her expression and he wondered why he opened this vein only to bleed anew from old hurts.

"Who told you this? Her family? His?"

Twisting, he slung a look over his shoulder that said this conversation was at an end.

"So you get to ask all of me, and I naught of you?" He remained silent. "We won't be talking much, I see." Sighing, Willa looked down at the box on her lap, her fingers whispering over the set. It was fine, finer than anything she possessed, and she wondered about the woman who bore him. And the man he called father.

"Unless you'd like to regale me with why you were in the tavern."

"Have you not guessed?" She worked the knots from her hair. "I was looking for information about my son." 'Twas the truth, she thought, except the information she sought started with tracking her husband's last steps. Misery, sudden and held at bay, engulfed her, and her eyes burned. How was she ever to get back to Calcutta and discover what Alistar had done, whom he'd spoken with, and where, God help her, he had hidden Mason? The trail was drying up, and she was dying with it.

"Why there?"

"A young boy was seen on the deck of a ship. I'd learned slavers drank there, and that witch of an innkeeper would deal in the selling of spirits and flesh . . . in any form." She shot him a hard look. "And do not chastise me again for my foolery, pirate. I have experienced more than its depths today."

Willa set the comb back into the box and took up the brush, dragging it mercilessly through her hair. 'Twas her own fault. She should have paid someone to discover the information for her. But Manav had warned her not to trust anyone, and she feared she'd have offered her coin again and again and never gained a word of news. And now there was no chance of even that. No chance. Nay, she thought. She would not give up. She was the only hope Mason had, and he was hers.

Wrapping her legs in the too-large robe, she drew them up, pressing her forehead to her knees. She wished he would leave her in peace. Hearing his footsteps, feeling him so close, unnerved her. She wanted to scream and wail and sob in privacy, but she knew from experience 'twould not ease the emptiness in her soul. She coveted comfort and succor from this terrible ache in her chest, and unexplainably she longed to find it in Raiden's arms, from the very man who'd taken her freedom. That she hated and wanted in the same breath confused her, and she throbbed to the center of her being for more than she was destined to have with this man. She turned her face to the window, to the black night and glittering ocean.

But he was there, behind her, his reflection as clear as if her gaze fell upon him. Tall and broad and decadently handsome. Her captor. A pirate who claimed she was a liability to his life, his crew, yet oddly, wanted to keep her from harm. A deeper reason, a darker one, lay beneath, she feared. He hunted Royal East India vessels, and he suspected she'd found information. She did, but she was not giving it over. Not when it meant revealing her lies. His fury was a power she could not withstand.

Willa felt as if a house of cards was about to fall, and all she did was shove another card into place, praying 'twould keep her world from crumbling. If only he would help her. She would not ask again, and though begging for his help, for her son's life, was not above her, she knew he would not aid her.

I am lost, she thought, choking back a sob. *Without my child, I am nothing.*

Raiden moved closer and slowly eased into the space on the bench beside her. "Willa?"

"Leave me be, Raiden. Go sail your damned ship and burn another into the sea." She tipped her head back slowly, meeting his gaze. The look in his eyes brought memory and sensation, again and again. She wanted none of it, not the feel of his tongue on her lips, the suggestion of his warmth and power, nor the fire she felt in the pit of her stomach every time she thought of being swept into his embrace and protected. She crushed the need and held tight to her anger. He kept her from her son. "You are a man without a heart, Black Angel. Without mercy in your soul. Go."

Yet he did not move, did not blink. "I know of every ship that sailed from Calcutta in the last fortnight. What is the name of the one you suspected carried your son?"

Her words dripped contempt. "I was about to discover that when you so gallantly interrupted."

Damn, he thought. Damn and blast. "You need to rest." He gestured to his elaborate bed turned down for her.

"I would sooner perish than lie upon your sheets."

He arched a brow, his lips curling in a cynical twist. "We shall see," he said, and she heard the threat in his tone. She flinched when he stood, yet he walked to the door, stepping though the hatch and closing her in, alone. Only then did she give in to her sorrow.

Raiden stirred from sleep, instantly sitting upright, a pistol in his hand. An unfamiliar sound blistered the silence and when recognition dawned, he carefully released the hammer, laying the weapon aside and leaving the bed. Naked, he moved across the cabin to where Willa lay on the divan of pillows on the floor near his desk. And she sobbed in her sleep.

For two days, she had moved listlessly about, declining even a stroll above decks. She'd refused all but the minimum of food, refused to look at him, respond to him, and dismissed the offer of his bed. He suspected she'd thought he'd join her. He would not, for he knew what lying with this woman would do to him. He longed to see her fire, the strength of her will. And to know her secrets. She was in grave danger, and yet he was no closer to discovering why than he was when he carted her aboard.

Damn him, but he did not want the responsibility of her, to care about her, to wonder over her life before now and what would occur in the future. He knew that if he let his desires unfold, his heart would follow. And that was the last thing he needed. To want when his days were numbered.

He reached, smoothing a tear off her cheek. She whispered his name and turned her face into his palm. Raiden swore his heart stopped just then. The texture of her skin, her breath, made him feel unexplainably powerless, and for a moment, a fraction of time, he savored the feeling. Then suddenly he shook loose and plowed his fingers into his hair. This was madness, he thought, covering her before turning back to his bed. And in the morn, he'd find a way to end it.

He didn't. And the hollow look in her eyes tossed him between anger and regret. Raiden had never known such frustration. She'd dismissed the gown laid on the chest for her, the tray prepared. "Dammit, Willa. Eat."

Eat this, wear this, sleep here, Willa thought, adjusting the robe at her throat. He'd been ordering her about all day. She did not care. Without the hope of finding her son, she found no reason to comply with anyone's demands but the ones in her heart. She was helpless, trapped, a prisoner, and she held to her vow to make his life miserable, because she already was.

"I can force you."

"It seems to be your way, Raiden. And if you touch me, you shall feel the sting of my teeth."

" 'Twill be better than this childishness!"

She shot him a venomous look. "What know you of children!" Her voice fractured, and something hard flickered in his eyes just then. "You search for prey and more wealth you do not spend." She waved to the opulent cabin. "Yet when I ask for help in finding something worth more than all your damned riches, you refuse. The prize is all you want."

"There are many prizes to be had." Hovering over his desk, his palms braced on the surface, he stared at her until she read the look in his eyes.

"Never." She was not the spoils of war. How could he refuse to help her and expect her to fill his damned bed!

A knock rattled the door, and she shifted toward the window, giving him a view of her stiff back and the cascade of flaming red hair falling nearly to the floor. Raiden ground his teeth and returned his attention to the spread maps and charts. "Enter," he barked, and the door swung open, Tristan stepping over the raised threshold, frowning at his captain, then the woman.

"Raiden, be a good lad and introduce me."

Willa turned her head. A truly handsome man, she thought. Tall and well built, from beneath a shock of chestnut-brown hair he stared at her with eyes bluer than the robe she wore.

"Mistress Delaney, may I present Mr. Tristan Dysart, of West Suffolk." Raiden waved distractedly between the two, his gaze on the map. "My first mate and quartermaster."

Tristan bowed, and Willa instantly noticed the polish in his moves and the tidy care to his worn garments. "A pleasure, sir." Her brows drew down. "By chance any relation to the Earl of Bridgeton?"

Raiden's head snapped up, his gaze slamming between the two.

Tristan barely smiled as he placed the rolled maps on the desk. "My uncle, I'm afraid. Don't tell him I'm misbehaving, please."

"How do you know of him?" Raiden demanded. How could she be acquainted with an earl known for his seclusion?

Willa's gaze swung to his. And though she kept her expression bland, she recognized her mistake. She'd given him the bone he'd sought since her capture. She was not English, and her Carolina accent confused him. She turned her face to the window again.

Raiden threw Tristan a *"See what I must endure?"* look, and the quartermaster hid a smile and turned his attention to the maps. "Southeast winds are kicking mad, so the storm will toss us off course for a day, I fear."

Raiden dropped into his chair with a curse. He needed to be in Malacca in a fortnight to beat Dunfee. "No sign of the *Regard?*"

Willa twisted around to stare. The *Queen's Regard.* An East India flagship.

Tristan shook his head. "I think Winston was lying."

Raiden agreed. The weasel of a man would sell his own mother if it would better his lifestyle. "Keep watch. We do not want to confront more than one Indiaman without sufficient armament and ships to escape."

Willa paled. They were planning an attack. And what would become of her, should they lose? 'Twould behoove her to know her options.

"Are we set with provisions?" Raiden asked, and when Tristan didn't respond, he looked up from charting a new course. He followed the direction of the Englishman's gaze to Willa. Though she sat tucked in her isolated corner, her arms wrapping her middle and legs tucked to the side, the large robe had slipped off her shoulder, exposing flawless skin, the plump swell of her bosom.

And Tristan was feasting on the sight.

Possession goaded him, and Raiden smashed it down. "Pay attention, Quartermaster."

"I am." Tristan leaned down, his gaze still locked on Willa as he whispered, "By the gods, Rai, how can you tolerate being so near her and not sample that . . . that bounty?"

"She's a pretty rose with abundant thorns," he muttered, throwing down the astrolabe. "We will take this up at another time. You are dismissed."

Tristan's brows drew tight, and Raiden recognized the silent inquiry he'd no intention of answering. "Damn, she's a sight better than those pigs above decks," Dysart said. Then, leaving the maps, he quit the cabin.

Raiden waited till the door closed before he said, "Dress, Willa. My crewmen move in and out of this cabin daily."

She tipped her head, the hollows around her eyes cutting him like a hot blade through tender flesh, and it angered him, this despondency, this listlessness and he wondered if she truly wanted to find her son. She was losing flesh, her eyes dull, and he could scarcely concentrate with her about, and knowing she mourned her child tore at him. He tossed aside the graphite stick and crossed to the gown, snatching it up and hurling it on her lap.

"Dress now. I'll not have you tempting my crew in so revealing a garment."

She threw him a frosty look.

Raiden's anger boiled. "Damn you, Willa, would you waste away and have naught left?"

" 'Tis all you have left me, pirate. You have taken my last chance to find Mason."

Sweet Christ, did she have to say his name? Guilt swept over him in heavy, pounding waves, and as hard as he ignored it, nothing stopped the crushing memories of fear and loneliness, of living without hope or a mother's love and security. If the boy was alive, he was terrified. If he was dead, he died alone. He cursed this day, this moment, and whatever tore the boy from her arms. But he had too many to answer to, too many crewmen who could vote him down. "I will dress you myself," he warned, trying to maintain a shield against her pleas.

Her look dared him to try.

God above, he wanted to shake her. "I cannot go about hunting a child most likely dead," he ground out. "I have plans of my own that must be met."

The flicker of indecision, whether in his tone or nay, pushed her to her feet. "He is not dead and you could find him. I know you could. You are the only one who can." She held his gaze for a moment, and then, seeing the denial there, she abruptly turned her back on him.

Raiden battled a war deep inside himself. He loathed seeing her like this, almost willing herself to die, and yet her faith in him was unfounded. He could no more find the boy than he could pull the moon from the sky and let her wear it about her neck. Nor could he be swayed by a pretty face and sweet body. Or a sad story. He'd heard too many to care overmuch.

But 'twas her fearlessness, her confidence in him that gave her the power to taunt him when he'd a gun pointed at her head. He'd actually tossed about a plan to accomplish his mission, and hers, but he did not want her to think him noble, for his motives were purely selfish. If he did anything, 'twas for the information he could gain. She knew of Barkmon's affairs, and the director was the pulse of the Royal East India. Yet the woman drew him, sapped emotions he'd suppressed for years, and Raiden knew he'd only one recourse to keep the lines between them. Lines he needed. Offer her a bargain. One that would force her from this lethargy, yet make her compliant. For her anger he could understand and deal with; 'twas her compassion and her desire he could not. Aye, a bargain, one she would never accept and vile enough to make her hate him.

"I will help you find the boy."

She spun around, her eyes filled with fresh hope. Her smile brightened the room and clawed at his heart. God, he wanted to be worthy of someone so virtuous and willing to die for a sliver of hope.

"For a price."

Her brows knitted, and she glanced at the gold-filled chest on the floor. "But you have refused my jewels. I have naught to offer."

"Aye, you do." He advanced slowly, his dark gaze sliding in a lazy prowl over her body, lingering at her breasts before rising to greet her.

She inhaled, her skin coloring deeply. "You cannot possible mean that I—that you and I—"

"Become lovers," he finished when she could not. "Or more precisely," he added, stopping inches from her, "you, little fox, shall become my mistress."

Seven

Mistress.

The word tumbled from his lips, offering a flood of forbidden images, of tangled sheets and writhing bodies locked in primal pleasure. He did not know what he asked, could not. The shock of his suggestion battled with her morals, with a secret desire to experience more than she'd known with any man, no matter the cost. Though her vows were watered down by her husband's behavior, she was still married, and whilst that meant little to Alistar and his trail of whores since their son was born, it meant something to her.

Vows were sacred. She was forever tied to another. Yet within her reach was the chance to find her baby when she had none before. The price was high, and she hated him for dangling it before her like a meal before a starving person.

She glared up at him. "You cannot force me."

"I will not have to." His glance was hot and penetrated her garments.

She scoffed, stepping back from the imposing lure of him. "You are too full of yourself, Raiden. You are a thief and an outlaw and as ill bred as any man I've known to make such a disgraceful offer." His eyes narrowed dangerously, but she ignored the hazard of taunting him. "In this, you believe you will win, but 'tis you who will be disappointed. Bedding with you will not be a sacrifice, but as with my husband"—her green gaze scored him with disgust—"a chore."

He took a step. "Guard your tongue, woman."

She threw her arms wide. "You force me to bargain with my body, pirate. What shred of decorum remains to me?"

"Mayhaps I should remind you that you are a lady."

She laughed. *"You* remind *me?* You who offer to degrade me for a price? A lady does her duty for a child, and I find naught appealing in the getting of them."

So, her husband failed her in their bedchamber, Raiden thought, then banished the notion of proving the fault lay in the man. This was a false bargain. He'd achieved his desire; her hatred and disgust was a wall between them. So why was the tempting challenge still looming like a hull full of precious spice?

"I find it most appealing," he said in a husky pitch. "And I assure you, I will see to it that 'tis worth your *sacrifice.*"

She scoffed. Not once had Alistar cared for her feelings, her desires; for the most part he had berated her for showing them to him.

"Shall I tell you how?"

Willa stared, her features impassive, yet Raiden saw a challenge he could not resist. He stepped closer, impressed that she did not cower or back away. Inches from her, he bent and held her gaze. "I will taste you, Willa, unveil your luscious body and put my mouth in places you never dreamed of." Her breath quickened, and he savored her reaction, and the teasing he would never fulfill. " 'Twill be my utmost concern to make you scream with pleasure."

Willa broke eye contact, turning away. Images clouded her mind, of his hands on her, of being loved and finding the rapture always out of her reach when she had no right, *no right* to want any of it from him. He moved up behind her, and she flinched when his hands rested on her shoulders with gentle weight, resisting the unbelievable urge to sink back into him.

"You will not have to swallow your pride," he murmured in her ear, the breath of his words skating down her throat and tightening her breasts. "I would not have you come to me in any fashion other than willing." A little moan escaped her and she closed her eyes, wanting and hating him in the same breath. "And you *will* come to me, without reservation or aversion."

His gloating tone shattered the spell and she rounded on him, her eyes sparking with anger. "I hear only idle boasts, Raiden."

He shrugged carelessly. " 'Tis a bargain. An agreement. I shall give you"—he cocked his head, thoughtful for a moment—"a fortnight to grow accustomed to me and the idea."

Why, the presumptuous bastard! "And I give you a fortnight to make me want you!"

His smile was slow and devilishly seductive. "I accept the challenge."

Willa's eyes widened and she wished the words back. What had she done? To lay a gauntlet at this man's feet was to ask for a passionate war she could never win. She hated him for making such an offer, so degrading when she thought there was at least a measure of respect between them.

Yet her child's life was her only concern, and she knew this was the one man who could help her now. Would she not take a pistol shot meant for her son? Would she not offer her last coin to see Mason's safe return? At least she had a fortnight before lying with him, and even now she frantically sought a way out, praying a miracle would present Mason into her arms, so she'd not have to fulfill such an arrangement.

"Your answer, my lady?"

Her voice was dull when she said, "I have no choice."

His heart sank like a stone in his belly, apprehension slithering through him. Surely she would not accept.

She was quiet for a moment, staring at the Persian carpet before her bare toes. "You have laid within my grasp the only solution to finding my son. Whatever you asked of me for the chance, I would do it." She lifted her gaze to his. "You have your mistress."

He schooled his features and nodded, snared in a trap of his own making.

"However, you must prove yourself, prove you can help me first."

His expression darkened. "I am not above honor, Willa."

She made a nasty sound. "You have asked me to whore for you, Raiden. Whilst history writes of the Black Angel"—his eyes flared—"and his feats of daring on the high seas, my name will be naught but a slur for my son to bear!"

"Then in this, we have a common bond, for I *am* the slur of my father's actions." He turned toward the door.

A bastard, was he? "Well, then, this blackmail has confirmed you have not risen above it," she snapped, hurt that he would force her to this.

He stopped and turned, his features taut. Suddenly he advanced on her like a dragon let loose from his cave, swooping down on her, his arm shooting out to snare her waist and slam her flush to his length. "Did I not warn that you swam in waters too dangerous for you?"

She stared defiantly back, shoving his chest, and his grip cinched tighter as he backed her up against the bedpost, imprisoning her. Green eyes narrowed, her breathing quick and shallow. "You will regret this, Raiden."

"Montegomery," he added for her, and her brows rose. "Raiden Montegomery. Bastard. Thief. Outlaw."

"Kidnapper, flesh peddler," she shot back. "Is there no end to your debauchery?"

"Apparently not." He insinuated his knee between hers, unbalancing her, yet he kept pushing deeper, the motion erotic, spreading her, hard muscle grinding against her intimate softness till she straddled his thigh, the robe loose and parting for his will.

Her fingers dug into his chest as she fought for her anger, fought against the decadent feel of her bare skin dampening his rough breeches. "You will not win me like this."

"I do not have to." His free hand rode her shape from hip to breast, and she squirmed. "You, my lady, have agreed to the price."

Damn him! "A fortnight, you said!"

Suddenly he ducked, his mouth slashing heavily over hers. She was stiff and unyielding, her head twisting to avoid him, and he clamped a hand in the cloud of red hair and feasted on her lips. Then, in the space of heartbeat, she softened, and a dagger of fire shot through his blood. He jerked back, stunned by the power of their clash, and met her angry gaze. He expected, anticipated, the claw of her nails, the bite of her teeth, yet he saw confusion, disbelief, and when she suddenly plowed her hands into his hair, gripping handfuls, Raiden knew he'd fallen into a cavern with no way to the surface. With a yank, she drew him down and devoured his mouth, drowning him in the flood of excitement and her passion spilling over him like boiling wine. He should have known she'd give no quarter, and like a siren luring him to his death, she plundered wildly, impatiently. And brigand that he was, he stole more, needed more. He held nothing back. He drove his tongue between her lips and she sucked it deeper, sending bone-shattering heat down to his groin. He groaned with the pleasure of it, accepting this insanity even when he knew her anger pushed her, knew she'd hate him more when this was done, and he wrapped her in his arms, crushing her to his chest.

She whimpered and rocked his thigh, the liquid heat of her torturing him through his clothes. He wanted to touch her there, taste her, and feel her take him inside her in complete possession. But Willa was a woman he could not possess, not with sex or prison, or threat. She'd turn it against him as she was now, weakening him with her lush mouth, her forbidden body, and driving the madness of passion through to his core until he could do no more than surrender.

His masculine power surrounded her, mastering her, engulfing her like a dense vapor, hot and smothering, the haze of her own hunger tumbling her into an oblivion she never knew existed, not for her. She should berate and slap him, curse him for opening this locked door, but it was useless. His first touch shattered her resolve, her insides pulling like the sharp gather of fabric, folding one sensation onto another. She felt out of control, her breathing too fast, her hunger ungodly, as if she needed to take him inside herself or she'd die. Her heart pounded heavily as his hands hurriedly found the curve of her buttocks, pulling her into his hardness and imprinting his arousal on her skin. The glorious feel of it catapulted images of him filling her, stroking her, and lips and tongue dueled in a frantic, erotic war. And she let him, because despite everything, she wanted to be plundered, wanted to explore him, the beast of her passion destroying her good sense. She'd known it would be like this, savage, unstoppable, dragging her down with him, making her greedy for the forbidden.

And showing her the price of his help, the cost of her defiance. Vows bound her to another. Lust sealed her in an illicit contract.

Willa shuddered violently, the barrier of her vows torturing her desire and fighting her for supremacy. Her oath won, and she tore her mouth free, pushing him back.

Her gaze locked with his, their breathing harsh.

Raiden struggled to gather his scattered senses and call on the words that would rebuild the barrier they'd just destroyed. "Your complete surrender will be easier than I anticipated."

"*Ahh!*" she raged, shoving him hard, hating the truth, hating that he could wound her with it. He released her abruptly and strode to the door, leaving a dastardly chuckle in his wake as he pulled it closed behind him.

Her legs folded beneath her and she slid to the floor, drained of energy, gasping for breath. Her lips were numb, her body struggling under the pressure of her desire. She wrapped the robe tightly and dared herself to cry. She'd made a mess of this, giving him a weapon without armor to repel it. Aye, she had one, she thought. She was married. Wed before God and king. It did not matter that when she saw Alistar again, she would likely shoot him, but 'twould do her well to remember her vows, for she realized exactly how helpless she was to Raiden's touch. A slave to her own desire for a man she could not have, should not want. She was no better than he for her lies and agreeing to such a contract. She'd bargained with the devil and was in a sensuous purgatory that would lead them both straight to hell.

A contest of wills and passion. She would lose. If he touched her again, kissed her like that, she would lose.

The scent of cinnamon, nutmeg, curry, and mace thickened the air, his boots powdered with spice as Raiden paced in the belly of the ship, across what little floor space was left in the hull. His arousal throbbed, and he welcomed the pain, rubbing the back of his neck, cursing his stupidity. His underestimation beat him like a slaver's whip, hammering at his good sense. That kiss, he knew, was the gravest of mistakes. God above, how could he share a cabin with her, knowing that when they touched, everything crumbled beneath a potent explosion?

Ah, and what an eruption, he thought, his muscles flexing with a memory all their own. Her kiss was as sharp as her tongue, spiced and intoxicating, and he wanted more of it. To tame it, and savor it. But not force it. And he knew that for the rest of his days, the taste of her would linger to haunt him. He was a fool to make this wager. And after the way he'd spoken to her, he knew she'd avoid him as best she could. 'Twas just as well, and what he needed, he thought, for he'd other matters to tend to, a betrayer to uncover and now a child to find. Then he recalled the conversation before the bargain.

If she was in the tavern to find information on her son, then why did the captain try to kill her? How did the man know she was there other than to follow her? Did the captain not want her to find the boy, and if so, why not? How could a child be of such significance? If the child was stolen and sold into slavery, he could be anywhere. Raiden had spent countless times searching for lost crewmen, to no avail. And still, she could be lying about the boy. Yet he doubted it. She was not schooled in hiding her emotions, and her expression whilst she pleaded for her child suddenly filled his mind; tiredly, he sank down on a keg of stolen nutmeg, wincing at the pain sparking through his groin. He shifted carefully, wishing they were anchored and he could dive into the cold sea, then wishing he'd never met Willa.

"Your cabin not a place for privacy?"

Raiden glanced at Tristan making his way down the ladder.

"Nay, I see." Tristan jumped the last few feet, sending a golden cloud of spice into the air, clutching his side.

"If I wanted company, I'd be topside. How goes that?" He gestured to the wound, days old.

"It heals slowly," he said, distracted to other matters. "Your cabin mate being difficult?"

Raiden scoffed to himself. Having the woman aboard was difficult. Offering her a bargain he'd have sworn she'd never accept was an error in judgment. But then, he'd offered her child back to her, and he was mortally ashamed of himself for dangling so ripe a cherry in her face. What had he expected? For her to forego her child for him? 'Twas unthinkable. And he'd only himself to blame.

Placating her with lies was reprehensible, and with few shreds of honor left, his wisest course would be to seek information— and quickly.

"A ship approaches."

Raiden's brows furrowed and he looked up. "Colors?"

"None we can see as yet."

"Stand ready, it could be the *Sea Warrior*."

The ship heeled suddenly, and by the motion Raiden knew a gale brewed. He glanced around, at the kegs, crates, and chests lashed to the walls; then, satisfied they would not shift and breech the hull, he stood and headed to the ladder.

An hour later, he was high in the rigging when he saw Willa step into the hazy light. He should have been angry that she'd come topside without permission, but clad in the blue gown and slippers he'd laid out for her, she looked like a breath of morning sunshine under the clouding sky. Just the sight of her made blood pool in his groin, and a quick glance told him his men had the same reaction. Her wild curls were tamed, swept off her neck in twists of braids and offering a demure picture when he knew she was anything but innocent.

Jabari walked beside her, and she shielded her eyes as Tristan approached. They spoke briefly before she tipped her head and met his gaze across the distance. Raiden felt the pull of his desire spread beneath his skin. He could not look upon her again without remembering how she had come apart in his arms.

Willa tore her gaze away. Her skin seemed to light with excitement at the sight of him. Pish-posh. She'd seen half-naked men before, many of them working for her father. But bare chested, she'd never laid witness to the likes of Raiden Montegomery. Nothing prepared her for the ropy sculpture of bronze muscle and man, the ripple of sinew as he climbed down. Her heartbeat accelerated, her blood rushing with the memory of all that power wrapped around her and her torrid behavior in his embrace. She still couldn't believe how she'd reacted, and it scared her, this passion buried inside her—and the wrong man bringing it out. She looked back as he climbed down the rigging and dropped to the deck. He walked toward her, and she wondered how the simple act could be so seductive, damn his hide. He was the wrong man. He wasn't her husband, and she feared the moment when he'd learn the truth.

He stopped close, staring down at her with those impenetrable eyes, and her gaze fell on the tattoo circling his bicep. A black ring of thorns. She curled her fingers into her skirts against the urge to touch it. Though there was a cut below it, from the battle in the marketplace, healing nicely, she wondered over the significance of such a permanent mark, then met his gaze and wondered what he was thinking, leering at her like that. Had he cast off their kiss as a feat of his prowess? For it was certainly not attributable to his glowing charm. Was he gloating over her quick fall into his arms? It made her more determined to hold him to his portion of the bargain.

"The cabin too hot, my lady?" He gave her a mocking smile.

His innuendo landed like a hammer to her chest, and she snapped, "Do not call me that."

He arched a brow, accepting his shirt from a seaman and slipping it on. That was the second occasion she'd made such a demand.

"When do we make port?"

"We won't for a day or two." He inclined his head to the cloudy sky.

She folded her arms and gave him an impatient look. "How can you discover aught while on the sea?"

"Be patient, Willa. I will hold to my end of the bargain." His gaze lowered to her mouth, then the swell of bosom, before meeting those green eyes. "As I know you can fulfill yours."

"You first," she said, and with the back of her hand, brushed him aside and walked the deck, Jabari at her side.

Raiden chuckled to himself, watching her for a moment, then handed Tristan the threading hook and nodded to the tangle of halyard line no one could unfetter. Tristan went off as Raiden tucked his shirt in his breeches and headed to the quarterdeck. He scanned the horizon through the spyglass, studying the approaching ship. 'Twould be hours before it was in range and could do them harm. He'd rather not do battle in daylight before they met with the *Sea Warrior*, but if necessary he would.

"Kahlid," he called over his shoulder to the helmsman. "Dance a course till the sun lowers and we can put a name to her." Raiden sensed 'twas one of his own ships, since they were to rendezvous at these coordinates at the mouth of the

Hoogley River. And if it wasn't? Every man aboard understood the risks, yet his concern was for Willa and what would happen to her if he failed. He lowered the glass, closing it and tapping it against his lips. He had to assume someone would come looking for her, and that would mean twice as many English vessels dogging their heels.

He heard her laughter, bright and feminine and carrying on the wind, and he turned sharply. She was amidships, sitting like a flower on coil of rope, an audience of pirates around her. He almost smiled at the crusty men hanging on her every word, bringing her a cup of wine. A foot or two behind her, Nealy Perth stood like a sentinel, watching her closely. It put Raiden instantly on guard. Though aged, the man was big and held his own amongst the younger crewmen. Wind snapped the sails, and Raiden glanced up to where Tristan hung in the rigging, untangling a line whilst having a conversation with the woman below.

Her face tilted toward the sky, she smiled as he spoke to her and Raiden experienced an unaccustomed surge of jealousy. "Mr. Dysart!"

Tristan swung around to look at him.

"Either work or get the bloody hell down." The clouds rolled in like a black blanket unfurling. "Mistress, to the cabin."

She looked his way, her gaze narrowing, and his expression dared her to defy him. She tipped her chin and stood, curtsying to the pirates. Raiden ordered kegs and barrels secured, and as he made his way toward Willa, a crack of lightning cut a jagged blade in the sky and hit the water.

The *Renegade* listed sharply, and Willa lost her footing, falling against the rail, the impact knocking the breath from her lungs. She gripped the rail as the ship dipped frighteningly low.

An unsecured keg rolled, hitting the back of her legs, snapping her back, then throwing her forward. And Raiden saw her feet leave the deck. He shoved men out of the way, leapt over rope and kegs to reach her. But she was falling head first into the black waters.

Eight

A sudden hard jerk swept her from the dangerous edge.

She inhaled a huge breath, blinking into the face of Nealy Perth, his arm about her waist, a fistful of her gown in his hand. "My deepest thanks, sir."

"Not at all, m'lady," he said, setting her to her feet.

Raiden was there, taking her arm and pulling her from Perth. "Are you mad?" All he could still see was her falling headfirst into shark-infested waters.

"Oh, aye, Raiden, I make an oath with you and then in a fit of despair, forget my son and throw myself into the sea." She jerked free, unaware of Perth's interest in the conversation. "Do give me for credit for possessing a bit of backbone, pirate." She marched off. Raiden let out a harsh breath, rubbing the back of his neck. She was never coming topside without him again, he thought, his heart still pounding.

"Spirited lass," Perth said from his side.

Raiden snapped him a glance. "My thanks, Mr. Perth."

The sailor nodded, a move, Raiden thought, that was somehow regal and condescending. "My good fortune to be nearer, Cap'n."

"Her good fortune," he said. "Secure that keg."

"Raiden!" Willa shouted, pointing, and he followed the direction.

Tristan Dysart hung in the loose lines by his ankle, the wind banging him against the mast. Willa raced to him, calling out, Raiden on her heels and ordering a grappling hook and rope.

"Hullo, lass," he said, his face flushed red.

She craned her neck. "Dear God, Mr. Dysart. You're bleeding!" His coat had fallen open, his side dark with blood.

"It would appear so. An old wound. Do not worry yourself." He waved it off, then tried curling up to the rope and failed, sighing heavily. "Damned embarrassing, this. Give a lift, will you, Rai."

"Remain still, Mr. Dysart," Willa said. "You will only tear the wound further."

"I am touched by your concern, m'lady."

"You are touched to go up there wounded in the first place."

"I always obey orders," he said, and Willa looked at Raiden, but before she could speak, he shouldered her aside and swung the rope and threw, catching the grappling hook in the cross jack. He climbed with a speed she never dreamed he possessed, and when he reached Tristan, he gripped a fistful of his coat and pulled till Tristan could reach his line.

"Hold on tight." The rain grew heavier, the wind kicking them against the sails.

"Aye, of course. Thought never occurred."

After he had a grip on the rope, Raiden climbed to the cross jack. He knew when he freed Tristan's boot from the tangle of rope, the release would jerk too hard on his wound, tearing it further. Wrapping the rope around his arm a few times, he cut the line at a spot above his head, then slowly unwound it till his first mate was no longer upside down. Tristan swayed weakly, wrapping the grappling rope around his leg and slowly sliding down. He collapsed on the deck. Raiden shimmied down moments later and found Willa, drenched as she knelt to examine Tristan's side.

With glazed eyes, Tristan peered at his wound. "Damn, that won't leave a pretty scar to charm the ladies."

Willa's gaze flashed to his. "It needs to be cleaned and redressed." She touched Tristan's forehead; despite the cool rain, his skin burned. She stood, helping him to his feet, and Raiden lurched forward, bearing his weight and bringing him to his cabin. Crewmen filed in after him as Raiden settled him into a chair and Willa immediately went down on her knees and threw open his coat.

"Madam, if you wanted me to remove my clothing for you, you need only ask," he said cheekily.

"Hush, you rogue," she said, pulling up his shirt. "My word!" He was bleeding profusely from his side, and she quickly blotted the wound with the shirttails. "I need a knife, strips for bandages, shears, and any surgical instruments and herbs you might have aboard." She lifted her gaze to the crewmen, then Raiden.

"Do the lady's bidding," Raiden ordered and the crewmen left.

"Remove his weapons and get him on the table," she said as she quickly gathered Turkish towels, soap, pitcher, and basin.

"Balthasar can take care of this," Tristan said, allowing Raiden to help him to the table.

She cocked him a look, her hand on her hip. "Well, then, decide now if you wish him to attend you, Squire Dysart."

"His rough touch or your sweet, tender hands?" he said, taking one and pressing it to his side.

He was truly impossible, she thought, shaking her head. " 'Tis angry with infection." She met Raiden's gaze. "Give me your dagger and remove his boots." Handing the weapon over, Raiden yanked Dysart's boots off as she cut a slit in the hem of his shirt.

Tristan caught her wrist. "Madam, what are you proposing?"

With a jerk, she ripped the shirt clean in two.

"That's my best one!"

"I don't believe thieving another will be a problem."

Reclining on his side, he wiggled his brows. "You just want to see me naked."

"Hush your mouth or I will stitch that shut, too," she said tartly and gave him a push. He went down easily, his head thumping on the table. She winced, instantly stuffing a pillow under his noggin, then patting his cheek as she passed. She stopped before Raiden. "I need rum."

"Spiced or nay?"

Her lips curved. "Either, Captain." She leaned closer, and Raiden caught her scent, lemony and awash with fresh rain. "Get him besotted, for this will hurt."

Raiden looked over her head at Tristan, who was doing his best to appear relaxed, except for his clenching fists. "How bad is it?"

"He has a fever and I suspect . . ." She hesitated.

"Tell me the whole of it now, woman."

She heard the concern in his voice. "Something is wrong. 'Tis too shallow a cut for so much blood."

Nodding, he went to his cabinets for rum, bringing the bottle to his mate.

"Oh, God," Tristan groaned. "Your best stock. I'm finished." He tipped the bottle to his lips and drank heavily.

Crewmen and Balthasar appeared in the doorway, the Bedouin scowling at her like black thunder as he advanced toward Willa. Raiden's arm shot out, stopping him. "Mind your tongue and remember my words," he warned, and Willa breathed a sigh of relief.

Balthasar handed a rolled hide to Raiden, then stepped back, glaring, his arms folded over his bare chest, swirling tattoos bending over dark skin. Raiden laid the items she'd requested, unrolling the hide filled with surgical instruments. She washed her hands, demanded a candle, then ran the blade over the flame. She checked Tristan's pupils, then washed the wound on his side.

"I'm going to have to reopen it," she told him.

"I shall behave, I swear." He took another huge gulp, watching her moves.

She reopened the wound and Tristan reared off the table. "Sweet Mary Mother of—damn woman!" Blood pooled beneath him and Tristan looked at it, taking another huge sip. "I shan't eat off this table ever again," he slurred.

She looked at Raiden. "Hold him, please. I will have to open it wider."

"I have a better idea," Raiden said, and walked up to Tristan, took the bottle, then slammed his fist into his jaw. Tristan went down instantly.

"That was truly charitable, Captain," she said tightly, yet went to work.

Raiden watched her cut his friend, then slide her fingers in the wound, blotting, looking, feeling, blotting; then, with tongs, she pulled out a thin splinter. Of metal or wood, he could not tell for all the blood.

The ship heeled, crockery slid, and she staggered, unable to keep her footing. Raiden waved to Balthasar to hold down the patient as he moved up behind her, his hands circling her waist.

She flinched and shot a look back over her shoulder. "What are you doing?"

He braced his legs behind hers. "Steadying you so you do not stitch your fingers to Mr. Dysart. Or fall on your pretty behind," he added for her ears alone.

His eyes were unreadable, but his closeness made her uneasy, and though she did not need his help, there were more important matters to attend to just now than arguing with him. "Hold tight, for he may come to," she said to Balthasar, then pushed at the cut, forcing the infection out. The odor was fetid, but she did not flinch, her expression never changing as she pushed and blotted, using a fresh rag each time, then cleaned the wound with rum. As she bade, Raiden held a cloth tightly over the wound whilst she plucked a long hair from Tristan's head and threaded the thin needle.

"His hair, Willa?" His soft words sent a chill skipping down her throat.

" 'Tis an Indian remedy." She checked the wound. "From America. I learned it from a medicine man whilst visiting a friend."

"In America?"

She braced herself to stitch Tristan's flesh, and considering what she'd done to him thus far, now was not the time to quibble. "Aye. I was born there. In Charles Towne in the Carolinas."

So, that was why he could not place her accent.

"I hear 'tis a savage land," a crewman said, watching her intently.

"Oh, sir, 'tis beautiful, unlike any place I have seen since leaving."

"And when was that?" Raiden asked.

A wave of homesickness hit her, and she ducked her head a bit. "Five years ago."

The ship heeled again, sending her back into him, her firm bottom pushing intimately to his groin. Raiden resisted the urge to push back and barked to a sailor, "Tell Kahlid to sail into the wind," then anchored himself in an effort not to touch her. But 'twas impossible, his resistance failing as his fingers flexed on her waist, and he realized she'd not donned the corset he found for her. God above, was she completely naked beneath the gown? The enticement drove through him with a hard rush of heat, and he leaned closer as she took small, quick stitches. Then he noticed the tear sliding down her cheek. "Willa?"

She did not answer, completing her task, but her mind was for a moment lost in the past, in a time when she was still her father's daughter and never once feared for her safety. Despite Papa's doting, she was in control of her life then. 'Twas so long ago, she thought, an innocence she could never recapture. She knotted the final stitch, then looked directly at Balthasar. "Have you a remedy for this? A purgative?"

His black brows drew together, taken back by the asking.
"I do."

"Can you mix it and apply it whilst I make bandages?"

"Why would ye ask him?" a crewman said sourly. "He left
the piece inside."

Balthasar leveled the crewman a deadly glance, but before
they had words, Willa spoke up. "Balthasar's fingers are too
big to get inside, and who would have thought the blade left
a piece behind in so shallow a wound?"

"You did," Balthasar said, eyeing her.

Willa shrugged, unnerved by the man's heavy looks. "He
needs to rest." Her gaze slid to Raiden, her expression chastising him for punching the man. "In true sleep. And be watched."

With swift moves, Balthasar ground and mixed herbs, then
smoothed the poultice over Tristan's wound. He lifted the
unconscious man as she wrapped him. " 'Twas not my intention
to usurp your authority, sir," she whispered to the Bedouin.
"And I apologize if I've offended you."

The *Renegade*'s cook stared for a moment, then nodded as
a sailor appeared outside the hatch, wet and breathless. "Captain, the *Sea Warrior* approaches."

Raiden nodded. "Excellent. Keep her in sight. The rest of
you, man your watch." Men left, yet Balthasar remained, cleaning up the mess.

"Another prize?" Willa said, drying her hands.

Raiden looked at her. "Nay. Another of my ships."

"Yours? Yours alone?"

He eyed her. "Aye."

"Just how many do you have?" She moved closer as she
spoke, her gaze narrow.

He shrugged. "Mayhap a half dozen."

"Nine," Tristan said groggily, then groaned, clutching his
jaw.

"Good lord. The price on your head must be very high."

His lips curved. "Is that hope or concern in your voice,
lass?"

"Neither." She turned away and met Balthasar's gaze. "Can you carry him to his cabin?"

"I can walk," Tristan groused, shooting a nasty look at Raiden as he sat up and worked his jaw. "I think you loosened a tooth."

"You were braying like a mule."

Tristan flushed, but it vanished when Willa rushed to his side to help him. As Balthasar took the brunt of his weight, she pulled off the remains of his shirt, rolling it in a ball. "Careful. Nay, you've indulged enough," she said when he tried to take the bottle of rum with him.

"My thanks, mistress," he said, and leaned out, brushing a kiss to her cheek.

Willa pinkened and touched his abused jaw. "Such a brave lad," she teased, her smile tender.

Behind them, Raiden scowled. "Get yourself to bed, Dysart. I do not want to have to tie you to the capstan to prevent you from rolling overboard."

"He's always grouchy after a rescue," Tristan whispered loudly to Willa, winking, then allowing Balthasar to help him through the hatch.

"A broth, mayhap, after a few hours' sleep?" she said to Balthasar, handing him Dysart's boots. "And something to help ease the fever?"

"As you wish," he said with a respectful bow, and Willa froze.

Her gaze swept his strong features, over the dotted tattoos on his temples and cheeks, to the ones on his forearms. He was the most exotic-looking man, she thought, and like Raiden, he had a pierced ear, the Bedouin's adornment a single teardrop pearl. He wore chains of gold and silver, rings on his fingers and nothing on his feet. The billowy trousers of his homeland wrapped him from the waist down in yards of black fabric, the wide red sash showing off the twisted muscles of his stomach. He was as big as Raiden, and she realized how easily he could have killed her before, after her bath. And how much she suddenly valued this small alliance.

She touched his arm and whispered, "My thanks for your assistance, sir."

His dark gaze shifted to Tristan, then back to her. "You are most welcome."

He left with the quartermaster, fairly carrying the man to his cabin. Willa turned and found Raiden staring at her in a way that made her uneasy.

"So, where did you learn all that?"

"I told you, in the Colonies." She swept past, the bottle of rum in her hand.

"Well-bred ladies don't usually tend wounds."

She sat on the aft bench and gave him a thin look. "And you know a great deal about well-bred ladies?" She took a swig of the spiced rum, and it felt like warm sunshine sliding down her throat.

"Intimately."

She glared and sipped the potent Jamaican rum. "Boasting. How very male."

It seemed her tenderness was only for the wounded, Raiden thought. Of course, she was still angry with him over their bargain, and he did not expect that to wane until he produced her son.

Though he'd made the wager hoping she would not accept and therefore ease his guilt over not searching for a dead child, the agreement bound them in the strangest manner. She searched for a lost child she adored. He'd been a lost child with no one looking for him, no one loving him. Raiden scoffed silently, ignoring the tightness in his chest. There was no value in dredging up a past he could not change, he thought, when suddenly, the face of a child loomed in his mind's eye—red-haired and dimple-cheeked like her. By some twist of fate, had the boy survived? Did he know his mother searched for him? Did he know how much her love for him cost her? And who took the lad? For 'twas clear to Raiden she would never neglect her baby and lose him as one loses a scarf or ring.

Not for the first time since she'd told him of her boy, Raiden wondered after his own mother, the same questions he'd asked himself for the past three-and-thirty years torturing him. Had she wanted him and was denied the chance because of her family, her social position, and the scandal his birth caused? Had his father ever tried to locate him beyond the time he named him? And why did he not take Raiden with him? And what of the other Montegomerys, the rumors of Ransom, raised as Granville's own son in a world of education and privilege, only to discover, after killing a man who'd accused him of being one of their father's many by-blows, that he too was illegitimate? Raiden did not know which was worse: to discover who you were to be a lie, or to have never known who you were or whence you'd come.

Stolen lives and lost souls, he thought wryly, focusing on Willa as she took a healthy swig of rum. Raiden wondered how much she'd already consumed while he wallowed in the ugliness of his past.

"My father's brother is a doctor," she finally said.

"In the Carolinas?"

"Aye, and my mother is dead, my sister dead, as is my husband." That last lie stuck in her throat, and she washed it away with another draught of rum. "And all I've left is my baby."

Guilt crowding him, he crossed to her, reaching for the bottle.

She shoved his hands away.

"You will regret it in the morning."

"I do not care, so why don't you just take yourself off now, laddie." She waved, sipping again, and Raiden frowned at the Irish brogue working into her voice. He snatched the bottle from her, tipping it to his lips for a long pull, and when she reached for it, he held it away, corking it.

"Don't be denying me a wee nip."

"If you hide in this"—he jiggled the bottle—"they will have won," he said, not knowing why.

"They will always win." She eyed him from head to toe. "Like you, Raiden, they haven't any scruples over their actions."

"How is that?"

"Because of power." She left the bench, staggering a bit. He grasped her arm, steadying her, and she met his gaze. "Power and more than a wee bit of money."

"But you are a wealthy woman—"

"A pile of hooey."

His lips curved. "I see a woman of refinement and beauty."

" 'Tis but a package for the barter block, pirate," she said, curtsying unsteadily. " 'Tis the prettiest bauble that will be sold to the highest bidder, don't you know."

His features darkened. He heard pain and loneliness in every syllable. "Surely your father did not force you?" Though it was not uncommon.

Her gaze slid to his, showing him she was not as intoxicated as he thought. She snatched the bottle, and before he could stop her, she uncorked it and tipped it to her lips again.

"Enough, Willa," he said softly, gently taking the decanter.

Willa didn't fight him, her limbs already numb. "Aye." She moved away, strolling round his cabin, touching this and that, flicking her fingers over the hilts of swords lining the wall as she passed and making them rock. She walked closer, and when the ship heeled, she stumbled, latching on to the bedpost and swinging around to look at him. She blinked, and Raiden wondered if he could catch her before she fell on her face.

"When do we make port?"

He glanced at the windows, at the rain battering the glass. "After the storm."

"Splendid," she moaned, stumbling to the aft bench and plopping down. "The monsoons will toss this ship for a month."

"Not the season yet."

Her heart lifted, and her lips curved.

"When we make port, 'twill be east of the mouth of the Hoogley River."

She blinked blearily. "Do not jest with me." Near the Ganges. The little bit of information she'd gathered from Barkmon was that Alistar was supposed to travel east. And there were slavers there. " 'Twould be cruel."

"I will look for him, Willa." Raiden wondered if all mothers were so devoted and then wondered how he could even think of denying this child, even at the remote possibility that the boy survived, the chance to be in her arms. To be loved as he had never been.

"But he's been lost for so long."

"He is a child alone, what else do we need?"

We. A peculiar partnership, she thought, looking away. The time to tell him the truth was closing in. But first he had to find something on Mason. Would he withdraw his bargain, cast her out because there was nothing to offer him because she was married? Or would he even care that she was still bound to her vows? Would he hold her to their agreement if he found nothing? she wondered, meeting his gaze.

Raiden set the bottle on his desk. "In two days' time, I will expect you to tell me all I need to find this child of yours."

Willa understood that when he knew of her husband, he would realize she knew about the East India Company, and the horrible treachery infesting it. She suspected that was the reason the captain had come after her, for the absence of her husband and his control over her made her a threat.

Alistar was stealing.

She smirked to herself. A pirate of ledgers, she thought, then cocked her head. If truth be told, she preferred the ones of the sea.

"So my lord pirate—" She laughed shortly at her own words. "You're going to be attackin' a ship."

"You are aboard a pirate's vessel, Willa," he reminded her

unnecessarily. "There will be battles, and death and coin to be had."

"Coin," she said bitterly. Was that all he ever desired? "And if you lose?"

"Then you are free."

She scoffed and waved. "Then I am dead, or taken prisoner, or raped."

He flinched at the last. "If the English take us, Willa, they will return you to Calcutta."

Aye, she thought, they would once she told them who she'd fatally wed. Yet there was real danger there now, and Willa had not forgotten the captain sent to kill her. Was Barkmon capable of doing Alistar's bidding to that extreme? Murder was murder and the penalty great. Was spice worth it? She looked at Raiden, knowing he risked much to save her. She should be grateful, she thought hazily, and she knew that although her body was payment, she was safer with him than alone.

She did not know what she said with those eyes, Raiden thought, offering her a hand up. She looked at it, then to his face, accepting it, and he pulled her from the bench. She swayed against him, her body a soft cushion molding to a wall of stone, yielding where his would not. Like her kiss 'twas as arresting as it was powerful.

"Do you seek to take advantage of my inebriated state?"

"When I take you to my bed," he growled, "I want all your senses alert and singing."

His tone was so suggestive, Willa's knees softened. His hands slipped to her back, pressing her into him, and Raiden reveled in the feel of her body laid like warm velvet to his own.

"Of course, if you would like to fulfill your part of the bargain now?" he suggested darkly, loosening her gown. She twisted to see what he was doing, following the motion around like a dog chasing its tail until she faced him again. He smothered a chuckle.

She eyed him suspiciously, then realized her gown was falling and inhaled, clutching it to her breasts. "How dare you!" She stumbled back a step.

He caught her. "I am captain. I dare all I choose." He swept her up in his arms, carting her to the bed and laying her there. "The gown is too tight for sleeping. Rest."

"I am not tired," she slurred, already struggling to keep her eyes open.

Even besotted, she would not give in, he thought, pushing her down when she tried to sit up. "I do not want to tie you here, Willa. But if need be, I will." He was now glad she'd drunk too much, for he did not want her causing trouble when they took the *Weston* in a couple of hours.

Willa sank into the soft bed. "But I swore never to lie upon your sheets." Her brogue grew thicker.

"With me, I believe was the exact specification."

She waved to where he sat beside her. Raiden did not have to be told how close he was to her. He could almost taste her, and his gaze roamed her flushed skin, her red hair curling and spread over his pillows in wild abandon. She was an aphrodisiac, constantly temping him with the tiny gifts of her smile, the glimpses of her pain, and her compassion she tried so hard not to show. Though he'd promised not to take her to his bed for a fortnight and was still uncertain if he'd ever survive after being inside her, he wanted to touch her, feel her capped power. Every time he looked at her, the memory of their kiss, the heat and explosion, reminded him in a warm flush. Ah, loving her body would be giving up his soul, he thought and remembered that she was still lying to him.

Willa wiggled deeper into the bed, the liquor working through her blood, stirring everything she'd suppressed—her desire for this man, her unforgivable want for something more than a bargain, and mayhaps the ease of her unending loneliness. The loneliness was the worst. Without her child, her father, her home, and being an outcast in England, she was alone, the poor shipper's daughter marrying into title and respect. Respect. What drivel, she thought, and what a fool she'd been to want only for her family to survive and in return gaining nothing but misery with Alistar Peachwood for a husband. A man cruel enough to hurt his own child.

She looked away, at Raiden's arm locked and braced at her hip, angry with herself for not seeing the truth, angry with Alistar for playing on her fears for her father's life. Alistar was to blame, pushing her to this, forcing to barter with her body for the return of her son. A wave of despair swelled over her, making her ache to hold Mason, to smell his hair, to feel his tiny arms linking around her neck. To hear him call her Mama.

Tears glossed her eyes, and unwillingly her fingers wrapped Raiden's arm. The warmth of his skin, roughened with hair, offered comfort and strength, and she slid her hand higher over thick, twisted muscles. She felt them tighten under her touch and slowly dragged her gaze up to meet his.

His dark eyes smoldered with a heat she recognized, and for a moment she wanted to be held and kissed and assured none would die tonight and she'd soon find her baby.

"Be careful, Raiden."

"Concerned, lass?"

Her fingers flexed on his bicep. "You've a bargain to fulfill with me."

Raiden lowered his gaze, hungry for her and something so much deeper digging through him like an English blade. Having this woman for more than his mistress was a notion he could never entertain overlong, and when the rumble of cannons rolling into place vibrated the wooden ship, and the gun ports opened, the sound reminded him who he was with aching clarity. A bastard pirate with a price on his head who would suffer a gruesome death at the hands of the English. He could offer her nothing but coin, and a little help now, and yet, until she graced his life, Raiden had thought all he'd left in his heart had died years ago.

When he looked back and found her asleep, he took her hand, kissed the palm, then laid it across her stomach, grateful for the rum and that she would not see his crimes.

Raiden left her, heading above, and when he climbed the quarterdeck, he saw three of his ships closing behind the *Renegade*. Kahlid handed him the spyglass. Under the haze of the moon, and through the subsiding rain, he sighted over the port side at the Royal East India ship, the *Weston*.

"Battle stations," he said, and the order trickled through the ranks with excitement. "Signal the *Sea Warrior*."

The prize awaited.

Nine

Willa flinched awake seconds before she rolled off the bed and hit the floor. She groaned, grabbing her head, then rubbing her bruised hip. Pain split her skull, the throb deafening, as if it shook the timbers beneath her.

Then she realized 'twas the roll of cannons below decks.

She twisted, her gaze locking on the porthole behind her. Fire. Oh, God. The distant glow of it filled the darkness. She climbed to her feet, gripping the bed for support and cursing her stupidity for drinking so much as a wave of nausea hit her. Visions of being boarded, of Raiden dying, sent her rushing forward on unsteady legs to the glass porthole. She opened it and peered out.

A ship rocked in the water, dangerously close and afire, yet damage was above the waterline and only to the mainmast. Flames devoured the sails and the Royal East India Company flag vanished into charred tatters. Dead men lay strewn like tossed rags on the capstan, over hot cannons, the stench of burning flesh filling the air. Willa's stomach threatened to empty right then, and she closed the porthole, staring through the glass.

Raiden stood amidst the carnage, his bloody sword out, his men thieving the cargo and loading it onto the *Renegade*. She watched men swinging rope nets filled with chests or carrying kegs with surprising ease across planks slung between the ships. The captain of the captured ship didn't look at all pleased by the looting, she thought, and reluctantly smiled. The man's powdered wig was askew, his deep-blue coat shredded, bloody, and his tan breeches covered with soot. Yet even wounded, he fumed and raged at Raiden. She could almost hear the haughty ''I'll have your head for this'' spilling from his lips. He was short and stout and opposite Raiden, Willa could not help but notice what a magnificent picture the Black Angel presented. His stance casual, he looked as if he'd all the universe at his disposal. His torso was wrapped in a burnished leather jerkin reaching past his hips, and the wide belt circling his waist was studded with weapons, enhancing his grand size. The wind whipped at his long hair and ebony shirt sleeves, yet there was not an inch of fabric to spare in the fit of those dark breeches. Her pulse quickened at the sight of him, like the angel of death, compelling and haunting, come to reap his share of souls. It made her indecently weak just knowing he'd held her, kissed her so ferociously. He commanded her senses even when she did not want it.

He shouted orders, his sword point pressed against the captain's chest, and through the haze of smoke, she saw the captured crew rush to put out the fire. Willa frowned. The stories reported that the Black Angel leveled the decks, leaving none to tell the tale. But it appeared that nearly the entire crew was assembling on the decks. Would he take them captive, ransom them? Or be so cruel as to execute them all?

Anticipation and anger twisted through her. *Nay, Raiden, please,* she thought. *'Tis murder.* Yet he stood alone amongst the prisoners. He even lowered the weapon trained on the captain as he spoke to the crew.

Curiosity eating her, she tugged the laces of her gown tight enough for modesty and left the cabin, creeping out onto the deck. She did not want to be seen and edged the wall, her gaze first sweeping the *Renegade*'s deck. Men lowered the booty into the hull, and Balthasar tended at least two wounded. Hardly tremendous casualties for a battle, she thought, looking back at Raiden.

"Choose now," she heard him say. Choose what? Death? Marooning? Several of the captured crew eagerly walked toward him, all ragged and malnourished. Two men helped another walk. Raiden's features were pinched with anger as he nodded and the sailors boarded the *Renegade*. He watched them intently, his gaze slipping past where she hid. She lurched back. He could not have seen her, she thought, 'twas far too dark except for the light of the fire. She waited seconds, then peeked again. He faced the captain now, the pirate's voice strong.

"Do you beg for quarter?"

"Never," the English captain said.

"I expected as much," Raiden replied tiredly, then turned toward the rail "Maroon him. Give the ship to the others."

The captain charged his back, but Raiden turned, almost as if he'd expected it, and the captain impaled himself on the end of his sword. Raiden cursed. Willa's stomach rolled as he yanked the blade free. The man fell to the deck, and before she could disgrace herself, she dashed back to the cabin. Inside, she slumped onto the aft window bench, licking her dry lips and praying the vessel would cease rocking. After a few moments, she lifted her head, and her gaze fell on the scene beyond the bank of windows.

Three ships, as black as the ocean floor, rocked in the waters. Lanterns swayed, offering the only note of their presence. She rose onto her knees and cupped the glass, peering between her hands. The figurehead of the nearest ship was a merman, his right arm outstretched and holding a sword. The *Sea Warrior*. Well, 'twas little wonder the East Indiaman took minor damage and surrendered with few dead. She sat back, admiring Raiden's cunning. Even if he attacked alone, at night the ships were nearly invisible.

Her brows knitted, and she wondered why Raiden gave those sailors refuge. For a captured crew, marooning was a known act of piracy, and the tales said he'd left none alive. Yet everything she witnessed was to the contrary. The pressing of sailors was commonplace, and a horrendous offense, in her opinion. 'Twas the treatment of those men, stolen from their families and forced to serve whilst their families suffered, often for years, that was despicable. Apparently, the East India captain cared little for his crew. Could Raiden be stealing from the East India Company and rescuing sailors as he went? Had she misjudged him?

'Twas not so great a comfort as she imagined, for she wanted to dislike him, wanted—nay, *needed*—his heinous crimes like a barrier against this fresh desire she felt the instant she clapped eyes on the man. He was a thief, no matter the compassionate gestures. He made war on the Crown. Well, she considered that really did not bother her so much. Not when she'd married Alistar because the East India monopolized free trade and nearly put her father in the streets.

"Never come topside without my permission."

She whipped around, the motion sloshing her aching brain in her skull. She moaned and rubbed the space between her eyes. Even her hair hurt, she thought. And now he was angry with her. Splendid.

"Is it necessary to shout?" she whispered.

"Is that understood?" He stepped inside, closing the door with enough force to make it rattle. "Your hair can be seen for leagues and is enough reason to provoke an attack. We are not out of danger yet. English ships travel in pairs."

She hadn't thought of that and nodded, rising slowly from the bench, her gaze moving to the blood splattering his jerkin and coating the sword. "You are uninjured?"

Raiden followed the direction of her gaze and wished she'd not seen anything, wished his life was not so, then knew he could do nothing about it and would not spend the day defending himself. "Aye." He crossed to the ward table, laying his weapons down before moving to the basin. He washed, throwing down the towel and raking his hair back, then gripped the commode with both hands. He breathed hard.

Willa thought he'd throw it across the room, he was so tense.

He pushed off and strode to the cabinet beside the bed, unlocking it. He pulled out a decanter and glass, pouring, then quickly draining the contents without stopping.

"Raiden."

"Give me silence, Willa . . . please."

The plea in his tone spoke volumes. He refilled the glass and swallowed a healthy sip, then stilled, his fingers flexing on the tumbler. Minutes ticked by, and Willa could see the liquor had little effect. If anything, his shoulders tightened even more. He wanted silence. For how long? Words backed up on her tongue, and she couldn't hold them in any longer. "What do you plan to do with those crewmen?"

He said nothing, swallowing more of the brown liquor.

"Tell me you will not maroon those poor souls."

His head snapped to the side. "Do you think so little of me?"

"I do not know what to believe. Then are the tales of the Black Angel false?"

"Nay, they are not."

Now 'twas his turn to wear the name liar, she thought. "They looked like skeletons, so thin and frail," she said.

"Aye, and poorly fed, beaten for the slightest infraction or for none at all."

"You know from experience." 'Twas a statement.

Again he did not answer, loath to relive this part of his life. Yet every time they met with an English vessel, he found the crew in the same condition—starving with hopelessness and begging for death. No man should have to suffer such an indignity.

"Raiden. Tell me."

"Aye, aye, damn it. *Aye.*" With the last word, he squeezed, and the glass broke with a sharp pop. Willa sucked in a breath as blood blossomed on his palm like a budding flower. He stared at it as if he could not see it, and she grabbed a Turkish towel from beneath the commode and rushed to him. But his expression stopped her in her tracks. His face half shielded by dark hair, he looked the wounded beast, his eyes glowing with a rage she'd never witnessed.

"Do not come closer, for I am in a mood to kill."

Her breath snagged in her throat, his words deadly calm. "You would not hurt me, Raiden," she said with little confidence.

"You do not know me, woman. Do not presume," he sneered.

She approached slowly, courting the wild animal prowling inside him. "Then help me understand this rage in you."

" 'Tis not for a lady to hear."

"But you must say it. You seethe with torment. My God, I can feel it."

The muscles around his heart tightened as he stared at her. "I seethe with hatred, Willa. A hatred so deep, naught will relieve it. Can you understand that?"

"Aye. Men are not the only ones to be wronged." He scowled, and she ventured another step closer. " 'Tis not your fault, you know, the fate of those men." Grasping his wrist, she opened his hand. The glass had broken cleanly in two pieces and she set them aside, then inspected his palm and the slice in his skin. " 'Tis clean and will not need stitches, but you must rinse this."

"Leave off." He pulled free.

She met his gaze. "But there's glass in there still."

"I do not care."

"Aye, you do." She moved away to gather a basin, pitcher, and cloths. "Or you will when your wound goes bad and you lose that hand." Setting the items on the table, she motioned to the chair, and almost angrily, he dropped into it. "There's a good lad."

"Do not patronize me, woman!"

"And do not bark at me!"

They stared hard, Willa with her hands on her hips, and Raiden glaring up at her as if he'd swallow her in one bite. She was the first to concede, sighing and reaching to brush his hair from his face, slide her fingers down the side of his haunted features. Instantly his eyes softened, and something inside her shifted.

Raiden wanted to push her away, but the turmoil inside him begged for her touch, for something soft and gentle in his ugly world. He gripped a fistful of her skirt, pulling her closer, between his spread thighs.

The intimate position sent curls of heat spinning through her. "You are bleeding on my dress."

And bleeding inside too, he thought, and wondered when it would cease. What day would he find justice? How many years would pass before he could sleep without dreams and wake without anger? How long could he resist what spread through him when this woman was near? His hands slid up to circle her waist. He tugged her closer, crushing her skirts and aching for the warmth of her flesh. Then she gave it, her hand resting on his shoulder as she bent and pressed her lips to his forehead.

He squeezed his eyes shut, his fingers digging into her waist. Raiden didn't wonder over the gesture, only that he'd needed her tender comfort then. He ached to pull her onto his lap, take her mouth, but the savageness still shuddering through his body warned him he might hurt her. And as if she knew, she straightened, then moved away.

Hovering over the table, she placed his hand in the basin and poured water over it, then tilted it to the light, plucking at the slivers. As if he'd not held her so close, as if the hot imprint of his hands were not still on her waist. As if in that moment, he had wanted more from her than information and her body.

"Talk to me, Raiden," she said into the odd silence. "I am here to listen."

He hesitated. He'd not spoken of this in years. "I was an

English sailor, shanghaied off the streets when I was naught but ten.''

"A child," she said, her voice breaking.

"Not for long," he muttered and went on. "Children, old men, men with families, they care only for the bodies to man the sails. When a few died, they'd toss them overboard and seek out replacements, like a new dish or a pot.'' He cursed and raked his hair back.

" 'Tis so cruel.''

"I escaped when I was nearly seventeen.''

Seven years pressed into service. Seven years of torture. No wonder he was still so furious. No wonder he'd freed the sailors. "Where did you go afterward?" She sat in the chair beside him, her attention on his hand.

"First to Siam, then to Java.''

"And took to piracy?'' She rinsed his hand again, then patted it dry.

"Not quite.''

Only her gaze shifted.

"I lived peacefully for a few years.'' He stared blindly at his hand, flinching when the memories grew vivid and filled with agony. "Then I was shanghaied again and . . .'' Raiden swallowed, remembering blood and gunfire at close range, and the screams and pleas that would haunt him till he died. Till he wished to die.

"Raiden, unclench your hand.''

He blinked and focused on her. She was frowning, and he heaved a long sigh, rubbing his free hand over his face and unfurling the other. "I was without choice, yet one does not rise to a captaincy without great price. Especially with piracy.''

Mutiny, slaughters. Charred ships and fleeing for his life, she thought, wrapping his palm in a soft strip of cloth. Such a life he'd led, filled with brutality, and yet there was a center of kindness in him still. What strength he must have to endure and not only survive, but triumph. "How did you gain so many ships?''

"I am good at thieving."

"I was asking for specifics."

"Preparing to betray me with them?"

So much for her gentle thoughts of him. 'Twould teach her to mind herself around him and not let her attraction blind her to his faults. Which were apparently numerous. "Who would believe the mistress of a pirate? When I leave here, I am ruined."

Leave. The word struck through him with aching loneliness. "Not if none know where you have been."

She scoffed lightly, tying the bandage. "That will not matter. I am missing, and Barkmon knows how by now. I will either be the sad victim of a pirate's handiwork or a tainted woman. He has never been very discreet."

"Your lover would smear you?"

She sent him a tight smile, angered. "If that man ever touched me, he would be singing like a woman in short order."

Raiden felt as if a stone had been lifted off his back. "Why did you let me believe otherwise?"

"You chose to. And 'twas none of your business. Nor is it now." She stood, the motion making her stomach float loosely and she gripped the basin, carrying it to the commode. She dipped the cloth in the water, blotting her forehead, licking her lips as the rum from last night threatened to appear, then tried to remove the bloodstains on her gown. But there were too many, from Tristan's wounds the night before and now his hand prints.

"You are my business, *mistress*."

Her gaze flashed to his as he stood. So the languid moment was gone, she thought, battle lines drawn.

"Now and till you are gone from here. Even your dealings afore then threaten me."

"Barkmon is not a threat to you." She slapped the towel into the basin. "The admiral is."

His spine locked, his gaze clear and hard on her.

"He has a thirst for vengeance on the Black Angel that is unmatched."

"He is one of many who seek the price of my head."

"It increases with every passing month because your pillaging drives up the price of spice."

He shrugged carelessly. "They will harvest more. And I will take more."

"And you hurt more than the Royal East India." His gaze hardened on her. "Have you no thought for the companies that must buy the spice at inflated prices?" Like her father, she thought, and the result was her marriage to Alistar so Papa would survive. "And the people who need it and cannot afford?"

She was rather vehement, he thought, frowning. "I cannot be bothered with the repercussions on a few cooks. 'Tis the Royal East India that keeps a lock on the trade."

And her locked in a marriage because of it, she thought, itching to tell him how far East India and his own pirating reached, but she would not degrade herself to win his sympathies. "You are wealthy—why keep pirating?"

" 'Tis what I do."

"You lead men, Raiden. Surely you could—"

He cocked her an irritated look. "Could what, Willa? Fight for the Crown? To rape the wealth from countries who've thrived for years without England's aid, on the guise of bringing culture God-damned *England* thinks they need?"

"Well, nay, but . . ."

"I am a thief." He moved to his desk, rummaging through the maps spread there. "I have always been a thief."

Always? She waved that off. "Aye, and an outlaw, and a bastard of Lord Granville Montegomery. I have heard this afore and it makes no difference."

Only his gaze shifted up. "You know him then?" That did that not surprise him, given her regal breeding.

"There are not many in London who do not. Your brothers are rather notorious."

His brows furrowed. ''I know only of Ransom and one other.''

The eagerness hinting in his voice, no matter how he tried to hide it, was strong enough to make her hurt for him. ''Have you not met Royce Tremayne?''

He shook his head.

''He's a Virginian, but visits south of my father's home, in Beaufort, often enough that I have crossed his path.'' She tilted her head, smiling. ''He sails a ship, too,'' she said, amused that both brothers captained vessels. ''But 'tis all I know.''

Raiden didn't know whether to be angry or pleased. His rogue father traveled in her circles, not his. ''Have you met my father?'' came softly, his head bowed a bit, his hands on the maps.

''Nay. But I've been told he is very handsome, even for his age.''

He scoffed. ''Likely still breeding bastards across the continents.''

''You hate him.''

''I do not even know him.'' He looked at her through a curtain of black hair; then, not knowing how to respond further, he tossed his head, sending dark hair from his view. ''We will dock on the morrow.''

She sighed at his evasion, then frowned questioningly.

''The storm died quickly, and we are not that far off the coast.''

She would have sworn they were deep in the Bay of Bengal, and her spirits lifted. Would he now make good his promise to search for Mason? ''How in God's name do you find these ships so easily?''

''Easily? I nearly died to find their time of departure.'' Because of a betrayer, he reminded himself.

''That is not the answer I sought.''

''There are few who are familiar with these waters, especially the English. I have sailed them since I was a child. I know the tides, the seasons, and the route they take. 'Tis simply a matter of patience.''

"And the others?" She pointed to the retreating vessels, both of which remained with the burning English ship.

"They do as they will." He kept to himself that the others were used often as decoys.

Then mayhaps *those* captains left the decks leveled and all for dead, she thought. "And the captain of the *Sea Warrior?* Who is he?"

"My half brother."

"Ah, then you do have family."

"The year of my birth was a very good one, for the seed of Montegomery litters the lands." Sarcasm dripped from his words. "And he does not know we are related."

She was appalled. "How could you not tell him?"

"He is not ready to know. Nor do I want him to."

Raiden looked away, spreading his legs when the ship heeled. He did not want to care for anyone, nor did he want anyone to mourn him when he died. He'd done enough of that in his own life and would not put that on another soul. Grief was a prolonged death of its own. Yet he found himself deeply troubled over the life he led. Willa made him this way. Willa with her bright green eyes and witty remarks. With her flaming mane and luscious body. And with the heart she wore on her sleeve and pushed into his face, making him see how low he'd sunk.

"What?" he said, looking up. "Nary a pithy response?" He frowned. She looked a bit pale.

" 'Tis the late hour." She started for the water pitcher, then stilled, covering her mouth, swallowing repeatedly and hoping she did not disgrace herself. "Dulls my glowing wit."

"A little too much rum, then?"

He just had to rub it in, she thought; yet there was a teasing light in his eyes she found utterly attractive. She wanted to stay angry with him. " 'Tis rude of you to mention it." She sank onto the aft bench, begging her stomach to calm.

"I've never had manners. Ask Tristan." He moved to his

cabinets beside the bed, withdrawing three small corked bottles along with a mug. He filled the cup with water, added pinches of herbs, then paused, turning back to add something more, stirring as he walked to her. He held it out.

She peered at the concoction. It looked vile. "I do not think that will help."

"It will, trust me."

"I imagine you have imbibed more than I," she said, reluctantly accepting the cup.

"Aye, but I do not affect a charming brogue when I get drunk."

Willa blushed furiously. "I did not."

"Aye, me lassie, you did."

She hid her embarrassment behind a sip. The stuff tasted as ghastly as it looked, and she drained it quickly, shivering, then handed back the cup.

"There, that's a good lass," he said and her gaze flashed to his.

He was smiling, all the way to his eyes, and the impact of it hit her with a punishing blow right into her heart, blossoming through her with the warmth and heat of the sun. Lord help her, he was even more devastatingly handsome when he smiled, making her pulse jump just a little harder. And what had happened to the angry, bitter man of moments ago? she wondered. That side of him she could deal with without her senses intact. But when he teased—she was so vulnerable. Thanking him, she stood and, immediately lightheaded, sank onto the bench again with a moan. "Ooh, how long does that take to be effective?"

"A wee bit."

Only her gaze shifted. "Cease."

He tried not to smile, pursing his lips.

"Fine, laugh. Go ahead and get it over with." She waved him on. "But mind you, I will not be so sympathetic when the occasion is yours."

He chuckled.

"Make this ship stay still!" she snapped.

"Think of something else."

Something else? Was he mad? Everything around her pitched and swayed. Oh, lord a'mighty. She took a deep breath and tried. "Did you take a good bit of booty?"

He folded his arms over his chest, staring down at her bowed head. "Enough."

"So now you are filthy rich."

Raiden did not reveal that this prize was forfeit for her safety and his claim. "I suppose."

She looked up. "Then perhaps you should bathe in it." She gestured to the blood on his jerkin.

Raiden looked down, then stripped off his belt and jerkin, tossed them aside, and pulled her from the bench. "Get to bed," he said.

"I am not tired," she slurred, "and I will sleep here." She gestured sluggishly to the pillows on the floor beyond his desk.

"Nay, the bed." Gripping her shoulders, he practically dragged her there.

Willa could not fight him, her limbs feeling oddly heavy, and she climbed into the bed, dropping onto her stomach. Raiden unlaced her dress and she rolled over slowly, meeting his gaze. She blinked him into focus.

"You have drugged me."

"Aye," he said, helping her into a more comfortable position.

"Scoundrel." She gave his chest a playful shove. "You were losing the argument and cannot admit defeat."

He smiled gently as she wiggled into the mattress, her bodice slipping low. He started to turn away, for the temptation to sweep her into his arms and taste her mouth was nearly overwhelming, but she grasped his hand, pulling him down onto the bed. Raiden sat frozen beside her, and when her hand slipped to his jaw in a light caress, he told himself 'twas the herbs affecting her. Yet he reveled in her fingers smoothing his jaw, sifting into his hair. He could not move, nor could he look away.

"You are not who you seem, pirate."

"I am all that you see, Willa. A dead man breathing still."

She made a sound of sympathy and disbelief. "Do not court your death so eagerly, Raiden. You breathe rather well right now."

But he would die, soon, when he met his adversary on a battlefield of black water and exacted his revenge—or perish in the pursuit. Yet, she made him long for peace, and the look in her eyes now, soft with the sheen of desire, struck him in the chest with deadly accuracy. His heart pounded heavily. Her breathing increased with his, and when her hand slid down to grasp his, Raiden curled his fingers in hers.

"Willa."

She brought his hand to her lips, rubbing it to her cheek. " 'Tis not so rough, this hand that wields a sword." With her free hand, she swept her fingertip over his lips. " 'Tis not so harsh, this mouth that speaks of naught but death."

Damn and blast, he should not have drugged her so she'd sleep off the rum's effect, he thought, for lush and willing, she was a danger. Raiden reminded himself that their bargain was to keep her away, an offense to her dignity. But her touch lured him and in the same moment, made him distrust. What well-bred woman would cavort willingly with a pirate, a bastard? What was she hiding from him still? Yet the feel of her soft skin against the back of his hand sounded her siren's call, a cry for the touch of another human being he craved. He was not worthy of her, the young mother, this widow, his past filled with crimes that forever shamed him, but when her lashes swept up, her gaze locking with his, Raiden knew he would take all she had for the time she was with him.

"Did you drug me to steal me favors like you be stealin' the spice?"

His lips curved. As Irish as linen and whiskey, he thought. "Nay."

"Pity," she said then went suddenly slack, unconscious.

Raiden shook his head, chuckling to himself. God, he was ready to climb into that bed with her just then, even after all the arguing. Quickly, he disengaged himself from her and made for the door. He had to either find some information on her son or put her ashore. For she prodded his conscience. She lied to him still. And she tempted him more than his vengeance drew him. And that was the true danger. He would not be swayed, yet neither could he take this abstinence when the enticement of her lingered in his bed. She was not safe from this passion and, he realized, neither was he.

His soul, he felt, was suddenly in jeopardy.

Ten

West India
Near the mouth of the Ganges River

The scene that greeted her when his highness, Lord Raiden the drugger, deemed she could come topside, was nothing short of chaotic. They were docked in a secluded lagoon, with men everywhere, repairing sails, arranging chests and kegs, and climbing in and out of the forward hull. But it was the shore that had her attention. From two huge, bubbling kettles, Balthasar served something that would have smelled divine, had she a notion to eat. Regardless, the aroma was enticing, and the crew, including those taken from the *Weston,* were eating their fill, sitting on the ground or on fallen trees. The *Weston*'s men had washed and were decently clothed, looking a sight healthier than they had the night before. Freedom, she thought, had a distinct glow.

The black carriage and team of gray horses waiting just beyond the men confused her, and though the dock was disguised by trees surrounding the shore and the narrow road leading out to Lord knew where, it made her see again that Raiden lived on a dangerous edge, in secret, always evading capture and a hanging. And the reminder sent guilt running through her. She had lied to him, burying herself deeper in her falsehoods as the days passed, and she feared they would somehow threaten his life. She told herself she should not care, that he was a brigand who thought little of forcing her to peddle her body for his help, but could not forget what she'd witnessed the other night when he took the sailors aboard. And what she witnessed now. He was truly not at all what he appeared. Well, she thought, in at least one manner.

"Most beautiful morning, yes, my lady?"

She turned as Jabari neared. "Aye, lovely. You seem pleased with the world." He was dressed in dark livery, his turban stark white against the black suiting.

"I have food to eat, protection, and a place to sleep. I need no more."

"Aye, what more," she heard and Willa whirled toward the sound. Raiden stood on the quarterdeck, gazing down at her.

"My, aren't you the dapper gentleman," she quipped, despite the quick thudding of her heart. Clad in somber colors, he looked more noble than any lord she'd met, yet his clothing was without the satins and frills the peers wore; his simple long black coat trimmed in dark silver and fitting his torso to perfection, his breeches smoky gray and complementing the black jackboots, unscarred and polished to a frightening gleam. Yet it was the silk frothing from his throat in a neatly tied cravat, and his black and silver-brocade waistcoat that offered elegant grace to his grand size.

He made her lungs feel tight, and she decided her gown was too small.

"My lady." He sketched a bow, tucking the tricorn under his arm. "Ready to test your land legs?"

She blinked, her eyes wide with surprise as she glanced at the carriage. "You will allow me to come along?"

"If you behave." Donning his tricorn, he climbed down the ladder and dropped to the deck.

"I promise not to shoot a single person, if you do," she said, a curl of anticipation spinning through her as he neared. His lips curved as he stopped inches away and looked her over in a way that made the backs of her thighs tingle " 'Tis tight," she said, embarrassed by how much flesh showed, yet refusing to tug again at the bodice.

" 'Twill do."

"The color, Raiden, 'tis . . . outrageous."

He frowned at the blood-red gown. "It suits you well." God above, too well, he thought.

"Aye, 'tis the dress of a whore."

He scowled blackly, suddenly hating that he pushed her to this and that she thought of herself as naught but chattel. "See what you wish, for I do not. And we are not going to argue now."

"So you decree? Or will you simply drug me again?"

" 'Twas freedom from your viperous tongue I sought."

She knew that to be a complete lie, and suddenly smiled up at him. "I do not remember much." The other night, before she nodded off, was only a vague dream to her.

He arched a brow, his look speaking volumes she could not decipher. "Pity. You lay in my bed for more than two days."

She reddened as he escorted her to the rail. Mercy, had she done something untoward? When he didn't respond further, Willa decided he was teasing her. Sharing a bed with him was something she would definitely recall. She descended the gangway, waving to Balthasar as he served.

As they passed, men stood. "Thank you, Captain, for delivering us," one called out.

"Aye," the group agreed, several shifting from foot to foot, a few holding up their weakened comrades.

Raiden stopped, his gaze sweeping the men. "Those of you who wish passage back to your homes will have it. Those who wish to remain with us can do so. But understand the consequences.''

The men looked at each other, mumbling amongst themselves.

Raiden put up a hand. ''You need not decide this day. Regain your health first.'' They smiled, obviously relieved, and nodded. Raiden looked at the Bedouin. ''They are under your care, sir.''

The man nodded, his gaze slipping past him, and Raiden turned. Willa stared at him with the oddest look. ''Is something amiss, madam?''

She scoffed, as if he'd asked if the sky was blue, then turned away, grasped the mounting strap, and alighted into the black carriage. He followed and took the opposite seat.

Raiden tapped the roof, and as the carriage rolled slowly away, his gaze rolled over Willa. For the past days she'd slept like the dead, looking damn fetching in his bed, and yet now she appeared every inch the refined lady she was, the shade of the gown only deepening her coloring, regardless of what she thought. Every facet of her entranced him, from the braids piled on her head to the tilt of her body as she peered out the window to her glib tongue. And the confusion she could not hide.

'' 'Tis impolite to stare, sir.''

''You are mine to stare at.''

The cold reminder rankled her. ''Why the carriage?'' She turned her head to look at him. ''Why all this?'' She waved to the gown and reticule.

''You are a lady and deserve the comfort.''

Something warm and gentle blossomed in her breast just then. Alistar had once said she deserved nothing till she gave him an heir. And after she had, he continued to treat her as poorly as he treated the servants.

''And I would rather the world see us as aught but a pirate and his lady.''

Discretion, she realized, and was pleased. ''I am flattered you've gone to the trouble.''

He frowned. "So you think being my mistress entitles you to less?"

Her chin lifted. "I have never been a mistress, so how would I know the duties? As I'm sure you will enlighten me."

Ahh, her rapier tongue was in rare form again. "You are to be at my beck and call."

She scoffed, looking out the window.

"Feed me when I say, strip for me when I bid."

"Thou hast grand dreams, pirate."

"And accept my touch."

"Not till you find information on my son." She continued to avoid his gaze.

"But if you desire it regardless?"

"I do not."

"Liar."

Her gaze snapped to his. She was not going to match wits with him today. "Where do we start looking?"

This woman shifted like the wind, he thought, and knew 'twas best they did not get into particulars. For the thought of proving her wrong, of even feeling her body pressed to his, made him stone hard. "Three ships have docked here since we left Calcutta."

"How do you know that?"

"My men have been asking after your son since dawn."

Her brows shot up, a radiant smile bowing her lips, and Raiden felt it like a sweep of the sun. Pity he didn't expect to find anything here.

Anticipation raced through her. Oh, for even a morsel of information, to tell her if her son lived. Her heart lifted, and she felt the excitement in the outing she'd never expected.

"You are pleased."

"How can I not be?"

Her smile warmed him, and though he wanted to join in her happiness, he knew the chance of finding anything was slim, if a'tall.

The carriage rolled to a stop in the center of the small city, and Willa noticed few soldiers about. There were no East India offices here, for this port offered only a spot to gain supplies and stores for another leg of a voyage, yet it kept the commerce of the city vibrant. And it was vibrant. The landscape was lush with flowers and green palms, the air balmy from the sea as people moved through the market on their morning shopping. Men conversed in clusters, and vendors hawked their wares as if more in competition over their shouting than their products.

Jabari opened the carriage door and waited. Willa eased to the edge of the seat, but Raiden stopped her. She frowned as he fished in the pocket of his greatcoat, then withdrew his fist, holding it before her face for an instant before he let it unfurl. A ruby the size of a robin's egg swung from the end of a gold chain.

"Sweet Mary." Quickly, he fastened it around her neck, the warmth of his fingers grazing her throat and spreading goose-flesh over her skin.

He leaned back to admire the gem lying above the swell of her breasts. "The gown needed something."

"Aye, more fabric."

He chuckled.

Willa fingered the large gem. So beautiful to be just another bar on the cage holding her.

"It belonged to a Spanish princess."

"I'm sure she misses it."

"Hardly. She gave it to me most willingly."

She pursed her lips. "My, there are some wealthy homes you've graced, sir."

"Only their beds, Willa. Never their doorsteps." He slipped past, then, outside the carriage, turned to assist her.

Willa tried not to frown, but the bitterness underlying his tone caught her off guard. He spouted of cold deals and bargains, yet he'd bedded royalty like a concubine? "Am I to believe you were a kept man?" He folded her hand over his arm and led her toward a cluster of shops. When he did not respond, she jerked on his hold. "Answer me."

"For as long as one keeps a pet dog," he said, for her ears alone.

She stopped and shifted toward him, her breasts pushing deliciously against his arm. "Do not speak this way."

" 'Tis the truth."

"Nay, 'tis a degradation you do not deserve."

He arched a black brow.

"One does what one must to survive, Raiden. God cannot fault us for that."

Her compassion would kill him, he thought. "And what would you do to survive?"

"I think I have made that rather clear. And spare me details of your sordid heritage. I do not want to hear of it. 'Tis past."

He ushered her into a small shop, the proprietress rushing to help them. "The past haunts us all."

"Not me." *Well, not much,* she thought.

He paused just beyond the threshold, waving the shop owner off. "Then tell me about how you lost your son."

"He was taken from my home in . . . London." Revealing that Mason vanished from their temporary Royal East India home in West Bengal would tell Raiden more than she wanted to right now.

She lies again, he thought and wondered what kept her so desperately away from trusting him. "Then why believe he is here?"

She was taken back. "I do not. Why do you think I wanted to be ashore? I'd learned a child was seen taken aboard a ship, bundled in a rug or sack, and I was attempting to learn which vessel whilst in the tavern."

"Who took him?"

"If I were certain of that, then I would know where to look." The half truth was like a sweet caught in her throat, nearly strangling her with her sugared lies.

Raiden eyed her for a moment. "What will it take for you to trust me?"

She shrugged. "Proof of your commitment and mayhap helping me without making me become your mistress."

"But you are too enticing a woman to let pass."

"The fact that you make me a whore with it does not bother you?"

His eyes narrowed. "God, I hate that word and I do not want to hear it from your lips."

" 'Twill spill from mouths of others, Raiden, and will be firmly attached to my back in a fortnight's time."

Willa did not know which bothered her more—the threat to her vows by simply being with this man, or the fact that he thought she'd only come to him in lieu of payment. Did he think so little of himself that he imagined himself unworthy of affection, of being loved?

Raiden felt the trap of his own making closing in, and since he'd revealed his past to her the other night, he felt exceedingly vulnerable to her in the light of day. And part of him, a portion that was quickly overshadowing anything else, was craving so much more than a torrid bargain. He had to remember that he could offer her nothing beyond this moment, mayhap even this day.

"I will try to keep this secret, Willa. But I can give no promises."

"I know," she said sadly.

He sighed, then asked the shopkeeper to fit her for gowns.

"Nay," she whispered, tugging on his sleeve, just realizing where they were.

"Aye." Sweeping off his tricorn, he tossed it in a chair, then seated himself in the rear fitting room like a king awaiting his subjects. Or a husband, she thought. "Would you prefer to go about naked or wearing only my shirts?"

She hushed him, blushing furiously as she glanced at the woman who stood silent and discretely to one side. " 'Tis improper."

His lips curved. "Any more than the bargain we share?"

"You never cease to amaze me. What an utterly insufferable

cad you can be!'' She batted him with her reticule, then followed the seamstress into the rear rooms, ignoring his soft chuckle.

A few minutes later, Raiden felt his chest tighten when she emerged in a coal-black gown trimmed in silver. His breath left his lungs as she twisted and turned before the mirrors, and he recognized the excitement lighting her green eyes. It lifted his tired soul, and when she left and appeared in another, then another, Raiden wondered why men chose not to witness such a grand show.

''Sahib?'' the seamstress called, and Raiden dragged his gaze from Willa, clad in crisp deep-blue cotton, to the owner.

''The fit?'' he managed.

''Perfect, sahib. Unless madam is not pleased.'' She looked at Willa.

''I am well pleased.'' Willa's gaze shifted between the two. ''Which one?''

''All of them.''

The owner beamed.

Willa's jaw dropped. ''All? Nay, I could not possibly—''

Raiden left the chair, moving till he stopped before her. ''I insist.''

He was truly taking this seduction seriously, she thought. ''I need no gifts, Raiden. I have agreed.''

''Then you know that I want to do this,'' he said, his gentle expression falling a little. Part of him swore 'twas to simply clad her luscious body from scrutiny—his mostly—but 'twas the pleasure on her face, and that she felt she did not deserve it, that made him want to give it to her.

She looked to the seamstress. ''The simpler gowns, then.'' She glanced at him. ''I've little use for velvets and satins in this heat.''

He nodded agreement, then, whilst an assistant helped her change, Raiden motioned to the owner, paying her in gold and asking her to provide the necessary accoutrements for the gowns. He added a parasol and gloves himself.

Outside the shop, he sent half the parcels back to the ship

with a sailor and was handing the remaining few into the carriage when Willa appeared to his right.

Beneath the shade of the shop's awning, she touched his sleeve, gazing up at him. "My thanks, Raiden. 'Tis generous of you." Without thought, she rose on her toes and brushed a kiss to his cheek.

The gesture took him aback for an instant, and he slid his arm around her waist, stroking his knuckle across her delicate jaw. "You are welcome, lass."

Her breath came faster, her heart doing that same leap in her breast that it did every time he looked at her like this, as if he would devour her whole.

"My debt to you is growing larger."

" 'Tis easily repaid." He bent, his mouth brushing lightly over hers, once, twice, before the eruption caught him. He claimed her mouth with the power of thunder. He molded, plundered, a slick erotic slide of lips and tongue, his fingers gripping her jaw as his tongue pushed between her lips. And she responded, clutching his lapels, her mouth hot and eager beneath his assault. She opened wide for him, arched into him, under his command, and Willa thought her legs would melt beneath her when a shout broke the private interlude under the awning. He jerked back, his gaze raking her features, his breathing labored.

Willa inhaled, stunned and trembling.

"Consider the latest debt well paid."

She gasped and shoved his shoulder playfully. "You really are a rogue," she said, yet smiled nonetheless.

"A pirate," he said in a seductive whisper, pushing the silk parasol into her hand, yet refusing to release her. "We thieve whenever valuable prizes are about."

She pinkened, glancing about for onlookers, then snapped the umbrella open before he led her into the sun and the markets. As the carriage followed far behind at a sedate pace, they strolled and he purchased cups of wine from a vendor, sweetmeats and pastries from another. *Mason would love these,* she thought, sadness sweeping her. She should not be enjoying a thing till her child was home, she thought, handing back the cup. She ignored his questioning frown and forced a smile. He introduced her to the people, the culture, showing her how learned he was. He spoke more than four languages, overpaid the merchants with aplomb, and talked to her of anything but their situation, as if for this moment he wanted her to forget. And she did, her attention focused on the handsome man beside her, his hand at the small of her back as they maneuvered around the carts and people.

He offered her a sweet, pushing it between her lips himself and when she nipped his finger, he grinned. She chewed the delicate confection as he sampled it himself and complimented the old woman selling them. Willa realized that she'd never spent a moment like this with her husband. Alistar would never converse with servants and vendors, nor would he consider a walk in the markets. Their time together was rare and more suited to host and hostess than husband and wife. Alistar never saw her, only what she represented. Raiden saw only the woman. She did not want to think how much that pleased her, especially when her lies would catch up with her and destroy this small sliver of peace.

Suddenly a little boy raced past, bumping into her, and Willa whirled, her gaze following the child.

Raiden noticed it, the way she stretched her neck to see the boy, the pain and longing in her eyes. "Enjoy the day and try to be patient."

She met his gaze, her anxiety clear. " 'Tis not your son who is lost."

His features sharpened, then quickly smoothed, and she wondered if she imagined that brief flicker of pain. Everything about him, from her rescue from the tavern to the freeing of sailors to this moment, left her confused and nearly exhausted with wondering just who this famed pirate was.

"You do not expect to find a thing here, do you?" she said unhappily.

"I can only try, for I know you do not tell me all I need to know."

"I cannot." His help was all she had left, and no matter the sensual bargain looming ahead, she needed his protection and knowledge. 'Twas selfish and unfair, but Willa could see no other way. Mason's life depended on her.

"Then how can I help you?"

There was a tinge of hurt in his voice and she swore she was mistaken, but when Willa thought of his rage when he discovered her lies and the further danger she likely put him in, she could not speak. He motioned to Jabari, and the child climbed from the footman's seat and raced to him. He slipped coins into his palm and whispered to him. The lad nodded and took off.

"Is that wise, to let him run alone?"

"He is armed."

She did not have to ask if Raiden was. She felt the weapons poke her when they walked.

"As should you be." With a dip into his coat and the flick of his wrist, he produced her folding blade. She smiled, accepting it, then opened the blade with a move so skilled that Raiden's brows shot up in surprise. She checked the edge, closed it, then started to put it in the reticule he'd provided earlier before discreetly sliding the blade into her bodice between her breasts.

She looked up to find him staring at her oddly.

"What?"

"There is much to know about you, Willa Delaney."

"Aye, such a fascinating creature I am," she said dryly.

Shaking his head, he folded her arm in his, but before they'd gone a yard, Jabari returned, chattering to Raiden in a language she could not understand, and she nearly shouted at the boy to speak English. But Raiden pulled the child aside and spoke to him in his native tongue. It irritated her.

"What? What has he found?"

He held out his hand to silence her and continued to speak.

Then he sent Jabari off, and Willa's gaze followed the boy for
a moment, then lit on Raiden. He took her hand and led her
quickly to the carriage.

"Raiden!"

"Inside first."

In the black leather privacy of the carriage, she wrung her
hands, wanting to throw him against the squabs and demand
he tell her what he'd discovered. The driver snapped the reins,
and the carriage moved down the avenue. Still he did not speak.

"Raiden," she gasped. "Please, I am going mad."

He looked up and found her teary-eyed and anxious. "How
old is Mason?"

"Only four."

God, a baby, and he thought of how frightened and alone
he must feel.

"Describe him."

She did, with loving detail.

"Does he bear a mark from birth, a freckle, aught that would
identify him?"

The color drained from her face. "Identify? Oh, lord, 'tis a
body they've found?" She trembled, raising a shaking hand to
her mouth, and Raiden instantly slid into the seat beside, gripping her hands.

"Shhh," he said. "Nay, we do not know that as yet."

"Tell me."

"A child was brought to the surgeon. A white child. There
are too few to ignore that."

She nodded, tilting her face up, and Raiden felt his heart
clench as tears threatened to spill. "Nay, lass, do not weep."
He smoothed loose strands off her cheek and gazed into her
eyes. "Now tell me, does he bear a mark that would set him
apart?"

"Aye." She sniffled. "A crescent scar." Tenderly, she
touched the one on Raiden's jaw. "Like this, but not so deep.
'Tis on his right leg near the ankle. He got it running through
the bramble playing hide-and-seek with me."

Raiden tried to imagine her chasing a small child through the thicket, her skirts high and her face beaming with mischievous laughter. Did all mothers love so eagerly? "That will help," he finally said, and as the carriage rocked, he drew her into his arms, her head pillowed on his chest. Her fingers flexed and relaxed on his arms as she fought her fears. Raiden prayed the boy lived, for he did not know what it would do to her if this information only confirmed his death. He could not bear to see the grief he knew would destroy her.

The thunder of hooves brought her upright as several riders joined them, flanking the carriage, and Willa recognized Vazeen, Sanjeev, and Nealy Perth. "Do you think we are in danger?"

"There is always a hazard," he said and out the window spoke to his men, before they rode on. 'Twas nearly a half hour before the carriage stopped outside a small home, modest and rather English.

Willa reached for the door, but he stopped her. "I must!"

"Nay, stay here. And do not forget that whoever tried to kill you might have done so to keep you from your son."

She blinked. The remark told her he'd thought hard and often about all she had revealed. And she couldn't help wondering what he would make of the entire mess if only she were able to tell him the whole of it.

He left the carriage. The guards positioned at the door and the concealment of the interior comforted as well as scared her. Expectation crept up her spine, tightening her skin as she watched him enter the dwelling and the door close behind him. She called to Jabari, but the boy had obviously been ordered not to respond. She fumed for several minutes, then anxiously gripped the windowsill when Raiden stepped out and, on the threshold, spoke to a thin man. The man looked directly at her, but she felt as if he did not want to see her, as if he looked through her. Raiden pressed coins into his wrinkled palm and turned away, slipping back into the carriage. The guards moved on ahead, and the conveyance started a new journey.

"I swear if you do not speak now, I shall make use of my knife."

He lifted his gaze slowly. "A child was brought here, to this doctor. He was gravely ill, Willa."

"But he lives?"

"When the couple left with him, aye, he was."

"His illness?"

"Malaria, he suspects."

She paled.

"He's been given quinine. 'Tis the only recourse."

"Did they call him by name?"

"Nay. And the physician felt 'twas in secret they'd come."

She nodded, fidgeting nervously. "Who brought him? Who was this couple?"

"A young black man and an old woman."

"Was the woman Irish?"

He nodded.

"It must be his nurse, Maura. She vanished with him."

"Willa—" He looked away briefly, then met her gaze. "He said the child was dying."

"Nay! He is wrong! I would know!"

"We will keep looking. I swear," he said, still shocked to have discovered this much. "Is there something you are not telling me about the boy?"

She reared back, frowning.

"The doctor said this child had . . . other problems."

"Mason does not speak. There is naught unusual with that," she said, defensive.

"I am not saying there is." He spoke softly, feeling her tensing to a fevered pitch. "But his mind—"

"He . . . he is locked in his own world, Raiden. But he is a good boy." She crushed her reticule. "He responds to love and tenderness." Bowing her head, she murmured in a voice so lost, "I fear the longer we are apart, the further he will go from me."

Raiden swallowed over the sudden knot in his throat. "Willa, look at me.

She lifted her gaze.

"Do you not see? It *was* Mason they brought. There is hope."

Her features stretched tight before she covered her face with her hands, hiding it from him, and Raiden reached for her, scooping her into his arms and cradling her on his lap. Suddenly her tears could not be contained, and she gripped his coat, sobbing helplessly.

"Thank you," she whispered. "Oh, Raiden, thank you."

He rubbed her spine in slow circles. "The doctor heard them say something about Kedah."

She tilted her head to look at him.

"And that is, by chance, where we are going."

She gave him a watery smile, then sagged into his arms, desperate to grasp the sliver of hope he offered. And so very grateful that Raiden Montegomery had stolen her away.

In the carriage, Willa dozed against his side, and Raiden leaned his head back on the leather squabs, his head lolling with the rock of the carriage.

Impatience rode him. They needed to get far away from this city, and quickly. Rumors had reached him that troops were amassing in Calcutta against an uprising. The Siraj-ud-dulah rebels would attack, mayhaps this week, mayhaps in a month, but it would occur, and if they took the city, hundreds would be slaughtered and within days Clive and the East India Company Army would begin a retaliatory sweep across India all the way to the Mongol boarder. The tribal kings were a fickle bunch, warring on each other whilst the English raped the riches as they'd done in Bombay and along the spice route.

But the Company would prevail. They were too numerous, well fitted, and prepared to launch an attack to consider otherwise. And on the sea, Dunfee would be in command. But

Raiden wanted that match to be on his terms, at his chosen time. Another reason to get to the *Renegade,* for if it were seized, his life would be over.

And just when he thought he did not care, he found he wanted to live.

He'd done all he could to find Mason, he assured himself and nestled Willa a little tighter to his side, hoping she knew he was committed by more than their bargain. He'd purchased considerable vials of quinine to add to the stock aboard the *Renegade,* and although they could use more medications, he could not delay now. The quinine would help her survive the disease rampant in the jungles, and if Mason truly suffered from malaria, there was little hope, but he would take along anything necessary. He was almost jealous of the love she had for the lad, and the image of a small, sickly boy, crying out for his mother and not knowing how to communicate what ailed him, plagued him hourly. The only thing that eased his conscience was the twenty men who'd scoured the city for a description to match the one the doctor gave, to learn how Mason, this Irish nanny, and her only escort, left the city.

The name of a ship would do nicely and he was thankful now that he'd ordered the men to report back to the ship instead of seeking him.

"You look terribly pensive."

He looked down as she blinked sleepily up at him.

God, she was beautiful. "I must always think ahead, my fox."

Willa was terribly grateful for the news and her heart did a tiny jump when she realized Mason was alive. Hope was all she had left, and Raiden had given it to her. "Have I thanked you properly for finding information on my son?

His entire body tensed with sweet anticipation. "That depends on how one defines *proper.*"

His brows wiggled rakishly and she laughed, soft and full of feminine purpose, as her hand swept up across his chest and curled around his neck. "Believe me, Raiden, I am well schooled in *proper.*" She pulled him down to her and he went, most willingly.

His mouth crushed over her in a hot wave, and he shifted on the squabs, shifted to feel the full impact of her kiss and the soft yield of her body against his. His arms closed around her, and for a brief instant he wondered if she offered herself to his feasting mouth because she was grateful or because she wanted the man. In the next breath he swore he did not care.

A shout cut through their desire and Raiden pulled back, then leaned toward the window, looking out. A foul curse spilled from his lips.

Willa wrenched around to see. "Oh, dear God. We are finished."

Eleven

The *Renegade* had sailed. Without her captain.

He called out and the carriage lurched to a halt. "Unhitch the horses," he ordered of Perth, then tossed his tricorn aside. "Vazeen, Kahlid, scout the area. Jabari, stay down."

Willa was stunned, yet as soon as the coach rounded the dirt road to the shore, Raiden had known they were in grave danger. Fires still burned at the campsite. Kettles were left behind, overturned in haste, the grounds scattered with spilled food and debris. This was second time in four months his ship had been forced to sail. The second time someone tried to hand him over to the authorities. The *Renegade* had already made the tide. At least it had not been seized. 'Twas another part of a riddle he could not understand. He'd lived for years without many incidents because he suspected everything and trusted but a few. Betray the captain and 'twas instant death. Betray the crew, and nine ships' worth of men would swarm to take a piece of the betrayer like disease to the leper. What could the authorities offer a man that would be worth betraying his captain and crew? For any man had the right to walk away with his wealth unharmed.

"I cannot believe they left without you," Willa said, looking out the window before Raiden pulled her back.

"The first responsibility is to keep the ship safe. As for us, the danger might still be there." Though he didn't see blood, and there were no bodies on the shore, he would not risk moving out into the open.

He checked the load of his pistols; then, gesturing at the cushions of the opposite seat, he said, "Take up those and conceal whatever you can."

Willa slid to the floor, looked inside, then reached in the chest for the powder horns and sacks of provisions. "You knew they'd sail."

"Aye." Weapons loaded, he dropped down beside her. "If there is trouble, 'tis an understanding to sail no matter who is left behind." Briefly, he glanced up, his gaze lingering on her calves where she'd hiked up her skirts. "We are constantly hunted. And this means—"

"We have been betrayed?"

"Most definitely." He took inventory, laying items on the seat. "And I do not know if the betrayer is on the ship," his voice lowered, "or with us." The fact remained that someone had given them up to the authorities, for the ship was harbored in so treacherous and secluded a spot, even the locals did not venture here.

"I am sorry."

He frowned.

"I have brought you to this."

He shook his head whilst he stuffed a British Army knapsack. "The soldiers in the marketplace in Calcutta knew I would be there. This has naught to do with you. Nor is it the first occasion someone has come close to catching me."

"But you could escape without me."

"I am not leaving you here, Willa."

"You have fulfilled your bargain."

"Nay, I promised to find the boy." Into the sack, he jammed

ammunition, cured beef, and the vials of quinine he'd managed to procure. "And you know too much."

"Your life is at risk, and I will slow you down."

"You are coming with me," he said with finality. He could not think of leaving her behind, for any reason. "We must travel by land to meet the *Renegade.*"

"This has happened before." There were far too many provisions hidden under the seat cushions for him not to have anticipated this.

"I . . . the Black Angel is hunted by more than the Royal East India, my lady. And now my presence is known in this city. Our only hope is that whoever seeks me so diligently believes I am on that ship." Raiden considered it was Dunfee or Waston's spies, but then, were either man this close, the entire fleet would be filling the Bay of Bengal. And if they were amongst the men beyond this coach?

"They will blast it?"

"They may try, but Tristan is a fine seaman. That lagoon was difficult to negotiate."

"But he is also still very weak."

"In body, not in mind." He handed her a satchel. "Take your new clothing from the boxes and stuff them in this, quickly."

Willa did as he bade whilst he lashed the leather knapsack closed. He handed her a loaded pistol and she stared at it, realizing the magnitude of danger they were in, then slid it into her skirt pocket.

Climbing to his feet, Raiden tied a rolled blanket to her satchel, then left the carriage, turning to help her as Perth brought the carriage horses forward. "You and Jabari ride double," he said to the big sailor. "He is not an accomplished rider, and we will have to move quickly."

"Aye, sir," he said, then held his arms out for the boy hiding in the driver's cab. "Come, lad, we've an adventure to find."

Raiden paused, glancing at Nealy Perth and frowning as the boy leapt into the man's arms and he swung him onto the animal's back. A sensation of a vague familiarity rippled up

Raiden's spine. And yet, Raiden was certain he'd never met the man before. Tucking the knowledge in the back of his mind, he pressed on to more important matters—escape.

Willa glanced at the others. Sanjeev, Vazeen, Kahlid, and Perth were already armed, any sign of the earlier refinement in their attire now gone. Kahlid, she admitted, was the fiercest looking, with a huge scimitar strapped to his back in a harness, a kayffia draping his head.

"Can you ride?"

She looked at Raiden and smiled. "Aye." She walked up to the horse, petting its nose before she led it to a fallen tree.

"Without a saddle?" Watching her, Raiden removed his coat and loosened his cravat as she swung up onto the animal's back—God help him—astride. "I was right, you must have been the bane of your father's existence." He hoisted the knapsack onto his back.

"As I am yours now," she said, smiling, then adjusting her skirts over the rump of the horse.

By God, Raiden thought, the woman was looking forward to the peril! After quickly securing the satchel to the remaining horse with rope, Raiden mounted, motioning Willa to his side. " 'Twill be a hard journey," he said gravely.

Her chin lifted. "I will endeavor not to disappoint you."

He smiled briefly, then looked at his helmsman. "Kahlid, you take the point. Perth, forward left flank." He gestured to Sanjeev and Vazeen to move ahead to the right. Raiden hated that he could not trust these men, and put his faith only in Kahlid. They'd served nearly a decade side by side as he had with Tristan. Yet regardless, the only person he could truly trust—was Willa.

For hours they traveled at an unrelenting speed, taking deserted roads, circling villages, but always following the shore. It was as if Raiden could not survive being too far away from it. Ahead, Kahlid cleared a path, his long, curved scimitar

slicing open a hole in the jungle like a gate into hell. Though
the sun still hovered in the sky, it was dark, the heat oppressive,
heavier with the warm mist of the forest. Her gown felt like
another body all its own, drooping, clinging to her skin and
making her wish for the sari. Nearly abreast of her, Raiden
rode, his gaze flicking to the dense vegetation, then to her,
before returning to the wall of vines and fronds surrounding
them. Astride the gray mare, the reins held loosely, he appeared
relaxed, yet even at this distance, tension radiated from him.
Anger, disappointment—she wasn't sure, but she understood
betrayal all too clearly. Though his hair was still fastened with
a black ribbon, his shirt clung wetly to his back, the knapsack
lashed to the satchel and slung across the horse's rump like a
saddlebag. Hours ago, he'd released the pack horse into the
wild to make better time.

To where, she'd no idea, but she did not want to discuss it
aloud when he distrusted so many right now. She could see
how much it bothered him as he eyed the other men when they
weren't looking. Whilst Willa was looking at him. Helpless to
aid her son and knowing she'd only work herself into a fit with
worrying, she told herself there was little else to ponder as they
moved through the forest. She needed the distraction, and by
God, he was pleasant to look upon. The thought of spending
the night with him in the jungle sent her mind off on a shame-
lessly erotic tangent.

When he slowed, staring at her with that knowing smile, she
knew she'd been caught wearing her feelings on her face.

"You've something to say to me?"

She looked straight ahead, avoiding those dark, probing eyes.
"Nay."

He leaned, his voice low in her ear. "Then cease looking at
me as if you wish to be taken against the nearest tree."

She reddened, swatting at a bug buzzing close. "I did no
such thing."

"You did, Willa, and so much more."

Slowly she turned her head to meet his gaze. "Am I so transparent to you?"

"In that, aye." The hot glow in her eyes made him hard, made him want to drag her onto his lap and map every curve of her body beneath the red silk.

"And what, pray tell, do you see now?"

"A woman who still hides many secrets. Even from herself." He cocked his head. "Have you not learned to trust me?"

It was not him she distrusted, but herself. She wanted to keep Alistar's image at bay, wanted to forget that pitiful existence and remain here, where she felt alive and wanted. Mentioning even a word of her former life, admitting she'd lied, would break this newborn friendship she had with Raiden. And she could not bear to lose it. 'Twas the richest thing she possessed right now.

Willa looked quickly away, suddenly remembering her jewel bag and the papers hidden there. She hadn't expected to flee for her life, stashing the bag in the window bench. But oh, if anyone found them beneath the aft window cushions, she was done for.

"I see panic."

"This situation is grave. I am frightened."

His gaze narrowed for a moment before he sighed, shaking his head. She was no more afraid than the horse she rode. How he longed for her to open her thoughts to him, let him help her, for whatever kept her secrets well hidden terrified her. It locked her away somewhere he could not touch, and the denial of it made him want to crush through this bastion of womanhood and see all that lay beneath. He reached, grasping her hand, and for an instant her fingers wrapped his. "We will find Mason, and then . . ."

She arched a tapered red brow. "Then?"

"—I will make good my promise."

To make her scream with pleasure, she remembered, and her warm skin tingled with anticipation she'd no right to feel but every reason to want.

* * *

Another three hours passed before they could no longer see clearly in the dark and Raiden called a halt. Dismounting, he was about to help Willa down when she slid from the horse's back with an agility that surprised him, especially in all those skirts and petticoats. He dragged the knapsacks and satchel from the animal, then dropped them at her feet and knelt. He rifled through them, removing pouches and securing them with his weapons in the waistband of his breeches.

"Where are you going?"

The tinge of panic in her voice cut him and he stood. "To get my bearings and mayhap hunt." Briefly he looked over her head at the men making camp, then met her gaze. "Is your pistol loaded?" She nodded. "Fire off a shot if you need me."

"Hopefully, 'twill be in the air and not at anyone."

Though it was him they wanted, Raiden could not forget that if anyone chose, they could use her against him. And likely win. The fact made him see how vulnerable she'd made him. But there was little to do about it now. His days of denying she meant anything to him were past. "There's a spring on the other side of those trees." He inclined his head as to where. "When I return I will take you there."

"You are patronizing me, Raiden."

His lips curved sadly. "I am trying to reassure you."

Her chin went up a notch. "I am capable of taking care of myself, pirate. Just be about it and quickly." She shooed him like a child, smiling. "Or is it you who needs assurances?"

Despite her light manner, he knew she was unsettled by all this and did not want to leave her, even for a moment, but he could trust no one to tell him what he needed. "That saucy tongue is going to gain you much trouble someday."

"It already has," she said. "I have a pistol and a scream of my own, Raiden."

"A deadly enough combination." He took a step away, but she gripped his arms and shifted closer.

"Please be careful." Willa wanted his arms around her, wanted more than a few words that spoke of his return. She received neither.

He bent and pressed his lips to her forehead, afraid that if he took her mouth beneath his as he wanted, he'd never leave. Forcing himself to step away, he gave strict instruction to his men, then called Jabari to his side. In a low voice, he said, "Sit with my lady, will you? She's afraid and in need of your company."

Jabari nodded, serious and adultlike. "I will protect her, Captain," he said, then withdrew his knife and marched to where Willa stood under a canopy of trees. Before Raiden slipped into the forest, he caught a glimpse of her, reaching for the boy and cuddling him close. Jabari's fierce facade melted under her tender touch, and like Raiden, he absorbed the loving he'd never known.

Willa knew he was gone the instant he blended into the darkness, his white shirt the last to disappear. She felt defenseless, in spite of the armed men surrounding her, and her gaze slipped over the clearing, watching Kahlid make it wider with his mammoth sword. Nealy Perth scrounged for dried wood, tossing the scraps into a pile. Sanjeev and Vazeen stood at opposite ends, their weapons ready for anything, staring into the moving darkness. Willa did not want to think what wild creatures lay beyond that wall of jungle.

"Let us find stones to border the fire," she said to Jabari, and together they searched. Jabari was taking his assignment a little too strongly, refusing to let her look under a palm or fern without his inspection first. Willa felt a presence behind her and spun about.

"Kahlid." She clapped a hand over her frantic heart.

"Forgive me, my lady," he said with a bow. "I did not mean to frighten you."

Willa tipped her head back and met his gaze. "I do not think you have a choice in the matter."

His solemn face broke into a smile, white teeth against dark skin. "A place to rest," he said, gesturing to the stack of fronds laid just back from the fire.

"That was rather nice of you, Kahlid." She was surprised by the kindness.

He sheathed the sword, the curved blade hissing into captivity. "You are Montegomery's woman."

Montegomery's woman, indeed, she thought. Part of her wanted to be his woman, not the bane of his existence. Yet she would not gainsay Kahlid. Like Balthasar, he could snap her neck with one hand. Kahlid, however, had gentle eyes, despite his tremendous shoulders and arms.

"Is this large enough?" came from somewhere to her side, and she looked down at Jabari and the stone he held.

"Splendid choice."

Jabari looked up at Kahlid. "We need water. Come with me to the stream?"

The Moor smiled, rubbing the boy's head. "Yes, I will escort you, little warrior."

Jabari scowled. "I need no escort," he scoffed. "I need someone big enough to carry the hides."

His hand on his sword, Kahlid laughed, a rich sound. "Finish your task first."

Hiding her smile, Willa glanced around and found Nealy watching them as he struck flint to dry brush. Squatting by the fire, he fed the blaze, keeping it low and nearly smokeless as she and Kahlid moved closer.

Jabari bent to place the stones and inspected the design. "Three more I think, madam."

"I agree, sir."

The boy marched off.

Shoving back his tricorn, Nealy ducked his head to hide his grin. "Ah, he's got himself a tenderness for you, lass."

She eyed him. "He's just taking his duty seriously. He owes Raiden too much not to."

Nealy quirked a brow.

"Ibn Montegomery rescued him from a slaver," Kahlid said,

his stance, at Willa's right, daring anyone to come near. A fierce protector now, Kahlid would be a dangerous enemy if crossed.

"I was not aware," Nealy said.

She lowered to the stack of fronds. "The captain does not lend to boasting." She glanced to where Jabari was hefting two rocks, the decision over which would serve his purpose taking his complete attention. "He is a sweet child."

"It's the motherin' he hungers for."

"What child so neglected and discarded does not?"

Nealy's gray brows drew down, and he rubbed his hand over the lower half of his face. Before he could respond, Jabari raced up, laid the stone down, then gestured to Kahlid. The tall Moor lightly touched her shoulder, and she nodded. Kahlid and Jabari gathered the skins and moved off into the woods.

"Do you not believe that?" she said to Nealy when they were alone. "About children, I mean?"

"I was raised to believe that mums only bred the heirs. Papas and 'ardship bred the men."

Willa thought of her parents, the love they showed openly, and how devastated her father had been after Mama's death. He'd ignored his business and she'd had to take over till he'd handled his grief. "Mayhaps your father thought this would make you stronger?" Though she did not know exactly how.

He scoffed. "My father beat the bloody hell out of me with the slightest infraction, and when I was old enough, ma'am, I left."

"Forgive me for prying, sir." So much pain in this world, she thought and wondered how Mason fared without her.

His wave dismissed her sympathy. "I swore I would never treat me lads that way."

"Is that why you sail instead of making a home?"

"Nary a woman would have me as a husband."

"I would not be so sure, Mr. Perth." He was a handsome man, she thought, his physique more dangerously lethal than one thought at first glance.

"Oh, the ladies would have me, lass, just not for overlong."

"Are you certain 'twas not you who could not remain?"

The sounds of movement through the forest gave Willa a start, and she twisted, her hand slipping into her skirt pocket as the rustling grew louder. Kahlid and Jabari appeared out of the darkness, the Moor carrying the boy on one broad shoulder. Jabari unknowingly spilled water from the skins on the man, but Kahlid patiently disregarded it.

"Thirsty, my lady?" he sputtered over the water dripping into his mouth, smiling as he lowered the child to the ground.

Willa rose, her foot catching in her skirts, and she would have toppled backward into the fire if not for Nealy's quick moves. He swept her from the blaze, setting her gently to her feet. "My thanks, sir," she breathed. " 'Tis twice you've saved me."

" 'Tis me duty, m'lady, and in the weight of that"—he gestured to the gown—"I am surprised you do not sink into the sand."

She plucked at the droopy, soiled fabric. " 'Tis a bit impractical, is it not?"

"Then mayhap you should change."

Willa turned at those words, a harsh breath sinking her shoulders as Raiden pushed through the vegetation. She'd never been so glad to see him, as if she hadn't taken a decent breath till now. He stopped on the edge of the light, his strong gaze moving heavily over her, then to each man before he walked over to Jabari and took a water skin. Holding it high, he poured a thin fountain of water into his mouth, then offered it to her. She came to him, taking the skin and noticing the bundle slung on his shoulder.

"You found a village?" She took a long drink, then studied the man. Something in his expression told her he knew exactly where they were and where they were headed. And the bundle told her he'd found what he sought.

"Aye." He dropped two dead monkeys at her feet.

She lurched back, glaring at him and sweeping her skirts aside. "I am not eating those creatures."

"You will or go hungry. You will need your strength for the journey. As do we all," he added, and she frowned at his brisk tone. He strode to her satchel, then back to the edge of the forest. "Come," was all he said, holding his hand out to her.

"If you will excuse me, gentlemen," she said with a glance at the others. "The captain apparently feels the need to be exceedingly rude." Then, lifting her chin, Willa slapped her hand into his and he pulled her into the forest.

Just out of sight, his grip softened, his fingers lacing with hers, and a blistering surge of anticipation burned though her as the jungle closed behind them.

Twelve

In the darkness of the jungle, Raiden dropped the bags and spun her into his arms like a hot curl of wind, enveloping, smothering, his mouth on hers, heavy and rolling. He gripped her jaw and thrust his tongue between her lips, a slide and push of unchained heat and passion. And she moaned in response, battling against him, with him, plowing her fingers into his hair and taking all that he gave of this power, this ungodly hunger.

Then, just as quickly, she yanked on his hair and tore her mouth away. "Do not think to order me about so crudely again, pirate. I am your mistress, not one of your crew." She shoved at his chest, but he jerked her back.

"Then do not let me find you in Perth's arms again." He claimed her mouth again, this kiss as strong and as powerful as the last, upending her world, for it teamed with jealousy. Even if he did not want to admit it, she felt it, in the possessing press of his mouth, in the way his big hands mapped her spine as if he wanted to dive under her skin.

He pulled back enough to growl, "And you are not my mistress—yet."

Yet. Expectation coiled in her belly, taunting her with what they'd shared, making her crave when she should not. "You are speaking of apples and applesauce now."

"Is that an invitation?" His hand slid to her lower spine, and he pressed her to his thickening groin.

Willa's body ignited with another heavy pulse of warm desire. His mouth neared hers, and she scraped up every ounce of control and said, "Nay, 'tis not," then shoved out of his arms. She couldn't look at him, not and see the glow of passion in his eyes, and want to explore it when he was forbidden. Oh, but he'd already shown her what Alistar never had . . . her own unchained need. And the denial of it made her angry. Withdrawing her pistol, she marched toward the sound of water, batting vines and branches out of her way—despite that her legs were liquefying beneath her.

Raiden blew out a harsh breath; then, scooping up the packs, he followed on her heels. "I could be most accommodating in the dark. This tree will do nicely," he teased, patting the trunk as he passed.

She glanced back, leveling him an irritated look. "Don't be vulgar."

Compared to her, he was vulgar, he thought, tossing down the packs again. "Have you experience from which to judge?" That delicate chin went up, and he knew she hadn't.

"Romantic intentions are not your forte, I see." She strode to the bank, kicking off her muddy slippers. "What do you propose, Raiden, to throw my skirts up and roar like a . . . a *man?*"

Ah, she was in a temper, Raiden thought, smothering a smile she wouldn't appreciate. He'd expected it, wanting to see her fire, feel it, to get her mind off the danger and her lost child if but for a little while. She had suffered the difficult ride and heat in silence, never complaining, and Raiden admired her stamina, for he was ready to drop where he stood and sleep for a century.

"Shall I woo you with flowers?" Willa looked up as he

plucked an exotic orange flower from a bush, offering it. "Or simply do as I've promised." He tossed the bloom aside.

"Men speak easily of promises when it's convenient for them."

He had no promises to offer, he thought sadly as he gathered dry fronds, bundling them around a branch. "Challenging me again, I see. I shall have to do something about that."

The possibility showered her with anticipation, and just as swiftly, her vows washed it away with denial. "Why do you insist on baiting me this night?"

"Because you are too easy to rile."

His voice sounded strange, tight, and she wished she could see him clearly in the moonlight.

Raiden continued to tie the dry, willowy vines of his make-shift torch, then struck flint to the brush, and jammed the torch into the ground. The silence stretched, the area flickering with shadows as he straightened.

With a frustrated sound, she laid the pistol aside before reaching behind herself to unlace her bodice. She stilled, meeting his gaze. "I need privacy."

"And have someone stab you whilst I give it? Nay." He shook his head.

Willa chewed her lips for a second, then turned her back. "Unlace me then."

Raiden almost groaned at the prospect, then undid the laces quickly.

Clutching the bodice to her chest, she glanced over her shoulder, pursing her lips. "My, how skilled you are."

He simply smiled.

"Beastly man," she muttered, not liking that he'd had enough women to be so knowledgeable when she had known the attentions of only one man. Without a choice, she loosened the skirts and petticoats, pulling them off over her head.

Raiden glanced, then his eyes went wide. She had the provisions and powder horns tied to the pannier cage like ornaments on a Christmas tree. Clever. "Good lord, that must be heavy."

She fussed with the tapes. ''Then find a way out of it. 'Tis tangled.''

Raiden withdrew a knife from his boot and sliced the tapes. The cage fell in a hard plop at her feet.

Her hands on her hips, she met his gaze. ''Well, I could have done that,'' she said sourly.

''You cannot ride comfortably in it anyway.''

That meant she'd have overlong skirts to battle with again. ''You enjoy destroying my clothing, I think.'' She stepped out of the pile, not at all sure what to do with her hands.

He eyed her blush. ''I have seen you in less, and besides . . .'' Her chin went up, and Raiden wanted to nibble on it.

''Aye, and you have had your hands up my skirts, I know. You are positively wicked to keep reminding me of our bargain.'' She marched to the stream, knowing she'd little choice. She'd agreed to be his mistress for information on her son. He'd performed his part of the bargain. Her turn would come. Willa had never found intercourse pleasing before and wondered why men seemed so preoccupied with the act, yet if she didn't find her son, she would lie beneath him. The very idea of this big man taking her brought torrid images that were a far cry from Alistar's hurried attentions.

Yet she could not betray her vows.

Just as she knew she had few options—and little time—left.

Her back to him, she removed her folding knife and wrestled with the bodice of her gown, its absence offering overwhelming relief from the heat. She plucked at the chemise clinging to her skin.

Raiden swallowed hard as she bent to roll down her stocking and offer him a delicious view of her round behind in the thin batiste. God above, was the woman trying to drive him completely mad? When the garters and hose lay in a pile, his gaze climbed over her bare legs to her torso cinched in the lacy corset. Her back was to him, and he strode closer and cut the laces.

She spun, clutching it to her breasts. ''Raiden!''

"I know you do not bathe in that contraption, so why now?"

"Because you are here."

He stepped nearer, the sparse clothing creating very little barrier and letting body heat simmer between them. "I am not leaving." He grasped her wrist, pushed a cake of soap into her palm, then yanked the corset off her. She crossed her arms over her chest, green fire flashing in her eyes. He seemed not to care, directing her to the stream as if she'd lost her way.

Willa glared at him as he leaned indolently against a boulder, watching her, and she was about to step in when she stilled and looked back at him. "Is it safe?"

" 'Tis running water. There won't be any snakes."

She lurched back. "Snakes!"

"Just fish." He would never let harm come to her.

Well, if she didn't bother the fish, mayhap they would not bother her, she thought, and not wanting to be a coward, she dipped her toes in. The cool relief beckoned and she walked into the little stream, sinking down and letting the water spill over her. 'Twas no more than hip deep, the bottom filled with smooth stones, yet the current was strong.

Raiden kept his distance as she unwound her hair and lathered the curling mass, then swam underwater to rinse it. When she emerged, he pushed away from the boulder and knelt on the bank, rinsing his hands. He dunked his head, tossing his hair back and shaking like an animal, then let his gaze roam the forest for predators. Raiden toed off his boots and sat on the bank, submerging his feet in the cool water. He continued to scan the jungle for movement, his weapons within reach. This area was populated with tigers, leopards, and the deadliest snakes, all swift creatures that could strike without warning. He brought his gaze back to her, and every thought of war and vengeance fled, everything inside him gone still. She was floating, coming nearer, the chemise hiding little, her hair unbound and, in the dark, looking like ink bleeding in the water. He curled his fingers into fists, his knuckles popping with the effort not to reach out and embrace her. She waved her arms gently, spreading water over herself in an undulating surge. Her body bobbed on the surface, her full breasts peaking with cold, and Raiden looked away, rubbing his hand over the lower half of his face. His hands fairly itched to touch her again, feel the fire of her kiss, the softness of her skin. She'd become a strange addiction, almost like air. Necessary for his immediate survival. One he wasn't aware he needed till it was missing. God above, he was in trouble. Even her scent clung to him, taunting him with a sweetness he'd never dared want, for he'd always known she was a woman he could never have. He looked back at her, and denial faded under the grip of relentless craving.

Suddenly he stood, shedding his shirt and stepping into the water.

She came upright instantly, floundering for balance and looking at him with wide green eyes. ''What on earth are you doing?'' She sank to her neck in the water.

His lips curved as he took the cake of soap from her, creating lather in his palms, then spreading it over his chest.

Willa watched, entranced, her gaze following the path of his big hands. Dear lord, he was a magnificent-looking man. Wet, dark hair webbed his shoulders, dripping water over muscles hewed tight and ropy, over the circle of thorns blackening his bronzed skin.

''Why did you do that?'' She nodded to the tattoo.

He paused in passing the soap over his stomach, then said, '' 'Tis a reminder.''

''Of what?'' She hugged herself, wanting to touch him so badly.

''The reason I turned to piracy.''

She nodded, though she did not truly understand. He'd told her of being pressed into naval service as a boy, and although she felt it went deeper than that, by his silence she knew he wasn't prepared to reveal it.

''Is all you do an act of vengeance?''

''Aye.''

She blinked. The admission came so easily, almost resolutely. "You do not see a future beyond a noose. 'Tis sad to have no hope."

"I've committed crimes against a government. I expect punishment."

Would it matter to anyone that he freed sailors pressed against their will and were treated no better than animals? Her throat tightened. Whatever they shared, these moments in time were just that, she thought, moments, and the hard realization that she would watch him die cut through her heart with unbelievable pain. Her eyes burned, and she wanted to scream at him, but it would do no good. What was done was done. His ruthlessness and cunning kept him alive and now was helping her find her baby. His only hope of survival was to cease pirating and fade away into history as a legend. But convincing him to give it up, to see that he lived because she cared that he lived, would meet with obstinacy. Raiden worried little beyond this day and another chance to blast the English out of the Bay of Bengal.

"I will likely be put to death for stealing you away," he said softly and she lifted her gaze.

"I would not allow it."

He scoffed a laugh, scrubbing his shoulders. "You would not have enough influence."

She took the soap and floated behind him, then stood. "Doubting my charms, hmm?" She lathered his back, and Raiden moaned as her fingers dug deep into his aching muscles. "Should I be insulted?"

"You could charm a snake," he said easily. "But the English are vipers."

"I know," she said sadly. "Lower into the water a bit." He obeyed, and her hands plowed into his hair; gently, she lathered his hair, rubbing his scalp, his temples. He tipped his head back, his eyes closed.

Willa tilted her head and smiled. He was almost purring, she thought, and shifted closer.

Slowly his eyes opened, his gaze greeting hers, then sliding to her breasts outlined in the wet batiste. A hot current whipped through her, and she stilled for a second, then rinsed his hair. He sank under the surface, then came to his full height inches from her, facing her. She stepped back.

He caught her to him, flesh pressed to flesh.

"Raiden." Her hands splayed his chest.

"Aye."

"I know I owe you—"

His features sharpened with something akin to pain. "I do not want you to let me touch you because you *owe* me, little fox." His gaze watched his hand as he pushed her hair back off her face, off her shoulder. Her hair was so bright, alive like red smoke. He felt her tremble, her heartbeat in every pore of her and thrumming through the water to penetrate his skin. "I lied. I do not seek to steal the prize"—his gaze shifted to hers—"I seek the gift of it."

It was a humbling thing for him to say, she thought, when he could take anything he desired so easily. "Oh, Raiden."

He tilted his head back, gazing at the star-splattered sky as he battled with his need and the loneliness of three-and-thirty years. The confession weakened him and he knew that with British troops no more than three miles away, he might lose more than his life. Yet he ached to hold tight to this moment, to have something for the time when he awaited his execution in the belly of a prison.

Slowly he tipped his head, and with a sigh, he pressed his forehead to hers. "You have bewitched me."

"Again come the grand dreams," she whispered, her heart pounding at the tenderness in his eyes. Her hands on his chest flexed, and he covered one, and Willa felt a pull that rooted in her soul.

She tipped her head and, without hesitation, brushed her mouth over his.

Raiden needed nothing else. His arms tightened around her, gathering her high against his chest as he took her mouth with exquisite hunger. He moaned at the torture of this kiss, this woman, and he stole all he could, his hand seeking the warm curve of her breast. And when he touched, she pushed into his palm, offering. He cupped her, thumbing her nipple to a glorious peak, aching to wrap his lips around the tender nub and hear her cry out in pleasure. Exquisite pleasure. Potent, untamed. Savage.

He bent her back, his mouth grinding quickly over her throat, her chest, the swells of her bosom. He pushed the chemise down, exposing her to the moonlight, and she plowed her fingers into his hair before he wrapped his lips around her tight, rosy peak and drew it into the hot suck of his mouth. She cried out and he paid lavish homage to its plump mate until she was panting. Then he straightened, taking her mouth again and again, tasting, teething, wanting more and more and knowing they'd think differently when they regained their senses. So he never ceased, sweeping her from the water and laying her on the blood-red gown strewn on the bank, then lowering himself down beside her.

He let his gaze glide over her body, ripe and round and soft, and a hard shudder wracked him to his heels. He was so undeserving of this moment and stole the privilege, meeting her gaze as his hand slid down to her spine, her buttocks.

With exquisite pressure, he pulled her against the thickness straining his breeches and Willa kissed him harder, arched to fit closer, feel more. She knew she shouldn't, but he seemed to will her into his arms, under the power of his touch. She clutched at his massive shoulders, heat coiling tightly in her belly, wrapping her waist and slipping lower, behind the path of his hand.

"Touch me, Raiden," she whispered against his lips. "I . . . I cannot bear another moment without it."

"Nor can I." He hovered over her, his mouth ravaging her lips as his hand dove under the hem of the chemise and between her thighs. He found her, cupped her, rubbing the warm apex, and she moaned, her hand sliding down his arm to where his hand lay. She pressed, almost ashamed at her boldness, then knew that with Raiden, she'd needn't be. He parted her damp flesh, his fingers thrusting deeply, and she cried out against his lips as he held her for the touch she could never deny. He withdrew and plunged again, stroking the bead of her sex, and Willa opened wider for him, drawing her knee up.

Raiden was rock hard for her, and needed to be inside her, stroking her with his body, but when he had Willa, it would not be in the jungles of India where his men could come upon them. It would be in seclusion, on beds of scented silk, with nothing but time to explore her. Yet now he let his lips and fingers delve, feeling the soft folds of flesh, his mouth drinking in her quick pants. He gazed down at her, adoring that she was too overcome to see him watching her every move, and he let his gaze slide over her bare skin.

She was a savage beauty, her passion overtaking her refinement as she twisted and writhed, her gaze locked with his as she dug her fingers into his arm, curled toward him, throwing her thigh over his. He pushed his fingers deeper, wishing it was his arousal so heavy with blood.

The pleasure was drugging, making Willa greedy for the sensations always out of reach for her in the past, in her marriage bed. Dead vows screamed that she should push him away, but new passion pulled her closer to him. And when her hand trailed his chest to the waist of his breeches, her palm sliding over his arousal, he swept her tightly against him, whispering her name, and thrust with a rhythm that only heightened her senses. She was so close, her body clawing madly for what she'd never known, never experienced. And she wanted it, the summit looming.

"I want to taste you there," he whispered in her ear, listening to her pants, feeling her body rush toward rapture.

She made a little helpless sound and rocked harder.

"I will. I will have you, Willa. I shall push my tongue into your very softness and drink of you like no other man will."

His words sent her hurling toward the edge. "Raiden, please. You torture me."

''Then succumb and die a little for me, Willa,'' he said, and she held on to him as waves of pleasure burst through her blood and seared her skin. She bowed, gasping for breath, and Raiden fought the tremendous urge to open his breeches and drive into her. He stroked her furiously, adoring the shudders and flexing, the grip of her muscles. He held her tight, the flood of desire softening, and she quaked for long moments, then sagged into his arms.

Willa buried her face in the curve of his shoulder. Raiden battled with control of his breathing, his body. He slammed his eyes shut, pressing his lips to her temple. Then he realized she was, very quietly, crying.

God above.

The *Renegade*'s sails open, and her crew at battle stations, Tristan sighted on the British vessel trailing them. The *Renegade*'s hull filled with stolen spice, she was sluggish, and he had his doubts whether they could outrun their pursuers. He'd no right to dump any cargo without a vote, and right now, not one of them had the time to discuss the matter.

''Orders, sir?''

Mr. Cheston stood at the helm, Balthasar beside him.

''I am open for suggestions, Mr. Cheston. For we will be captured if we do not gain some speed.''

''Lightening the load?''

He felt three pairs of eyes land on the quartermaster. ''No time.''

''Turn and fight?'' Balthasar suggested, his hand on the hilt of his sword.

''Those are the options I've considered,'' he muttered dryly, lowering the spyglass.

Earlier that afternoon, the watch guard in the jungle learned of the troops skulking close. He'd made the decision to sail, and no sooner than they'd caught the tide, British soldiers fired on the *Renegade*. They returned it, of course, and evaded capture only to encounter this vessel hours later.

"Raise the Union Jack."

Balthasar frowned.

"And lower sails. Let them approach, but do not let them get ahead of us, and have a look at the masthead." Tristan handed him the spyglass and headed to the quarterdeck ladder.

Balthasar loomed over the rail as Tristan lowered himself to the deck. "What do you plan, sir?"

"What else is left, my friend, but"—he shrugged—"to bluff."

Thirteen

Raiden pushed her back, and when she met his gaze, a wave of relief washed over him. She was smiling. A rather catlike curve of her lips.

"Thank you," she breathed and cupped his jaw, kissing him delicately.

She'd never experienced such before, he realized suddenly, and kissed her back, a gentleness he did know he possessed unfolding inside him.

"I am glad you were pleased, little fox. Just watching you find pleasure is nearly enough satisfaction."

In the dark, she felt her cheeks warm. "*Nearly* enough?" she said, her hand sliding down his chest to the bulge in his breeches. He moaned and pressed, then withdrew her hand, kissing the smooth back.

"Have I unleashed a hellion?"

"Aye," she said, shifting to her elbow.

Her bare breasts were temptations in themselves, and he drew her chemise strap up onto her shoulder. "Not now, not here." He brushed his mouth over hers, her quick seductive response driving a bolt of fresh desire down to his already throbbing groin. Reluctantly he climbed to his feet and strode without pause into the stream, sinking under once, then standing in the flow, his hands on his hips.

Willa stared at his broad back, unsure of what she was feeling and, practical female that she was, tried to find a proper spot for the jumble of sensations fighting inside her.

She couldn't and focused on the most prevalent.

So, that was what was missing, she thought, smiling, stretching. A remaining tremor peeled deliciously through her and she shivered, wanting more, knowing there was more. Leaving the makeshift pallet, she righted her chemise and walked to the river's edge. She washed, only the trickle of water sounding in the little copse. A barrier had been broken tonight, she thought, the intimacy stripping away the unfamiliarity and giving her something she'd never possessed—awareness of her body.

She was not ashamed that the discovery was with him, for it felt as if she'd been wrapped in cloth since her marriage, muffled away from being a complete woman, smothered by society and judgments till the moment Raiden had first kissed her, touched her.

And yet with the pleasure he gave her came the guilt of wanting more. She'd let a man who was not her husband touch her. It did not matter that Alistar had taken her body often and when it suited him, with a cold indifference that always left her filled with humiliation and feeling like his whore. Vows gave him that right. And tonight, her heart gave the right to Raiden. The realization rushed through her, and she knew more than pleasure lay at its root.

She lifted her gaze, letting it rest on his broad, naked back. How could just looking at a man give her so much pleasure? How could seeing his rare smiles fill her with such joy?

"Raiden."

He simply put up a hand for silence.

She frowned, apprehension slithering over her, and she

waited for what felt like an eternity before he faced her. His gaze glided over her from head to foot as he raked his wet hair back.

"You've grass in your hair."

Her shoulders lifted and fell.

"And you are nearly naked."

"My, how perceptive you are."

He chuckled to himself, leaving the water, pausing long enough to kiss her, then walk past.

Again, she frowned as he went to the packs. "Raiden Montegomery!"

"Aye." He carried the packs to her.

"Look at me."

He did.

"Why are you suddenly so—cold? What did I do?"

He made a painful sound and drew her into his arms. " 'Tis naught you've done, but me."

"What you did was rather splendid," she said.

He smiled, her head tucked under his chin. "Such high praise." He let out a long breath. "I had no idea how innocent you were."

She scoffed. "Innocent? I am not a virgin."

"In the ways of passion, aye, you are."

"Is that so bad?"

"It is when I have taunted you so mercilessly."

She tipped her head back and met his gaze. "There is naught to forgive." The lines in his face softened. "For the taunting, I will admit, was as much pleasure as your touch."

Raiden's smile was slow, and he shook his head, knowing he would never understand women, especially this one. He felt inexplicably honored by her words. He kissed her, yet before his desire overcame him and he pulled her down to the ground, he patted her behind and pushed her toward the packs. "Dress. The others will come hunting for us soon."

The prospect of being found clad in only her chemise sent

her hurrying to collect her clothes. She held up the ruined corset.

He chuckled to himself and she looked up, making a face. "Change into these," he said, tossing a bundle.

Willa caught it, untying the shirtsleeves he'd used to bind the garments. There was a boy's shirt, breeches, a pair of short leather boots, and heavy stockings, all worn but clean. "Breeches?"

"Aye, like your hair, that gown and your figure in it are too noticeable." He tossed her a cap. "And we cannot run if you are so encumbered."

She pulled the shirt over her head and her hair from beneath its collar. "You expect to be doing a bit of running?"

"There are troops in the area."

Her eyes went wide and she froze, one leg in the breeches. "Here? But 'tis so sparsely populated."

He scoffed lightly. "There is a city about four miles from here. We have less than three days to reach the rendezvous point, and 'twill be through British and French ports. England's battle with the French and their animosity toward the Dutch will not gain us any courtesies."

She dropped to the ground to don the stockings and boots. "Then it seems rather stupid to make a rendezvous point right in the middle of it."

"At the time I did not have a woman with me." By God, he enjoyed the bloody hell out of watching her dress, he thought. "And aye, 'twas a greater risk, but offered less suspicion."

"They wouldn't dream you'd appear under their noses, therefore they did not look, hmm?"

Nothing escaped this woman, he thought, gathering weapons, stuffing her gown in the pack, and then hiding their trail.

"How could they know where we were? Someone had to get word to them whilst we were in the city." She pulled on the boots and stood, stomping into them.

"Mayhap 'tis a fellow who knows my plans."

"Are they spoken about aboard the *Renegade?*"

"Aye. All are involved in the choices," he said.

"Then it could be anyone." She tucked in her shirttails, then buckled the belt.

"Aye. Therefore I do not want you speaking overmuch with my men."

"Would it not seem even more suspicious if I ignored them? Would they not know that we suspect them?"

She had a point. "Aye."

"Would it not benefit us if they were lulled into carelessness and then mayhaps they'd reveal themselves?"

"Nay," he barked, his expression darkening as he came to her. "Do not risk yourself." He gripped her arms. "Is that understood?"

She blinked up at him. "Raiden, be calm."

He let her go, mashing a hand over his face. She pulled his hand away and stepped into the circle of his arms. "I will try not to do aught that will get you hung." Her smile was bittersweet.

It wasn't himself he was worried about. "Then you intend to behave?"

Her smile widened to a grin. "Of course not." She rose up on her toes and kissed him lightly, then scooped up a pack and shoved the pistol in the waist of her breeches and the knife in the side of the boot.

Raiden grabbed the torch and the heavy satchel as he glanced at the clearing, then ushered her toward the camp. His gaze lowered to her figure shaped in brown broadcloth.

"Those things are indecent," he muttered. The breeches were snug and showed every bloody hill and valley.

She glanced back, smiling at how his gaze remained on her behind. "I like them. I think I will wear breeches from now on, for they are certainly more comfortable and practical."

Raiden groaned. She looked even more enticing than before, and without pounds of clothes between them, how was he to keep his hands off her and his men from gawking? They stepped into the clearing and heads came around. The men were gathered around the fire, Jabari asleep on a pallet of fronds.

Nealy's eyes narrowed as he gave her attire a thorough look and Willa tipped her chin up, daring him to comment. Then he smiled inside his bushy gray beard. She didn't know why his judgment meant something, but it did, and the notion cautioned her, for he could be the traitor. Kahlid glanced covertly at her as she slid to the pallet of fronds and she suspected he was snickering.

She wondered if the past moments in Raiden's arms were stamped on her face, for when she looked up at him, he seemed to remind her of it with that sexy, crooked smile. Raiden offered her a large leaf filled with warm, cooked meat and Willa took it, looking dubiously at the slice, then around for the carcasses. There were none. She bit into a piece, ignoring the odd taste and washing it down with water. He settled down beside her to question the men as he shared her meat.

Sanjeev sat across from them, chomping into the monkey or whatever it was, the whites of his eyes bright against his dark skin. The gold around his neck glittered in the firelight, the rings on his fingers many and heavy with gems. He wore a tightly wrapped black turban, and Willa could not tell where the fabric ended and his hair began. Beside him, Vazeen stared at her as if she were a better meal than they shared now, his gaze falling constantly to her breasts thinly shielded in the coarse shirt. She waited till he lifted his gaze to her, then pulled her hair forward to cover herself and let him know she was aware of his scrutiny. There was little difference in the appearance of Sanjeev and Vazeen, both Indian, yet Vazeen, the younger of the pair, kept staring as if she were a conquest to be taken, whilst Sanjeev looked on her indifferently, yet with respect.

Willa scooted closer to Raiden, and he glanced at her, then followed her gaze. He leaned close to her to whisper, ''He looks at you like that because he wants to bed you.''

She reddened, staring at her lap. ''Should I be flattered?''

"Not really. He is still discovering the pleasures of women, and frankly, any one will do."

She looked at him through a curtain of hair. "Now I know I am not flattered."

"Good," he said, and she met his gaze.

His look was possessive, and in it she saw the delicious feel of his fingers playing over her flesh, the hot sensation when he'd put his mouth on her breast. Her skin flushed, and she ached with a new longing for him. His gaze darkened with understanding, his unsatisfied hunger sharpening his features.

"He should be afraid of you," he said lowly, brushing the backs of his fingers across her cheek, "for you are a dangerous beauty, little fox."

She nuzzled his palm briefly, his smoldering tone leaving her wonderfully breathless.

Unable to pull his gaze from her, Raiden snapped his fingers to get Vazeen's attention off Willa, then focused on the lad. A warning in his eyes, he flicked his fingers for the flask the lad held. Vazeen quickly passed it to Raiden and he sipped the rich Madeira, then offered it to her.

"Since you have a penchant for the stuff."

She shook her head. "To be honest, I rarely imbibe."

"But I want to hear your brogue." His smile was teasing.

"My father paid for many schools so I would lose it."

He frowned. "Why?"

She rolled her eyes, sinking down on her side. "The cream of Charles Towne society does not want to be takin' a wee bit o' tea"—she offered a heavier dose of her Irish lilt in her next words—"with a lass that spakes like the housemaid."

Raiden stared, watching her eyes drift closed and realizing how much he'd misjudged her over the past days, never considering what her life was truly like before now. He'd often wondered over the kind of man she had married, but her words that time she drank too much, that she was the prettiest bauble sold to the highest bidder, told him more than she said herself.

Had she ever grown to love her husband? She'd already said

she cared nothing for the marriage bed, yet their moments spent in the privacy of the stream told him that her man had failed her. Her husband had been a fool not to want her, he thought, his groin rushing with blood as he remembered the sweet pulse of her climax beneath his touch. With a groan, he slid down beside her, his pistol on his chest. Sleep eluded him, yet his body screamed for rest. His arousal flexed, the unsatisfied need slow to fade. He turned his head to look at her, her shape silhouetted against the fire's light. The light spirited through her hair, making it appear alive and glowing

She could have fled any number of times today. She could have turned him over to the authorities at any moment. But she had not. He wondered if 'twas the danger that kept her here, or the prospect of finding her son—or him. A little of each, he thought. Yet what troubled him over and over was that who he was had put another woman's life in jeopardy. Painful memories threatened, and he rubbed his forehead, banishing them. He did not want to care, but he did, deeply. He did not want to be a hunted man, but he was. He wanted her gone from here, to safety, for a woman like her should not have to hide in the forest, wear breeches, and dine on scraps.

He lowered his hand to look at her, her face serene in sleep. She blinded him to things he'd done, to the ugly vulgar past that owned him and preyed on his soul. Her spirit was a thing of beauty, yet it was her determination to win, to succeed, that drew him. She fought for what was hers. And he wished he was worthy of such a battle.

"He is here. I can almost smell him," Admiral Dunfee growled, his feet braced wide apart for balance on the rolling deck.

"Sir, we have scoured the area for days now."

Dunfee shot a look at the officer. "Then we scour it again, Lieutenant."

"Aye, sir."

The young officer turned his attention to duty, and Dunfee snapped his fingers for the spyglass. Someone produced it in seconds, and he sighted on the open waters. There were several ships in the area—a French brig that he could attack, and two Dutch schooners—yet it was a black vessel he sought. And he would not rest till he sank the pirate ship. The Black Angel was too long marauding against the Company. The sea was filled with filth that needed cleaning, he thought. He'd already sunk two pirate craft this month.

His thoughts shifted to another prey, another man he had to find, and the notorious Black Angel needed to be in irons before he could finish his pursuit of Raiden Montegomery.

Granville's bastard would meet his death, and then Percival would have all he needed. His title, his lands awarded him for his valiant efforts on the seas on behalf of England and the East India Company. He bloody well deserved it and Montegomery was the only thing stopping him from accepting the king's rewards now.

For he was the only one left who had witnessed his crimes.

Willa sat near the campfire, her gaze drawn to Raiden. Squatting, he balanced on the balls of his feet, his elbows braced on his thighs. He looked more native than sea captain, his hair loose, sweat glistening on his bare chest. The tattoo jumped and flexed as he drew in the dirt, informing his men of his plan to get them past the British troops and to the *Renegade*. In the morning, they would take the final leg, and Willa knew she could not step onto his ship without telling him the truth.

It plagued her, these lies. She wished she was not wed; she wished Mason was with her and could know Raiden, his strength, his sense of humor.

Ah, God, what have I done? she thought, hugging herself. For the past two nights she'd woken to find herself curled around him, safe and protected. And for two nights she'd tried to say the words she knew would destroy the closeness they'd found. It broke her heart to look at him and know she'd deceived him so handily, and that he trusted her.

That would hurt the most, she thought.

She swallowed past the rock in her throat and looked away, into the black jungle. A bird hawked somewhere close by. She'd grown used to the noises, the sensation of pairs of golden eyes watching them. She brought her gaze back to Raiden and caught his quizzing look.

Smothering her anxiety, she smiled and bit into a piece of fruit before the ants got to it. He rose slowly and she tipped her head back. His breeches rode low, worn and stained and as he moved around the men who tended roasting meat and their guard positions, her gaze played over his body. He had a walk that drove her mad with desire, lazy, almost prowling, and for an instant he reminded her of the black leopard they'd seen yesterday. Dark, still so mysterious—a predator only when he hungered. And like the panther, as the natives called it, Raiden approached cautiously. She held out her hand to him and he sank down beside her.

"Hullo," she said, and he smiled hesitantly, his gaze searching hers.

"I know you must be tired of this—"

Briefly she covered his lips with two fingers. "Do not worry over me, Raiden. I can withstand the discomforts, as long as it brings me closer to my son." Her smile was slow as she lowered her hand and said, "Actually, 'tis a grand adventure. Won't the ladies in Charles Towne be jealous that I had the opportunity to traverse the dark recesses of the jungle with a famed pirate?"

His lips quirked, yet little humor lay in the gesture.

This journey had shed nearly all sense of propriety, since he would not let her leave his side, even to relieve herself. After the first occasion, Willa gave way to her embarrassment. She would rather suffer it than be killed.

"I have the dawn watch."

"Then you should rest now," she said, scooting back and offering her satchel for a pillow.

Smiling at her tender gesture, Raiden reclined, his shoulders braced, his hands behind his head.

Nealy Perth stood, tossing the remnants of his meal into the blaze, then snapped out a handkerchief and wiped his fingers and mouth. Willa tipped her head, watching. 'Twas a courtly gesture, not in the cleaning but in the manner of it, she thought, especially when, beside him, Vazeen smeared the back of his wrist across his mouth.

"Cap'n. Ma'am," he said to them with a nod.

"Be careful, Nealy."

"I will, but you needn't worry, lass. I slept in the saddle."

Raiden chuckled briefly, and when the seaman was gone, melting into the jungle to his post, he turned his gaze to Willa and the fruit she pared. She plied the folding knife with a speed that defied logic, the fruit peeled, sliced, and absent of its nut center in seconds. He lowered his arms.

"How did you learn to handle a knife so well?"

"My father." She cleaned the blade, closed it, then slipped it into her boot before looking at him. "He wanted a boy, as any man does, and—"

"Not necessarily."

"Come now—heirs to the wealth, a way to prolong your image?"

"Some of us do not care."

"You?"

He shrugged, and when he didn't expound, she said, "Papa knew he wouldn't be around to defend me, so he taught me how to use this knife. 'Tis small and not as deadly as that." She pointed to the curved dagger still sheathed at his waist. "But I've carried it since I was ten and three, and it's become like an appendage, another part of my hand, I suppose."

"Well-bred ladies wielding knives," he muttered. "God save us."

She gave him a playful shove. "I've done it unconsciously and scared a few matrons."

"And suitors?"

"I didn't have any."

He arched a brow. "I find that difficult to believe."

She blushed at the compliment. "I was bartered away. Rather, I let myself be bartered away." She eased down beside him, propped on her elbow

"Why?"

"My father's business was failing, and we needed money. My husband had it and wanted to invest." Alistar wanted a brood mare more, she thought. "I was the trade. So you see, pirate, I am worth only a few hundred pounds sterling."

"What kind of business is it, Willa?" Caution laced his tone.

She met his gaze. "Imports, exports."

"No wonder you are so familiar with ships."

"Not as much as you would surmise, but at least I do not get seasick." She paused, watching her own finger as she drew in the dirt. "When you rob the spice, it makes it that much more expensive and rare. And my father's company, I fear, will fail despite my husband's money."

"I regret that, but there are hundreds who steal the scented coin. I cannot cease for you alone or I would have mutiny on my hands."

"I know."

He shifted to his side, facing her, and ran his hand down her arm.

"Why was your son stolen?"

A pained look passed over her features. "I am not certain. Ransom mayhap. But I fear that my husband's family may want to be rid of him."

"That I can understand."

She looked up. "I beg your pardon?"

"If he is the only male heir, then he is a stone in the path to the seat of family power."

Her expression turned sour. "I do not see the value in making one child more important than another because he was birthed first. Each babe is a gift and should be cherished.''

"Would that were true of all," he said.

"Did you not think that your father might have had reason to—"

"Discard me?"

Oh, the bitterness lying there! "Mayhap he thought you were dead, Raiden. Have you considered that?"

"As a boy I did. I could not fathom why a man would ignore his own flesh and blood, but as I grew older, and learned of Ransom and the others, I understood that Granville Montegomery was a potent male who did not care where his seed sprouted or within whom."

Willa understood his feelings, for Alistar ignored his own son. "Have you ever loved, Raiden?"

He was taken back by that. "As any can love in the immaturity of youth."

"Have you loved more than once?"

"Aye."

"Then how can you not see that mayhaps Granville loved more than once? That he loved your mother and was just as crushed when she died?"

His dark brows knitted tightly. "I suppose 'tis possible."

She made a face. "At least that is something."

"Why do you defend him when you admit to never having met the man?"

" 'Tis not he I care about." She held his gaze, her meaning clear. "I am loath to see you filled with such hatred, especially when the one you hate is not aware of it." She slid her hand into his. "It accomplishes naught but to make you miserable."

Raiden sighed, plowing his fingers into her hair, and cupping the back of her neck, he drew her close. His heart leapt as she came willingly into his arms, snuggling in the shelter of his body. "How did you become so wise, little fox?" he whispered, pressing his lips to the top of her head.

"I have known love and hate. The latter ruins the former. I

chose the prospect of love and being loved in return, even if 'tis for a short time''—her grip on him tightened just then— ''over a hatred that could last a lifetime.''

The muscles around his heart clenched, and silently Raiden admitted she was right. The chance to love was far more precious than the need to hate.

''Besides,'' came muffled against his chest, ''hatred would turn me into a shrew.''

''Turn?''

She pinched him, and when he made a show of great pain, she soothed it, tilting her head back. Her gaze searched his and something warm spread through him at the look in her eyes.

''Kiss me into my dreams, pirate lord.''

''Only if you will take me with you,'' he said, ducking, the warm press of his mouth making her tremble. Aye, he wanted to be in her dreams, inside her innocent happiness, filled with plump children, whereas his were still nightmares filled with black thoughts and a vengeance that was slowly destroying him. Could he give up his quest, relinquish the very hatred that drove him into her arms? And what if she was his last chance to know love before he died?

Fourteen

Utter foolishness.

They might as well be astride elephants for all the subtlety they produced, Willa thought while riding down the main street, bold as you please. The area teemed with British troops and East India soldiers, yet the pirate parade took little notice. A jacket hiding her figure, her hair tucked in a cap, she glanced left and right, keeping directly behind Raiden. He'd said they needed to make up for lost time. Time lost, she was certain, that was her fault. And going through the city was swifter than riding miles around it. And they'd already covered ground that would take a fortnight to travel otherwise.

They were northwest of Syriam, in Burma or Siam, she didn't know, and was too exhausted to care. It was a Dutch-ruled port till recently and stretched up the jagged coastline. Yet   was no different than the dozens of other villages they'd p.
and the people were darkly tanned, with engaging smiles. Of course, they were half naked, she thought, their dress more sparse than a sari. The women wore ankle-length sarongs, the

men, drapes of fabric or mere cloths around their waists. And she'd never seen so many bare chests and thighs before.

"Try not to stare."

She glanced at Raiden as he moved abreast of her. "They look more comfortable than we in this heat," she said.

He heard the wistful lilt in her voice. "They are."

She blinked at him. "You have dressed like that? Half naked?"

"On many occasions."

"Barbarian," she muttered, smiling privately. That she would like to have witnessed, she thought as they passed taverns and shops, fisheries that reeked so bad her expression soured. Men in *prahns* lined the shore, pulling the slim, flat boats onto the sand, then heaving nets filled with fish and bloody sharks onto the shore. Women raced to collect the ocean's harvest, and Willa suddenly longed for so simple a life.

Wouldn't Mason love the beach. She could almost see him chasing crabs and catching his own fish. Her throat closed with misery, her eyes burning. *It's been too long,* she thought. *We've been apart for over a month.* Oh, the damage Alistar could do in that time to Mason's mind with his rancid attitude.

With a sigh, she turned her gaze ahead, praying they would not be caught. Ships bobbed in the harbor, their origins too numerous to consider, yet the East India crafts were easy to spot, flying the East India banner arrogantly above England's own. Was Alistar on one of them? she wondered, yet knew there was no hope of finding out whether he was here or had gone further south. They rode out of the city, and at the edge, she recognized the Royal East India crest gracing a pair of doors to a tall stone building. She was instantly on guard, for she hadn't been aware of East India offices established here, only that it was a port of call for stores and such. She glanced to the side, at Raiden, and wondered if he was simply taunting his own capture or if this was truly the only way out. Wagons full of unmarked kegs and men crowded the street, the throngs so heavy, they had to pick their way carefully around them.

For Raiden, dressed in the fine clothes he had worn before their escape, they cleared a path.

"You are positively mad," she whispered.

"Just a little while longer," Raiden said and smothered the urge to reach out and touch her. Briefly, he glanced back at Perth. The man rode behind Willa, his weapons exposed, his gaze hard on anyone who approached the caravan. Being on land made the seamen impatient for the feel of the deck beneath their feet and yet, in the past days, each one had performed admirably to keep them safe and away from prying eyes. Although he'd liked to have kept to the jungle, where he had more control, now they were running out of time. The *Renegade* would be farther east of Syriam by nightfall, moored in a tributary deep enough to accommodate the ship, and if Tristan was as smart as Raiden assumed, he would not wait for them. If they did not make it, they would be forced to steal a vessel. And the harbor looked ripe for the picking, though his crew complement was a bit light.

He glanced to the side, frowning at the pained look on Willa's face. As if sensing his attention, she lifted her gaze and Raiden was struck hard with the misery in her beautiful eyes. She seemed about to speak twice, mustering courage, and apprehension raced down his spine.

Just then they passed the company offices and a pair of doors flung open, soldiers and officers spilling out. The crush of men hurrying out of their path and the shouts startled Willa's horse and it shied away. Willa struggled for control, to maintain her balance and keep the animal from trampling a man.

"Come on, lad, you can do it," Raiden said, keeping up the pretense of hiding her femininity.

"I am trying." But there was no saddle, nothing to grasp, and the carriage horse, unused to freedom, would not be contained, rearing, pawing the air.

Raiden reached and caught the bridle. But not before Willa toppled off the back, hitting the ground with a teeth-clicking thud. Pain shot up her shoulder. Sharp hooves did a dangerous dance around her head and she curled into a ball, praying they'd back off. Blood filled her mouth. Then, suddenly, a hand clamped on her arm and she was hauled to her feet.

"Are you a'right?" Raiden demanded. "Are you hurt?"

She shook her head, swiping at the blood on her lip as she looked up at him. "Forgive me, I tried—" His eyes widened as she felt her cap slip off.

Quickly, he reached, but it was too late. The coil of bright red hair spilled down her back.

"Well, mates, looky wot we got 'ere," a man said, approaching, but a look and Raiden's dagger pricking his belly sent him back. His crewmen crowded around her, a circle of firepower to discourage all but the most foolish.

Quickly Raiden gave her a leg up, then remounted his horse. She stuffed the length of hair inside her jacket, and grasped the reins. She smiled apologetically at Raiden, then glanced around. The troops continued to shout taunts and teasing, but she didn't hear it. All she saw was the man, a familiar man, filling the doorway and looking right at her.

Barkmon.

"My lady," he said with a courtly bow, then stepped off the porch. "How good of you to appear like this. Saves me from sending another contingent in search of you."

Willa swallowed and forced herself to look at Raiden.

His expression was so remote, she felt a chill despite the heat.

"*Lady?*" he gritted, glancing at Barkmon.

"Aye. And who might you be?"

Raiden looked down at the round man too stupid to forgo a powdered wig in this ungodly heat. "Her kidnapper," he said, then planted his boot on Barkmon's chest and shoved. Whilst the director tumbled backward into the crowds and cart, Raiden swept Willa from the gray mare, dropping her before him on the bare-backed horse, then drove his heels into the animal's side.

The mare bolted, people scattering for cover as they fled into the trees.

Gunfire erupted behind them, and he heard pairs of hooves hot on his trail.

He hoped it was his own crewmen.

"Raiden."

His tone sizzled with anger as he growled, "Do not speak, *my lady.*"

The ride was merciless, Raiden driving the animal at a breakneck speed, leaping fallen trees and streams, all the while angrily slashing his sword through the heavy jungle thicket. Willa could feel his rage building with every yard they covered.

They rode into open country, then back into the jungle along the shore.

"Cap'n," Perth called, not far behind. "A squad follows."

"Only a squad? How generous of Barkmon," he muttered in her ear, then yanked back on the reins and spun the horse around in the direction they'd come. The rest of the crew leapt from their horses, pistols smoking.

"Get down," he told Willa. "And hide."

She slid off and he didn't spare her a glance before riding forward to meet his men. She slipped behind a tree, gripping her pistol.

"Try not to kill them," Raiden ordered, then fired at a soldier, clipping his shoulder. The man clutched his wound and ran back into the trees. Several more soldiers appeared, but well-placed ball shots sent half of them running, the others diving for cover. The English charged and the pirates dropped two men before the rest retreated.

Raiden looked down at the dead soldiers, then lifted his gaze to Vazeen. "Damn it, man, I said wound them! Now we will have more on our trail!" With a sound of disgust, Raiden motioned to Kahlid. "Make sure they run back to the city," he said and after depositing Jabari with Perth, the Moor rode into the forest. Silence permeated the air along with gunsmoke as they waited, watching.

"They have already mounted up and turned back, *Sajin,*" Kahlid said the instant he returned. "Like children." He spat in the Englishmen's direction.

"If I know Barkmon, he will send another squad." Raiden glanced back over his shoulder at Willa, his lips pulled into a flat line, then he addressed the men. "Kahlid, remain here with Jabari and destroy our trail. Sanjeev and Vazeen, take aught you find off the dead, hide the bodies, then guard the path we took. Perth, post yourself a few yards from the mounts and watch the sea."

He turned his horse toward Willa, and when she stepped out from behind the tree, he dismounted and pulled her along toward the shore.

Willa wrenched her arm free, glaring up at him. "I am capable of walking on my own."

Raiden looked around, squinting at the rapidly setting sun and hoping the *Renegade* would show. "And quite capable of lying." He turned his head to look at her.

"I had no choice but to lie."

"In the beginning, mayhap."

"Always."

"You think too little of me, my lady," he said, his voice tight and thick.

"You made no secret of the fact that you would do little to help me find my son."

"And yet, we are looking for him."

"And I would do naught to stop that."

His features sharpened with impatience. "Tell me the truth, Willa. I will have no more secrets between us."

Willa swallowed hard, wrapping her arms across her middle. "You will hear my secrets," she said in a defeated voice, "and want only distance atween us."

At the sudden tears glossing her eyes, his tense shoulders sagged. He blew out a breath and stepped close. "It will not matter."

"You say so now."

Lightly, he grasped her arms, rubbing, pulling them from her waist and grasping her hands. "What could be so bad? So you were married to a titled man—"

"Nay. Still *am* married to a titled man."

Raiden stared into her beautiful green eyes, searching for a hint of denial, a thread that said he'd misunderstood. And when he found only the harsh light of truth, he dropped her hands and stepped back, anguish crushing through his heart.

For days, he'd let himself believe in her, clinging to tattered shreds of hope of some kind of future with this woman, however short. Yet now they had nothing, vanquished beneath her web of lies.

He wanted to howl. He wanted to rage at her for giving him the sweetest taste of tenderness and compassion, of making him know that his heart was not dead, only to destroy it with two words. *Still married.*

"Damn you." He crowded her vision, glaring down at her. "You let me kiss you, hold you, touch you as only a husband should, yet you spoke not once of vows to another!"

Sorrow bled through her, at the anger and hurt he could not hide. "At first I feared you'd use me against others or ransom me. Or worse, ransom me to a man who would not pay. Then, after a time, I was scared you'd react like this!"

That was meaningless beneath the onslaught of her crimes. "You never intended to fulfill the bargain."

"If forced, who is to tell? But vows are sacred, Raiden, and though my husband does not observe them, I must."

He sneered. "You weren't observing them very well by the stream, woman, when you were panting in my arms, begging for your pleasures."

A flush of embarrassment rode her cheeks before she lifted her chin and declared, "Because I wanted to be there. I wanted you to touch me."

That did not satisfy the anger and hurt running rampant in his blood now. "My God, have you no conscience, no morals?"

She looked as if she'd been slapped. "Morals?" she scoffed.

"You are one to talk, pirate. Does your conscience bother you when you thieve on the seas? You dare speak to me of morals when you forced this horrid bargain on me? I did not ask for it, nor your help until you refused to set me free!"

"You could have told me sooner, when I asked, countless times!"

"Under your constant threats? My very welfare, my hope of ever finding my baby lay in you!" Anxiety swiped hard across her beautiful features. "And after your offer, I did not believe you would help me if you knew I was wed. I had naught to bargain with. *You* gave me no choice!"

"Do not blame me for your lies! And the fact of the matter is, I offered the bargain believing you, a lady, would refuse to spread your soft thighs for an outlaw and would keep your distance in anger." His icy tone bit into her as he added, "I was wrong. You'd open for any man."

His gaze raked her, the crudity of it stinging her with hurt, and she wanted to slap him. "For my son's life, I would lie with the damned devil!"

"Ah, but you had your chance, Willa. Now tell me your real name."

"Willa Delaney . . . Peachwood."

His features stretched taut.

"My husband is—"

"I know who he is." His gaze slid over her as if looking at her anew. "So, Lady Eastwick, you have yourself a very powerful husband. I shall send you back to him immediately."

He walked away, each step like a blister on her soul. She spoke quickly, her words tumbling from her lips on a tide of pain. "I was a fool to believe in you, to trust you. No honor among thieves, eh, Raiden? I should have kept the lie going, for at least I had the pretense of your caring! 'Tis you who have lied, with your kisses, with your touch!"

He whipped around, advancing on her, his handsome features sharp.

Fear skipped up her spine, and she stepped back.

He stopped, his scowl growing blacker. "Why do you retreat from me? Have I ever hurt you? Have I once raised my hand to you? I am not your goddamned husband! And I do not abuse women."

"Well, he does." Her lip trembled. "And he abuses his son. In Alistar's eyes, Mason is imperfect and not fit to be the Eastwick heir." She clutched his sleeve. "He took my son to lose him in the jungles. To let the dangers kill him so his hands remain clean."

Raiden gazed down at her, sympathy for her child and a dark hatred for his father simmering inside him. Rage split him in two. Part of him wanted to kill the son of a bitch for raising a hand to her or the boy, another wanted to send her back to his lordship so he would not have to look upon her and feel the devastation of his loss.

"He is already ill, Raiden. And you know Alistar did not see to his care himself."

He continued to stare, ever silent.

"You know I speak the truth."

His lips curled with disdain. "Truth? You would not know the truth if it were tattooed on your backside, Lady Eastwick." He plucked her hand from his arm, throwing it back at her, then turned his back on her.

It felt like a door slamming in her face, wounding her more than his words. Willa blinked back unshed tears, a dull throb in the place of her heart. She'd lost everything—his trust, his help, and mostly whatever tenderness he had for her. All he felt now was fury, betrayal.

Suddenly gunfire echoed from the trees.

Raiden ran toward the horses as Kahlid and the others burst onto the beach. "Kahlid, race up shore and see if the *Renegade* is near." As the Moor rode off, Raiden swung up onto the animal's back, pulling her mount with him as he rode to her. "Get on the horse."

She shook her head, tears threatening. She could not remain

and bear the brunt of his anger. "I think this association is at an end." She turned away, not knowing where she'd go.

Instantly he dismounted, and in three strides was upon her. He clamped his arm around her waist. "Oh nay, my lady." He pulled her off her feet and hauled her back to the horses. "It ends when I say it ends. You will *not* be leaving."

She kicked out to no avail. "We have naught more to say."

"Aye, we do. We are not finished, Willa, not by a league," he growled in her ear, then tossed her onto the animal's back. "And you are still a threat." He swung up behind her.

"I would not reveal you."

"And you expect me to believe you? Nay, you will never have the chance. You are worth more to me now . . . as a hostage."

Her heart fractured, a cut so harsh, she gasped for air. He did not truly care about her. And he would use her as much as the man she'd married had done.

"Damn your black heart, Raiden," she choked on a sob, refusing to give him the satisfaction of seeing how severely he'd wounded her. "You are no better than Alistar."

Her words left a burning trail in his soul, deeper than the ocean floor, for Raiden already knew of the depth of her hatred for her husband.

And now, it seemed, he was finally equal to a peer of the realm.

Director Barkmon walked over to the cart, viewing the stack of uniformed bodies with a disgusted glance. Blood dripped through the wagon's slats, and he stepped back. His gaze locked on the whiskerless face of one young lad, and remorse he could not afford to feel rushed at him. He turned away, a perfumed lace cloth pressed under his nose. Godforsaken country, he thought, and wanted desperately to be assigned some place more civilized, like Bombay, or blessedly, to be returned to England. The crown did not pay him enough for this kind of suffering.

"Orders, sir?"

Barkmon hastened toward the offices. "Hail the ship. He'll be interested to know what has transpired."

The young officer paled. "Aye, sir."

"Question the men and the townfolk, see if anyone recognized those men."

"I have, sir, and no one claims to know him."

Barkmon looked at the lieutenant. "Claims?"

"I don't believe they would tell if they did, sir."

"Humm." Barkmon grunted, striding toward the newly installed offices, furiously brushing the barbarian's bootprint from his waistcoat. Lady Eastwick stolen. Again. Right out from under his nose! By the rod, he would not pay for this, he thought, fighting down the string of fear tugging at his spine. The woman's unrestrained behavior would be his death, and he was sick of chasing the little colonist across the country. If his lordship couldn't control his wife, then 'twas not up to Barkmon to do it for him. And from the look of that hedonist astride the gray mare, she would not be in safe company. Mayhap he should just leave her to that brigand. He glanced back at the ships in the harbor. He would do best to report his findings and pray Eastwick was somehow pleased. Barkmon would not attempt to assume his lordship's thoughts. So far, he'd been wrong every time. Dangerously wrong.

The ship moved swiftly through the water, and Raiden was pleased that Tristan had unloaded some of the cargo onto another of his ships. They needed to shave a day off their time to reach Malacca before Dunfee. He still wondered what Barkmon was doing in Syriam, with soldiers. And what was in those unmarked kegs? Spice nuts and seeds normally had lime residue on the kegs to keep anyone from taking the seeds out of the Indies and undermining the East India trade. He scoffed to himself. He had a crate of nuts in the hull, but germinating them was impossible. Regardless, Barkmon and the unusual number of ships in Syriam was a cause for concern.

"Take a dead reckoning," Raiden ordered and sailors scrambled to drop the knotted line into the water. He needed to know exactly where they were. His boot sole propped on the quarterdeck bench, he didn't spare anyone a glance, his gaze on the black water foaming after his ship. His thoughts immediately fell on Willa. He'd yet to discuss the situation—or rather the turn of events—with anyone, for he felt she was withholding a few surprises.

"Damn," he muttered, bracing his forearm across his thigh and rubbing his hand across his mouth and chin. He'd deposited her in the cabin the instant they boarded and had not seen her since. Nor did he care to. One look in her disappointed eyes and Raiden would relive again how much he'd lost.

"I know you are not one to be chatty, but you've hardly said a word since you returned," Tristan said. "And anyone with eyes can see something's amiss with Mistress Delaney."

"Peachwood," he corrected without taking his eyes off the water.

Tristan's eyes rounded. "As in Eastwick?"

Raiden nodded.

"I can't picture her with that—that pisshole of a—"

Raiden reared back and arched a brow in his direction. "You've crossed paths with him?"

Tristan shook his head. "My second cousin was compromised by the man, and I think he did it a'purpose, for my uncle's vote in Parliament on some such matter swayed the others, away from Peachwood."

"Hmm," was all Raiden said.

"Kahlid said there was trouble in Syriam."

"Aye, Barkmon was there and recognized her ladyship. And the *Persephone* was in the harbor."

Tristan's brows shot up. "So Pendergast lied."

Raiden gazed out into the night. "Or we are simply too early or too late. Sailing time is not an exact science." But what of the *Persephone*'s sister ship, and where was it headed? When he saw it, its hull was near empty, for it rode high in the water. And why there?

"There is still the *Queen's Regard* on its way to Malacca."

Raiden's head jerked to the side, his gaze honing in on Tristan. "Did you see it?"

"I know 'tis near the straits, for Killgaren spied it, a day back."

At the mention of his half brother, Roarke, something riddled his spine. There were so many men to be considered, as suspects and friends. Could Roarke be a spy? Did Roarke know they were related? If he should tell him the truth of his lineage, would his brother reconsider his association with him?

Raiden did not know what to think, for in the back of his disturbing thoughts lay Willa and the wall her marriage created between her and his tattered honor.

But not between her and his heart.

Fifteen

Raiden never spoke to her. Nor did he look at her.

'Twas as if, in his mind, she no longer existed. She felt like a pariah and almost wished for a battle of words. It would ease the slow shattering of her heart. He slept elsewhere, abandoning all pretense of sympathy. Willa admitted she missed his presence, even an angry one. She sighed dispiritedly, blinking to clear her watery vision as she took a careful stitch in the fabric spread across her lap.

Jabari tended to her, and although she lacked for nothing, the situation confused the child. And the odd looks from his crew as they moved in and out of the cabin were further stings to her composure. She felt so completely alone.

Yesterday, Raiden had handed her into another cabin, and without a word of explanation, locked her inside for nearly two hours. And where was she to go, for pity's sake? Who was she to tell? 'Twas a burning slap, that he no longer trusted her, and Willa knew the search for her son had come to a painful end. In his anger at her, he would leave her son in Alistar's cruel hands. And they'd been so close.

Mason was near, Willa could feel it. But just as she experienced the rush of hope, it was dashed with the reality that Raiden would never help her now. For days this interminable silence went on till her own anger foamed to a crushing level. Who was he to judge her so coldly? She had not taken a life. She had not stolen so much as a ha'penny. One lie was not so dark a crime.

Ah, but 'twas a big lie. Vows bound her and excluded him completely. She jammed the needle into the fabric, pricking her finger. Sucking the tip, she breathed deeply and tried banishing the useless emotions. She was marooned here and would make the best of it till a plan came to her. If they ever made port again.

Tucked in the corner of the aft bench, she scarcely felt the bob and rush of the stern cutting through the water, the ship was moving so fast. A pitch-black night blanketed the sky beyond the bank of slanted windows and she twisted toward the lanternlight, stitching the shirt for Jabari. The boy needed some clothing that fit him better, and her thoughts tumbled to Mason and the last time she'd fitted him for a shirt. A nightshirt, she recalled, and smiled at the memory of his fidgeting. Her expression instantly fell, Alistar's reaction replaying in her mind as he'd insisted he was wealthy enough for her to have them made, not make them herself. Alistar's image unfolded in her mind, a picture of cool, emotionally remote English aristocracy. Such was her life with him. And her son had suffered the most, she thought. How often did her son reach for his father only to have Alistar recoil and act as if Mason did not exist. Oh, the hurt in her little boy's eyes, she thought, her body suddenly trembling with anger. Even with Mason's limited understanding, he knew his father didn't want him. He simply did not know why.

Her eyes burned and, the sewing forgotten, she tipped her head back, smothering a scream of frustration. She wanted to do Alistar harm for hurting her baby's feelings, and deep in the corner of the bench, she slipped her hand beneath the cushions, feeling for the velvet bag of jewels. The papers hidden beneath the lining crackled softly, and with a sigh of relief that they'd not been discovered, she shoved them deeper under the cushions, then picked up the shirt fabric again.

I will have my day, Alistar Peachwood. I will.

The door thrust open and she jolted, looking up as Raiden stepped inside.

He hesitated on the threshold, and across the room his gaze focused on her like a glance through a spyglass, his expression offering nothing but cool disdain. Yet she drank in the sight of him and instantly noticed his unshaven beard, his wrinkled clothes. It made him appear more sinister than the dark clothing and complement of weapons he wore.

Five crewmen entered behind him, ignoring her and quickly taking their business to the ward table. All that was missing from their jungle entourage was Mr. Perth, and she wondered if Raiden still distrusted the man.

Kahlid met her gaze across the distance and nodded politely. "My lady," he said.

She managed a smile. "You fared well after the jungle?"

He chuckled. "But for regaining my sea legs, yes."

Without looking up, Raiden said, "If you are through chatting with my hostage, Kahlid, join us."

Willa's anger flared. "You'd deny me even a bit of conversation?"

Raiden looked up, his expression telling her she was less than welcome and to keep quiet. Willa turned into her spot on the bench. The ship listed horribly and the rain battered the windows like tacks on a wood floor. Monsoons were coming, and when they did, the force of the wind would push the ship faster than anyone imagined, right into the Spice Islands.

The men talked amongst themselves and Willa listened, knowing the information she heard would further seal her fate with these men. Restlessly, she stood, stretching her legs, then strolled about the room, studying his selection of books, plucking a pillow off the bed, then sitting there without conscious thought.

Raiden pulled out a chair, turned its back to the table, and straddled it, his chin resting on the top as he scanned the maps.

"We port here for provisions," Tristan said, tapping the map. "Then sail onto Malacca, for the *Regard*."

"Do not be hasty, mate."

"A man who gluttons will surely die of it," Kahlid said.

"Then we die happy and rich," Vazeen added, grinning.

Willa cleared her throat. Raiden glanced up and, seeing her there, on his bed, sent a familiar curl of heat through his gullet. God, was there no relief from this female?

"You will not find the *Queen's Regard* in Malacca."

Six men swung around to stare at her.

"Your information is false," she said.

Raiden straightened. "And how did you come by this?"

Tossing the pillow aside, she stood and walked closer. "I dined with Barkmon three nights afore my bodyguard was slain." Manav's image burst in her mind, and the muscles around her heart squeezed. "I chanced to see . . . something to the contrary."

"And what might that be?"

His nasty tone angered her. There was no reason to be so rude, especially before his crewmen. "Did you ever stop to think why Manav was killed, why that soldier tried to shoot me in the tavern? Why Barkmon was in Syriam, of all places, and so quickly?"

His gaze thinned.

"I see you have."

"And?"

"Barkmon does as Alistar bids, and it means he's near, which means Mason is near."

"You reach for straws." He looked back at the maps.

She refused to believe Mason was gone, and she hated Raiden for trying to squash her hope. "Alistar seeks to silence me."

He looked at her. "To what purpose?"

"I own half of Delaney Shipping." His brows rose and he straightened in the chair. " 'Twas my dowry."

"Then it is now his."

She shook her head. "Only if I die." She folded her arms across her middle. "Lord Eastwick knows next to nothing about ships and imports, but he saw the opportunity with those greedy colonials, as he used to say." Her gaze moved over the others, then focused on Raiden. "He was sent to India to investigate Clive's work, for the Crown could not fathom the success of the East India and thought Clive was profiting too well, especially with the *jagir,* the stipend paid by the Mogul leaders. He was to take some control. Alistar found a prosperous and fruitful company—one with grand opportunities to make him a fortune." She scoffed. "Only if a man could order troops to slaughter anyone who opposed him."

"There are plenty who would follow such an order," Kahlid said.

Raiden waved impatiently. "What could reports to the Crown have to do with you?"

"His reports are false."

"He gave the Crown false documents?" Tristan said, his gaze shooting between Willa and Raiden.

Raiden stood, glaring at her. "You lie again. 'Tis a threat to his life for such a crime."

"And worth the threat to Alistar when there is more coin at stake. He is stealing. I think he is dumping spice to drive up the price, or diverting it and fudging the ledgers."

"You have proof of this?"

She nodded, turning to the window bench. Lifting the cushion, she heard Raiden's soft curse as she removed the velvet bag and opened it, spilling the jewels, then digging in the bottom for the paper slipped under the lining. She unfolded it carefully, then held it out to him.

Moving around the ward table, Raiden crossed to her, taking the parchment. He read. "Sweet Jesus, Willa." He lifted his gaze from the paper.

"Manav died for those. So did that captain. I did not think Alistar had the stomach for such acts, but I do not doubt that he is giving Barkmon orders for a split of the profits. He might be using one of Papa's ships, for he could never take command of an Indiaman." She rubbed her temple, confused. "Alistar could do this and mark my father as a traitor to the Crown," she mumbled to herself, then looked up, her hand falling to her side. "So you see, keeping me hostage will gain his wrath, for I would not put it past the lot of them to hunt you down, simply to kill me."

Raiden didn't know whether to believe her or not. And Lord Eastwick did not know who held his wife. He looked down at the papers, three of them, signed and bearing Eastwick's seal. "They make no mention of spice."

"Of course not. He is greedy, not stupid. He could claim it was bolts of fabric if caught and within days produce enough evidence to cover his story."

His gaze narrowed. How much more was she keeping from him? "You stole these letters? Or did you fabricate them to get even with Eastwick for stealing your son?"

She sent him a bitter smile and snatched back the papers, folding them meticulously. "I admit I've had some delicious thoughts of humiliating the man for all he's done, but I only want my son." She stuffed them in the dainty bag. "I will grant him aught he wishes if he will just give me Mason."

"And what if you are wrong and he does not have the boy—what then?"

Misery swept her features and she turned away. "I will keep searching."

"You forget that you are my prisoner, alone, and without funds." He hated the cruelty of his own words, instantly regretting them.

Over her shoulder, she sent him a look, the narrow glance of a tigress defending her cub. "Make no mistake, I will do as I must."

"Even, mayhap, betray me?"

"You count my lie to protect my son a betrayal to *you?*" The idea was preposterous. "I am not the outlaw—you are."

Raiden crossed to her, forcing her to face him. "Why did you not tell me of this sooner?"

"A trap?" Tristan said, his eyes narrowing.

She looked around Raiden to Tristan. "With myself in the middle of it? Don't be absurd. I would like to live long enough to see land again and find my son. If I die, Mason will have no one." She wrenched out of Raiden's grasp, laying the blame at his feet, then went to the table, glancing over the maps. "I tell you, if you choose this route, then you will all die. Or be taken prisoner."

"We have been doing this a sight longer than you, woman," Raiden scoffed, moving up behind her.

"Long enough that one would think you'd appreciate valuable information." She looked at him. "Mayhaps you are growing careless." He fumed and she shifted her gaze back to the maps, studying them for a moment and realizing that Raiden's were far more detailed than Barkmon's. "There are no less than four man-of-war patrolling these waters." She circled the parchment with a manicured fingertip. "And here"—she pointed to a spot at the mouth of the Malaccan Straits—"they will have at least four vessels, Naval ships, not East Indiamen, ready to blockade the Malay Peninsula." She lifted her gaze to Raiden's. "Watson commands the *Regard,* not Dunfee. That posturing oaf is on the *Yorkshire* and hunting for you."

"I am well aware of that."

"Really?" She flipped her hair back off her shoulder and regarded him. "Then you know he thirsts for vengeance against a Montegomery. His chase of the Black Angel is more for sport." She waved airily. "The man is to be knighted in the fall of this year and would want to stay alive till then at least."

Raiden exchanged a glance with Tristan, and whilst the others were focused on the maps, Willa caught it.

"So why does this man want you? A man known only as a bastard sailor, if his memory serves him that well?"

Raiden's expression turned black, almost evil. "One could only imagine." Without taking his eyes off her, he said, "Gentlemen."

The crewmen gathered the maps and left. Raiden remained, gazing down at her, silent. An odd light flickered in his dark eyes. She took a step. His spine stiffened, and again she felt his emotions simmering on the surface. Emotions he refused to show her anymore.

He spun on his heels and strode to the door, pausing on the threshold to look back. "Batten yourself down, Lady Eastwick." The address rolled off his lips with the sharp edge of an ugly slur. " 'Twould not do to have my prize bruised."

"I am not your prize, remember, I am your hostage." Anger swelled in her. "Speak to me again like that, *pirate,* and you will have bloody good reason to be watching your back!"

The roar of cannons and the screams of the dying went on for days. No ships sailing near the Straits of Malacca were safe. The noise was deafening, the recoil terrifying, and when the *Renegade* shuddered violently, Willa sank to the floor, unable to look out the window. But she knew what she would see. In the black of night, debris trailed the *Renegade,* the *Sea Warrior,* the *Lady Rajah,* and another vessel Raiden could claim under his command.

He'd attacked relentlessly, this time leveling the decks till the brigs and barkentines were nothing but long boats. Her skin chilled at the thought of him exhausting his vengeance against her on those unsuspecting vessels. English, East Indiamen, French. He did not care. His hull, no doubt, overflowed with riches. She glanced about at the new chests, the bolts of silks and canisters of rare saffron. How many had died for that damned chest?

The battle waged on above decks, and she could tell when it was nearly done. First the cannon fire, the screams, then the deadly silence before they raped the vessels. It turned her stomach, and although once, when she'd looked out the leeward portal and had seen him help men from chains, she wished to God Raiden would cease this dangerous life.

She covered her face, crouching low to avoid any shattering glass. The stench of smoke told her the *Renegade* had not fared well this time.

Then blessed, terrifying silence reigned. The ship creaked and Willa thought she'd go mad with the suspense. She stood, picking up fallen objects and storing them, then she paced, refusing to be concerned about a man who gave no thought to plowing through the seas and ravaging them dry. She did not care anymore. She would not, she thought, but when the door opened, relief swept her and her legs nearly folded beneath her.

Raiden stepped through the hatch, smudged with soot, splattered with blood, and her heart skipped to her throat as he crossed to the desk, laying his sword there. He lifted his gaze to hers, but said nothing, his expression vacant. And yet he commanded every fiber of her being, this fierce-looking man, and she could not look at him without remembering his searing kisses and the tender intimacy of his touch. But nothing of those fragile moments remained now. Even his black kneeboots and breeches spoke little of the man she'd held in the forest, his chest bare but for the dark leather jerkin wrapping his torso and revealing his thickly muscled arms. The wide belt was again stuffed with weapons, bloody weapons, as if to remind her exactly what kind of man she'd angered.

Raiden stared at her upturned face and watched an emotion he could not name fade from her features. Like a shutter closing. His gaze swept her briefly, the gown of deep blue Egyptian cotton a contrast to the yards of red hair spilling over her shoulder. She had not pinned it up since they'd returned, and behind his anger he could admit how much it pleased him to see the wild curls—and remember his hands fisted in them when he last kissed her, when she gave to him on that riverbank in the jungle.

Damn her, he thought. Damn her for lying so grievously. Damn her for the vows that gave him ideas and images he did not want to see, images that stole the precious memory of her pleasure in his arms when he wanted it for himself alone. Did she let Eastwick touch her like that? Did she cry out wildly for—With a snarl of disgust, he banished the questions. They only served to wound him deeper.

"Why do you do this?" She gestured to the wreckage beyond the walls. "Must you live up to your reputation by crushing these vessels?"

"I do as I must."

"How much more do you need?" She flicked a hand at the chests of loot. When he did not respond, she sneered, "You disgust me now, pirate."

"You assume *we* attacked?"

"How can I not! I warned you the vessels were here! You could have gone around them."

"We were hunted. Because Mason was the reason the *Renegade* had to depart so quickly last week. Questions brought interest, and my men were followed."

"Then we've sailed away from the source." She glanced at the windows, then to him. "Mason could still be in the Ganges or at Chittagong."

" 'Tis doubtful. They found no information."

"Then why are you telling me this now? You will not turn back. Do you hate me so much you would steal my hope, crush my heart even more?"

Her volley struck home, and Raiden's lips tightened in a flat line.

"Why do you not simply tie me up, deny me food and water?" she flung bitterly.

"Consider yourself fortunate that I do not throw you in the brig."

Standing at his desk, Raiden wondered why he'd even bothered to come in here. Just to hear her voice and the loathing coating it made him burn with anger.

"Mayhap you should. 'Twould be a sight better than seeing you destroy half the ships on the sea!" A pause and then, "Why do you wreak havoc in the night like this?"

"Have you forgotten already? I am a buccaneer, a thief."

"Aye, and usually you are more discreet! You risk more than your own life by coming through the straits." She drew in a long breath. "You do this in anger at me?"

He scoffed. "You hold yourself far too high."

Willa saw only the hollowness in his eyes as she gazed back at him. "Did you not listen to me? Dunfee is not on the *Regard*."

"You lie too well to be trusted, Lady Eastwick."

"Nay, Raiden, only *you* doubt me. You will get yourself killed and all these men with you if you do not heed my words."

"I do as I please." He inspected the edge of his blade, wiping a drop of a dead man's blood with his thumb and sanding it.

She saw the motion and knew he'd done it to push her further away. "Nay. Your concern is only for your bruised pride."

His gaze flew to hers, and Willa felt it like the sting of needle. Did he not realize she bore only malice for her husband, that only a slip of paper kept her from giving him more than just her body?

"Pride is worthless."

"Really? Pride keeps you from forgiving—not just me, but your father. Pride keeps you from telling your brother he is not alone. Pride has sent you a life of crime and now a battle of pure vengeance!"

"You know naught of me!"

"I know plenty, Raiden Montegomery. You rescue pressed sailors because no one rescued you. You want riches beyond imagination so you will never go hungry again and always have a warm place to sleep." She drew a long breath. "And you strike with a lethal rage till you are so feared, no one could dare look down on you as less of a man!"

Her words struck with deadly accuracy, and his features burned.

"You would be very wise to hold your tongue," came with deadly calm.

She met it, matched it. "I am not afraid of you! You threw a bargain of lust because you wanted beneath my skirts and hoped I would oblige."

He scoffed meanly. "Believe as you will."

"I believe what I know, and I see more than you want."

"And I see a woman who wanted to lie beneath an outlaw. Like all the others, I mean no more to you than the heady risk of crossing into another class—"

"Class? What know you of class, pirate? I am true to my heart," she said, thumping her chest, "whilst you volley atween corsair and gentleman and the tiny shred of honor you have keeps you from giving way to the past and offering *anyone* a shred more than you want. If you were truly as notorious as your reputation bids, you would—"

In a single stride, he was against her, pressing her back to the nearest wall, his hips grinding suggestively into hers. "Would what, my lady fox?"

She gazed into his tortured eyes and saw the beast screaming to be set free. "You would have fulfilled your promises."

"Damn you, Willa!" He slammed both fists to the wall on either side of her head and she flinched. "Do not test me," he snarled, "for I could easily rape you against this wall as take you on the floor."

He'd said that to hurt her, to push her away, she knew, and she marshaled her feelings to say, "Your base-born breeding does not scare me, Montegomery."

"It should."

He kissed her, hard, a punishing crush of lips and tongue, and she accepted, fought back with all the wildness still locked inside her. And in it she told him she was not afraid of his anger, nor the ugliness of his abandoned soul. His hands found their way beneath her skirts, and he cupped her bare behind and jerked her against his hardness.

Then she captured his jaw in her smooth palms, the feel of her unblemished skin to his stubbled beard, the tenderness with which she touched, was like a piercing shaft bolting straight into his soul. For a second, his kiss softened.

"You believe you possess only a wicked heart," she breathed against his lips, "with no room for love."

Love. *Ah, God above.* "Love is for drunken poets."

He took her mouth again, his tongue thrusting hotly and seeking to ease a pain so deep, he wanted to roar with the agony of it. Even without her vows, she was denied him. Because he would kill a man, in cold blood, exact his revenge, and die in peace. "Do not love me, Willa. Never." It would be her death.

"My vows," she whispered, "do not rule my heart."

He reared back, his eyes black as the skies beyond. "Do not fill your head with fantasy, Lady Eastwick. For I will destroy it."

He thrust from her, snatching up his bloody sword as he strode to the door.

She flinched when he slammed it shut behind him.

Willa blinked away hot tears, swiping her hand across her bruised mouth as she dragged air into her lungs.

It was over. There was no reaching him.

Sixteen

Banda Aceh
Gateway to the Spice Islands

She stood at the rail, never feeling her isolation more than she did now. One woman surrounded by dangerous men. Loneliness and fleeting hope engulfed her as the ship rocked, the creak a mournful bale in the darkness. Not even the distant crash of waves soothed the ache in her chest. Raiden had locked her inside the cabin when they'd docked, and it was nearly nightfall before anyone had come to release her. And then it had been Jabari, bless his innocent heart. He did not know why the door was barricaded and said he believed it was to keep her safe if they were boarded. Willa knew otherwise.

"Do you want to leave?" a voice said from behind her, and she inhaled, startled. "Do not turn around," came sharply when she tried to look. "Do you?"

Willa tried to discern who was speaking, then realized it did not matter and finally nodded. She had to leave. She needed to find her son, and Raiden had become a man she scarcely recognized.

"Gather your things and toss them in that longboat to your right, then hide inside."

She nodded. Was this the betrayer? Why was he helping her? Did he not realize Raiden would kill him for this? Willa touched the blade secreted in her bodice. She trusted no one now. The only thing that had not failed her was her love for her son.

"A quarter hour, no more," he whispered.

She felt him depart from her presence as a cool wind moved across her back. She did not look to see who remained near and hurried to the cabin, her heart breaking with every step.

Willa looked left and right, then slipped into the longboat, immediately curling into the forward hull and pulling the rain tarp over herself. She let out a slow, quiet breath, unsure of who stood near.

She'd had a devil of a time getting above decks without being seen, even in the dark and wearing the breeches she'd worn in the jungle. Her hair braided and tucked down her back under her shirt and coat, she lay still as the vessel was lowered away. The instant it hit the water, several men crowded in, talking softly, and when someone dropped a pack on her, she bit her lip to keep from grunting aloud.

Oars slid and scraped into their brackets, and then they were moving, rushing to shore under secrecy of a black, still night. The men talked of plans, of seeking out someone named Futar and hoping they came away with their fingers. She did not recognize a single voice, nor could she imagine who Futar was or why their fingers were in jeopardy. She just wanted to be away from them all. Away from Raiden and the heartache of what might have been. It seemed like forever before the longboat scraped the shore, then it rocked as men leapt to the ground and dragged it on shore. She heard the rustle of brush and dry leaves and realized they were hiding it. She didn't dare move,

even when the voices and noise faded. She had to be certain
no one lingered who might discover her.

Several minutes later, the rustle came again.

"Get out."

The voice again. Willa pushed the tarps and packs off herself
and struggled to sit up. A figure was shadowed in the darkness,
and she strained to see. From her position, he looked incredibly
tall. She climbed to her feet, pulled the pack onto her back,
and looked at him again, yet she could scarcely see her hand,
let alone identify him.

"Be quick about it."

He spoke precisely, hiding any trace of an accent that would
reveal his identity. He led the way, and with no other choice,
she followed, her legs struggling to keep up in the wet sand.
After a few yards, he pulled a hood over his head. Was it Perth?
she wondered. Or someone she'd never met? For the *Renegade*
and the *Sea Warrior* were both anchored in the isolated harbor,
each with over a hundred-man complement.

"Why do you aid me?"

He did not answer.

"You know he will find out," she said.

"Nay, he will not."

She scoffed. "He suspects everyone."

"Except you."

"There, you are very wrong."

She saw two horses tethered under the trees, and he shoved
the reins to one into her hands, then swung up onto his saddle.
Willa didn't bother to tie the pack on, and with it heavy on
her back, she climbed into the saddle. She sent the *Renegade*
an indecisive glance, the black vessel scarcely visible in the
dark, and wondered what he'd do when he discovered her
missing. Would he seek her out? Would he simply cast the
thought of her aside?

Reining around, she followed her accomplice. They rode for
over an hour, and when the glow of village lights reached them,
he reined up and handed her something rolled in oiled hide.

Frowning, she accepted it, unwrapping the parcel. Inside, lay a pistol, powder horn, and shot.

"There is a Dutch hotel two miles down that road." He pointed, his long arm and his gloved hand looking like the damnation of the Grim Reaper in the dark. Fear skipped up her spine again. What was she thinking to venture out alone with a man she could not even identify? But Raiden had left her with no other options, his bitterness driving her to this. And now there was no turning back.

Slowly he rode off in the opposite direction, leaving her in the dark, and Willa urged the horse toward the village, realizing how unwise a move this was. But she could no longer bear the pirate's anger. Not and have her heart survive.

Even at this late hour, there were dozens of people milling about, some going in and coming out of a tavern across the dirt road, a few wandering the streets, obviously intoxicated. East India soldiers strolled, their red lapels and waistcoats contrasting sharply against the blue of their broad-cuffed coats, their presence a deterrent against brawls amongst the sailors and natives. The sight of them made Willa extremely wary as she reined up outside the inn and slid from the saddle. Though she doubted even one would recognize her, she worried over being able to protect herself and find a way to pick up Alistar's trail.

It all seemed so hopeless right now.

Standing beside the horse, she pressed her forehead to the warm saddle and let out a long breath. Was she truly doing the right thing? Lord, if anyone discovered she was a woman, there would be no saving her. And what could she accomplish without Raiden's help?

Damn him for being so heartless. Did he not understand she cared for him more than she had ever done for her husband? And she missed him. Lord a'mighty, she missed him and longed to see the man who'd teased her mercilessly, who stole kisses outside the dress shop, whose touch drew her body to a passionate explosion in the darkness of the jungle. She'd never felt so aware of being a woman than when she was with him.

The muscles around her heart contracted as his image unfolded in her mind. She choked on a breath, tears searing her tired eyes.

She stiffened when she felt a presence behind her.

"A rather dangerous move, isn't this?"

She spun around, her knife clutched in her hand. "Do not come any closer." She flipped the blade out.

"I will not harm you."

She scoffed. "Show yourself."

A tall, broad-shouldered man emerged slowly from the darkness, and her breath caught. For a moment, she thought it was Raiden.

Her gaze narrowed as she visually picked him over, from his shiny black boots and dark breeches to his snowy white shirt and dark broadcoat. He wore no tricorn, and his long dark hair was tied back. His face—what was it about his face that unnerved her? She wished he would step into the light, then wished he was gone from there.

"Lady Eastwick," he said ever so softly.

Her gaze flicked around them. There was no one near enough to overhear them and realize she was female. "I'm afraid you have the wrong person."

He shook his head slowly, and disregarding her knife as a threat, he stepped close, under the torchlight coming from the inn. "When an English peer takes an Irish bride, the word travels all the way to Erin."

She frowned. His accent held just a lingering hint of Ireland. "Who are you?"

"I am Roarke Killgaren, captain of the *Sea Warrior.*"

She inhaled and took a step back. Raiden's brother. The resemblance was not so great that he could be a double for Raiden, but 'twas enough. Two handsome brothers, she thought, and wondered if the others had like appearances and were all as big as trees.

"What do you want?"

"Only to see that you are unharmed."

"You have seen. Now go." With the knife, she gestured somewhere to the right.

He did not move, his chiseled lips curving in a ghost of a smile. "You truly want to lose his protection?"

"Protection? I was his captive, again."

He folded his arms over his chest and gazed down at her like a father at a troublesome child. "Only since he discovered you're married."

She groaned, irritated. Did the entire crew know their business? "Does the length of time in a prison matter?" she asked. " 'Tis still a cage."

"Do you want to leave?"

"I must," she said and swallowed the stone of agony that lodged in her throat every time she thought of never seeing Raiden again. If only it were a matter of wanting, she'd never leave.

"Why?"

"I can not bear his anger another day. I thought he had a heart, but the man is positively wicked down to his boot heels, and he's made it clear he loathes me for lying. He has disregarded our . . . agreement completely, blasting his way across the South Seas, and I cannot wait for him to find whatever it is he seeks with such venom, for I must find my son."

"Ah, so that is why he's kept you this long."

She frowned, unsure of what he meant.

"Raiden has a problem with lost souls."

"Not any longer."

"Do not discount my brother, lass."

Her tapered brows rose. "Raiden is not aware that you know of your relation."

"Oh, I ken that well. But 'tis Raiden who is not ready to have family in his life." Roarke shrugged. "When he is, I shall be near enough."

She smiled sadly. "I am pleased, then, that someone will be there for him when he needs it."

"But my lady," he said with a knowing smile, "you just tried to tell me you cared naught for my brother."

Her chin lifted. "He has made his feelings clear, Captain Killgaren. I am lawfully wed and that is that."

"Call me Roarke," he said, and she nodded. Great God, even in boy's clothes, she was beautiful, and he understood the reason behind the recent changes in Raiden. In the times that he and Raiden had talked whilst she was aboard the *Renegade*, he'd recognized them in his brooding half brother, a lightness of heart Raiden rarely showed anyone, least of all him. Raiden would be very angry over her escape and that she'd fled his prison spoke of an accomplice, for she could not have handled this alone. Roarke wondered who'd risked his life to help her leave—and why. Mayhaps someone thought to help her escape, then take her again, and offer her back to her husband for a price? Eastwick might pay a hefty sum for her, but nothing equal to what each pirate took in spoils. Especially after their most recent acquisitions. Nevertheless, she was courting her death being anywhere in this city alone.

Brotherhood and conscience bade him do something about it.

With a deft move, he snatched the blade from her grasp, but he'd underestimated the woman, for a second later, a pistol appeared under his chin.

"Give it back."

When he hesitated, she drew back the firing hammer.

"Very resourceful, my lady." He offered the knife and an admiring smile.

"A lady does what she must." She took it, gesturing with the pistol for him to step back. He obliged her, and Willa wondered how to get away from him. Surely, given the chance, he would take her back to Raiden.

"He feels more for you than you believe, lass."

"Locking me in the cabin is a peculiar way of showing it."

" 'Twas for your own protection. This port is dangerous, and the further we travel into the Indies, the worse it becomes. Why do you think the British sail in pairs?" He stepped close, and Willa tamped down her fear and listened. "The natives are vicious. One infraction of their customs could mean instant death."

"But I have to find my son," she whispered.

"Had you a little patience, Raiden would have cooled and returned to the search." She gazed up at him, with so much hope shining in her teary eyes that Roarke wondered how Raiden could have missed the love she bore him.

"I am not so certain of that," Willa said.

"I am."

"How can I believe that? He was so angry and . . . hateful."

"If he did not care so deeply, he would not be so distraught over learning of your marriage."

Anguish skipped across her features. "He has no forgiveness in him, Roarke. None."

"But can you say you feel naught for him?" he asked softly.

Willa gazed up at him, into his beautiful, deep-blue eyes, and the truth spilled from her lips. "Nay." She lowered the pistol, pushing it into her waistband. "Nay, I cannot." She looked away, at the distant harbor and the ships' lanterns winking in the dark. The gloomy night stretched out before her, and her soul felt just as empty and barren, with only her love for her son to comfort her.

She should never have left Raiden. Everyone had left him— his mother, his rogue father. He'd been discarded and forgotten all his life. He seemed so invincible, shielding himself in cool indifference against feeling too much or growing too close to anyone, and yet he was still so alone in his misery. His wounds were clear enough for anyone to see. Yet no one had ever looked. They showed in his face when she'd told him the truth, his tender concern turning to hurt, then to outrage. And in the way he taunted her the other night, vulgar and lurid, as if to prove to her that her vows were not the only thing that separated them.

She didn't care if he was a bastard, a thief, and a hunted

outlaw. For the man she knew cared for the hopeless, and struggled to overcome tremendous odds to survive. The legendary Black Angel was only a portion of the man she'd come to know. A life with him, however short, was far better than one without him. She d been a fool. Of course Raiden would help her find her son. He wouldn't turn his back on a defenseless child for the sake of anger. And now she'd left him just like every other person in his life.

Willa turned away from Roarke.

"Whoa, where are you going?" he said in a hushed voice, following on her heels.

"Back to the ship."

He heard the tears in her voice. "And how do you plan on getting aboard—swim?"

She collected the reins. "I grew up on the coast. I am capable."

Roarke stopped her when she tried to mount. "Lady Eastwick," he said lowly, and she turned her head to look at him. "Willa. The waters are infested with sharks. And those creatures are less dangerous than those you'd find on land, if someone should realize you are female." His gaze lowered purposely to her bosom outlined in the thin shirt. She closed the jacket, glancing about and blushing.

Roarke merely arched a brow, and Willa wondered if all Montegomery men possessed such a haughty affectation.

"What do you propose I do? I've no notion of when he will return, and I would rather he not discover I'd left a'tall."

"I will take you." He looked over her head at the darkened streets. Men spilled out of taverns, looking about for more mischief. "Leave the horse. This way." He pointed. She followed.

Yet their escape was halted when a wagon rolled to a stop beside them, kicking up dust and sand and blocking retreat. A commotion came from behind, and she turned to see two men carrying a pallet and working their way out the inn's front door.

"Oh, my word," she whispered. They carted a body. Instantly Roarke was in front of her, blocking the view as they tossed the cadaver in the back of the wagon.

"You don't need to see that."

"Unfortunately, I am well schooled in death and wounds." When the men climbed into the back of the cart, removing jewelry, which was often their payment for collecting corpses a flash of something caught her attention.

She pushed around Roarke.

"Willa, please don't."

She waved him off, and Roarke muttered, "It is little wonder he locked you in," as she stopped at the back of the cart.

"What have you there?"

The man hid his fist behind his back, glaring at her.

The click of a pistol hammer interrupted the silence, and Willa glanced at Roarke. Gone was the congenial man, and before her stood the warrior, prepared to defend. "Show us."

The man offered his hand, palm up and open. At the sight of the silver bracelet, Willa's heart slammed to her stomach. Instantly she rushed to the side of the wagon, gently pulling back the muslin cloth. She moaned, tears filling her eyes.

"Oh, nay," she wailed softly. "Maura."

Roarke gripped her shoulders from behind and whispered in her ear, "You knew her?"

She nodded, sniffled, then said, "She was my son's nanny."

Roarke gazed down at the body; the old woman's face was swollen with disease, her skin ashen. "Was there a child with her?" he demanded of the men.

"Nay, guv, she was alone. Been this way for a day or so, I figure." The man scratched himself rudely.

"Was there anything a'tall in the room?" Willa asked.

The second man shook his head, running a dirty sleeve under his nose. "Not even clothes, miss. It was them that sent for us." He pointed.

Willa turned, her gaze searching the dark, and when a figure emerged, she felt her heart slide right out of her chest to her knees. Oh, God.

"Alistar."

Seventeen

Raiden swung his leg over the side of the ship and dropped to the deck, then strode toward the passageway. Behind him, men swarmed over the railing like rats scurrying to their positions without the aid of light. He paused for a second, cocking a look behind, his gaze searching the decks. It was hard to see, but he knew every inch of his ship like his palm, and instantly he realized that a longboat was wet, where it should never have touched the water. His features tightened and he called for Tristan.

When the man appeared, Raiden said, "Who was instructed to remain behind?"

Tristan thought for a moment. "Dobbs, Van Pool, Riggs, Cheston, Perth, Kahlid, Vazeen, Sanjeev, maybe three more." He frowned questioningly, and Raiden gestured to the water on the deck, yet the two longboats they had taken had not been hoisted aboard yet.

"Take account of every man and have those men report to me. Now."

"Aye, aye," Tristan said, scowling as he spun on his heel, snapping orders.

Raiden ducked into the passageway and froze outside his cabin door. The lock was sprung, and the barricade missing. Instantly he thrust open the door, his gaze scouring the lit interior. The empty interior. Quickly, he stepped over the threshold, moving directly to where she'd kept her belongings near the aft window bench. The satchel was there, but his knapsack was missing. Her East India pistol was still locked in the chest. She had no weapon but her knife. He rifled through her things, finding most of the clothes he'd bought her still there. But the boy's garments were painfully absent.

His heart pounded, and with each passing second, it grew harder and harder until it nearly choked him.

Jesus. She's left me.

Did he expect to keep her forever? Did he really believe she would suffer his insults and rage without rebellion? Raiden swallowed, the muscles in his throat scraping like broken glass, and he sagged against his desk, her nightrail fisted in his hand. *Oh God. What have I done?*

Raiden hadn't thought losing her would hurt so deeply. But it tore through him like a hot blade, slashing at the heart he'd tried so hard to ignore. He'd pushed her to this and now her life was in grave danger—with no one to blame but himself. He straightened suddenly, the nightgown falling to the floor as he wondered if she'd left to inform the authorities. He plowed both hands into his hair, gripping his skull, his mind and heart battling for supremacy. Would she betray him? For he'd given her no reason to believe there was anything left between them. Sweet Christ, to find her son, she would do anything! Had she not said as much? Why wouldn't she hand him over if the reward was her boy?

Kicking the gown aside, he strode to the hatch, barking orders for a complete search of the ship. But it was useless. She was gone, and he knew exactly how she'd left.

"Lower the longboat," Raiden commanded, taking Tristan's weapons and calling for powder horn and shot.

"Raiden—"

He checked the loads. "She is gone."

"What? How can that be? She was locked inside."

"Obviously someone released her." Raiden glanced over his shoulder at Jabari cowering in a corner, then without a word returned his attention to Tristan. "And someone took her ashore."

Tristan scowled at the wet deck. "I can understand why she wanted to leave," he said with an assessing look. "But why would any man here help her? Betray you? Us?"

"How the bloody hell should I know why?" he snapped, snatching the horn and shot bag from the seaman "Money? Amnesty? He was wooed by her pretty face or he thought to sell her or to ransom her himself? But I swear," he said with a look over his crewmen, "I will kill the man who helped her escape." His gaze scanned the men, assessing the few who were missing and hating it. "Remain here and find out who is not aboard and exactly who was in that longboat. If anyone arrives, throw him in the brig. I go ashore."

"Raiden, be reasonable. You cannot do this. We have only five or six hours of darkness left. In the light of day we will be seen for miles!"

"Then we have five hours to find her. Or you must do as you must."

Tristan understood, but he damn well didn't like the thought of sailing without Raiden again. The seasons were changing, the monsoons were coming, and if they were caught at sea, they would not see him for weeks. And Tristan admitted he was not as skilled a sailor as Raiden. "You would risk all our lives for her when you have dismissed the woman for days now?"

Regret pounded through his blood. "Aye. Have you not considered that she could be speaking with the authorities at this moment and revealing our location, our plans?"

"If she has, then you are the one to blame for this," Tristan said in a low hiss. "You could not even be civil to her, and now she's fled right into one of the most dangerous ports of—"

Raiden's head jerked up, his gaze hardening on him. "I know exactly what lies beyond the dark, Mr. Dysart."

"She is going to be killed or at best sold into slavery!"

"Not if I find her first."

"You are a fool if you think anyone will offer her up to us. She will fetch the highest price, Raiden, that hair and fair skin, that temper. By the time you find her she will be a shred of the woman you knew."

Raiden stilled for a second, one leg over the side of the ship as he looked back at the quartermaster. "Your lack of expectation is rather vexing, Tristan." *God help the soul who lays a hand on her,* he thought.

"Since when have you ever held hope so dear?" Tristan scoffed.

Raiden slid over the side of the ship. "Since now," he said before disappearing from sight. Aye, since Willa, he thought and clung to shredded hope as he repelled down the web of ropes. Her peril was his fault. She'd risked death to escape him, running full force into God knew what kind of danger, and it proved to him that his battery of anger had hit a deadly mark. And how dearly they would all pay if he was wrong about Willa.

He had to find her before trouble did.

Rage spread through Willa like an uncoiling serpent as she glared at her husband. "Where is my son?" she demanded and would have clawed him if Roarke hadn't put his hand on her shoulder just then.

Alistar walked closer, a spine-stiff stride born of breeding. "Our son," he corrected, leveling a pistol.

"You cannot claim him, Alistar, not when you never even held him, spoke to him."

"What was the point, when he could not answer back?"

His expression blamed her, and Willa's temper went white-hot. She'd wed herself to a complete and utter fool. "I swear, Alistar, if he's harmed, I will—"

He laughed, softly, elegantly. "What could you possibly do to me?"

Her eyes glittered like fractured glass. *"Kill you,"* she said with deadly intent, her hand closing over her pistol stock. She took satisfaction in seeing him pale a little and his features slacken. An instant later, his look was a formidable mask.

The men with the digger's cart scrambled up the driver's seat, snapped the reins, and rode off, spinning dust in their wake.

Alistar watched them for a moment before his gaze flashed to Roarke, then back to Willa. "Is this your lover?"

Willa glanced at Roarke, and when his hand shifted to his weapon, she shook her head ever so slightly. Alistar had Mason, and if he died in a gun battle, she'd never find her child. She looked at her husband. "I abide by my vows, Alistar. Which is naught to say of the trail of whores you've left behind."

He shrugged. "Such is a man's right."

She flushed with outrage.

"Calm yourself, Willa," Roarke said from behind.

"I hate him."

"I think he knows that."

"You need to get away. I do not doubt he would kill you to get to me."

"I can take care of myself," Roarke assured her.

She looked up at him, tears of anger filling her beautiful eyes. "I know."

A shot fired at her feet, and an instant later, Roarke put himself between her and her husband, leveling his pistol. "Careful, your lordship."

"Give me my wife."

"She does not wish to go with you."

"Who the bloody hell are you to interfere with a man and his wife!" Alistar's skin turned molten with outrage.

"I am her friend. I need no other reason."

"Don't do this, Roarke."

"Do you wish to go to him?"

"Nay, but—"

"Then hush, woman."

Were all Montegomery men so dictatorial? she wondered fleetingly, clutching his coat. "He is devious. Have a caution."

"Come. *Now,* Willa," Alistar demanded, his hand out.

She peered around Roarke. "Are you mad?"

His smile was thin with impatience. "Do you want to see your son?"

Inside, Willa crumbled. He knew exactly the marks to hit and wound her the deepest. She moved around Roarke, but he put out his arm to stop her.

"I cannot let you leave with him," Roarke said, his gaze on Eastwick. "Great saints, Willa, Raiden will never forgive me if aught happened to you."

"You cannot stop me. This is my child, my flesh and blood, we speak of. I would go to the gates of hell with the devil himself if it meant finding Mason."

Roarke kept his gaze on Eastwick and his pair of lackeys. "That's exactly where you are going, madam."

"I beg you . . ." She swallowed heavily. "Ask Raiden to find it in his heart someday to forgive me."

"Shoot him," Alistar ordered and his man aimed.

A flash of light in the darkness, a crack of gunfire, and Willa jumped in reaction. Roarke flinched, his pistol shot firing in reflex and going wild.

Willa's eyes widened as blood blossomed on his chest like a fresh rose.

"Damn," he muttered and sank to his knees, the spent pistol slipping from his grasp.

"Oh, God, Roarke!" She pressed her hand to the wound,

kneeling and glaring at her husband. "Damn you, Alistar, that was not necessary!"

"He impedes my plans. Of course it was." Alistar handed the pistol over to his man and said, "Reload it," then strode to her. He grabbed her arm, yanking her to her feet.

"Roarke!"

"We will find you," he said, clutching his wound. His eyes were glassy, blood fountaining between his fingers.

"Nay, you will not," Alistar said, then looked at his men and flicked his head toward Roarke.

Willa understood completely. "Nay!" She fought him. "He is innocent in this—nay!"

But her husband was bigger and stronger, despite his elegant ways, and wrapping an arm around her waist, he dragged her from Roarke. "Have a little decorum, madam."

"Please do not do this, Alistar, I'm begging you."

Lord Eastwick paused, looking down at her. "Beg? Now there is a first occasion for that. What will you give for his life?"

"Name your price."

"Your own life? Your son's?"

She hesitated, and Alistar looked back at the wounded man. "Do forgive me. Priorities, you understand," he said to Roarke.

Willa screamed for him, scratching and clawing at Alistar's hold around her waist, her gaze never leaving Raiden's brother. Roarke managed to get to his feet just as the two men approached. Alistar quickened his pace, hauling her down the road and into the darkness. Still looking back, she could see no more than figures under the dim torchlight. A shot cracked into the silence, and her heart broke with it.

Roarke. Oh, Lord help him.

"I will see you dead, Alistar Peachwood." She reached for her pistol only to find it gone.

"Your threats are as empty as your pockets, and you have caused me quite enough trouble, wife." He threw her down on the road and glared. "Why didn't you stay where you belonged?" He advanced.

She scooted back on her behind. "You are a fool to even ask that."

"The boy is dead."

"Nay!" she howled and lurched to her feet, charging him.

Alistar sighed tiredly, then clipped her on the side of the head with the butt of his pistol. She dropped like a sack at his feet. He gazed down at her as he drew a handkerchief from his sleeve, snapped it out and wiped her blood from his wooden stock. God, what a troublesome woman.

Raiden stole a horse and rode through the small city, leaving human debris in his wake, battered and terrified. He bore a bloody slash across his stomach, a representation of a man daring to cross his path. He moved methodically, from tavern to inn, coming closer and closer to the wharf. To the one place he could be recognized. But he no longer cared. All he wanted was Willa safe and spitting fire at him again.

He stormed out of the last tavern and past a cart stacked with corpses. The stench of fresh death was unbearable, and Raiden quickened his pace, halting when he came upon a small cluster of British soldiers standing over a body sprawled in the street. His heart thundered as he swung from the saddle, pushing men out of his way, uncaring if he were spotted. He stared down at the lifeless form, instantly knew it was not her, yet he rolled the man onto his back.

The blank eyes of a dark-haired man stared up at him

"You know him?" a soldier asked, giving him a wide berth.

Raiden shook his head.

" 'Ad a bit of gold on him—sovereigns."

Raiden jerked a look at the solider, and the man stepped back. Gold. The local currency was usually East India Company script. "Was there aught else?"

Most just shrugged and looked away, moving off, and Raiden

surmised that the gold had already been distributed. The digger's cart rolled up aside the group, and as two men climbed tiredly down, the troops dispersed.

"This be five in one night. Ain't gots no more places to bury 'em," one griped.

Raiden grabbed him by the collar of his jacket. "Were any of the dead women?"

"Aye, one," the older of the two said.

Raiden's heart did a slow tumble in his chest, and he swallowed repeatedly. "Show me," he managed in a whisper.

Frowning, the diggers moved to the back of the cart and rolled a body over. Raiden's expression softened with relief as he looked upon the swollen face of the old woman. "Have you seen a lad, traveling alone?" He lifted his gaze to the scraggly-looking men. "A small fellow?" He did not want to alert anyone that a lush female lay beneath the boy's clothing.

The pair glanced between themselves, then to him. Raiden tossed a coin at each man. They snatched it midair. "We saw a lad with a big fella, size 'a you, I'd say."

"Aye, I'd say he was." The other frowned. "What you want with the boy?"

"What else did you see?"

"We didn't hang around when the others showed up."

Raiden questioned them, offered more coin, but the odd pair claimed innocence beyond accounting for three men, this dead man being one of them. He turned back to his horse, mounting and heading west. Was Barkmon here? Who had she encountered? Who had taken her to shore? And who were these "others" that left a body behind?

Yet, as the hours snailed along, the deeper his fear grew, dredging up horrible images no man had a right to envision. They fed his anxiety, his guilt, and he plowed through the crowds, grabbing up anyone remotely fitting her size and wearing like garments. Men dashed out of his path, and Raiden was unmindful of the commotion he stirred. He questioned dozens at the point of his sword, daring anyone to lie or taste their own blood. He rode to the farthest end of town, confronting natives and merchants, Portuguese and Dutch sailors. Silently, he admitted his wits were frayed, his emotions testing his control, and in a tavern, he grabbed an East India soldier by his coat lapels and brought him up to meet his face.

"A lad, small, green eyes. Have you seen him?"

Violently, the man shook his head, his eyes wide. Raiden poised the sword high, prepared to drive it through his throat. He completely ignored the pistols aimed at his back.

"I swear, guv! I ain't see no lad!"

"I did," a deep voice said from behind.

Raiden turned sharply, refusing to release the soldier, the motion knocking over tankards and a chair.

"Who speaks? Show yourself!"

A figure staggered into the dim, smoky light.

"Roarke." Raiden's gaze fell on the blood coloring the man's clothes to his knees and he thrust the soldier aside, then pushed through the patrons to his brother. Instantly he took his weight, slinging Roarke's uninjured arm across his shoulder.

"Hurry, man, we have to get to the sea." Roarke did his best to walk upright as Raiden cleared a path with his sword.

Outside, Raiden propped his brother against the nearest wall and examined his wound. "Sweet mother," he said. The shot went clean through.

" 'Tis not that bad." Roarke closed his eyes, willing the blood to cease flowing and give him the strength he needed.

"Aye, if you'd lie still. How long have you been walking about?"

Roarke shoved his hands away and took a halting step. "We have to get to the wharf." All he could remember was the look on Lord Eastwick's face as he dragged his wife into the dark. He was going to kill her. And enjoy it.

"Not now, man, you're no good like this."

Roarke staggered. "I promised." He grabbed his brother's shoulder, and despite the pain, dug his fingers in. "I promised her."

Raiden did not have to ask who; the look in Roarke's eyes told him more than he wanted. He swallowed heavily. "Oh, God. He found her, didn't he?"

Before Roarke could respond, his eyes rolled back in his head and he collapsed against his older brother.

In the corner of the cabin, Roarke lay in Raiden's bed, in a hot sweat, deathly still as a fever wracked his big body.

Across the room, his elbows propped on his desktop, Raiden sank his fingers into his hair and clutched his head. His thoughts raced between his brother and Willa, unable to find peace or watch Roarke suffer. The wound was poisoned with infection, the hole in his brother's shoulder festering quickly. Within hours, Roarke thrashed near death's door over a wound that should not have laid him so low. He could not bear the thought of losing Roarke as well as Willa.

Anguish riddled him like a living thing, pouring into his blood and making him stew in his own guilt. She'd trusted him to keep her safe, and he'd broken her trust because her vows had wiped away any dream of a future with her. Until she'd told him the truth, he'd never realized how much he'd desperately wanted one. Short, uncertain—dangerous—any way he could have her. God above, he'd been so furious. That he'd wanted to hurt her, wanted her to feel his loss when she at least had her son to hope on. He was truly unworthy of such a woman, he thought. He'd tried to make her see that, and apparently, he had finally succeeded.

He had to find her.

There was no question that he would interfere in the most grievous ways, hunt the bastard down, and take Willa back. If only to make things right with her, for her.

The longer they were apart the less chance he had of finding her. He'd gained no more information from Roarke other than that Lord Eastwick had taken her. By the rule, he should not interfere. Eastwick was her husband. Oh, the thought of that man touching her, taking his rights with her when she had given herself up to his touch, tore at Raiden. He lowered his hand and thrust back into the big chair. His gaze settled on the bank of slanted aft windows, and he remembered her sitting in the corner of the bench, her head tipped to the glass. It stung his soul to even conjure her image. But it came regardless, her defiance, her smiles, her biting wit—oh, God, her tears and tenderness when he was cruel and vulgar. No one dared lock horns with him as Willa did and Raiden's lips curved in a sad smile.

I miss her.

She'd been right about too many things. She knew him better than he knew himself. Just as she knew that Eastwick was hunting her, and somehow tied up with Dunfee. His association with Barkmon was a given, yet he would not have meshed the three men together until he'd had some proof. And it came in Willa. She'd been right about the man-of-war guarding the straits, and the armada of vessels littering the harbor. The *Queen's Regard* was to be in Malacca, but Willa suspected it was the *Yorkshire* that sailed with Dunfee at the helm. But Raiden had to consider that since Barkmon had been following her, her information, some of it at least, was falsely given.

Raiden shifted his gaze to his brother. He could not stand being idle and shoved out of the chair, then moved to the door. He flung it open and shouted for Balthasar. Jabari, who'd been punished for disobeying an order, arrived first, his head hanging low.

"Remain with him till the Arab arrives." Jabari tipped his head back, and Raiden's heart sank at the rare tears in his dark eyes. He squatted, eye level with the lad. "Did she ask you to set her free?"

Jabari shook his head.

"Speak, son, I cannot hear your brains rattle."

"No sir. I just . . . just thought it was unfair and too hot and you should not have made her cry!" came in a powerful rush.

The corner of his mouth quirked. "I see that now, boy."

Jabari held his gaze. "You will find her, yes?"

"I will try." Raiden straightened.

"You must do better than that, Captain," the child commanded, his tone still colored with anger. "She is your lady."

My lady. Raiden closed his eyes, the muscles around his heart clamping down like an invisible fist. He would not wish for what could never be. He could not. Expecting more only meant he would be hurt later. As if he was not in agony now, so shamed by his actions. Yet in the recesses of his heart, bruised and battle-worn, he dared hunger for more, and wondered, if he did, would he find the same fate he'd tasted over a dozen years before? Would he again know love and lose it in the most heinous ways?

He bowed his head, gripping the door frame. This time he knew he would never survive.

Balthasar's approach stirred him from his thoughts, the sound of his voice in the quiet making him flinch.

"Captain?" Looking inside the cabin, he frowned at Roarke, then returned his gaze to Raiden's. "I am going to open it again, like Lady Eastwick did." He hefted a tray laden with supplies to change the dressing. "It is the same, I think. Something is not right in there."

Raiden nodded. "I will be above decks. Send for me if there is any change." He stole one last look at his younger brother and headed to the brig.

Raiden didn't bother to look at the men in chains, the small cell keeping them in the dankness of the hull.

"We didn't know she was in the boat, Cap'n."

" 'Tis the only way she could have escaped," Raiden said, his hands locked at the small of his back as he paced the small corridor before the cell.

"Unless she's shark fodder," Cheston said.

Raiden stilled, his gaze sharpening on the snickering man. "Captain Killgaren attests that she made land. That means someone went ashore, without permission, leaving the *Rene-*

gade unguarded.'' He continued to pace, his stride slow, methodical, and though he knew it unnerved the prisoners, that was his intention, and it calmed the storm of emotion raging inside him.

''There was plenty men aboard,'' Vazeen said.

Raiden stopped, his head whipping to the side. His gaze cut into the men like shaved ice. ''You disobeyed direct orders!''

The five men paled. It meant a whipping at the least, and marooning at best.

''You will remain here on bread and water until I and the rest of the crew can gather testimony and decide your fate.'' They sank deeper into the flooring, aware their time was limited. ''If Captain Killgaren dies, I will hold you responsible.''

''Why? Wot we to do with that,'' Dobbs snarled.

''If you had not stolen the longboat and gone ashore, risking detection, by the by, Lady Eastwick would have had no way to get to shore. Captain Killgaren would not have had to defend her and possibly lose his life.'' Raiden headed to the ladder, pausing briefly to add, ''And if his life is lost, there will be no mercy.''

Raiden climbed the ladder, praying Roarke survived, and praying for information, the piece he knew was missing from the puzzle that would lead them to Willa. He wished he could form a plan beyond sending Tristan to captain the *Sea Warrior* and order the other ships far from the straits and the south bay, away from the heavily guarded port. But without a lead to take, he would never find Willa in the Banda Islands.

His steps faltered on his way to above decks. God above, what would become of her? In Peachwood's hands, he could sell her, trade her, kill her with a tiny dab of poison, and no one would question him. Raiden's urgency drove him to take the ladders in one hike. Sailors backed out of his way, flattening against the wall to let him pass. He was used to doing things his way, and now he had to rely on God, Balthasar's healings, and Roarke's will to survive.

His brother, his only family, was his single greatest hope of ever finding Willa.

Eighteen

Roarke felt movement, someone touching him, and he opened his eyes. His gaze fell first on Balthasar tying off the bandage on a fresh dressing, then shifted to his brother, slumped in a chair, his feet propped on the foot of the bed.

Even sleeping, Raiden looked incredibly weary, his hair untied and looking as if he'd run his fingers through it a hundred times. He called to him and Raiden flinched, blinking like a sleepy child, then pulled his feet from the bed.

"You look better," he said, coming to his feet.

"You look like bloody hell."

Raiden shoved his hair back and started to tuck in his shirttail, then gave up.

Roarke inclined his head to the Arab. "You allowed this tattooed barbarian to cut on me?"

Balthasar snickered, hiding a smile. "This barbarian saved your stupid Irish hide . . . sir," he added when Roarke arched a brow.

Finished, Balthasar helped him sit up, but Roarke waved him off. "God, you'll be killin' me with your tenderness, man."

Balthasar straightened indignantly.

"You always were a better fighter than a nursemaid."

The Bedouin gathered his things. "I'll bring you something to eat. Perhaps it will keep your mouth occupied before I cut out your tongue, infidel."

Roarke sent him a sideways look. "Great Erin, I hope you are a better cook then."

"He is the best I have."

Roarke's gaze flew to his brother's. "The best you had, Raiden, you let go."

The man stiffened, his expression suddenly as sharp as glass.

Roarke remained silent until Balthasar left them alone. "There were three men. She has only her blade for protection because after I was shot, I took her gun."

"Damn you, Killgaren. How could you leave her so defenseless!"

Roarke sneered at him. "They would have stripped her of her weapons in any case, and if I hadn't taken it, I would be dead and we could not find her now, Captain. My shot went wild and there were two men."

"One is dead."

The flash of a grin said Roarke knew that. "And the other is gravely wounded," he assured. "Now . . . I will do you this one favor—"

Raiden frowned. "Your favors are becoming infamous, Killgaren. Why do you do it?"

"I have my reasons."

His expression clouded, reminding Raiden that he might have served with Killgaren for three years now, but there was much still he did not know about the man and his motives.

"And I expect them to be repaid," Roarke replied, a cynical twist to his lips. "At my discretion."

Raiden folded his arms over his chest and regarded him. "So, what is this favor you ask of me?"

"Not *of* you, really. One I will grant you."

Arrogant cub, Raiden thought. "I need no favors from you."

''Really? Then I've your permission to court Lady Eastwick once you've found her?''

Raiden's expression turned molten with slow anger.

''I thought not. So . . . I will forego pursuing Lady Eastwick, which I would thoroughly adore doing, mind you.''

His implication was like a knife in his ribs. ''Did she invite your . . . suit?''

Roarke's ice-blue eyes narrowed, hard and frosty. ''I would not dare assume without first speaking to you. I am a man of honor.''

Raiden scoffed. ''Amongst thieves?''

Roarke smiled with tender humor. ''Nay, amongst brothers.''

Raiden sank slowly into the nearest chair, stunned. ''How long have you known?''

''Years. Since you and I were boys. Father told me.''

''So you've spent time with the bastard.''

''Bastard no, time aye. He's not such a bad sort, you know.''

''Really? Did he marry *your* mother?''

''Nay, nor did he love her for long. He loves Sayidda.''

Raiden frowned.

''Ransom's mother.''

''I am thrilled for him,'' he said dryly.

Roarke ignored that. ''He has always loved her most, but then, have you not loved two women at the same time?''

''Nay. I have not.''

''Pity.''

''What has this to do with Willa?'' Raiden ground between clenched teeth.

''Naught at all. I just like seeing you squirm.''

Raiden shot him an indignant look. ''I do not squirm.''

''Nor do you see what you have till it is gone.''

Raiden looked to argue, then released a long pent-up sigh. ''Aye.'' He stared at the floor, rubbing his face with both hands and silently admitting that he felt brutally incomplete without her. ''I beg you, brother,'' Raiden said softly, pleadingly. ''Give me a crumb to appease this torment.''

Roarke's features slackened with sympathy. "She was alive when he took her," he said, knowing it was not enough to soothe his brother's anxiety. "And there was something about Lord Eastwick that gave me great concern."

Lowering his hands, Raiden met his gaze. "Other than he ordered you slaughtered?"

Killgaren sent him a look that said the man would pay dearly for that. " 'Twas his eyes, the color of his skin."

"He is ill, mayhap?" Raiden hoped the man was crusted over with lesions and withered like a leper.

Roarke shook his head. "He did not act ill, nor was he staggering, his speech impeccable. But his skin looked . . . I don't know . . . almost transparent."

"Had you seen the man ever before now?"

"Nay."

"Mayhap 'twas just his usual appearance."

Roarke nodded, as if agreeing, but Raiden could see he didn't. "How did she get to shore?"

Shoving out of the chair, Raiden told him, his anger building with each word. "She's a fool to risk her life like this." *And 'tis my fault,* Raiden thought, *mine.*

Killgaren tipped his head back on the pillows, studying his brother. "She'd decided to return to you before we met Eastwick."

Raiden whirled, his brittle gaze pinning him.

"She wanted to get back afore you found her missing," Roarke added.

"Why?" He had to ask, though he worried over the answer.

"She wanted her freedom. She had it."

Roarke looked at his brother and decided he was a simpleton if he could not see the truth. "She wanted you more."

Raiden's legs folded beneath him, and he sagged against the ward table. *She was coming back. To him.* What made her change her mind after the dangers to get ashore? Why would she want to return to his cabin and captivity? Especially after the way he'd treated her. Oh, God, the things he'd said to her.

Sighing hard, he pinched the bridge of his nose, and when he looked up, Roarke was staring at him with an odd little smile.

Raiden sent him a speculative look and arched a brow.

"I'm savoring the moment," Roarke said. "I've watched you for years, invincible, bullying your way across the seas to be, by far, the richest, most feared pirate afloat. To see a simple gesture from a woman make you crumble is not something I shall enjoy again."

Raiden straightened. "Repeat that and I will have you flogged."

A slow grin spread across Killgaren's face. "You just try, old man."

"Old? By God, you impudent whelp—"

Roarke laughed, softly and to himself. "Ah, 'tis nice to have a brother."

That brought Raiden up short, and he stared at Killgaren, wondering why he'd thought to keep their relationship from him. Then realized his concern was not for his Irish brother, but for himself, the distance keeping the emotions at arm's length. It had not mattered, Raiden thought, for seeing him so badly wounded had nearly driven him mad with worry.

"Aye, it is," he said, then cleared his throat. "This is a discussion that will keep till later. You wanted to get to the wharf—why?"

"I heard the men say they were in a hurry to kill me, so they could get back to the *Persephone* afore she sailed."

Raiden cursed, grabbed up his charting equipment and maps, then spread them on the ward table. "The *Persephone* was in the Syriam harbor. No wonder Barkmon was there. He was aboard."

"Was Eastwick with him then, you think?"

" 'Tis very possible, but I think that Barkmon was meeting him somewhere. And Willa encountering him was more chance than aught." His fingertip swept over the thin hide map, pausing here and there.

Roarke struggled to sit up, then swung his legs over the side of the bed.

Raiden glanced. "Should you be doing that?"

Roarke's expression said that even if he wasn't, he wouldn't be stopped. His brain felt like mush and his legs trembled. God, he hated this.

"How long have I been here?" Roarke asked.

"Nearly three days."

Roarke stood, gripping the bedside table when his vision shifted. "We have to hurry then. He could be taking her anywhere."

"I will see this done."

Roarke scoffed. "Since when have you gone into battle without me to watch your back, brother?"

Raiden smiled slightly.

"Who is sailing my ship?" Killgaren asked.

"You mean *my* ship."

"Now you are talking the difference atween apples and applesauce."

Raiden's blood seized in his veins and his throat filled with a hard knot. Willa had said exactly that, and with the words came the memory of living with her in the jungle, how she rose to the dangerous occasion, and how gloriously warm and right she felt tucked in his arms. "You are right. I give the *Sea Warrior* to you."

"I beg your pardon?"

Raiden looked up and smiled at the shock painted over Roarke's face. "She's yours. Sink her, sail her, sell her. I do not care."

"My thanks, but why?"

Raiden returned his gaze to the maps. "Because, little brother, you will need something to start your new life."

Roarke's spine stiffened. "I like my life just fine."

"A brother of mine is not going to be a pirate when he has the brains for more."

Belligerence lit Roarke's features. "Ever since we met, you have tried to tell me what to do."

"That is because I am older and wiser." He lifted his gaze from the maps. "And I want you to live for a long time after I am gone."

Gone. Merciful lord, Roarke thought, his lips tightening with understanding. "You are going after this Admiral Dunfee, and you are willing to die to take him out of this world!" Raiden's silence was more confirming than spoken words. "What of Willa?"

"I will find her and her son and I will—"

"Leave her a widow or make her your wife?"

"Never my wife. She will not bear the shame I have."

"The shame of being born a bastard is not yours. The sum of living as one is. And there is no virtue in making her your damned whore! What pride is there in that? Do you not care enough for her to give her your name?"

Raiden stared at his brother, itching to throttle him. "Of course I care!"

"Horse shit." Roarke flicked a hand. "If you did, you would not do the lady such a grave disservice. Do you want another Montegomery toddling around without a father, a name?" Roarke took hope in the tension flexing Raiden's shoulders, but when the silence lengthened, his own temper rose. "Your caring ends with this vengeance you hold for Dunfee, and you enjoy being a bastard when I am proof that it has never altered my life! Because I *chose* not to allow it. You have let it make a difference and 'tis your failing."

Raiden glared at him. "My concerns with Dunfee are not yours, and you have no notion of the life I led afore our meeting."

"Because you refuse to share it or any part of yourself. I met Willa only once, Raiden, and I know she will not tolerate having half a man!"

Raiden's fingers curled into fists. "You cross the line, *brother.*"

Roarke ignored the threat. "Do you like living so isolated?"

"I am a hunted man and I would see you out of this afore your head ends on a pike."

The redirection of purpose did not escape Roarke. "I can take care of my own bloody damn head, Montegomery."

Raiden sighed. He did not want to get into a battle of wills with Roarke, not now. "I know you can," he said softly. "I am alive still because you have seen to my back. Now, come over here and look at these maps. We must figure out where to look first."

"You think her husband will kill her, don't you?"

Not looking up, Raiden's fingers flexed on the protractor till he almost bowed the metal. "If all Willa has told me thus far is true, aye. He will take her life. She knows too much that would destroy him." Slowly he tipped his head back to meet Roarke's gaze. "And he will enjoy it."

His eyes burned and he looked away. But the images came, of her being mistreated, beaten, starved, and worse, left for the pleasure of a ship's crew. A hard shudder wracked his body. The graphite snapped in his grip. He knew he'd be useless to her if he did not regain control. He focused on the maps spread beneath his palms, studying the tiny islands scattered across the East Indies like stars in the sky. The odds seemed hopeless.

I will find you, love. I swear on my soul, I will.

Raiden had one advantage. He'd grown into a man on these islands, held his own fortress on the back coast of Java, undetected for years. And the English, no matter the cause, were impatient bastards when it came to dealing with the tribal kings and sultanates. After all these years, they understood little of ancient ceremony and protocol when dealing with the savages of Ceram and Banda.

They only wanted control of the spices.

And, Raiden knew, it would be their undoing.

* * *

" 'Tis not Balthasar."

Looking through his spyglass as the *Renegade* cut through the sea with a vengeance, Raiden cast Roarke a side glance. "You sound certain."

"Aye. The Arab would rather die than betray you or me."

"He knows we are brothers." It was more statement than question.

Sitting on the bench on the quarterdeck, Roarke nodded, his back braced on the aft railing. "You must look to the source. Who would benefit greatly from seeing us all hang? Any pirate could either fade away or take a bargain with the British, but most would still see inside a prison and go to trial regardless of offering any one of us up on a platter."

"Some have been made governors."

Roarke threw him an irritated look. "Morgan does not count. 'Twas nearly a hundred years ago, and he was affluent to start." Roarke waved that off. "All a matter of timing."

"I see your point, though." Raiden snapped the glass closed. "Perth is the newest member of the crew."

"And the oldest, I see," he said staring at the bearded old man as he climbed the rigging with an agility that surprised him. But then, Raiden would not have a crewman aboard who did not carry his duties.

"Feel free to question the six in the brig."

Roarke leaned forward to stand, favoring his side. Raiden reached for him, but Roarke shot him a look that made him freeze. "I am fine," he said, then groaned as pain lanced his shoulder.

"But I am indebted to you, Killgaren."

Roarke grinned, a debonair flash of white teeth. "Indeed? I shall have to consider how to take advantage of that."

Raiden smiled for the first time in days, then watched as Balthasar helped him down the ladder. His gaze shifted to Kahlid, and as if he could feel his captain's his eyes on him, the tall Moor twisted to look over his shoulder. The man frowned, then turned his attention to the sea ahead.

Raiden paced, tapping the spyglass against his thigh, trying desperately to focus on the situation and not his woman. His woman. *You dream, man,* he thought. She was still wed, and he knew Willa would not consent to an affair with him. Her abstinence and bargaining was proof of that. Nor did he want to think on bringing about Lord Eastwick's death, for the tormenting thoughts plaguing him now were enough to push him to kill the man.

But none of that meant a thing without her in his life. He wanted only to look upon her face again.

"Kahlid, assemble the men."

The Moor turned his duties over to a midshipman, then yelled "Avast!" and every man aboard froze.

Raiden waited impatiently as the crew of pirates assembled on the lower deck and then said, "I am going after Lady Eastwick. Those of you who do not wish to join me can board another ship. But I am going."

"Where?" someone shouted.

"To Ceram and the Banda Islands."

An odd silence grew, then there was talk, a few bowed heads as they considered their options.

"There be a prize?"

Raiden thought for a moment. "Only my gratitude." The men grumbled sourly. "I will likely have to pay all I have to get her back." A pause, and then he added, "Of course, we should encounter several ships laden with spice." He let his tone trail, hoping to entice their help. "Take what you will."

Perth was the first to speak up. "I'll join you, Cap'n."

Raiden met his gaze, wondering if a trap lay ahead.

Dozens followed, a muttered, "What else we got to do," and "I'd like me own East Indianman," added before the crew agreed as one.

Raiden nodded, pleased, and hoped he wasn't stabbed in the back for this bit of trust.

                              *   *   *

Roarke Killgaren leaned against the hull, inhaling the scent of cinnamon and cardamom, ginger and nutmeg. It was a harvest for the senses, with the exception of the stench radiating from the prisoners. Vazeen glared at him, his turban gone, his hair matted; Riggs, Santosh, and Cheston glared at each other. The Dutchman, Van Pool, looked patient and innocent while Dobbs sulked like a child. Their treatment was proof of Raiden's anger.

"Would you like to be free of this place?" Roarke said into the silence.

The men eyed him warily.

"I will free you."

"If?" Cheston said, glancing at his fellow inmates.

"If you join me in mounting a mutiny."

"Why?" Vazeen ventured, his expression neither agreeing nor denying the prospect.

"I am tired of pirating in the Black Angel's shadow."

The *Renegade* sailed beyond the equator and around the southern coast of Sumatra, cutting through the narrow Sunda Straits between Sumatra and the western tip of Java. The British ships never traveled this route, for they knew little of its existence, its depth at low tide, the rocky bottom. But the passage was familiar to Raiden, as familiar as his own voice, and he maneuvered the ship through the pass and sailed into the Macassar Straits. For days they rode the torrential seas past Borneo, the north coast of Java, Bali, Lombok, and the island of Celebes. The crew kept a vigilant watch for the native *prahas,* small, flat-bottomed boats, and the *kora-kora*, ten-ton outrigger war canoes, that were manned by a hundred warriors and that could move swifter than anything and attack with sudden and deadly accuracy.

Raiden had witnessed such a slaughter once too often to be carefree now. The closer they drew to the Banda Sea and the Spice Islands, the stronger the danger. France warred on England. England warred with any vessel they suspected would impede their monopoly on the trade. And lingering like maggots waiting to feed off the dead were Dutch schooners, unsanctioned by their country and daring to be near these waters after the slaughter of Ambon. Portuguese brigs and galleons passed them, unharmed, one offering a single-shot salute for their daring. Any captain worth his skill knew there were far more deadly adversaries to come.

Roarke stopped beside him and drew a deep breath. "By God, the air reeks of spice," he said. "I've never been this close."

"And you never will again."

Roarke arched a brow, studying him. "I beg your pardon?"

"Trust me when I say this is more danger than you could put in a single nightmare."

"You're afraid."

"Of dying afore I wish, aye." He slanted Roarke a glance "And so should you be."

Roarke simply rocked on his heels and said, "You worry overmuch."

Raiden scoffed. "I have earned the right, believe me. A hundred miles beyond lies Ceram"—he nodded to the blue water—"the very heartbeat of the Spice Islands. Naught is traded there that is not worth ten times the price in England or the colonies. And of all these islands, it possesses a natural deepwater harbor in the east and covelike inlets that nearly cut the land in two and leave it capable of secluding entire fleets."

Roarke's dark brows drew tight. "Fleets? How can they not be seen?"

"The jungle, little brother, is so thick that it once dulled my sword to useless. And within striking distance lie Ternate and Tidore in the north, an island spilling with clove."

"Banda is to the south?"

"Almost like my home in Java, 'tis a damned perfect fortress.'' He looked at Roarke, frowning at the bloodstain on his shoulder.

"I opened it, climbing," he said.

"Have Balthasar look at it."

"I am fine."

Raiden's lips quirked. "Take Mr. Dysart's cabin. I will call you when there is something to offer. Or when we can get you back to the *Warrior*."

Roarke nodded and turned toward the cabin. Raiden frowned at his back, then returned his gaze to the bright blue waters. He'd not sailed here in a few years, preferring to take ships after they left the straits beyond the Malay Peninsula. Although his home lay on the jungle side of Java, he knew he would not see it for a while. Not till he had Willa and, God willing, Mason with him. He hoped she'd taken the vials of quinine. He'd forced her to before she escaped, and though only one vial was missing, he prayed disease had not quickened in her.

The monsoons followed them, the hot-licking wind and rain virtually taking any ship daring to cross the corridors leading to the spices and sending it to Davey Jones. 'Twas the singular reason most explorers never returned from their search for the spices. The islands were clustered and confusing. One could walk ashore and be greeted like a king, or encounter savages so cunning and deadly, you didn't dare breathe, waiting for the poisoned dart that would kill a man in seconds.

Or you could be eaten alive at a feast for the dead.

He was much younger than Roarke when he'd made the mistake of sailing to one of those untouched islands and was served a death sentence in a dirt pit for a over a year, beaten, cooked in his own skin by the sun and tossed scraps like an animal. He'd never known ungodly fear until then. Oh, his life had been filled with experiences that took him near his death or starvation, but nothing had prepared him for the horrors of the savages he found there. But it was the customs and traditions he'd learned years ago, after his release, that he prayed would save Willa now.

"Avast," the crow shouted and Raiden whipped around. The lad pointed to the east. "Ship to leeward, Captain!"

Raiden ran to amidships, climbing the rigging, then grabbing a rope and swinging to the cross jack. He snapped out the spyglass and sighted on the ship.

"She flies England's Jack! Full sail, Mr. Perth. Let's give her a scare and climb up her arse."

"Aye, aye, Cap'n," Nealy shouted, ordering the bonnet unfurled. The extra sail would take them faster. The wind filled the canvas with a snap. "Release the bowline!"

Raiden grabbed the line, letting it unfurl and lower him to the deck, his feet hitting hard.

"Gun ports open, sir?" Perth called, and Raiden glanced back.

"Nay, but all hands make ready! Arm every cannon. But do not fire. Lady Eastwick could be aboard."

Raiden strode to the fo'c'sle, wanting a first look. He sighted through the glass, and a slow grin bowed his lips.

The *Persephone.*

Damn, if Willa hadn't been right on the mark.

When he boarded the vessel, he planned to beat information out of Barkmon.

And then again, mayhaps he'd show him mercy and feed him to the sharks.

Raiden lowered the spyglass.

Nay.

No mercy.

No quarter.

Nineteen

The Black Angel. God help them all, Barkmon thought, as the specter of sinister evil ghosted over the rough seas, drawing nearer with incredible speed.

The first blast had come out of the darkness like the smiting hand of God, leveling the deck with such precision that the crew had been spared, yet Barkmon wished God would take him now before the pirates boarded them. No such peace came. The second volley hit the captain in the middle of giving a command and sent bloody bits of him and two of his officers swirling into oblivion. Without the captain's stern hand, the crew would surrender. Especially when the crew of their sister ship had fled like cowards at the first sign of trouble, damn the sorry lot.

Barkmon looked about for an escape, a place to hide this out, but lost valuable time as the black pirate ship swiftly drew abreast of them, grappling hooks whirling through the air to catch on the *Persephone*'s rail, planks lowering. They offered no quarter, made little sound. Swinging from ropes and racing across planks, they came like a swarm of bees over the side of the ship. He backed against a wall, then turned toward the passageway. Let the bastards have the damned ship.

A hand on his shoulder stopped him, and he flinched around to find the largest, strangest-looking man he'd ever encountered. A Moor.

"My captain wishes a word with you."

Barkmon gaped at the dark-skinned man, tattoos dotting his temples and chest. He held a long curved sword that looked too heavy to be brandished so lightly. He forced Barkmon ahead and he went obediently, walking farther out onto the main deck, stepping over debris. The Moor shoved him and he stumbled, catching himself on the rail. He looked up and his eyes rounded as a man swung from a rope over shark-infested waters to land with a thump before him.

Instantly the point of a sword swept beneath his chin.

Barkmon swallowed, damning God for not letting him die in the first blast and cursing himself for underestimating the threat of pirates. The man, clad in black leather with wild, dark hair, was huge—and familiar. He was the same man he'd seen in Syriam, holding Lady Eastwick captive.

"Where is she?"

Barkmon licked his lips. "I am not privy to Lady Eastwick's comings and goings."

The pirate inclined his head, and several men headed into the passageway. "Bring me the ship's log. Search every inch." He smiled thinly down at Barkmon. "And rape her clean." Then he slapped a hand to Barkmon's chest and hauled him up to his face. "I will ask once more—where is she?"

"He—he will kill me if I impart a thing."

"I will kill you if you do not." His sword pricked his throat and Barkmon felt the burn, then a trickle of blood. "I am out of patience, English. Is she aboard?"

Barkmon shook his head. By the rod, Lord Eastwick would carve him down to the bone if he revealed anything.

"Speak, Barkmon, or I hand you over to the Moor."

Barkmon's gaze shifted to the tattooed man, and the Moor

sent him a slow, menacing smile that promised hours of torture. Barkmon felt his insides roll and churn with fear. Damn if he was going to pay for the Crusaders invading his country five hundred years ago now. "He mentioned," Barkmon stalled, knowing when he uttered the words, his life was done. "He's at Fort George. The—the old castle. But I have not seen his wife, I swear."

"Your oath is worthless." The pirate's black eyes, like dead pools, searched his. "Why does he take her there?"

"He didn't take her, he sold her. To a sultanate or a prince."

The Black Angel's grip on his coat tightened till his fingers went bloodless white and his knuckles cracked. "The boy, where is the boy?"

Barkmon frowned. "What boy?"

The pirate's sword sliced his throat a little more.

"I swear, there is no child!"

The pirate's brows knitted. "If Eastwick could take the life of his wife and his child, what, Director, do you think he will do to you?"

Barkmon's knees weakened beneath him, and with a shove and a sound of disgust, the pirate sent him hurling back against the passageway wall. Barkmon didn't dare move, and as men opened the fo'c'sle hatch and the midship grate, hauling out kegs and crates, he knew he'd be blamed for this. Eastwick would hunt him down, ruin his reputation, and come out smelling like his lady's linens. As keg after keg was transferred to the pirate vessel, Barkmon saw his life ending.

Especially when they discovered exactly what was inside the small barrels.

Raiden flipped through the logbook, reading quickly and assessing where this ship was headed, and comparing his conclusions to Barkmon's words.

"Captain?"

Raiden looked up in time to see Barkmon run to the rail and pitch himself over the side.

"Man over board!"

"Get him out of there, for the love of God." Raiden handed the log over to Kahlid and stepped to the rail, peering down. Barkmon, apparently, could not swim. "Come now, man, grab on," Raiden shouted, pointing to the rope within reach.

Obviously having a change of heart, Barkmon reached for the rope, then suddenly went stiff, his pudgy face masked in horror, a scream frozen on his lips before he abruptly vanished beneath the surface. He never reappeared. Yet the distinct shape of a fin pierced the water before gliding effortlessly away with its prize.

"Damn." Raiden slammed his fist against the rail, then turned toward the captain's quarters. He searched the room; then, with maps tucked inside his vest, he swung back aboard the *Renegade*.

"Very well done, Captain. With the exception of Barkmon, of course."

He shot an irritated look at Roarke. "That idiot must have more at stake than we first thought. Apparently Eastwick scares him more than I do."

Roarke's gaze lit on the sleeveless leather vest exposing his massive arms, then to the array of weapons that would make any man run and hide. "I find that hard to believe."

Raiden smirked. "The *Sea Warrior* is ready for your command." He nodded behind them, to the vessel sweeping near.

Roarke didn't bother to look and only nodded before his gaze scanned the decks, the overflowing prizes being lowered into the hull. "You are richer than ever."

Raiden's brows furrowed and he cast him a glance. "I take no share of this prize."

Roarke flashed him a grin. "I didn't think so." He stepped close, his voice low. "I don't believe your betrayer is in the brig."

Raiden reared back a bit. The sharp sting of betrayal worked through his thoughts, and his gaze shot to the open decks. "How are you so certain?"

''I asked the men in the brig if they wanted to mutiny with me, and they all nearly killed themselves to get at me.''

''That was foolish.''

Roarke shrugged, sheepish. '' 'Twas the only thing I could think of at the moment.''

''They will not trust you now, for simply suggesting it.''

''Aye, but I had to know.'' Roarke looked away, then back at his brother. ''And what of *your* trust?''

''Blood has its worth, Killgaren.'' He gave his uninjured shoulder a gentle squeeze. ''And blood I can trust.''

Roarke smiled, relieved beyond words. ''Take your ship and do as you will. Sail away with the crew or alone.''

''You think I am done pirating simply because you wish it?''

''I see that you do not enjoy life.''

''And you do?''

Raiden looked out over the vessel as the last of the cargo was loaded, then to the *Persephone,* cut loose with its crew alive. The men cheered and waved, and Raiden shook his head ruefully. It never ceased to amaze him how quickly pressed sailors could turn on England.

''Do you?'' Roarke prodded.

''Aye,'' he said easily. ''I have more wealth than any man could spend in a lifetime.''

''But you do not expect to live a lifetime.''

''My expectations and the hard truth are thoughts I've battled with since meeting Willa.''

''Then give it up, this vengeance.''

''I cannot. Either way I will not have peace till Dunfee joins Barkmon.''

Roarke sighed. ''You will have to make the choice, I think. And someday you will tell me why Right Admiral Dunfee enrages you so.''

Raiden's features hardened with pain. ''Mayhaps.''

The Moor approached, calling for Roarke. The brothers shook hands, and Roarke departed.

Raiden watched him, saw him pause and stare at Perth for a long moment, then swing over to the *Sea Warrior* with the help of Balthasar. Raiden swore the Arab was more devoted to his brother than to him. As Tristan returned to the *Renegade,* Raiden turned his gaze to the damaged ship, watching as the *Persephone*'s fire glow finally died, leaving a white smoke trail as the crew took charge. A new breed of pirates, he thought, then looked back at the *Sea Warrior.* He exchanged a salute with Roarke, then turned toward his cabin. In the passageway he stopped a sailor, ordering the brig prisoners released. They had disobeyed orders and would be fined with the crew's consent.

Inside his cabin, he tossed the maps onto the ward table and went immediately to his cabinets, unlocking one and withdrawing a heavy glass decanter and a glass. He poured, tossed back the rum in one swallow, then poured another, replaced the decanter and moved to his deck. He sat, propping his boots on the surface. He stared at the glass for long moments, thinking on Roarke's words and trying not to imagine Willa a prisoner to a sultan. The prince would make sport of her. Her life was meaningless, of no more value than a beast for the roasting.

He hoped Barkmon had been wrong, because killing the man was the only thing that would appease the lie. And the coward had taken that from him. He lifted his head, his gaze settling on the corner spot of the aft window bench, her spot, and he saw her curled to the side, her head bowed, her hair spilling down to nearly touch the floor. His heart contracted, muscles squeezing, and he gulped the spiced rum, remembering her smile and how her accent grew prominent when she was drunk. How deeply she kissed. How easily she climbed under his skin. How much he missed her. Dropping his feet to the floor, he pushed out of his chair and went to the bench, settling there, his hand smoothing over the cushions. He shifted around, his back braced on the wall, and stared through the long bank of windows. No wonder she liked this spot, he thought. It was as if he were the only person in the universe, the sea beyond the windows like an endless sheet of black glass. He leaned forward to stand and heard a sound, a crackling. Immediately he twisted and shoved his hand into the corner of the cushions.

His heart pounded as he withdrew a piece of folded parchment—addressed to him. He set his glass aside and opened it. His gaze swept the fluid script, his heart racing when he thought of when she'd written this.

Raiden,
*   How difficult it is to speak to you even through quill and ink. Ah, well, pirate, I'd hoped you could forgive me for lying, but I cannot bear to look at you and know you hate me so. My heart breaks when I think of how much time I've wasted in this life, and the chances I've missed. Had we met at a different time, Raiden, do you think we could have found a life together? For I will tell you honestly, love, your wicked heart possesses mine.*

Oh, God. Raiden blinked, his fingers crunching the parchment. He absorbed every word, every letter like a man starved for the sun.

I ask one last favor of you, my pirate. Enclosed are the papers I'd shown you earlier. Use them as you see fit, for I suspect that by the time you find this, I will be dead. Do me this little bit of justice, Raiden. Find my child, and take him back to his grandfather.

Raiden swallowed repeatedly and pinched the bridge of his nose, struggling for a clean breath. She was not dead, he thought, adding prayer after prayer to a God who'd forsaken him years ago. He blinked to clear his vision and looked down at the letter, folding it neatly and pushing it inside his vest. Then he studied the papers. There was a third sheet, her writing prominent once more.

I have my suspicions as to who has betrayed you all these weeks. Be patient and let me explain why I believe he would do such a thing. . . .

Raiden read it once, twice, then stood and walked to the lantern, igniting the paper. He watched it burn for a moment, then slid back an aft window and hurled the remains into the sea. Angrily he slammed the window shut.

Did she always have to be right?

"You are absolutely mad."

Raiden stood on the main deck, his hands braced behind his back. "I saw no other way."

"Firing a few rounds, blowing up the ramparts of the antique fort didn't occur?"

"Willa could be in there. And look around us, Dysart. We are in the den of snakes."

Tristan agreed.

French, Dutch, Portuguese, and English East India ships populated the harbor, yet every ship lay anchored nearly a half mile back, awaiting invitation into the cove. Only the *Renegade* had received the message to sail closer, brought by five armed warriors in an outrigger. Now the danger really began. "My point exactly." Tristan nodded. "Well, you got their attention."

Raiden ordered everyone back and most from sight as he watched the outriggers move toward his ship. Aboard a divan on the outrigger, the sultan reclined on a bed of pillows under the shade of an awning, bedecked in a turban with a large blue stone fastened in the center. Raiden swore the man wore every jewel he possessed, his fingers glittering from the distance as he waved to his warriors. He was one of many tribal princes, but he was the most powerful, having already wiped out several tribes to dominate the islands. His brother ruled Tidore and therefore the clove trade.

Within minutes, a warrior carried the prince up the rope ladder from the barge, and set him with the gentlest touch on the deck of the *Renegade*. Raiden immediately postulated, swallowing his pride, willing to do anything for the chance to get Willa back.

The sultan's warriors, clad in bright red-and-orange sarongs that reached no further than their knees, stood around his highness, blowpipes poised.

His highness commanded Raiden to stand. Raiden kept his gaze lowered.

"Lord Raiden. It has been a very long time."

"It has, your majesty."

Raiden could feel the prince inspecting him. Kahlid brought a small chest forward, setting it at the sultan's feet. The prince admired the contents, the pearls and sandalwood, then waved a servant forward to take it.

"You may look at me."

Raiden carefully lifted his gaze.

Prince Inaka stepped closer, poking his arms. "I see more scars. You will tell me about them."

Raiden's lips curved. "As you wish, your highness."

Prince Inaka studied him, as if trying to come to a decision, then said, "We think it is good that you have come to visit." The man with coffee-colored skin and bright eyes glanced left and right at the other ships. "Your daring knows no bounds, Black Angel."

"We endeavor to please your highness. If I may ask . . ." The prince nodded his permission. "I wish a private audience with his highness," Raiden said and bowed deeply, his palms together and held at his chest.

Prince Inaka eyed him. "You do not come to trade and feast?"

"I have taken plenty of England's spice."

"While I keep the coin."

"His highness is benevolent to all."

"Yes, I am." The grin appeared, but Raiden knew from experience not to trust it. He waited for the invitation.

"At sunset we feast. We would be most pleased to hear of your recent battles then."

The sultan's gaze swept his clothes, his distaste showing. Two thick-armed warriors approached, lifted the prince on to their shoulders, and carried him down the rope ladder, then laid him like an infant on his divan. A beautiful young girl swept a palm fan, cooling the royal hide. Raiden watched as the outrigger sailed back to shore, his eyes respectfully downcast.

"Do not approach me till he walks on the shore."

Tristan stilled near the passageway.

When Inaka stepped on the shore, Raiden let out a breath, then motioned Tristan close. "Keep everyone still and away from weapons. Do not make any kind of threat to the warriors. They will line that beach with outriggers and enough poison to kill us all without so much as a scream."

"You can't think to go alone?"

"I will be allowed two men to accompany me, but I need you here."

Tristan nodded. "He's the one that held you prisoner years back?"

"Aye. He was younger and given to moods."

"How many have died to his moods?"

Raiden didn't bother to respond. The agony he experienced years ago did not compare to what he was feeling now. He looked to the land, as if trying to see past the fortress, past the thick jungle. She'd never left his thoughts, nor had what Inaka would do to her if he was still privy to his odd whims. And if Inaka didn't have Willa prisoner, Raiden hoped he would offer assistance or direction to where she was. And if an enemy had her, he knew the prince would join in the battle.

He glanced at the other ships, aware that every captain had a spyglass trained on him. Regardless of the Royal East India Army on nearly every island, to control the natives that could not be controlled, they dared not breech the trade agreements. It was their own fault, being forbidden to arrive without permission. The East India trade monopoly was slipping, thanks to cunning merchants and a few pirates, and their only strong foothold was on the groves themselves. Too much was lost at sea.

But the Royal East India had never been patient when it came to adhering to protocol. The Portuguese had at least approached with respect and forbearance. Unlike the Dutch, the English bullied their way onto the islands, killing anyone in their path and thinking to control these people with fire power and religion. Yet the tribes ruled and the visitors learned quickly that a blow pipe had greater distance than any musket or long rifle. If they angered the kings or sided with the wrong one, the natives would put a torch to the nutmeg and mace forests just to spite the traders.

The threat kept them at a distance till Raiden had a chance to search the island. But it would not be long. He turned his gaze to the old fortress nestled in a small mountain; a mile beyond lay Gunung Api, a volcano that constantly trembled the earth.

He ordered a boat readied and filled with sacks of rice, fabrics, and anything remotely European. If he remembered correctly, the prince had a penchant for the finer things of the west. He just hoped he'd kept his hands and his men away from Willa.

He glanced over his crew, then beckoned only Balthasar close. "If anyone attempts to leave this ship," he said in a low voice, "shoot him."

Raiden had stripped down to his skin and donned a sarong, the blue-and-black batik fabric his own, from Java. The yards were ornately tied, snug and draped at his hips, his legs and feet bare.

The garment was familiar to him, making him wish for his home and Willa safe within its stone confines. The instant his bare feet sank into the wet sand, the tension he'd carried for days left him a little.

"Not a word," he warned Perth and Kahlid as the men flanked him. "Remain three paces behind me and do not look the prince in the eye."

The prince's people pulled the longboat ashore, quickly unloading the gifts onto a sedan, lifted the poles, and carried it farther inland.

A bonfire lit the sunset. A whole pig roasted over another fire, four small boys turning it, whilst women, tightly wrapped in sarongs, prepared a table on the ground. Hours passed, food and drink were devoured, and Raiden waited for the moment when he could make his request. But the stories came, the prince prodding for details lest he gloss over them, and Raiden prayed for patience.

"Why have you come to me? I am not stupid, Black Angel. I know you would like to kill me for the manner of your treatment on my island."

"I am a better man for it," Raiden said. "But I ask a favor of you."

The prince nodded.

"I seek a woman, a white woman with red hair."

The prince's eyes flared. "I have no such woman. You have been misled."

"Have I? I learned her husband sold her to you."

"Why would I need more women? I have plenty."

"Why indeed, your highness?"

Raiden dared stare at the prince, hard, and the longer he did, the more the prince fidgeted.

"She does not know her place."

Something akin to a fresh rain swept over Raiden, and it took everything he had not to reach across and wring that royal neck. "I know this."

"You wish to buy this troublesome female?"

"What is the price, my lord?" Raiden bowed.

The prince selected a piece of meat, gnawing on the edge, yet his gaze remained fixed on the pirate. "Years ago the English took my home by force and have since left their squalor in my father's palace." Inaka made a sour face. "Do you know they do not wash themselves daily, even before prayer?"

Raiden nodded, not at all surprised by the change of subject. The prince was toying with him. "I would give all I have to have her back, your highness."

Inaka burst with laughter and Raiden, despite the danger, scowled. "I will take all you have, Black Angel, and I will tell you to forget her and find yourself another woman." Inaka's gaze swept over a maiden standing close and offering him figs. He took one, ate it, then, with his eyes alone, told the girl she'd gained his favor and to sit behind him.

"I want only this woman."

The prince sighed and tossed the uneaten meat into the sand. "I see I did not beat the heart out of you years ago, son of Montegomery."

Raiden's patience snapped and he came to his knees. A dozen warriors suddenly aimed short swords at his chest. His gaze swept the weapons and he stood, defying all to look down at the prince. A warrior tried to shove him back down, but failed. "I have paid a price no man should, Prince Inaka. This, you owe me."

The prince stood, bracelets and necklaces clinking as he met his gaze. "This is my island, my people. I owe no one, least of all a white man."

"Am I not more native than the English, than the Dutch? Do I not respect your ways, your customs?"

The prince eyed him, thoughtful, then with a careless wave, said, "She is yours."

"With your permission."

The prince scoffed, his hands on his hips as a slow grin spread across his swarthy face. "You never needed my permission, Black Angel. For I do not hold her.'' The prince twisted, pointing to the castle. ''They do.''

Just then, the mountain, Gunung Api, rumbled, its roar sending white smoke into the darkness.

Twenty

Gun smoke followed him as Raiden strode down the dank stone corridor, shouting for her. Behind him, Perth and Kahlid, with five Ceram warriors, covered his back as he searched. And if she wasn't in here? If Inaka was toying with him and truly held her prisoner elsewhere? And if she was dead? His body thundered with anger and impatience, his boots splashing through the seawater and muck as he rushed from cell door to cell door.

Suddenly he slid to a stop.

For a moment he couldn't move, couldn't breathe for the relief ripping through him. Wearing nothing but a dull blue sarong, she sat on the dirt floor, hunched in the corner. There were rope marks on her wrists, a bruise on her bare right shoulder. She looked like a beaten animal and his imagination, of what her husband had likely done to her, took quick flight, engulfing him with a tide of anger.

"Willa." She didn't move and he gripped the bars, shaking them furiously. "Willa!"

Her head snapped up and she stared at him through a curtain of tangled hair. "Raiden?" Her voice was gravely, dry.

"Aye, love." He went down on one knee, eye level with her.

Her hand trembled as she pushed her hair back, gazing at him through troubled eyes. "You came for me." Astonishment hung in her tone.

That she thought he had abandoned her cut him to the core and he stood, pulling on the bars, his muscles bulging as he struggled to separate the crumbling mortar from the steel hinge. Slowly she came to her feet and pushed away from the wall, staggering toward him as the cell door yielded to his strength. Angrily, he threw the wood and steel aside, sending it crashing to the ground.

For an instant, she simply stared, looking too fragile to touch.

"God above, Willa, speak to me," he said, his voice hoarse.

Her gaze searched his and he heard her long exhale of air, saw her lips tremble. *"Oh, Raiden,"* she cried softly, reaching for him, and her legs folded beneath her. He gathered her into his embrace before she hit the ground, holding her tightly.

"Sweet mercy," he said, burying his face in the curve of her neck, his hands making a wild ride over her spine.

Willa clung to him, feeling his strength, his warmth, his big body quaking. *Oh, it was glorious to be in his arms again.* "I never thought you'd come for me," she cried.

He cradled her jaw in his callused palms and met her gaze. "I would go to the ends of the earth for you."

Her green eyes sparkled with tears. "This *is* the ends of the earth, pirate."

Her little smile fractured his tired heart, and he pressed his mouth to hers, the defenses in his soul tumbling into dust as he kissed her. Mouths melded, bodies fused, brief and thirsty with want and relief until Raiden wanted nothing more than to obliterate this entire castle into a pile of rubble and steal her away into the dark.

"Captain? Make haste, sir."

They drew back and Raiden brushed a kiss to her forehead, still holding her close. "Can you walk?" He couldn't stop touching her, his hands smoothing over her hair, her shoulders.

"I will damn well walk out of here."

He squeezed her gently, his cheek pressed to the top of her head as he said, "Somehow, I knew you would."

Leaving the cell, they moved quickly to the end of the corridor, where Perth stood watch.

"My lady," he said with a polite nod, despite his singed beard and the bloodstains on his shirt.

"Good to see you, Mr. Perth." She looked at Raiden, suddenly panicked. "Roarke? What happened?"

"He lives." It touched him, her concern. "He is the only reason I found you."

"Then I owe him a good deal."

"I'm sure my brother will exact the favor sometime in the future," he said with a cryptic smile. She frowned but didn't have time to ask questions as he ushered her along. She didn't bother to glance at the dead East India soldiers littering the end of the corridor. They'd taunted her for days, and the only circumstance keeping them from raping her was the cell door and the fact that Alistar had the key.

Kahlid emerged from the forward corridor, smiling at Willa, then addressing Raiden. "We will not have as much trouble leaving, I think," he said. "His highness has sent more warriors."

"His highness is indulging his bloody whims against the British." Raiden took a step in the direction they'd come, but Willa stopped him.

"Nay, this way," Willa said, tugging on his hand.

Raiden frowned at her, then the others.

"Trust me, Raiden. I was not drugged when he dragged me in here."

"Drugged!" All three men said, yet she looked only at Raiden.

"Aye. It took me a day to realize 'twas in my food, for the euphoria was so intense. He'd left me here to die."

Fury engulfed him. And she noticed it. Willa gripped his arm, gazing up at him, and she felt his tension quickly fade. " 'Tis done," she said, not wanting to dwell on the matter, yet the question of what he'd given her still lingered. "Let us leave this place."

He agreed, and they followed her for several yards.

"This passage takes a twist, then rises and keeps rising," she said, laboring on weak legs as the corridor grew steeper. "There is a set of stairs that lead to the hill side behind the fortress, I think."

"Think?"

She glanced back. "Well, they were not about to give me a tour."

" 'Tis the only chance we have. The entire fort is alerted now." Raiden took the lead, refusing to release her hand and pausing twice to inspect the passage before going on. And when he did stop, Willa touched him, his back, his arm, rejoicing that he was there.

"This is too easy," Raiden muttered as the staircase loomed ahead. Footsteps echoed in the corridor behind them, growing closer, and the three men turned to defend themselves as a dozen of Inaka's warriors rounded the corner.

"Flee, pirate! The English come!" the warriors called out, then turned back as fresh troops attacked. The native blowpipes were swift and accurate but no match for British firearms. Men fell as Raiden clasped Willa's hand and raced toward the stairs, sweeping her into his arms and taking the curved flight of steps two at a time to the top, where they stopped, their exit blocked by a closed hatch.

Cursing a blue streak, he set her to her feet, then rammed his shoulder into the planks twice before the rotting wood shattered. Sand poured down on them as Raiden shoved away the broken wood, crawled through, and then reached down for her. He lifted her out, then helped the others, several warriors joining them.

Raiden scanned the area. The chaos came from inside the castle, and from his position, he had a view of the entire fortress and the sea beyond. The instant any one of those British ships in the harbor got wind of this, there would be no stopping the war.

"Come pirate, this path," a warrior said, gesturing, and Raiden followed, Willa close behind. From his waistband, he offered her a knife, and with nowhere to hide it, she gripped it, blade down. They fled, ducking jungle vines and flowering trees, moving around the east side of the castle till they emerged on edge of the beach, the crash of waves and the winking light of the ships greeting them. The *Renegade* was scarcely visible.

The warriors herded them to the long boats. The shore was still decorated with the remnants of the feast, the torches and bonfire still lighting the beach, yet the prince was nowhere in sight.

"That prince threatened to cut off my feet, can you believe that?"

Raiden glanced back, his dark eyes smoldering over her. "That's all he wanted from you?"

She tipped her chin up. " 'Tis all he would get, by God. He's a spoiled brat."

"Aye, and these are his warriors," he warned in a low tone. "Now, get in the boat." He held his hand out for her.

She didn't take it, looking back at the castle, the jungle beyond. "We cannot leave."

Raiden smothered a groan. Would anything be easy with this woman? "Willa, we wouldn't be in this fix if you'd stayed on the ship."

Her hands on her hips, she stared up at him, her anger building. "And I wouldn't have had to leave if you hadn't been so . . . mean."

His expression crumbled. "Forgive me, love. I was so furious—"

She rushed to him, covering his lips with two fingers. "I know exactly what you were," she said sympathetically. "But we still cannot leave." She gripped his arms. "Mason is here. I know it. I heard Alistar speak of some cove on the other side of the island."

Raiden's brows drew tight. "Aye, there is one, just as there are a dozen ships that will see this uprising and sail right onto this shore."

"Raiden," she said softly, gazing into his concerned eyes. "Since the moment we met in the market, this is where I have been headed. *This* is where my son is hidden. How can you ask me to leave without looking?"

He smoothed her hair back off her face, curling his hand around her nape and drawing her nearer. "I wouldn't. You know I will help you." He brushed his mouth across hers. "I cannot refuse you."

She smiled against his lips, her hand on his bare chest and itching to play there. "And you shall be generously rewarded, my love," she whispered and heard him moan.

My love. His heart ceased beating, he swore, his gaze raking her upturned face. "Willa—"

"Well, isn't this cozy."

Willa spun about to see Alistar astride a white horse and riding toward them. Raiden drew his pistol, and the crewmen and warriors followed suit, daring even one of Alistar's men to move.

He shielded Willa, waiting for the worst because Lord Eastwick was accompanied by four men, Inaka's deadliest enemies—cannibals.

"Careful, love," Raiden whispered when she inched around him.

"Didn't I shoot you once already?" Alistar said, gesturing to Raiden.

"My brother bears your wound"—Raiden carefully pulled the firing hammer back—"for which I owe you."

Alistar shrugged. "It couldn't be helped." His gaze shifted

beyond, to the ship rocking in the water, and recognition dawned. "Ah, the Black Angel." He looked at Willa. "Illustrious company, wife, hmm? Was his bed as soft as ours?"

"Shut up, Alistar, you're showing your stupidity." Willa glared at the man she'd been forced to marry, loathing that superior look of his. It had always made her feel less than adequate. Now it only angered her, made her seethe with ungodly hatred. He was pompous and vain and although sitting regally astride the horse, Alistar's blue damask coat and impeccably tied white cravat looked ridiculous in this heat. He was still handsome, his blond hair neatly combed into a ribbon, his features fine enough to make any woman swoon and fawn over him. But not her, never her. For his cruelty showed in his ice-blue eyes, in his long-boned hands that could wield such pain. How many times had he struck her, then acted as if it was her fault he could not control his temper, or given her a trinket to appease his conscience? How often had he treated her as less than a human, less than a woman?

"Come, wife." Alistar gestured with a riding crop as if she were no more than his pet.

Her disdain showed in every pore. "Nay. You are no longer my husband. You have destroyed any vows atween us." She inched toward Raiden, feeling any reservation fade with just his nearness.

Alistar's gaze thinned, shifting between the two. "Legally we are wed, and you are my possession."

Raiden chuckled shortly, humorlessly. "Possession." He chanced a brief look at Willa. "There in lies your folly, Eastwick."

Alistar's gaze fell on her hand on the pirate's arm, the way his wife looked up at the brutish pirate with such devotion, and he seethed with anger. Did she think he would give her over to the barbarian and be pleased? If anyone got word that he could not keep his own wife under control, he'd be finished in British society. Served him well for taking the brash colonist to wife, he thought. She couldn't even breed a child worthy of being his son. Alistar's stomach knotted when he thought of his son, the blank stares, the grunts serving as words. It was fortunate the boy had been kept a secret. No one would question his death. Nor the emergence of his mistress's babe in his place. But Willa was another problem. He'd needed her father's ships for his plans, and she knew too much. Though she'd never revealed exactly what she knew, there was a smug certainty in her, even in the dungeon cell, that unnerved him. Had she known all along that this man would come for her?

But it was the thought of any man having what he owned that sent him from the saddle. If he could not garner even an ounce of affection from her, then by God, the pirate would not have it either. And Willa would pay for humiliating him like this.

He strode across the beach, a loaded pistol aimed.

Instantly Raiden pushed her behind him and leveled his pistol at Lord Eastwick's chest. "Not another step, your lordship."

Alistar stopped, the look in the man's eyes gone deadly with retribution. "Willa, come to me at once."

She didn't move, couldn't move, and she felt as if her entire world hung in the balance between those two weapons.

"She is not going anywhere with you."

"You challenge me?" Alistar said, laughing, yet remembering the stories about this man and his attacks.

" 'Twill be my pleasure."

Alistar's gaze shifted to his wife. "I should have known you would choose such a vulgar man over me."

She looked him up and down, disgusted. "Refinement does not always breed a true gentleman, Alistar. You have proven that . . . consistently."

Alistar's features yanked taut, his lips tightening to bloodless white. His attention flashed to his rival. "Swords or pistols, pirate?" He would earn an earldom for killing the Black Angel. "I will see your head on a pike on the London Bridge."

Raiden flicked his fingers. "Come, try to take it."

"Raiden, don't do this."

" 'Tis time he pays." His eyes on Eastwick, he said, "Swords, your lordship? I want to savor this." He inclined his head to Perth. "Give him one."

Perth gave him his own weapon, snatching Eastwick's pistol from him when he was inclined to keep it. Alistar didn't wait for Raiden to draw his sword before shoving Perth aside and lunging at the pirate. The blade tip sliced Raiden's shoulder.

Raiden blandly looked at the cut, then to Eastwick, enjoying the man's paling skin. "First blood," Raiden said. "How good of his lordship."

"I shall add more to that!" Alistar swiped the air.

Raiden reacted instantly, his black cutlass clashing quickly against Eastwick's, the man's elegant fighting tactics no match for the seasoned pirate.

Nor for Raiden's strength. Alistar had no chance, and yet he could not see it, his eyes glazed with twisted rage, and Willa's heart pounded as they fought, her husband's slashes and parries missing the mark as Raiden sent him stumbling back across the shore. Raiden shredded Alistar's coat, yet did not make him bleed, each quick, relentless clash leaving Alistar winded. Yet he continued with a vengeance that made Willa wonder what truly pushed him.

Metal connected. Blades locked and slid hilt to hilt. Two men stared, each fighting for different reasons. One bound to Willa by vows, the other bound by his heart.

"Have you enjoyed my wife?"

"Her faith in her vows is unmatched, Eastwick."

"She'll breed you naught but addlepated idiots," Alistar sneered. "If you live."

Raiden's rage for the little lost boy exploded through him, pushing him to take this man out of existence. He did not deserve to live. Noble blood made him no better than the most vulgar of commoners. He shoved, sending Eastwick back again and again, the clash of his sword shooting sparks. Then, with a low growl, he brought his sword down, snapping Eastwick's blade in two. Eastwick looked from the broken blade to the pirate, then charged.

Raiden drew back his fist and drove it into Eastwick's aristocratic face. Bone shattered, cartilage shifted, and Eastwick went down on his back.

Raiden stood over him, sweeping his blade point neatly beneath his chin. "Do you beg for quarter?"

Eastwick glared up at him, the broken hilt falling to the ground, blood gushing from his broken nose. "I will see you hunted till the end of time!"

"Not if you are very dead." Raiden held the blade to his throat.

"Raiden, nay!"

His gaze flew to hers, and his chest clenched at the pleading in her eyes.

"If you kill him, I will never find Mason!"

Raiden knew she was right, always right.

Alistar chuckled. "Who has bested who now, pirate?"

Raiden stared down at the man and knew he would not tell them where he'd hidden the boy, his drug-induced state giving him courage. Opium, Raiden realized. And he was addicted.

"You are not worth the effort, Eastwick. A man who would try to kill his wife and attempt such on an innocent babe is no man at all." He sheathed his sword with an angry shove. "You will never regain your place in society, *Lord Eastwick*. Even now your letters of confession are on their way to England, and the *Persephone*'s cargo is mine." Raiden enjoyed the horror on the man's face, then strode to Willa. He barely reached her, touched her, when he heard a shout, and turned just as a shot blasted in the torch-lit darkness.

Eastwick sank to his knees, a small pistol that had been concealed in his sleeve, in his hand.

Willa's gaze dropped to the red stain flowering on his chest, and she rushed to him, holding him up. "Where is he?" She shook him. "Where is *my son*?"

Alistar's smile was slow, exposing bloody teeth, red foam

spilling from his lips before his eyes rolled back in his head and he sank to his side in the sand.

The Ceram warriors aimed, yet the cannibals fled as Raiden lifted his gaze to Perth, the smoking flintlock in his hand. Willa looked up, stricken.

"Forgive me, Lady Eastwick, but he was going to shoot my captain in the back."

"I am glad you were so quick, sir. My thanks," she said, then folded to the ground, dazed. "How will I find my son now?"

Raiden knelt, gripping her arms. "We are no worse off than afore. Eastwick would have told us naught, my love. If Mason is here, we will find him." She lifted her teary gaze to his. "I will find him. I swear it."

Willa searched his handsome face and knew he would not fail her. A peace and certainty spirited through her, and her smile was faint as she leaned into him to stand. For a moment he simply held her, rubbing her back and whispering soft assurances before he let her go and withdrew powder, shot, and another pistol from the hull of the longboat.

He donned his shirt as he spoke. "Perth, sail to the *Renegade,* return with supplies and firearms. But meet us at the far cove. Bring only Vazeen, Cheston, and Riggs with you." Raiden met Kahlid's gaze. "The charts are in my cabin. Be careful of the reef." Raiden was confident that his helmsman could navigate with the help of the charts. He looked at Willa. "Can you travel?"

"I have waited for this day for too long."

There was something in her tone that alerted him, made his insides tighten with anticipation. Her eyes spoke more than she was saying as they rode over him like a slow pour of warm oil, coating him before she spun about and headed up the beach.

He caught her hand, gesturing. "Nay, by boat." She looked at the outrigger, three warriors manning the craft, and she stepped gingerly to the front, her back to the bow. Perth nodded to Raiden as Kahlid pushed the longboat off the shore, then climbed in.

The British troops would be on the beach any moment, and though it would take Kahlid and Perth some time to reach the *Renegade* in the heavy longboat, the outrigger would get them to the other side of the island in mere hours. Raiden took lead position in the canoe, facing her, his knees outside hers. He dug the paddle into the water, working in harmony with the warriors. He was oblivious to the muscle-straining paddling, his gaze on Willa. She sat on her knees in the narrow canoe, her gaze so intense he didn't need the light of day to feel it. The outrigger moved silently, the rush of water and the swoosh of paddles the only sounds.

"I have missed you, pirate."

He swallowed hard, the emotions he'd capped till he'd found her rushing back to him. "And I you, little fox."

Willa's stomach tightened, and she leaned forward, cupping his face, and he ceased paddling, gazing into her soft eyes as the canoe swept over the glassy water. "Forgive me for leaving?"

"If you will forgive me for being such a blustering fool."

His bashful mutter touched her deeply, and she brushed her mouth over his. "I know you were hurt, Raiden, but I could not bear to feel your anger."

He slid the paddle beside him and leaned forward, gripping her waist. "I wanted you for myself, Willa. I wanted aught I could have from you even if it was for but a short time, and when you told me the truth, it stole even the hope from me."

"Oh, Raiden," she moaned sadly. "Don't you see? Alistar destroyed our vows long before he took my baby. I just didn't see it till I was on shore." She brushed her mouth over his, each pass growing stronger and stronger. "I was coming back. I wanted what time we could have."

"I know. Roarke told me." He savored her soft mouth rolling over his like a fine wine at a rich feast, stirring the dark heart of his desire. God. He wanted to hold her so badly, wanted to banish the foul memories of her imprisonment and give her sweet dreams. "Willa, I can offer you only—"

"Your heart," she whispered into his warm mouth. "I want only your heart."

"Ah, love." He swallowed heavily, gazing into her eyes "You have had it from the first moment."

"Raiden." She pressed her mouth harder, moving in slow, hot deliberation, her tongue sliding across his lips, then pushing inside. He tugged her closer, his fingers tightening on her waist, sliding toward her breasts.

"Good God, you are naked under that." Raiden felt weak and vulnerable—which he could ill afford with Inaka's warriors in the canoe with them.

She smiled against his mouth. "Would you like to know exactly how naked?"

"Oh, God." His kiss grew heated, lush, and when they rocked the outrigger, someone cleared his throat. Reluctantly, Raiden eased back, taking up the paddle and unconsciously pushing it through the water. His gaze never left her, skimming her body in the sarong. Tied over one shoulder, it was wound around her like the wrapping of a comfit, and though he'd seen many women wear them, especially on Java, none affected him as greatly. In the moon's light she looked at ease in so little clothing, as if she'd worn the like all her life.

It showed him that society and wealth meant nothing to her and how easily she could shed her past and create a new life. He looked away, at the paddle passing into the water, and he wondered when he could do the same, when he would find the strength to leave his past behind. And what she would say when she learned he would leave her soon.

"We can take you no further, Montegomery," a warrior said a couple hours later as the canoe slid onto the shore, the scraping sound loud in the stillness.

Raiden climbed out, then helped Willa onto the shore. When he turned back to give the outrigger a push off, the warrior, their leader, pressed into his hand a blowpipe and a small leather bag he knew was filled with darts and powdered poison. Raiden frowned.

"For a man willing to defy our king for a woman," he said with a smile and an admiring glance at Willa. Raiden nodded, thanked him, then gave the outrigger a push into the current.

He turned to Willa, ushering her off the shore and into the jungle. "The sun will be up in a couple of hours. We are on the west tip of the island and it will take us half the coming day to travel to the cove."

"There are more tribes here, aren't there?"

"Aye. Cannibals."

She looked up at him with wide eyes, then down at the knife he'd given her earlier. "Lord a'mighty, Raiden, how can we survive? And what of Mason? Oh, tell me they wouldn't have—"

He caught her, gazing into her eyes, willing her to be calm. "I will be honest with you, love, I do not know. Boys are often taken as slaves and mayhaps they will not harm Mason, since he cannot speak." Raiden prayed there was some tribal belief that cannibalizing a child like Mason would bring bad luck and the boy was still alive. He held tight to hope, for 'twas all they had left. Eastwick was evil enough to kill his own child and that they could be chasing a ghost did not escape his concern.

Willa released a breath, willing the fear back. She would be no help to him if she panicked. "Do we travel at night?"

"Nay. We will be on our own till dawn." He held a tangle of vines aside for her, and she ducked through. "Even then, the *Renegade* crew has strict orders not to land a boat till the next evening." He pointed ahead. "A stream lies yonder, with a waterfall. 'Tis too noisy to hear anyone approach, but there is a cave."

"You have been here, aye? When you were prisoner?"

"When Inaka finally released me, I drifted in a *praha* for what felt like days only to realize I'd merely taken the riptide around the island." He shook his head, the sound of rushing water bringing memories. "I'd wandered and came upon the tribes quite by accident. I knew they were cannibals. Inaka had threatened to give me over to them often enough. I ran back toward the shore, determined to swim to my freedom, sharks be damned, when I found the cave and hid.''

Willa stepped into the dappled moonlight and froze. The sight took her breath away, silver beams mixing with the spray and casting the green jungle in blues and yellow. It must be incredible in the sunlight, she thought. The water spilled from a point high in the mountainside, foaming in the pool.

She frowned, seeing no way to get behind it. ''Must we swim in it?'' She remembered the snakes in the Ganges.

''Aye. Remember the current moves strongly.'' Walking ahead of her, he stepped into the water, then turned, offering his hand. She stepped in, the rush of cool water soothing her tired bare feet. His hand in hers, he held his weapons and powder out of the water, wading into the fall, then stepping under it. For a moment he was gone, only his hand clasping hers, then Willa slipped under the hard rush of water, pausing for a moment as it beat down on her thinly clad body. He tugged and she climbed the slick, smooth rocks. His hands on her waist, he lifted her to the mossy floor. Willa gazed up at him, aware of the privacy, of the man and the restraint he showed. His fingers flexed on her waist, and his breath came quickly. Then suddenly he released her and placed his weapons and horns in the rear of the cave, away from the spray.

''We can hide here and be safe for the night.''

She cocked her head, watching as he pulled off his wet boots and tossed them with the weapons. ''Doubting that you can protect me?''

''We will need more manpower to search,'' he said, pulling off his shirt and draping it on a rock. The cut Alistar left was barely visible on his broad shoulder, the tattoo of thorns calling to be touched and tasted. ''And protecting you is not my worry.''

''What is your worry then?''

He looked at her sharply, through a drape of wet, dark hair, his eyes smoldering as they raked her from head to foot and back. The heat there flared the fire ever simmering inside her to ungodly proportions, and a quick tingling wound up the backs of her thighs, diving between, and she nearly moaned at the hunger engulfing her.

"Of wanting you so badly that I might hurt you," came in a voice harsh with desire.

Willa slowly lifted her hands to the knot of fabric on her shoulder, loosening it.

Raiden straightened, his gaze never leaving her.

Her hands trembled, her body quaking with tremors of want, and she knew she'd explode and burn into dust the instant he touched her. She wanted him that badly, longed for his touch with a surge of desire so strong, it was agonizing to be apart from him. Her body as much as her soul begged for release, begged to feel him touch and taste her. To push his body inside hers. A hard shudder passed through her down to her bare heels, and she fairly screamed for satisfaction.

The sarong slid down her over her damp breasts, past her waist, exposing her naked flesh to his heated gaze.

Raiden moved toward her, absorbing every glorious inch of her bare skin as he stopped less than a foot away. He looked his fill, his fingers curling and uncurling into tight, hard fists. His breath quickened, and he dragged his gaze up to lock with hers.

"Give to me all you have, Raiden Montegomery," she whispered. "Make good your promises."

He swallowed, the beast of hunger beating at the threshold of his desire.

He reached for her.

And passion erupted.

Twenty-one

They came together in a stormy clash, skin to skin, savage with lust. Ravenous for completion.

He thrust his knee between hers, opening her for his pleasure, and his fingers found her, wet and tight, and at the first touch she surged against him, eager with desire. He played and probed, loving how she rocked into his touch and whispering how much he wanted her, that just to look at her made him hard, and how he longed to fill her body with his.

Willa whimpered, his soft, seductive words splintering her composure and she nipped the gold loop piercing his ear, scoured her hands over his bare chest. his ribs, and his stomach on the way to his breeches.

She was no maiden; no shyness lingered. And she knew what she wanted. Raiden had never doubted that. And when she outlined his erection, then quickly thumbed open the buttons of his breeches, each release felt like a gun shot through to his heels. He thought he'd explode with the exquisite pleasure of her touch. He tore his mouth from hers, smoothing his hand roughly over her hair, her jaw, tipping her face to his. His breathing labored, he gazed into her eyes for the space of a heartbeat and read more than he had a right to see, to want from her.

"Willa," he whispered, his voice rough with desire. "This power, it takes us." She covered his hand, drawing it to her lips and laying a kiss to his palm. Raiden briefly closed his eyes, the gesture unmanning him nearly as much as the passion boiling through his blood.

Willa never thought to see him hesitant and knew he feared she could not withstand the strength of his passion, the heat of it. "Then let it, Raiden, let it," she said as she drew his hand to her breast, folding his fingers over her rounded flesh.

He came unhinged, kneading the lush globe and taking her mouth with the ferocity of a man given a second chance to live. A second chance to love. He held nothing back, letting her know he would take all she offered and never give it back. And in that moment, he knew he'd spent his entire life coming to this point, to this moment when he joined with the woman of his soul. Her body was not all he wanted. He craved her heart, ached to the depths of his being to be loved by her.

And the emotions hidden in his heart spilled into his touch.

Hot and primitive, a craving so deep and dark, Raiden feared it would destroy him.

His hands charged an erotic ride across her bare skin, as if to melt her into his palms, as if he were dreaming and she'd vanish into vapor and he would be left alone and vulnerable without her. Yet she was here in his arms, climbing higher on his thigh, rocking luxuriously against his hardness, her womanly softness burning him through the layer of fabric. Raiden trembled with his own hunger, and he broke their kiss, hoping for some control, then relinquished it again to the delicious task of licking a path down her slender throat, bending her back over his arm. His lips closed wetly over her plump nipple and she cried out, the rich sound melting into the stone walls as he flicked his tongue wildly over the tight bud, circling once, twice, before drawing it deeper into the heat of his mouth.

She clutched his head, glorying in the feel of his mouth, the play of his broad hands over her flesh, his erection pulsing against her heat. He feasted on her, the slick of his tongue sending spirals of pleasure radiating to her fingertips, and she couldn't catch her breath fast enough, and wished he would devour her. She felt it was the only way she'd have sweet satisfaction.

This would never be enough. Never.

No movement was wasted, for neither could spare a second to breathe, to wonder—only to take what they'd denied each other for so long. He buried his face between the soft, lush mounds, then dipped lower, scoring his teeth over the tender underside of her breasts, licking a moist line down to her navel as he sank to his knees. He made her mindless, his lips and tongue playing over her ribs, dragging over the marks left by her son's growth into this world. He nipped her hip, whispering her name, pushing the sarong to the ground, then smoothing his hands up the back of her thighs to enfold her buttocks.

Her trembling ripped through him, and he wanted her breathless, wanted her screaming for him and, when he tipped his head, meeting her gaze as he slicked his tongue over the swell between her thighs and made his sensual threats a reality.

He peeled her open and took her femininity with his mouth.

Her scream of pleasure echoed off the walls, hushed under the pound of the waterfall. "Raiden, oh, lord a'mighty, Raiden!"

"A concern you wish me to address, my lady?" he paused long enough to say, chuckling over her squirming, delighting in it.

"Beast!" She sank her fingers into his hair, arching into his touch, and he held her, drawing her thigh up over his shoulder and pushing his tongue deeper.

Willa thought she'd shatter, her limbs liquefying as he stroked the slick bud of her desire, dipped his fingers between the lush folds. She gasped for air, then collapsed, sliding onto his lap, straddling his thighs and kissing him greedily, her fists trapped in his hair.

"You torture me," she said against his lips.

"Nag, nag," he muttered, then devoured her mouth.

She tasted him, tasted herself on his lips and could stand no more. She drove her hand inside his breeches, enfolding him, freeing him fully into her palm.

Raiden flinched, lavish pleasure slashing through him as she slicked her fingers over the moist tip of him. "Sweet mercy, woman."

"No mercy," she whispered, pushing his arousal down, letting the tip of him graze her damp flesh. "No quarter."

"And none taken," he growled, gripping her hips and thrusting upward, entering her in one hard stroke. "I surrender."

"Oh, Raiden," she cried, wrapping her arms around his neck, desire building as he gave her hips motion, retreating and thrusting deeply. She chanted his name, rising and falling onto him.

With each thrust he lost a piece of himself. With each kiss he abandoned more than his body to the rip and crush of pleasure.

Yet Willa could feel his restraint. "Give me," she said in a husky whisper that sanded over him like raw silk. "Give me all, Raiden." She wrapped her legs around him, leaned back, pulling him down onto her, onto the mossy bed, the motion driving his body deeper into hers.

He let out a low growl, squeezing his eyes shut, and braced above her, he gazed into her green eyes. "I will hurt you."

Her fingertips swept the passion-harsh lines of his handsome face, trickling down his chest. "Nay. Nay," she said, then gripped his hips, pulling him back. "You only hurt me by withholding yourself."

His control snapped and he groaned, arching, thrusting deeply. He withdrew, then plunged, sheathing himself over and over, her feminine muscles gripping him in a wet glove of desire. She pulsed like a sleek wave, her hair spread like a halo of fire about her as her hips undulated to greet his. Her hands wouldn't be still, her thumbs circling his nipples, then sliding down to touch where they joined. And he groaned like a tortured animal, arching to drive deeper, yet it was not enough. He wanted to climb inside her, know all of her, and he felt every nuance—her quickening breath as she ravaged his mouth, the convulsing of her muscles, the wet, slick slide of him inside her, and her body clawing for his return. On the mossy ground behind a curtain of clear water, moonlight spilled over her, coating her in silver as he loved her with smooth deliberation.

"Look at me, love. Let me see it in your eyes."

Gazes locked. Their bodies moved in lavish rhythm, glossy with mist, delicious friction carrying them to the brink of maddening rapture. Their tempo increased, frantic, raw, the pale skin of a lady melting in the dark with her sun-bronzed pirate.

The flawless cradling the scarred.

Luxurious femininity and masculine power.

She abandoned herself to him, clawing him, locking her legs around his waist as his hips slammed into her, the rush of sumptuous heat and sensation shattering through them. He saw it in her eyes, felt her rapture unfold like a tropical storm, hot and fast, the throb and clench of feminine muscles taking him over the edge. With a dark groan, he shoved hard, grinding to her as his warmth spilled and she cried out, bowing like a sea siren beneath him, her fingers digging into his chest.

He howled her name, the sound torn from his throat.

For a moment he held her suspended off the ground with one arm, holding her on the edge of pure bliss and letting her feel all there was of him, of her own pleasure, gazes locked as bone-wracking tremors fused them in waves of wicked pleasure.

His hard shudder passed through him and into her, and they shared a deep kiss, a wet slide of lips and tongue and the promise of more. Willa felt boneless, a tingling racing through her blood with a madness that defied explanation, even as he lowered her to the ground, even as he still pulsed inside her. Together, they sagged to the mossy earth in a tangle of arms and legs and sated bodies, unable to utter a word, trying to regain their lost breath. He smoothed her hair back and showered her face in kisses, wanting to remain thusly till the haze was long gone and night turned back into day. She kissed him gently, tenderly, and he nuzzled her throat.

"Ah, love," he growled into the curve of her neck. "You have a way about you."

"I am glad you found it, then."

He smiled against her skin, then lifted his head to look at her. God above, she was beautiful, he thought, loving her satisfied smile and how easily she responded to his kisses. And how easily he could want her again with the same earth-shattering force of moments ago. He held dear the knowledge that this woman found rapture under his touch, and after he shed his breeches, he rolled to his side, pulling her thigh over his.

Instantly Willa curled into the warmth of his body, her fingers playing over his sculpted chest. She'd never experienced anything quite like that, and she knew 'twas more than just carnal pleasures that gave their joining such devotion. She felt forever anchored to this man and could not tell if 'twas in Calcutta, or in Malacca, or the days alone in her prison when she'd recognized that she loved him. Truly, madly loved him. He'd captured her that day in the tavern. He'd cared enough to keep her from dying, cared enough to hunt after her child and defy her husband.

She never wanted to be parted from him, and it hurt to even think on it, yet he was an outlaw, hunted, and they both knew the authorities would catch up with him someday. Raiden had always claimed he was beholden to no one, especially his heart, and she realized he might not want to hear her feelings. Her gaze swept over his features, and as if sensing her, he cocked his head to look where she lay on his chest.

Raiden curled his hand in her hair, bringing a lock to his lips and trying not to frown at the question in her eyes. "What are you thinking, little fox?"

Her throat tightened. How she wanted a forever with this man. But Raiden Montgomery lived by the day, by the hour. By the sword. She would not ask for more than she had now. For he could not give it. "I was wishing we could stay here."

"We can, till the morrow." He bent and tipped her head, worrying her lips. "So rest, love. We are safe. Let me hold you through the night as I've been wanting to do for so long."

"How long?"

He smiled as she snuggled into his embrace. "Since I saw you sitting in the window sill of your hotel in Calcutta."

She wiggled closer, yawning. "I knew you were there, you know," she said on a fading whisper. "Watching over me then."

"Ah, love." He rubbed her naked spine. "With you, I am as transparent as glass."

She sighed sleepily. "With me, Raiden, you have naught to fear."

But he did, for he knew he loved her. And whilst he was wont to hide away with her and forget his past and the mission he'd yet to complete, he could not. Sighing, he pressed his lips to the top of her head, savoring the feel of her naked body wound with his. He wished he could say the words, to give her all she deserved, and he admitted he was afraid. Afraid she did not want a life with him, that a part of her saw him only as an adventure, even as a voice in him contradicted the notion. And he was deathly afraid loving her would destroy them both. The vulnerability of it left a hole deep in his heart that had taken ten years to fill again. He tipped his head and looked down at her, her features soft in sleep, and he brushed her hair off her cheek. She turned her face into his palm and whispered his name, and Raiden's chest tightened.

Ah, God, you give me love when I still have so much yet undone.

When he could die on the morrow and leave her, quite possibly, with his unborn child.

He squeezed his eyes shut, the thought of her bearing his babe without him cutting to the core of his being. He could not allow it. He'd not follow his father's legacy, by God, and he'd find a way beyond this, find a way to have it all. A home, a safe harbor with her, and a quiet, sedentary life with no one pursuing his head for reward.

And in the seclusion of the cave, behind the rush of water, away from the creatures of the jungle hunting the night, Raiden held Willa against his scarred chest and knew only in her the poignant desperation of wanting a place to rest his soul. And knowing of no way to have it.

Her arms braced behind her, Willa lay supine on the smooth rocks, the hard beat of water erotic against her bare skin. It soothed tender areas, stirred others, and she rolled on her side, the small plateau of rocks offering a pool of still water between her and Raiden. She lifted her gaze to where he lay sleeping, his muscular body taut even in repose. She stood, walking closer, her gaze sliding over his long hair, the scar on his jaw, the earring that hinted of his profession. His chest and arms were striped with scars, badges of his bravery, yet not one deterred from the sleek grace of his body. A polished savage, she thought, for he bore the refinement of a gentleman, yet his rough side, the part of him born on the streets, without love, fighting to survive, rose often. As it had when he boarded a ship and freed the pressed sailors. And when he'd spoken cruelly and wanted to push her away.

She wrung out her hair, watching him, her body yearning for more of his loving, and she tossed her hair over her shoulder and settled near. For an instant, apprehension slithered through her; then she pushed aside caution and decided Raiden must be repaid for his sensual torture all these weeks past.

Raiden stirred from sleep, groaning at the familiar tightness working hard through his groin. He drifted in and out of an erotic dream, then forced his eyes open, and his mind to associate sensation with reality. A low growl rumbled in his chest.

"My God, woman, what are you doing?"

"I do not think it needs explanation."

Her mouth played over his arousal, drawing him deeply, and a hot, molten shudder wracked him to his toes.

He arched, thrusting. "You are mad!" He opened his eyes and looked down, watching her tongue snake over him. Nothing in his life was ever so torrid. "You do know there is a price for this."

"I've been agreeable to your bargains thus far, Montegomery."

His lips quirked, and then all teasing vanished as he sat up, unable to stand much more. And then he did. The pulsing increased, her rhythm driving all thoughts from his brain, and Raiden felt the rush of blood and desire speed through his veins. He quaked with hard tremors, unable to keep still. Then suddenly he gripped her under the arms and dragged her up the length of his thighs, shoved hers apart, and in a heartbeat, he was inside her, bucking her, refusing to let her have motion. In seconds he reached his climax and spilled his seed.

When the cloud of passion dissipated, he realized she was laughing. Laughing!

"Willa," he said, looking affronted.

Her arms above her head, she stretched, cat-pleased. " 'Twas good to see you come apart like that." It gave her an incredible sense of her power.

He clutched her roughly to his chest. "I will show you coming apart, woman." He pushed her to her back and began his assault, loving her laughter, her chatter, and especially the moment it ceased on a shuddering breath and she could do no more than let pleasure take her.

The morning sun glittered through the curtain of water and into their privacy as Raiden watched her sleep in naked splendor. The lady was gone, his temptress appearing during the night, and his gaze swept down her lithe body, her hair spilling over her back, one leg hiked as she lay on her side on the moss.

A little smile curved his lips. He felt drained, gloriously replete, yet he only had to look at her to want her again.

I will want her forever, he thought and wished he had that kind of time. But Raiden was not so blinded by his heart that he did not see the dismal future ahead. He was an outlaw, hunted by Dunfee and most of the British Navy. He'd committed crimes in the name of justice and most in the name of piracy.

A thief of the first water.

What kind of life was that for a lady?

Sunlight bred a new vein of thought, as he pulled on his breeches, fastening them. He stuffed his weapons into his boots to keep them as dry as possible, then moved to Willa, kneeling and shaking her gently. She moaned as she twisted and stretched, the rivers of red hair exposing her plump breasts. Raiden grit his teeth against the urge to suckle her rosy nipple and slip back into her arms.

"Wake, sweet."

She opened her eyes, smiling up at him. Willa reached as she sat up, drawing him to her mouth and kissing him.

"Good morn," she said.

"How can it not be?" he murmured against her mouth. "I had you screaming for me last night."

She scoffed playfully. "Shall I remind you who howled?" She slid her hand down his broad thigh to his manhood shielded in dark breeches.

He caught her wrist, bringing it to his lips. "I concede defeat."

"Ah, victory," she murmured, then noticed his boots in his hand, the weapons tucked inside. "Where do you go?"

There was no panic in her voice, only concern.

"I must search for food and scout for tribes."

She nodded. "Be careful."

He kissed her once more, hard and quick, then stood and walked to the left of the fall.

"You will get soaked, as will your weapons."

"There is a narrow ledge of rocks that edge the cave." At

her frown, he added, ''Last night, I was in a hurry to get us to safety, but now that I can see, this way is quicker, if treacherous.''

She stood, walking toward him in naked glory. She peered around him, to the narrow passage. He would get wet regardless because he was so big.

''Do not try it. You have no shoes to protect your feet.''

She nodded, then looked up at him, and his gaze toured her ripe figure, the memory of last night returning with a quick rush that made his body tighten.

''Hurry back.'' She rose on her toes to kiss him, and his arm locked around her waist, dragging her against him as he molded his mouth to hers.

''Stay hidden.'' He released her and stepped to the ledge.

The light of day lent caution. Aside from food and to assure him of their secrecy, he needed to cover their tracks and see if the *Renegade* was near. And the British Navy was not.

As he sidestepped around the tidal pool, toward hard land, Raiden hoped the East India Company didn't balk at Inaka's interference in Willa's rescue, for to anger the prince would destroy relations over the spices. One woman was not enough reason to go to war. Raiden strode toward the sea, wondering over the man who'd betrayed him, and praying that he hadn't incited a mutiny and that they would not be left on this island to die.

''I can carry you.''

''I can walk.''

''But you have no shoes.''

''I have no clothes, so what is the bother?''

Raiden's gaze dropped to her round bottom tucked in the blue-and-green sarong, the fabric wound tight and molding every curve of her figure. He'd been accustomed to seeing women in such a garment, just not Willa, and the thought of

his crews looking at her, thusly clad, made him want to cover
her again in pounds of clothes.

"The garment suits you," he admitted.

"I adore it. I feel as if I've been . . . liberated from a drudgery
I'd no idea I'd suffered." She walked swiftly ahead of him,
pausing occasionally to take his direction. The scent of the sea
grew stronger, the sun setting quickly behind them.

"Willa, about last night, and this morning."

"And in the pool," she said with a seductive look over her
shoulder.

"Aye."

She stilled and faced him, frowning. "Do not tell me you
did not enjoy that."

"Oh, nay." He kissed her sweetly. "You know that I did,
but 'tis the result of such loving that concerns me."

The result. A child. She looked at the ground, at her bare
toes, her eyes stinging suddenly. She'd almost forgotten. "I
cannot bear any more children." She lifted her gaze to his. "I
nearly died birthing Mason."

It pained him to see the sudden agony in her eyes. "A
physician told you this?"

"Aye, and Alistar reminded me of it constantly. And that if
I could, I would give him another imperfect child."

Damn the bastard, Raiden thought. "Then do you not think
that possibly 'twas Eastwick who truly spoke the words and
not the doctors? 'Twas clear the man did not want his own
son."

"Aye, I've thought of that."

"You've had cycles."

Her cheeks stained pink and she eyed him. "Aye, but they
are not monthly." Hurt stung her voice. "You needn't worry
over breeding a bastard in me, Raiden."

She turned away, but he grabbed her back, gazing deeply
into her wounded green eyes. "Do you think you are less of
a woman for this tragedy? Because I do not. Breeding babes

does not make you a woman. It makes you simply a mother. Do you think 'twas all I cared about when we made love?''

"Nay, I know 'twas not."

"If that were true Willa, I would never have touched you."

Her tight features softened, and Raiden realized she'd held far too much stock in her ability to offer children. He wanted to beat the bloody hell out of Eastwick again for making her feel this way, and he drew her into his arms, holding her snugly.

"My God, Willa, can you not see how much I adore you?" She nodded against his chest. "I do not believe I will ever survive without you," he said very softly, squeezing her, his throat growing tight. She tipped her head and his lips crushed over hers as he mapped her curves, pulling her into him. "I want you again, little fox. I will die wanting you."

"Do not speak such words!" she rushed to say, cupping his face and kissing him heavily, quickly. "Do not give up, I beg you."

Her optimism was infectious. Because he wanted it to be. And he kissed her savagely, wanting some of it, more of it, enough to banish the hopelessness he felt whenever he thought of the future, whenever he thought of her learning the price he was willing to pay. Part of his soul would never be at rest if he didn't fulfill his vow. He dreaded telling her and instead pushed her up against the nearest tree, lifting her, pushing her legs around him, his hands riding her thighs and taking the sarong with him as he cupped her buttocks.

She rocked against him, her hands fumbling around his weapons for the buttons of his breeches. She freed him, and he was inside her, filling her in one long thrust. She gasped, tightening her legs around his hips, never breaking eye contact as he withdrew and retreated. Her breath shuddered against his lips, his ragged and thready. He quickened, the force of his passion pushing her up the tree.

"Forgive me," he whispered, aware he was hurting her.

"I do not care," she said, holding his gaze. "Can you not

see? Naught you do will push me away, my love.'' She was his, no matter what came. The measure of time was unimportant.

''Oh, God, Willa,'' he groaned, burying his face in the bend of her shoulder, loving her more for her compassion, more for her generous heart he didn't deserve. Heat surged in his veins, and she cried out as he shoved once, twice, then took her with him in his climax, the echo and pulse of blood and body shattering through them. Flesh gripped and throbbed, their cries startling a covey of colorful birds, drawing in the humid heat of the jungle to coat and swell over them in a shield of privacy.

Moments ticked by, seconds he wanted to recapture, yet neither could, and Raiden knew the only step he could take was to give her what she truly desired above all. What she'd need to survive when he was gone.

Her child.

Twenty-two

Raiden pressed a loaded pistol into her hand. "Do not ask, Willa. You know I cannot take you with me."

"I will not sit on the ship and wait, Raiden, please."

Her teary eyes cut him to the quick. "Shh," he hushed, glancing briefly at Perth and Balthasar and Kahlid, then drawing her aside. "Listen to me, love. We risk much with you on this island still. The cannibals prize white slaves, especially women, and your hair alone is enough to make us visible. Our only chance is that of surprise." He waited for her to weigh the consequences, and when she nodded sadly, he went on. "Kahlid and I have scouted three villages, and this is the only one where we've heard any mention of a white captive."

Willa's heart thundered with hope and fear as she looked to the glow of firelight in the darkened jungle. Drums beat a disturbing tattoo, the sound growing louder and quicker with each passing moment. Vines hung from trees like a spider's web, trapping the bizarre cult in a mysterious shroud. Cannibals. Flesh eaters. Oh, Lord, the horror of it. She could not argue the matter. With the *Renegade* anchored off shore and under the cover of night, she'd already waited most of the day with Perth, Vazeen, and Balthasar whilst Raiden and Kahlid and several others searched the cove and jungle. Dawn would come in less than two hours. There was no more time.

"Mason might not come to you," she said.

He sighed, relieved. "I will not give the lad the choice." He offered a weak smile. "His mother wants to see him."

Her eyes filled rapidly with tears. "Oh, Raiden, do you really believe he is alive? He was sick in Kedah—"

"Aye, I do," he interrupted firmly. "You have too much hope in you for him not to be, love." His brushed a kiss to her forehead, squeezing her briefly, praying to God her boy was alive. It would destroy her if he wasn't. "Perth will stay with you," he said, then reluctantly turned away, facing his crewmen. After a weapons check, Raiden armed himself with the blowpipe Inaka's warrior had left him, slipping the harness on his back, careful of the sack of poison dust.

Willa looked down at the weapon in her hand, the East India crest on the stock glaring in the moonlight. He'd kept it all this time, she thought, remembering when she'd found it in Barkmon's carriage. It felt like a century ago. Instinctively, she checked the load, then shoved it into the waistband of the borrowed breeches Perth had thoughtfully brought for her along with a shirt and a pair of boots. She'd sworn that after a sarong and breeches, she would never wear a gown again. The thought made her smile slightly, and she looked up to find them all staring at her.

"What?"

"No matter what you hear, do not leave this spot."

Her eyes widened. "Why? What do you mean?"

He stepped close. "You must trust me, Willa."

"You know I do."

"Good." He kissed her lightly. "I did not want to have to tie you to a tree."

"You think that would hold me?"

He arched a speculative brow, all male arrogance.

She produced her jackknife, flipping it out, then folding it closed and slipping it into her boot in one smooth motion. "Try me, pirate."

He glanced at Perth. "My job will be less dangerous, I fear, than yours."

Perth chuckled to himself as Raiden followed the others into the heavy forest of bramble and vines. Then suddenly he stopped and cocked a look back over his shoulder at her. He stared for a moment, his gaze moving over her from head to foot and back, and Willa saw rawness in his features. He turned, and in three strides he was before her, sweeping her into his arms and carrying her into privacy.

"Raiden!" Surely he didn't want to make love to her now.

He released her legs, holding her against him. Cupping the delicate curve of her jaw in his rough palms, he stroked his thumb over her lower lip, watching the motion and knowing he'd confused her.

She covered his wrists. "Raiden, speak to me. What is it?"

His gaze flew to hers. " 'Tis hard to leave you, even for a moment, even when I have a purpose that begs for my complete attention. But I could not go without—" He swallowed, his gaze raking her flawless features, his chest aching for just the right words. "I love you, Willa Delaney."

She inhaled sharply, her tears suddenly flowing.

"I love you so much it strangles me."

She breathed his name, gripping his waist.

"I do not care if you love me back—"

"—I do."

He stilled, searching her eyes.

"I do love you," she said, reaching up to stroke his cheek, push his hair back.

He shuddered, a release of years of lonely hunger. His eyes were glossy in the dark, a sheen of emotion that threatened her breathing.

"I love you, Raiden Montegomery."

"Willa." He whispered her name like a prayer before he kissed her, delicately, reverently.

Wrapping her arms around his neck, she held him, whispering her love.

Nearby someone cleared his throat. "The sun rises in an hour, sir. If we are to do this, the time is now."

Raiden stepped back, his gaze locked with hers even as he acknowledged Perth.

Her arms slid from his neck, and she rested her palms on his chest for a moment. "Go. Bring me my baby," she said, marshaling her courage.

He touched her tear-stained cheek, smiled, then walked away.

Perth remained near, waiting for her.

Willa brushed at her tears, then pushed away from the tree, walking with him to the clearing.

Raiden and the others were already gone.

Raiden had selected Balthasar and Kahlid for two reasons. They were twice the size of the natives and would scare anyone when they first encountered them, yet despite their size, they moved without a sound. Vazeen was crafty, and from his position Raiden watched the slim Hindu move like a spider through the trees and grounds, searching each thatched hut for the prisoner.

The tribe was celebrating, and Raiden wished he understood their language better. It was not unlike Inaka's and yet had a decidedly Arabic note. Raiden moved back deeper into the woods. The cannibals were feasting now, the dawn meal a ritual prior to attack. Inaka's tribesmen did something of the like. Raiden prayed it was not the *Renegade* they were to attack and not the boy they were eating.

His stomach clenched when he thought of how frightened Mason must be. Unable to communicate, unable to understand. The men were alert to listen for cries, a child's whimper. Raiden could not stand watching any longer. He skirted the village, meeting with Vazeen and Balthasar and finding nothing. Had he been wrong, had he misinterpreted the language?

Through his spyglass he scanned the grounds, the wide area for ceremonial grounds, for council meetings and sacrifice. Around a bonfire, nearly naked men and women danced, palm fronds and raffia covering little. Tall, narrow drums stood in a long row on the far side of the clearing, young men pounding a constant beat meant to carry on the wind and frighten their enemies.

The heavy scent of burning mace stung the air, burning his nostrils. If the East Indiamen could only see this, he thought, raising the spyglass toward the trees. Nutmeg and mace, groves of them.

He dragged the glass to where he'd last seen Vazeen. Balthasar almost blended into the vegetation, his tattoos and dark skin giving him a ghostly appearance. Raiden's gaze lighted on a thin young man carrying a wide elephant leaf filled with fruit. Carefully, he closed the glass and backed up, following. He signaled the others. Catching up with the food-bearing boy was difficult, for each snap of a twig could alert the tribesmen. They would need a diversion, he decided, and he took up his powder horn, meeting with Balthasar and explaining what he wanted. Then he headed to the farthest edge of what looked like a street. Years ago, Inaka had kept him in a pit with a cagelike cover, a place that filled with rain during the monsoons, where snakes sought his warmth, and every day of his life had been a struggle to survive till sunrise. Raiden considered that these cannibals would do the same and leave a captive in a pit.

God help the child, he thought, if they had.

"Eat something, m'lady." Perth offered a strip of dried beef and sea biscuits.

"I can't." Sitting on the ground, her back braced on a tree, Willa cast a look behind her, into the dark. She heard nothing but the drone of drums. The incessant beat was giving her a terrible headache and stretching her last nerve as taut as a violin wire. Tears she refused to let fall burned her eyes. All she loved lay in the forest, hopefully in that village.

"Have I thanked you for saving Raiden's life?" she said suddenly, her gaze darting to him.

"You mean for blasting a hole through your husband."

Willa flinched at that. "Well, aye. That too."

Perth waved. "He was a cruel man, my lady. Not well liked regardless of his station. So I wouldn't waste your grief on him."

She cocked a look at him where he sat a few feet from her, his elbows braced on his bent knees. "I won't."

He shifted uncomfortably beneath her gaze. "You've somethin' on yer mind, lass. Yer starin' a might hard."

"I was thinking about how your accent comes and goes."

His features tightened. "As does your Irish lilt."

"Only when I drink," she reminded him. "You, on the other hand, sound rather English. Quite the aristocrat, as a matter of fact."

He scoffed, stabbing at the ground between his boots with his knife.

The drums pounded; birds squawked overhead.

Her voice was soft, sympathetic, when she asked, "When are you going to tell him who you really are?"

His head jerked up, his eyes narrowing. "And who might that be?"

Willa stood, dusting off her behind. "His father."

He chuckled, but the sound held no merriment. "You've a wild imagination, lovey. I've been a seaman—"

"Do not trifle with me!" she cut in sharply, her temper and patience already strained to the breaking point waiting for Raiden to return. "I can see the resemblance even that beard and long hair cannot hide. Not to mention the way you dine, the way you walk, ride a horse." She drew in a breath. "Your speech."

He continued to dig in the ground with the blade.

"You are he. You are Granville Montegomery."

He lifted his gaze to her, and Willa saw years of regret glimmering in his eyes.

"Aye."

She nodded and asked, "Is a curtsy required in the jungle, my lord?"

He scoffed, climbing to his feet to tower over her. "Spare the formalities, Lady Eastwick."

"Please don't call me that. I've never considered that lineage made one noble."

He laughed to himself, dryly, and Willa saw a different man emerge. "I am proof of that."

Willa stepped closer, grateful for the distraction, yet feeling sorry for him. "Why have you joined his crew?"

"To know my son, of course."

She'd thought as much. "You seem to have quite a few."

His gray brow lifted, so much like Raiden's, yet she didn't smile, for all she could see was the pain Raiden had suffered because of this man's callousness. "What possesses a man to discard his baby and go off on adventures, breeding bastards all over the world?"

"You have no right to speak to me thusly, Lady Eastwick."

Willa was up in his face. "I have every right. I love Raiden, and he loves me. And you have caused him naught but agony. He was thrown aside, he lived on the streets, a beggar, eating scraps if he ate at all. 'Tis the very reason he is a thief!"

Granville sighed hard, his ears tuned to the sound of drums, to any odd noise, but his mind lay on her words.

"I did not know he was discarded," he said, and she heard the sorrow in his voice. "When his mother, Lady Elise, learned she was carrying, she married the first man she could, afore I knew 'twas my child. I saw my son once after his birth and gave him a name. His mother's husband was out of the country at the time," he added at the question in her eyes. "She died not long after birthing Raiden, and I thought the babe would be raised by her husband. Raiden was nearly two when I learned he'd been given over to a servant by her husband, and by then I'd lost all account of him.''

"That is no excuse for not watching over the child all these years, my lord.''

He eyed her, a pinning stare. "I think you have chastised me enough to call me Granville," he said. "And you are right.''

"Then why now? Why enter his life now when you have had more than thirty years to find him?''

Granville fell back against a tree, tired. "I learned he took my name and not that of his married mother. How he learned the truth, I do not know, nor does it matter. But that name has put him in danger.''

"He is always in danger. He's been evading the law since he was a boy. Because you never cared enough.''

He straightened. "Watch your tongue, Lady Eastwick.''

"Do call me Willa," she snapped back.

"I have always cared, Willa. I love all my children. What man would not admire the strong men they are?'' A little pride crept into his voice then. "But Raiden is good at what he does, and by God, he is a hard man to track. Furthermore, no one knows the Black Angel is a Montegomery—''

"Bastard. Say it aloud, Granville. A Montegomery bastard," she sneered. "Like the half-dozen others you've made, he bears the stain of it whilst you dally over the continents creating more.''

"I was not careful in my youth, I admit that, but I have been cautious for the past thirty years. Overly so.''

Willa felt only her regret for Raiden. For the horrible, lonely life he'd led because of his father's potency and callousness about within whom he spilled his seed. But like the man she loved, his father could not be blamed for the past of his youth. "So, why would the name Montegomery put him in more danger?''

"Because my enemies have become his.''

Willa's gaze shifted to the spot where the drums thundered. "Who?" she said almost absently.

"Percival Dunfee."

Her gaze flew to his, and she inhaled a sharp breath. "The admiral?"

Granville nodded, pulling off his cap and pushing his hair back. "He was the man Elise married. He's never forgiven me for bedding the woman he loved, and he hates Raiden, for the boy's birth caused his wife's death."

"Granville," she said carefully, staring him down. "Raiden has some bone to pick with Dunfee. Could this be it?"

"You do not know?"

"I am not privy to everything in his life, yet."

"Dunfee wants a Montegomery. I do not think he knows he is the Black Angel."

"Oh, I know he does not, for I've met the admiral and the man thinks of capturing the pirate as no more than sport."

An explosion shook the earth, and Willa stumbled.

Granville dragged her to the ground, his gun out. The drums stopped.

"Sweet Mary, what was that?"

" 'Twas not gunfire. Nor cannons."

It came again, the night suddenly as bright as day, the ground beneath them trembling.

"A quake?"

"Then what is that?" He climbed to his feet, helping her up and gesturing with the pistol.

Willa looked. The jungle was alive with sound and flashes of light, and she recognized gunfire.

"They've been discovered. Oh, God!" She took a step toward the chaos, but Granville grabbed her back.

"Nay. You promised to remain here."

"He needs me." Willa struggled against his hold.

Granville locked his arms tightly around her and said in her ear, "What can you do but get yourself killed? He is skilled, woman, a master at evasion. Trust him."

Willa knew he was right. She'd promised. Her panic would serve no good. Yet she could only watch and listen. Screams of agony, of the dying, colored the air like the shriek of exotic birds. Smoke puffed through the dense jungle, painting the magenta dawn with white ash.

The cracks of pistol shots made her flinch, and she wrestled against Granville. *Please, God,* she prayed. *Don't take them from me.* Her throat tightened, burning with smoke and tears. A figure raced toward them, a native, and Granville fired, dropping him before he plunged a war ax into her head. He backed up, pulling her with him, but Willa refused to go, digging in her heels. No matter the danger, she couldn't leave Raiden.

Suddenly the earth roared and Willa saw it—the red-gold glow of molten lava, the spray of heavy ash sinking through the trees.

"Lord save us."

The volcano bellowed. Fist-sized stones hurled into the sky, then fell to the earth, smashing through the leafy canopy as a spume of melted rock poured over the crust.

"Sweet Christ, come on." He pulled her toward the shore, toward the *Renegade.*

"Nay." She yanked free. "I can't—how could you leave him?"

"I swore an oath!"

"He is your son!"

"Aye," Granville groaned, yet he grabbed her again and dragged her back through the jungle toward the shore.

She screamed for Raiden until her throat was raw, and still there was no answer. Willa couldn't take her gaze off the one spot where Raiden had disappeared.

Show yourself, she thought. *Damn you, Raiden, show yourself.*

Just then a man stepped through the jungle.

"Wait!" she cried, digging her heels into the soft dirt. "There!"

Granville turned.

It was Kahlid, then Balthasar, and young Vazeen. And still no

Raiden. Willa's heart started to shatter, their glum expressions offering nothing.

''*Raiden!*'' she cried out, her plea echoing through the trees.

For the space of a heartbeat, the chaos ceased, the cries stopped, the jungle red with dawn and tranquil. The volcano's blood spilled over the land. Willa choked on a sob, covering her mouth, wanting to run, to cry, and unable to do either. Her heart thundered fast and furious.

Smoke swirled, leaves rustled; then the jungle vines parted as if by an invisible hand and a dark specter emerged, his face blackened, his shirt torn and bloodstained.

''Raiden,'' she breathed, her legs nearly folding beneath her. She ran to him, then stopped short when he lifted his arms and offered her the limp body of her son.

Twenty-three

"He lives," Raiden said, pouring the child into her out-stretched arms, and Willa sank to the ground, clutching her baby, feeling him for wounds.

Oh, Lord, he was so thin.

She sobbed helplessly, overjoyed, and when Raiden knelt, she clutched at him. "Thank you, thank you," she cried.

Raiden stroked her hair, her shoulder. "He is underfed and weak, but he is well."

She cried harder, releasing Raiden to examine her son, cataloguing every cut and bruise, every grain of dirt. He didn't stir, his eyes still closed, and she shot Raiden a panicked look.

"He's in a faint. I think I scared him." Raiden's anger flared again. He'd found the child in a caged pit of murky water. The hollow look on the lad's face as he stared up at the sky, as if waiting for an angel to have mercy and take him to heaven, had torn through him with pity. When Raiden had jumped down into the pit, Mason didn't move, didn't speak; only his round eyes screamed with terror. When he'd touched him, he'd fought him, squealing like a trapped piglet and raising the alarm. Then he'd gone limp.

"Come, we must hurry." Raiden helped her to her feet, ushering her along through the jungle.

Perth and Kahlid ran ahead to signal the *Renegade* and draw the longboat from its hiding place. Raiden took Mason from her and they ran, the jungle suddenly alive again with shouts, the pound of drums. War drums.

They'd scarcely made it to the boat and into the water when the shore filled with savages like ants pouring over rancid meat. Spears and rocks flung in slings rained down on them; twice Perth and Vazeen were hit with the hail of stones. But they continued to row as Raiden stood in the boat, signaling the *Renegade*.

In a burst of firepower, the *Renegade's* gunners bombarded the beach, explosions of fire shredding the shore and sending sprays of sand and warriors into the air. Under the barrage, Mason stirred in her arms, and Willa looked down as his eyes opened.

At first there was no recognition, but when the truth dawned, his tiny arms looped her neck, and she heard the word, the only word he'd ever said, "Mama."

The sound gave her life.

"Oh, Mason, my sweet. *I have missed you.*"

He squeezed her in response, giving her a comforting pat, and she laughed through her tears, rocking him, sobbing with joy.

Alive. He was alive and in her arms. *Oh, sweet mother of God, thank you,* she thought, raining kisses over his dirty auburn hair. Over his head, she met Raiden's gaze, and he smiled tenderly, his own eyes bright with unshed tears. "I love you," she mouthed under the roar of the cannon's blast.

"I know," he said and bent. "It warms my soul to see you so happy, my love."

"Oh, Raiden, the joys you have given me," she said, kissing him. They broke apart when Mason twisted in her arms to